C8 000 00

ONE
NIGHT

SENSUAL
BARGAINS

ONE NIGHT OF
CONSEQUENCES COLLECTION

October 2017

November 2017

December 2017

January 2018

February 2018

March 2018

ONE NIGHT

SENSUAL BARGAINS

JENNIE
LUCAS

SUSANNA
CARR

MAUREEN
CHILD

MILLS &
BOON

All rights reserved including the right of reproduction in whole or in part in any form. This edition is published by arrangement with Harlequin Books S.A.

This is a work of fiction. Names, characters, places, locations and incidents are purely fictional and bear no relationship to any real life individuals, living or dead, or to any actual places, business establishments, locations, events or incidents. Any resemblance is entirely coincidental.

This book is sold subject to the condition that it shall not, by way of trade or otherwise, be lent, resold, hired out or otherwise circulated without the prior consent of the publisher in any form of binding or cover other than that in which it is published and without a similar condition including this condition being imposed on the subsequent purchaser.

® and TM are trademarks owned and used by the trademark owner and/or its licensee. Trademarks marked with ® are registered with the United Kingdom Patent Office and/or the Office for Harmonisation in the Internal Market and in other countries.

Published in Great Britain 2017
By Mills & Boon, an imprint of HarperCollins*Publishers*
1 London Bridge Street, London, SE1 9GF

ONE NIGHT: SENSUAL BARGAINS © 2017 Harlequin Books S.A.

Nine Months to Redeem Him © 2015 Jennie Lucas
A Deal with Benefits © 2014 Susanna Carr
After Hours with Her Ex © 2015 Maureen Child

ISBN: 978-0-263-93189-1

09-0218

Our policy is to use papers that are natural, renewable and recyclable products and made from wood grown in sustainable forests.
The logging and manufacturing processes conform to the legal environmental regulations of the country of origin.

Printed and bound in Spain
by CPI, Barcelona

NINE MONTHS TO REDEEM HIM

JENNIE LUCAS

To Krystyn Gardner, my friend since childhood, maid of honour at my wedding - the bold, fearless soul who moved halfway round the world and convinced me to meet her there. Thanks, you crazy girl, for blazing a trail, and for always being in my corner.

Jennie Lucas grew up dreaming about faraway lands. At fifteen, hungry for experience beyond the borders of her small Idaho city, she went to a Connecticut boarding school on scholarship. She took her first solo trip to Europe at sixteen, then put off college and travelled around the U.S., supporting herself with jobs as diverse as petrol station cashier and newspaper advertising assistant.

At twenty-two, she met the man who would become her husband. After their marriage, she graduated from Kent State with a degree in English. Seven years after she started writing, she got the magical call from London that turned her into a published author.

Since then life has been hectic, with a new writing career, a sexy husband and two small children, but she's having a wonderful (albeit sleepless) time. She loves immersing herself in dramatic, glamorous, passionate stories. Maybe she can't physically travel to Morocco or Spain right now, but for a few hours a day, while her children are sleeping, she can be there in her books.

Jennie loves to hear from her readers. You can visit her website at www.jennielucas.com, or drop her a note at jennie@jennielucas.com.

PROLOGUE

THIS IS ALL I can give you, he said. *No marriage. No children. All I can offer is—this.* And he kissed me, feather-light, until I was holding my breath, trembling in his arms. *Do you agree?*

Yes, I whispered, my lips brushing against his. I hardly knew what I was saying. Hardly thought about the promise I was making and what it might cost me. I was too lost in the moment, lost in pleasure that made the world a million colors of twisting light.

Now, two months later, I'd just gotten news that changed everything.

As I went up the sweeping stairs of his London mansion, my heart was in my throat. *A baby.* I gripped the oak handrail as my shaking steps echoed down the hall. *A baby.* A little boy with Edward's eyes? An adorable little girl with his smile? Thinking of the sweet, precious baby soon to be nestled in my arms, a dazed smile lifted to my lips.

Then I remembered my promise.

My hands tightened. Would he think I'd somehow gotten pregnant on purpose? Tricking him into becoming a father against his will?

No. He wouldn't. Couldn't.

Could he?

The upstairs hallway was cold and dark. Just like Edward's heart. Because beneath his sensual charm, his soul was ice. I'd always known this, no matter how hard I'd tried *not* to know it.

I'd given him my body, which he wanted, and my heart, which he hadn't. Had I made the biggest mistake of my life?

Maybe he could change. I took a deep breath. If I could only believe that, once he knew about the baby, he might change—that he might someday love us both…

Reaching our bedroom, I slowly pushed open the door.

"You've kept me waiting," Edward's voice was dangerous, coming from the shadows. "Come to bed, Diana."

Come to bed.

Clenching my hands at my sides, I went forward into the dark.

CHAPTER ONE

Four Months Earlier

I WAS *DYING*.

After hours of being cooped up in the backseat of the chauffeured car, with the heat at full blast as the driver exceeded speed limits at every opportunity, the air felt oppressively hot. I rolled down the window to take a deep breath of fresh air and rain.

"You'll catch your death," the driver said sourly from the front. Almost the first words he'd spoken since he'd collected me from Heathrow.

"I need some fresh air," I said apologetically.

He snorted, then mumbled something under his breath. Pasting a smile on my face, I looked out the window. Jagged hills cast a dark shadow over the lonely road, surrounded by a bleak moor drenched in thick wet mist. Cornwall was beautiful, like a dream. I'd come to the far side of the world. Which was what I'd wanted, wasn't it?

In the twilight, the black silhouette of a distant crag looked like a ghostly castle, delineated against the red sun shimmering over the sea. I could almost hear the clang of swords from long-ago battles, hear the roar of bloodthirsty Saxons and Celts.

"Penryth Hall, miss." The driver's gruff voice was barely audible over the wind and rain. "Up ahead."

Penryth Hall? With an intake of breath, I looked back at the distant crag. It wasn't my imagination or a trick of mist. A castle was really there, illuminated by scattered lights, reflecting in a ghostly blur upon the dark scarlet sea.

As we drew closer, I squinted at the crenellated battlements. The place looked barely habitable, fit only for vampires or ghosts. For this, I'd left the sunshine and roses of California.

Blinking hard, I leaned back against the leather seat and exhaled, trying to steady my trembling hands. The smell of rain masked the sweet, slightly putrid scent of rotting autumn leaves, decaying fish and the salt of the ocean.

"For lord's sake, miss, if you've had enough of the rain, up it goes."

The driver pressed a button, and my window closed, choking off fresh air as the SUV bumped over ridges in the road. With a lump in my throat, I looked down at the book still open in my lap. In the growing darkness, the words were smudges upon shadows. Regretfully, I marked my place, and closed the cover of *Private Nursing: How to Care for a Patient in His Home Whilst Maintaining Professional Distance and Avoiding Immoral Advances from Your Employer* before placing it carefully in my handbag.

I'd already read it twice on the flight from Los Angeles. There hadn't been much published lately about how to live on a reclusive tycoon's estate and help him rehabilitate an injury as his live-in physical therapist. The closest I'd been able to find was a tattered book I'd bought secondhand that had been published in England in 1959—and when I looked closer I discovered it was actually a reprint from 1910. But I figured it was close enough. I was confident I could take the book's advice. I could learn anything from a book.

It was *people* I often found completely unfathomable.

For the twentieth time, I wondered about my new employer. Was he elderly, feeble, infirm? And why had he sent for me from six thousand miles away? The L.A. employment agency had not been very forthcoming with details.

"A wealthy British tycoon," the recruiter had told me. "Injured in a car accident two months ago. He can walk but barely. He requested you."

"Why? Does he know me?" My voice trembled. "Or my stepsister?"

Shrug. "The request came from a London agency. Apparently he found the physical therapists in England unsuitable."

I gave an incredulous laugh. "*All* of them?"

"That's all I'm allowed to share, other than salary details. *That* is sizeable. But you must sign a nondisclosure agreement. And agree to live at his estate indefinitely."

I never would have agreed to a job like this three weeks ago. A lot had changed since then. Everything I'd thought I could count on had fallen apart.

The Range Rover picked up speed as we neared the castle on the edge of the ocean's cliff. Passing beneath a wrought iron gate carved into the shape of sea serpents and clinging vines, we entered a courtyard. The vehicle stopped. Gray stone walls pressing in upon all sides, beneath the gray rain.

For a moment, I sat still, clutching my handbag in my lap.

"'Consider a carpet,'" I whispered to myself, quoting Mrs. Warreldy-Gribbley, the author of the book. "'Be silent and deferential and endure, and expect to be trod upon.'"

I could do that. Surely, I could do that. How hard could it be, to remain silent and deferential and endure?

The SUV's door opened. A large umbrella appeared, held by an elderly woman. "Miss Maywood?" She sniffed. "Took you long enough."

"Um…"

"I'm Mrs. MacWhirter, the housekeeper," she said, as two men got my suitcase. "This way, if you please."

"Thank you." As I stepped out of the car, I looked up at the moss-laden castle. It was the first of November. This close up, Penryth Hall looked even more haunted. *A good place to heal*, I told myself firmly. But that was a lie. It was a place to hide.

I shivered as drops of cold rain ran down my hair and jacket. Ahead of me, the housekeeper waved the umbrella with a scowl.

"Miss Maywood?"

"Sorry." Stepping forward, I gave her an attempt at a smile. "Please call me Diana."

She looked disapprovingly at my smile. "The master's been expecting you for ages."

"*Master*..." I snorted at the word, then saw her humorless expression and straightened with a cough. "Oh. Right. I'm terribly sorry. My plane was late…"

She shook her head, as if to show what she thought of airlines' lackluster schedules. "Mr. St. Cyr requested you be brought to his study immediately."

"Mr. St. Cyr? That is his name? The elderly gentleman?"

Her eyes goggled at the word *elderly*. "Edward St. Cyr is his name, yes." She looked at me, as if wondering what kind of idiot would agree to work for a man whose name she did not know. A question I was asking myself at the moment. "This way."

I followed, feeling wet and cold and tired and grumpy. *Master,* I thought, irritated. What was this, *Wuthering Heights?*— The original novel, I mean, not the (very loosely) adapted teleplay that my stepfather had turned into a cable television miniseries last year, with a pouty-lipped starlet as Cathy, and so much raunchy sex that Emily Brontë was probably still turning in her grave. But the show had been a big hit, which just went to show that maybe I was every bit as naïve as Howard claimed. "Wake up and smell the coffee, kitten," he'd said kindly. "Sex is what people care about. Sex and money."

I'd disagreed vehemently, but I'd been wrong. Clearly. Because here I was, six thousand miles from home, alone in a strange castle.

But even here, between the old suits of armor and tapestries, I saw a sleek modern laptop on a table. I'd purposefully left my phone and tablet in Beverly Hills, to escape it all. But it seemed even here, I couldn't completely get away. A bead of sweat lifted to my forehead. I wouldn't look to see what they were doing, I *wouldn't*...

"In here, miss." Mrs. MacWhirter led me into a starkly masculine study, with dark wood furnishings and a fire in the fireplace. I braced myself to face an elderly, infirm, probably cranky old gentleman. But there was no one. Frowning, I turned back to the housekeeper.

"Where is—"

She was gone. I was alone in the flickering shadows of the study. I was turning to leave as well when I heard a low voice, spoken from the depths of the darkness.

"Come forward."

Jumping, I looked around me more carefully. A large sheepdog was sitting on a Turkish rug in front of the fire. He was huge and furry, and panting noisily, his tongue hanging out. He tilted his head at me.

I stared back in consternation.

Was I having some kind of breakdown, as my friend Kristin had predicted? I *had* seen enough funny pet videos online to know that animals could be trained to talk.

"Um." Feeling foolish, I licked my lips. "Did you say something?"

"Did I stutter?" The dog's mouth didn't move. So it wasn't the dog talking. But now I wished it had been. Animal voices were preferable to ghostly ones. Shivering, I looked around me.

"Do you require some kind of instruction, Miss Maywood?" The voice turned acid. "An engraved invitation, perhaps? Come forward, I said. I want to see you."

It was then I realized the deep voice didn't come from beyond the grave, but from the depths of the high-backed leather chair in front of the fire. Oh. Cheeks hot, I walked toward it. The dog gave me a pitying glance, tempered by the faint wag of his tail. Giving the dog a weak smile, I turned to face my new employer.

And froze.

Edward St. Cyr was neither elderly nor infirm. No.

The man who sat in the high-backed chair was handsome, powerful. His muscled body was partially immobilized, but he somehow radiated strength, even danger. Like a fierce tiger—caged...

"You are too kind," the man said sardonically.

"You are Edward St. Cyr?" I whispered, unable to look away. I swallowed. "My new employer?"

"That," he said coldly, "should be obvious."

His face was hard-edged, rugged, too much so for conventional masculine beauty. There was nothing *pretty* about him. His jawline was square, and his aquiline nose slightly off-kilter at top, as if it had once been broken. His shoulders were broad, barely contained by the oversized chair, his right arm hung in an elastic brace in a sling. His left leg was held out stiffly, extended from his body, the heel resting on a stool. He looked like a fighter, a bouncer, maybe even a thug.

Until you looked at his eyes. An improbable blue against his olive-toned skin, they were the color of a midnight ocean swept with moonlight. Tortured eyes with unfathomable depths, blue as an ancient glacier newly risen above an arctic sea.

Even more trapped than his body, I thought suddenly. His soul.

Then his expression shuttered, turning sardonic and flat, reflecting only the glowing embers of the fire. Now his blue eyes seemed only ruthless and cynical. Had I imagined the emotion I'd seen? Then my lips parted.

"Wait," I breathed. "I know you. Don't I?"

"We met once, at your sister's party last June." His cruel, sensual lips curved. "I'm so pleased you remember."

"Madison is my *step*sister," I corrected automatically. I came closer to the chair, in the flickering light of the fire. "You were so rude…"

His eyes met mine. "But was I wrong?"

My cheeks burned. I'd been working as Madison's new assistant, so had been obligated to attend her posh, catered party. There'd been a DJ and waiters, and a hundred industry types—actors, directors, wealthy would-be producers. Normally I would have wanted to run and hide. But this time, I'd been excited to bring my new boyfriend. I'd been so proud to introduce Jason to Madison. Then, later, I'd found myself watching the two of them, across the room.

A sardonic British voice had spoken behind me. *"He's going to dump you for her."*

I'd whirled around to see a darkly handsome man with cold blue eyes. *"Excuse me?"*

"I saw you come in together. Just trying to save you some pain." He lifted his martini glass in mocking salute. *"You can't compete with her, and you know it."*

It had been a dagger in my heart.

You can't compete with her, and you know it. Blonde and impossibly beautiful, my stepsister, who was one year younger, drew men like bees to a honeypot. But I'd seen the downside, too. Even being the most beautiful woman in the world didn't guarantee happiness.

Of course, being the ugly stepsister didn't guarantee it

either. I'd glared at the man before I turned on my heel. *"You don't know what you're talking about."*

But somehow, he *had* known. It haunted me later. How had some rude stranger at a party seen the truth immediately, while it had taken me months?

When Madison arranged for Jason to get a part in her next movie, he'd been thrilled. Working as Madison's assistant, I'd seen them both every day on set in Paris. Then she'd asked me to go back to L.A. and give a magazine a personal tour of Madison's house in the Hollywood Hills, and talk about what it was like to be a "girl next door" who happened to have Madison Lowe as my stepsister, a semifamous producer as my stepfather, and up-and-coming hunk Jason Black as my boyfriend. "We need the publicity," Madison had insisted.

But the reporter barely seemed to listen as I walked her through Madison's lavish house, talking lamely about my stepsister and Jason. Until she pressed on her earpiece with her hand and suddenly laughed aloud, turning to me with a malicious gleam in her eye. *"Fascinating. But are you interested in seeing what the two of them have been up to today in Paris?"* Then she'd cut to reveal live footage of the two of them naked and drunk beneath the Eiffel Tower.

The video became an international sensation, along with the clip of my stupid, shocked face as I watched it.

For the past three weeks, I'd been trapped behind the gates of my stepfather's house, ducking paparazzi who wanted pictures of my miserable face, and gossip reporters who kept yelling questions like, *"Was it a publicity stunt, Diana? How else could anyone be so stupid and blind?"*

I'd fled to Cornwall to escape.

But Edward St. Cyr already knew about it. He'd even tried to warn me, but I hadn't listened.

Looking at my new employer now, a shiver went through

me, rumbling all the way to my heart, shaking me like the earthquakes I thought I'd left behind. "Is that why you hired me? To gloat?"

Edward looked at me coldly. "No."

"Then you felt sorry for me."

"This isn't about *you*." His dark blue eyes glittered in the firelight. "This is about me. I need a good physiotherapist. The *best*."

Confused, I shook my head. "There must be hundreds, thousands, of good physical therapists in the U.K...."

"I gave up after four," he said acidly. "The first was useless. I hardly know which was thicker, her skull or her graceless hands pushing at me. She quit when I attempted to give her a gentle bit of constructive criticism."

"*Gentle?*"

"The second woman was giggly and useless. I sacked her the second day, when I caught her on the phone trying to sell my story to the press..."

"Why would the press want your story? Weren't you in a car accident?"

His lips tightened almost imperceptibly at the corners. "The details have been kept out of the news and I intend to keep it that way."

"Lucky," I said, thinking of my own media onslaught.

His dark eyes gleamed. "I suppose you're right." He glanced down at his arm in the sling, at his leg propped up in front of him. "I can walk now, but only with a cane. That's why I sent for you. Make me better."

"What happened to the other two?"

"The other two what?"

"You said you hired four physical therapists."

"Oh. The third was a hatchet-faced martinet." He shrugged. "Just looking at her curdled my will to live."

Surreptitiously, I glanced down at my damp cotton jacket, sensible nursing clogs and baggy khakis wrinkled from the overnight flight, wondering if at the moment, I too was curdling his will to live. But my looks weren't supposed to matter. Not in physical therapy. Looking up, I set my jaw. "And the fourth?"

"Ah. Well." His lips quirked at the edges. "One night, we shared a little too much wine, and found ourselves in bed in a totally different kind of therapy."

My eyes went wide. "You fired her for sleeping with you? You should be ashamed."

"I had no choice," he said irritably. "She changed overnight from a decent physio to a marriage-crazed clinger. I caught her writing *Mrs. St. Cyr* over and over on my medical records, circling it with hearts and flowers." He snorted. "Come *on*."

"What bad luck you've had," I said sardonically. Then I tilted my head, stroking my cheek. "Or wait. Maybe *you're* the one who's the problem."

"There is no problem," he said smoothly. "Not now that you're here."

I folded my arms. "I still don't understand. Why me? We only met the once, and I'd already given up doing physical therapy then."

"Yes. To be an assistant to the world-famous Madison Lowe. Strange career choice, if you don't mind me saying so, from being a world-class physiotherapist to fetching lattes for your stepsister."

"Who said I was world-class?"

"Ron Smart. Tyrese Carlsen. John Field." He paused. "Great athletes, but notorious womanizers. I'm guessing one of them must have given you reason to quit. Something must have made the idea of being assistant to a spoiled star suddenly palatable."

"My patients have all been completely professional," I said sharply. "I chose to quit physical therapy for—another reason." I looked away.

"Come on, you can tell me. Which one grabbed your butt?"

"Nothing of the sort happened."

"I thought you would say that." He lifted a smug eyebrow. "That's the other reason I wanted you, Diana. Your discretion."

Hearing him say he wanted me, as he used my first name, made me feel strangely warm all over. I narrowed my eyes. "If one of them had sexually assaulted me, believe me, I wouldn't keep it a secret."

He waved his hand in clear disbelief. "You were also betrayed by your boyfriend and America's Sweetheart. You could have sold the story in an instant and gotten money and revenge. But you've never said a word against them. That's loyalty."

"Stupidity," I mumbled.

"No." He looked at me. "It's rare."

He made me sound like some kind of hero. "It's just common decency. I don't gossip."

"You were at the top of your profession in physical therapy. That's why you quit. One of your patients did something, didn't he? I wonder which—"

"For heaven's sake!" I exploded. "None of them did anything. They're totally innocent. I quit physical therapy to become an actress!"

Actress. The words seemed to echo in the dark study, and I wished I could take them back. My cheeks burned. Even the crackle of the fire seemed to be laughing at me.

But Edward St. Cyr didn't laugh. "How old are you, Miss Maywood?"

The burn in my cheeks heightened. "Twenty-eight."

"Old for acting," he observed.

"I've dreamed of being in movies since I was twelve."

"Why didn't you start sooner, then? Why wait so long?"

"I was going to, but…"

"But?"

I stared at him, then looked away. "It just wasn't practical," I mumbled.

Now he did laugh. "Isn't your whole family in the business?"

"I liked physical therapy," I said defensively. "I liked helping people get strong again."

"So why not be a doctor?"

"No one dies in physical therapy." My voice wobbled a little. I lifted my chin and said evenly, "It was a sensible career choice. I made a living. But after so many years…"

"You felt restless?"

I nodded. "I quit my job. But acting wasn't as fun as I thought it would be. I went on auditions for a few weeks. Then I quit that to become Madison's assistant."

"Your lifelong dream, and you only tried it for a few weeks?"

Looking down at my feet, I mumbled, "It was a stupid dream."

I waited for him to say, "There are no stupid dreams," or murmur encouraging or sympathetic noises, as people always did. Even Madison managed it.

"Probably for the best," Edward said.

My head lifted. "Huh?"

He nodded sagely. "You either didn't want it enough, or you were too cowardly to fight for it. Either way you were clearly headed for failure. Good to figure that out and quit sooner rather than later. Now you can go back to being useful. Helping me."

My mouth fell open. Then I glared at him.

"You don't know. Maybe I could have succeeded. You have some nerve to—"

"You waited your whole life to try for it, then quit ten minutes after you started? Give me a break. You're lying to yourself. It's not your dream."

"Maybe it is."

"Then what are you doing here?" He lifted a dark eyebrow. "You want to give it another shot? London has a thriving theater scene. I'll buy you the train ticket. Hell, I'll even send you back to Hollywood in my own jet. Prove me wrong, Diana." He tilted his head, staring at me in challenge. "Give it another go."

I stared at him furiously, hating him for calling my bluff. I wanted to grandly take him up on his offer and march straight out his front door.

Then I thought of the soul-crushing auditions, the cold reptilian eyes of the casting directors as they looked me over and dismissed me—too old, too young, too thin, too pretty, too fat, too ugly. Too worthless. I was no Madison Lowe. And I knew it.

My shoulders slumped.

"I thought so," Edward said. "So. You're out of a job and need one. Perfect. It just happens that I'd like to hire you."

"Why me?" I whispered over the lump in my throat. "I still don't understand."

"You don't?" He looked surprised. "You're the best at what you do, Diana. Trustworthy, competent. Beautiful..."

I looked up fiercely, suspecting mockery. "*Beautiful*."

"Very beautiful." His dark blue eyes held mine in the flickering light of the fire. "In spite of those god-awful clothes."

"Hey," I protested weakly.

"But you have qualities I need more than beauty. Skill. Loyalty. Patience. Intelligence. Discretion. Devotion."

"You make me sound like..." I motioned toward the sheepdog on the rug. The dog looked back at me quizzically, lifting his head.

Edward St. Cyr's lips lifted at the edges. "Like Caesar? Yes. That's exactly what I want. I'm glad you understand."

Hearing his name, the dog looked between us, giving a

faint wag of his tail. Reaching out, I scratched behind his ears, then turned back to glare at his master.

His master. Not mine.

"Sorry." I shook my head fiercely. "There's no way I'm staying to work for a man who wants a physical therapist he can treat like his dog."

"Caesar is a very good dog," he said mildly. "But let's be honest, shall we? We both know you're not going back to California, not with all the sharks in the water. You wanted to get away. You have. No one will bother you here."

"Except you."

"Except me," he agreed. "But I'm a very easy sort of person to get along with—"

I snorted in disbelief.

"—and in a few months, after I can run again, perhaps you'll have figured out what you truly want to do with your life. You can leave Penryth Hall with enough money to do whatever you want. Go back to university. Build your physical therapy business. Even audition." He shook his head. "Whatever. I don't care."

"You just want me to stay."

"Yes."

Helplessly, I shook my head. "I'm starting to think I might be better off just staying away from people."

His eyes glittered in the firelight. "I understand. Better than you might think."

I tried to smile. "Somehow I doubt a man like you spends much time alone."

He looked away. "There are all kinds of alone." He set his jaw. "Stay. We can be alone together," he said gruffly. "Help each other."

It was tempting. What was my alternative? And yet...

I licked my lips, coming closer to his chair near the fire. "Tell me more about your injury."

His handsome face shuttered as he drew back.

"Didn't the agency explain?" he said shortly. "Car crash."

"They said you broke your left ankle, your right arm and two ribs." I looked over his body slowly. "And also dislocated your shoulder, then managed to dislocate it *again* after you were home. Was it from physical therapy?"

He made a one-shouldered gesture that would have been a shrug. "I was bored and decided to go for a swim in the ocean."

He could have died. "Are you crazy?"

"I said I was bored. And possibly a little drunk."

"You are crazy," I breathed. "No wonder you got in a car accident. Let me guess. You were street racing, like in the movies."

The air in the dark study turned so chilly, the air nearly crackled with frost. His hand gripped the armrest, then abruptly released it.

"Got it in one," he said coldly. "I raced my car straight into a Spanish fountain and flipped it four times down a mountain. Exactly like a movie. Complete with the villain carted off in an ambulance as all the good people celebrate and cheer."

His friendliness had evaporated for reasons I didn't understand. Wondering what had really happened, I took a deep breath. "Too soon to joke about your accident, huh? Okay, got it." I bit my lip. "What really happened? What caused it?"

"I loved a woman," he said flatly. Jaw tight, he looked away, staring out the window. It was leaded glass, small-paned and looked very old. The last bit of reddish sun was dying to the far west.

"I find the topic boring." He looked at me. "How about we agree to forget about the past—both of us?"

It was the best plan I'd heard all day. "Deal."

"Jason Black sounds like an idiot in any case," he muttered.

The memory of Jason's warm eyes, his lazy smile, his sweet, slow Texas drawl—*Darlin', aren't you a sight for sore eyes*—made pain slice through me like a blade. Folding my arms tightly over my heart, I glared at my new employer. "Don't."

"So loyal," he sighed. "Even after he slept with your stepsister. Such devotion." Deliberately, he rested his eyes on his sheepdog, then turned back to me suggestively. I scowled.

"How do I know you won't toss me out tomorrow, for some trumped-up reason, like all the others?"

"I'll make you a promise." His dark blue eyes met mine. "If you'll make one to me."

As our eyes locked in the firelight, my whole body flashed hot, then cold. His deep, searing blue eyes made me feel strangely shivery. My gaze fell unwillingly to his mouth. His lips were sensual and wicked, even cruel.

And just the fact that I *noticed* his lips was a very bad sign. Mrs. Warreldy-Gribbley definitely would not approve.

Stay professional, she'd ordered in Chapter Six. *Keep your heart distant when you're physically close. Especially if your employer is handsome and young. Keep your touch impersonal and your voice cold. See him as a patient, as a collection of sinew and bone and spine, not as a man.*

Looking up, I said in a voice icy enough to flay the skin of a normal man, "You're not flirting with me, are you, Mr. St. Cyr?"

"Call me Edward." His eyes gleamed. "And no. I wasn't flirting with you, Diana." His husky voice made my name sound like music. I tried not to watch the flick of his tongue on his sensual lips with each syllable. "What I want from you is far more important than sex."

It had been an insane thing to worry about anyway—as if a gorgeous, brooding tycoon like Edward St. Cyr would ever look twice at a girl like me! "Oh. Good. I mean... Good."

"I need you to heal me. Whenever I'm not working. Even if it takes twelve hours a day."

"Twelve?" I said dubiously. "Physical therapy isn't an all-day kind of endeavor. We'd work together for an hour a day, maybe three at most. Not twelve..." I tilted my head. "What is your work?"

"I'm CEO of a global financial firm based in London. I'm currently on leave but a sizeable amount of work from my home office is still required. I'll need you available to me day or night, whenever I want you. I need you to be available for my therapy without question and without notice."

Dead silence followed, with only the crackling of the fire. Caesar the Sheepdog yawned.

I stared at Edward. "It's a completely unreasonable demand."

"Completely," he agreed.

"It would make me your virtual slave for months, possibly, at your beck and call, with no life of my own."

"Yes."

Considering the mess I'd made of my life myself, maybe that wouldn't be all bad. I looked at his leg, propped up on the stool. "Will you quit on me when it gets difficult?"

His shoulders stiffened. Putting his foot down on the floor, he used one hand to steady himself on the back of the chair, and slowly rose to his feet. He stood in front of me, and my head tilted back to look him in the eye. He was a foot taller. I felt how he towered over me, felt the power of his body like a broad shadow over my own.

"Will *you*?" he said softly.

I shook my head, looking away as I mumbled, "As long as you don't flirt with me."

"You have nothing to fear. My taste doesn't run to idealistic, frightened young virgins."

I whirled back to face him. "How did you—"

"I know women." His eyes were mocking as he looked down at me. He bared his teeth in a smile that glinted in the firelight. "I've had my share. One-night stands, weekend affairs—that is more my line. Sex without complications. That is how I play."

"Surely not since your accident—"

"I had a woman here last night." He gave his one-shouldered shrug. "An acquaintance of mine, a French lingerie model came down from London—we shared a bottle of wine and then we... But Miss Maywood, you look bewildered. I guessed you were a virgin but I expected you'd at least have *some* experience. Should I explain how it works?"

My face was probably the color of a tomato. "I'm just surprised, that's all. With your injury..."

"It's not difficult," he said huskily, looking down at me. "She sat on top of me. I didn't even have to move from my chair. I could draw you a diagram, if you like."

"N-no," I breathed. He was so close. I could almost feel the heat from his skin, the power from his body. He was right, I didn't have much experience but even I could see that this man was dangerous to women. Even idealistic young virgins like me.

Edward St. Cyr was the kind of man who would break your heart without much bothering about it. Casually cruel, like a cat toying with a mouse.

"So you agree to the terms?"

Hesitantly, I nodded. He took my hand. I nearly gasped as I felt the warmth of his skin, the roughness of his palm against mine. A current of electricity went through me. My lips parted.

"Good," he said softly. We were so close, I smelled his breath, warm and sweet—like liquor. I saw his blood-shot eyes. And I realized, for the first time, that he was slightly drunk.

A half-empty bottle of expensive whiskey was on the table by his chair, beside a short glass. Dropping his hand, I snatched them up. "But if I'm going to stay and be on call for you every hour of the day, you're going to commit as well. No more of this."

His dark eyebrow raised. "It's medicinal."

I didn't change my tone. "No drugs of any kind, except, if you're very nice to me, coffee in the morning. And no more late nights with lingerie models."

Edward smiled. "That's fine."

"Or anyone else!" I added sharply.

He scowled, folding his arms like a sulky boy. "You're being unreasonable."

"Yes," I agreed. "So that makes two of us."

"But if you take away all my toys, Diana," he looked me over, "what else will I have to play with?"

My cheeks burned at his deliberately insulting glance. "You'll have hard work," I said crisply, "and lots of it."

Edward leaned back, his handsome face cold. "You still yearn for Jason Black."

The cruelty of his words hit me like a blow. With an in-take of breath, I looked towards the window at the deep-ening night. I saw my plain reflection in the glass, against the red-orange glow of the fire.

"Yes," I whispered, and was proud my voice held steady.

"You lo-ove him," he said mockingly.

My throat choked. Madison and Jason were probably making love right now, in their elegant suite at a five-star

Parisian hotel. I said in a small voice, "I don't want to love him anymore."

"But you do." He snorted, looking over me with contemptuous eyes. "You'll probably forgive that stepsister of yours, too."

"I love them." I sounded ashamed. And I was. What kind of idiot loves people who don't love her back? My teeth chattered. "People…can't choose who they l-love."

"My God. Just look at you." Edward stared at me for a long moment. "Even now, you won't say a word against them. What a woman."

Silence fell. The wind howled outside, shaking the leaded glass in the thick gray stone.

"You're wrong, you know," he said quietly. "You *can* choose who you love. Very easily."

"How?"

"By loving no one."

At those breathtakingly cynical words, I looked at his powerful, injured body. The hard jaw, the icy blue eyes. Edward St. Cyr was the master of Penryth Hall, handsome and wealthy beyond imagining.

He was also damaged. And not just his body.

"You've had your heart broken too," I whispered, searching his gaze. "Haven't you?"

Edward looked me over in a way that caused my body to flash with heat. He took a step closer, and his muscular, powerful body towered over me in every direction.

"Perhaps that's the real reason I wanted you here," he murmured. "Perhaps we are kindred spirits, you and I. Perhaps we can—" he brushed back a tendril of my hair "—heal each other in every way…."

Edward pulled closer to me. I felt the warmth of his breath against my skin and shivered all over. My heart was beating frantically. He started to lower his head toward mine.

Then I saw the sardonic twist of his lips.

Putting my hands on his chest—on his hard, muscular, delicious chest, warm through his shirt—I said, "Stop it."

"No?" Taking a step back, laughing, he mocked me with my earlier words. "Too soon?"

"You are *a jerk*," I choked out.

He shrugged his one-shoulder shrug. "Can't blame me for trying. You seem so naïve, like you'd believe any line a man told you." He considered me. "Kind of amazing you're still a virgin."

Outrage filled me, and new humiliation. "You claim you're desperate to be healed—"

"I never used the word *desperate*."

"Then you fire your physical therapists, and waste your days getting drunk—"

"And don't forget my nights having sex," he said silkily.

"You're already trying to sabotage *me*." Narrowing my gaze, I lifted my chin. "I don't think you actually *want* to get better."

His careless look disappeared and he narrowed his eyes in turn. "I'm hiring you as a physio, Miss Maywood, not a psychiatrist. You don't know me."

"I know I came a long way here to have my time wasted. If you don't intend to get better, tell me now."

"And you'll do what? Go back home to humiliation and paparazzi?"

"Better that, than be stuck with a patient who has nothing but excuses, and blames others for his own laziness and fear!"

"You say this to my face?" he growled.

"I'm not afraid of you!"

Edward stared at me blankly.

"Maybe you should be." He fell back heavily into the chair and stared at the fire. The sheepdog lifted his head, wagging his tail.

"Is that what you want?" I said softly, coming closer. "For people to be afraid of you?"

The flickering firelight cast shadows on the leather-bound books of his starkly masculine study. "It makes things simpler. And why shouldn't they fear me?" His midnight-blue eyes burned through me. "Why shouldn't you?"

Edward St. Cyr's handsome face and cultured voice were civilized, but that was a veneer, like sunlight over ocean. Beneath it, the darkness went deeper than I'd imagined. In spite of my earlier brave words, something shivered in my heart, and I suddenly wondered what I'd gotten myself into.

"Why should I be afraid of you?" I gave an awkward laugh. "Is your soul really so dark?"

"I loved a woman," he said in a low voice, not looking at me. "So much I tried to kidnap her from her husband and baby. That's how I got in the accident." His lips turned flat. "Her husband objected."

"This is why you wouldn't allow the agency to give me any details," I said slowly, "not even your name. You were afraid if I knew more about you, I wouldn't come, weren't you?"

His jaw tightened.

"Was anyone hurt?"

His expression suddenly looked weary. "Only me."

"And now?"

"I've left them to their happiness. I've found that love, like *dreams*," he said the word mockingly, "offers more pain than pleasure." He turned to me in the firelight, his expression stark. "You want to know about the depths of darkness in my soul?" His lips twisted. "You couldn't even see it. You, who are nothing but innocence and sunlight."

I frowned at him. "I'm more than that." I suddenly remembered my own power, what I could do. The glimmer of fear disappeared. "I can help you. But you must promise to do everything I say. Everything. Exercises, healthy diet, lots of sleep—all of it." I lifted an eyebrow. "Think you can keep up with me?"

His lips parted. "Can *you* keep up with me? I've broken a lot of physiotherapists," he said dryly. "What makes you think I can't break you? I…" He suddenly scowled. "What are you smiling at? You should be afraid."

I *was* smiling. For the first time in three weeks, I felt a sense of purpose, even anticipation as I shook my head. The high-and-mighty tycoon didn't know who he was dealing with. Yes, I was a pathetic pushover in my personal life. But to help a patient, I could be as ruthless and unyielding as the most arrogant hedge fund billionaire on earth. "You are the one who should be afraid."

"Of you?" He snorted. "Why?"

"You asked for all my attention."

"So?"

My smile widened to a grin. "Now you're going to get it."

CHAPTER TWO

"YOU CALL THIS a workout?" Edward demanded the next morning.

I gave him a serene smile. "Those were just tests. Now we're about to start."

We were in the former gardener's cottage, which Edward had recently had converted into a personal rehabilitation gym, complete with exercise equipment, weight benches, yoga mats and a massage table, with big bright windows overlooking the garden. I had him lift his arms slowly over his head, saw the pull in his muscle, saw him flinch.

"Okay." I squared my shoulders. "Let's begin."

Then started the stretches and small weights and balancing and walking and then driving him to the nearest town recreation area so he could swim. I nearly brought him to his knees, literally as well as figuratively. I think I surprised him by pushing him to his limit, until he was covered with sweat.

"Ready to be done?" I said smugly.

Now he surprised me, by shaking his head. "Done? I'm just getting started," he panted. "When will the real workout begin?"

Leaving me to grit my teeth and come up with exercises that would continue to strengthen him, or at least not cause him injury.

As the afternoon faded into early evening, he never once admitted weakness or exhaustion. It was only by the grip of his fingers and the ashy-pale hue of his skin that I knew.

On the second day, though, I knew he'd be sore. I expected him to plead the demands of business, and spend his day with ice packs on his aching muscles, relaxing in his home office and talking on the phone. But when I told him to meet me in the gardener's cottage after breakfast, he didn't complain. And when I went down to set up, I found Edward already at the weight bench, lifting a heavier weight on his shoulder than he should have.

"Linger over your kippers and eggs, did you?" he said smugly. And then the second day went pretty much like the first, except this time it felt like he was a step ahead.

So the third day, determined to regain a sense of control, I had an early breakfast and went down to the gardener's cottage, at nine. I was able to greet his surprised face when he arrived five minutes later.

The fourth day, he was already there stretching when I arrived at eight forty-five.

We fell into a pattern. Any time Edward wasn't working in his home office, on his computer or the phone at odd hours talking to London, New York, Hong Kong and Tokyo, he demanded my full attention. And as promised, he got it. Each of us trying to prove we were tougher than the other. A battle of wills, neither of us willing to back down.

And now, almost two months into our working together, it had come down to this.

I'd woken up at five this morning, cursing myself in the darkness, when any sensible person would have drowsed in bed for hours longer. I'd been woken by Caesar, who'd trotted into my bedroom to heft his huge fluffy body at the foot of my bed. The sheepdog had become my morning alarm, because he only came to visit me after Edward was gone. When the dog woke me, I knew the day's battle was already half-lost.

Now, snow was falling softly outside as I hurried toward the gardener's cottage. I pulled the hood of my sweatshirt more tightly over my head, shivering as the gravel crunched beneath my feet. It was still dark, as was to be expected at five o'clock in December, the darkest day of the year.

I'd thought I could bring Edward St. Cyr to his knees? Ha. I'd thought I would make him beg for mercy? Double ha.

I'd worked with football players, injured stuntmen, even a few high-powered corporate types. I thought I knew what to expect from the typical arrogant alpha male.

But Edward was tough. Tougher than I'd ever seen.

Shivering down the garden path in the darkness, I pushed open the cottage door to discover that, just as I'd thought, Edward was already there. Doing yoga stretches on the mat, he looked well warmed up, his skin glowing with health, his body sleek in the T-shirt and shorts as he leaned forward in Downward Dog. My eyes lingered unwillingly on his muscular backside, pushed up in the air.

"'Morning." Straightening, Edward looked back at me with amusement, as if he knew exactly where my eyes had been. I blushed, and his grin widened. He stretched his arms over his head, then spread his arms and legs wide in Warrior II Pose. "Enjoy your lie-in, did you?"

"I didn't sleep in," I protested. "It's the middle of the night!"

He lifted his eyebrows and murmured, "If five is too early for you, just say so."

I glared at him. "It's fine. Happy to be here." I'd come at four tomorrow, I vowed privately. Maybe I'd start sleeping in the gym, instead of the beautiful four-poster bed down the hall from Edward's master suite on the second floor of Penryth Hall.

Edward looked at me with infinite patience. "Whenever you're ready...."

Scowling, I stomped to the equipment closet, where I yanked out a stairstep and some resistance bands. The bands got caught, so I yanked even harder.

"Maybe you should do some yoga," he observed. "It's very calming."

My scowl deepened. "Let's just get started."

I supervised his stretches, rotating his foot and his arm and shoulder, before we progressed to squats and knee lifts on the step, then thirty minutes on the exercise bike, then stretching again with the resistance bands, then walking on the treadmill, then lifting weights—carefully, with me spotting him. I helped him stretch and strengthen his muscles, stopping him before he could do himself another injury, or dislocate his shoulder again. But it was a constant battle between us. He worked like a demon at it, and his determination showed.

After nearly two months, he no longer wore a sling or brace. In fact, looking at him now, you wouldn't see a sign of injury. He looked like a powerful, virile male.

And he was.

Damn it.

Don't notice. Don't look.

We'd become almost friends, in a way. During the hours of physical therapy, we'd talked to fill the silence, and prove that neither of us was winded. I'd learned that his financial firm was worth billions, was called St. Cyr Global, and had been started by his great-grandfather, then run by his grandfather and father, until Edward took it over at twenty-two with his father's death. He'd tried to explain what his company did precisely, but it was hopeless. My eyes glazed faster than you can say *derivatives* and *credit default swaps.* It was more interesting to hear him talk about his cousin Rupert, whom he hated, his rival in the company. "That's why I need to get better," he said grimly. "So I can crush him."

Seemed a strange way to treat family. When I was ten, my beloved father had died, which had been gut-wrenching and awful. A year later, my mom had married Howard Lowe, a divorced film producer with a daughter a year younger than me. Howard's outlandish personality was a big change from my father's, who'd been a gentle, bookish professor, but we'd still been happy. Until I was seventeen, and my mom had gotten sick. Afterward, I'd realized I wanted a career where I could help people. And patients never died.

"You've never lost a single one?" Edward said teasingly.

"You might be the first," I'd growled. "If you don't quit adding extra weights to your bar."

But there were some topics we carefully avoided. I never mentioned Madison, or Jason or my failed movie career. We never again discussed Edward's car accident in Spain, or the woman he'd loved and tried to kidnap from her husband. We kept it to two types of talk—small and smack.

We'd become coworkers, of a sort. Friends, even.

Friends, I thought mockingly. *He's a client. Not a friend.*

So why did my body keep noticing him not as a patient, not even as a friend—but a man?

Beneath the rivalry and banter, I felt his eyes linger on me. I told myself not to take it personally. I'd cut him off from his sex supply. It was like denying gazelles to a lion. He was hungry. And I was handy. He couldn't help himself from looking, but I wouldn't fall prey to it.

And so I kept telling myself as we worked together in near silence, till the sun rose weakly over the horizon. Then I heard his stomach growl.

"Hungry?" I said in amusement.

Straightening from his stretch, he looked at me.

"You know I am," he said quietly.

I turned away, trying to ignore the sudden pounding of my heart. I tried to think of what Mrs. Warreldy-Gribbley would say. Looking at my watch, I kept my voice professional. "Time for breakfast."

But I couldn't stop looking at him beneath my lashes as we left the cottage to go back to the hall. Edward was so darkly handsome. So powerful and dangerous. So everything that Jason was not.

Stop it. Don't think that way. But I shivered as we tromped through the snowy garden, beneath morning skies that had now turned sodden violet in color.

A full English breakfast, prepared by Mrs. MacWhirter, was soon ready for us in the medieval dining hall. As I sat beside Edward at the end of the long table, I watched his hands pour hot tea into his china cup. I felt hyperaware of his every movement as he served himself bacon and eggs and toast. I felt him lift the fork to his mouth. I could almost wish I was bacon, feeling the caress of his breath and tongue.

This was getting ridiculous.

Shaking myself angrily, I dumped a bunch of cream and sugar into my coffee.

I couldn't let myself linger over the face and body of my handsome, brooding boss. But I couldn't stop. For weeks, my eyes had lingered over his chiseled jawline, often dark with five o'clock shadow. Lingered over the curve of his cruelly sensual lips. Over his wicked smile. Over his large hands, the thickness of his neck, his muscled forearms, dusted with dark hair.

And his eyes. When they met mine, I lingered there most of all.

As I sat next to him now at the breakfast table, pretending to read the newspaper, I couldn't stop being aware of everything about him. Every time he moved, every slight vibration from his direction amplified in waves. When the waves hit my body, they could have been measured on the Richter scale.

Sadly, there was no chapter in Mrs. Warreldy-Gribbley's book about how a nurse should quash her own lust.

Lust. I shivered. Such an ugly word, without love to make it pretty. Because I knew I didn't love him. I saw the darkness in his soul too acutely. He trusted no one, cared for no one. Especially not the women he'd taken to his bed. If he had cared for any of them, he would have written or called her. Instead, there was nothing. If he couldn't take a woman to bed, he wasn't going to bother with her. It was despicable, really.

But my hand still shook as I held my coffee cup. If he knew how easily he could seduce me...

Edward St. Cyr was a powerful man accustomed to satisfying his every desire. Sex-starved as he was, he might make short work of me right here, on this table. He'd lick me like salty bacon, pull me into his mouth like the sweet, plump imported strawberries. He'd satiate himself quickly with the offered treat—my body—and forget me an hour later. Just like what he was eating now....

Desperate for distraction, I snatched up the London newspaper he'd just finished. Edward looked up with a frown. "Wait—"

His warning was too late. As I opened the page, I saw a picture of Madison on a red carpet, smiling in a glamorous sequined gown as she attended the premiere of her latest blockbuster in Leicester Square. At her side, slightly behind her in a tuxedo, was Jason.

"Oh," I breathed, and even to my own ears it sounded like a choked, bewildered wheeze, the sound someone makes when they'd just been punched.

Something grabbed my hand. Blinking hard, I saw it was Edward's hand, holding mine tightly over the table. Was he trying to comfort me?

Abruptly, he dropped his hand. Lifting a sardonic eyebrow, he looked at the photo. "He looks like a trussed duck," he observed.

"She's dragging him behind her like a baby blanket."

"You're wrong," I said automatically, then looked more carefully. Hmm. Now that Edward had pointed it out, Jason did look rather like an accessory, rather than a man, as Madison clutched his hand, dragging him behind her.

"And that white toothy smile of his," Edward continued, rolling his eyes. "How much did he pay for those?"

"His smile is lovely!" I protested.

"The white hurts my eyes." He briefly covered them. "I've never seen anything so fake."

"Shut up!"

"Right. I forgot he's your dream man." Leaning back in the chair, Edward took a gulp of his black tea as he rolled his eyes. "See where love gets you."

For about the hundredth time, I wondered about the woman who had broken his heart in Spain. The one who'd made him care so much that he'd actually tried to kidnap her. What had been so special about her? I looked back down at the photo of my stepsister and Jason, beaming at the camera.

See where love gets you...

I set down my fork. "Let's get back to work." I tilted my head and said challengingly, "Unless you need a longer break…"

Edward's cup fell with a clatter against the saucer. His eyes were gleaming with the joy of the fight. "I've been ready for ten minutes. I was waiting for you."

An hour later, back at the cottage, he was walking on the treadmill at the slow speed he hated.

"This is boring," he grumbled.

"It's fine," I insisted.

"No." He turned up the treadmill speed.

"Don't!" I said sharply.

He turned it up even more.

"You're going to kill yourself!" Then my eyes went wide as I drew back, watching him—this man who at the beginning of November had walked with a cane—now jogging forcefully on the treadmill. Edward had improved more rapidly than any client I'd ever seen.

"It's almost superhuman," I breathed. I jumped when I realized I'd said it out loud. Praise wasn't part of our deal. I blushed. "I, um, mean…"

"No. I heard you perfectly." Still jogging, Edward turned his head to give me a triumphant grin. "I *amaze* you with my strength and power. You're in *awe*. You're wishing right now you could give me a *big fat kiss*…."

"Am not!" I said indignantly, my cheeks on fire.

"I can see it in your face." His grin widened. "*Oh Edward,*" he said mockingly in falsetto, "*You're incredible. You're my own personal hero—*"

His sentence ended when his ankle abruptly twisted beneath him. He slammed down hard, cracking his shoulder and head against the treadmill. In a second, I was on my knees beside him.

"Are you all right?" Luckily he'd been wearing the safety, which made the treadmill's engine stop, or the skin of his cheek would have been ripped raw. "Careful. Don't sit up so fast—"

Ignoring me, he ripped his arm away with a scowl. "I'm fine."

"It was my fault—"

"It wasn't," he said shortly.

"I distracted you."

Edward looked even more ticked off than ever. "Stop trying to take the blame. You didn't do anything."

"Your head's bleeding. We might need to take you to a hospital—" But as I started to run my hands along his head, he yanked away.

"Stop bothering. I said I'm fine." He put his hand to his scalp and his skin was covered in blood as he pulled it away.

Rushing across the cottage, I grabbed a clean white towel. Turning on the hot water in the sink, I got it wet and soapy then brought it back to him. Taking it without comment, he wiped his head. I put my hands over my mouth, almost ill with guilt.

"I shouldn't have let you push yourself so hard. It's my job to control you...."

"As if you could," he gibed. He snorted, and one corner of his lips lifted as he looked at me. "Seriously. Think about it."

Our eyes met. My shoulders relaxed slightly.

"That's true. I can't tell you anything, can I?"

He shook his head. "Not a thing."

Seeing the blood dripping down his forehead, my smile fell. "But you can't be strong all the time, Edward." My voice faltered. "Even you have moments of weakness...."

His smile changed to a glare. "*Weakness?*"

I recoiled from the blast of cold anger. "From your injury."

"Ah. Well. That's what I'm paying you for, isn't it?" He bared his teeth into a smile. "To wipe every trace of weakness from my body, to make me twice the man I was before she—"

He looked away, his jaw tight.

"Do you miss her?" I said softly.

"No," he bit out. He pulled the towel from his head.

"She was a good reminder of the lesson I learned as a child. Never depend on anyone."

What had happened when he was a child? I wondered. "You depend on *me*."

"To fix me? Yes. To keep my secrets? Yes."

"That's something, isn't it?"

"Yes," he said slowly, looking at me. "That's something." He abruptly turned away. Grabbing the handrail of the treadmill, he pulled himself to his feet. "The bleeding's stopped. Back to work."

"You're going to run more?" I stared at him in shock.

"Why not, are you tired?" he said challengingly.

I held up my hands. "Don't even! You're going to hurt yourself!"

"I know what I can handle." But as he stepped back on the treadmill, I saw the white of his knuckles as he gripped the handrails.

Edward was used to commanding everything and everyone. He was nearly killing himself to prove his strength. And forget the time a few thousand pounds of steel had crushed him like a blade of grass.

"A body needs time to heal." I put my hand over his. "Even a body like yours."

He tilted his head with a mocking smile. "Looking, were you?"

I blushed. "No. That is, yes, of course I was, but—"

"I like it when you blush." Turning away, he reached for the power button of the treadmill. He really was determined to kill himself.

"No more running for today," I said desperately. What could I possibly do to stop him? "Um—take off your clothes and lie down."

He gave a low laugh. "You really don't want me to run. Very well," he said gravely. "If you're determined to lure me away with sex, I accept."

"Take your clothes off for a *massage*. I don't want you to stiffen up…." The corners of his lips quirked, and I scowled. "Shut *up!*"

"I didn't say anything," he said meekly.

I pointed at the massage table. "You know what I want."

"Yes, as a matter of fact I do." Stepping off the treadmill, Edward looked down at me with a gleam of light in his eyes. "I'm just surprised it's taking you so long to admit it."

He was so close. And looking at me so intensely. My heart was pounding. All he had to do was reach out and take me in his arms.

"Admit what?" I breathed, trying to ignore the bead of sweat between my breasts as heat flashed through me. "Admit you're a colossal pain?"

"Have it your way." With a grin, he stepped back and reached up to pull his T-shirt off his body. "So you want me naked, huh? I knew sooner or later you'd be begging me to—" He flinched, and exhaled, dropping his arms. Gritting his teeth, he started to try again.

"Stop. Is it your shoulder?"

"It's fine," he ground out, an obvious lie. He must have hit his shoulder harder than I'd thought.

Coming to him, I ran my hands over his shoulder anxiously, then exhaled. "It's not dislocated."

"I told you." He started to reach up to pull off his shirt.

"Stop. Let me do it."

He tilted his head, his eyes gleaming. "Be my guest."

My hands shook as I lifted his faded cotton T-shirt upward, trying to ignore the warmth and steel of his tautly muscled chest and shoulders beneath my fingertips. I yanked it over his head, tousling his dark hair that my fingers longed to touch, to see if it was as silky as it looked.

He straightened. "Thanks."

"No problem." I couldn't stop my eyes from lingering

over his hard-muscled form laced with dark hair. I licked my lips.

Then our eyes met.

Our bodies were still so close together. The upper half of his body was now naked.

And Edward suddenly smiled.

Not a friendly smile. A dangerous one, full of masculine power that threatened all kinds of things. Things I would like. Things that would pleasure my body. Things that would break my heart.

But I'd already had my heart broken once. And if Jason Black had broken it, Edward St. Cyr would crush it, smash it, light it on fire and then laugh, as he watched the ashy remains float softly to the ground.

"Are you going to take off the rest of my clothes, or shall I?" His dark sapphire eyes gleamed. "It might assist in your massage to take off your own clothes as well."

A selfish man may try to tempt the unwary virgin into sensual pleasures beyond her imagining, Mrs. Warreldy-Gribbley had warned. *There is only one means of resistance. The weapon of icy courtesy.*

Coldly, I lifted my chin. "This isn't a *date*. Your muscles need to be massaged after all your exercise today, and the fall. Otherwise you'll hurt." Grabbing a large white towel, I flung it at him. "Don't lift your shoulder again today. Let me know when it's safe to turn around."

Folding my arms, I turned the opposite direction. Furious at myself.

Why did I let him have this effect on me? No other client, and there had been some good-looking ones, had remotely made me feel like this. Even Jason had never made me feel like this. The times he'd kissed me had been pleasant. But he'd never made me feel so confused, off-kilter, and well, *burning hot....*

"You can turn around."

I did so. And wished I hadn't.

Edward was stretched naked, facedown across the massage table, as I'd ordered, covered only by a white towel across his backside, between his powerful back, his slender hips and thickly muscled thighs. Leaning his elbow against the leather cushion of the table, he propped up his head and looked at me darkly.

"Isn't this what you wanted?" he said huskily. "Me naked and at your mercy?"

I opened my mouth for a witty comeback, but only a squeak came out. I coughed to cover, then nervously went to the table. *It's no big deal,* I told myself fiercely. I'd massaged him many times over the past few weeks.

But something felt different. Something had changed. My skittish sexual awareness of him had managed to penetrate the gym. Why? How?

Edward lifted a dark eyebrow. "Be gentle with me," he said mockingly. Closing his eyes, he propped his chin on his folded arms and waited for me to touch him.

Touch him.

I looked down at my hands, which felt suddenly tingly. I knew how to give a professional massage. Why were my hands shaking? I didn't feel like a competent physical therapist. I felt like what he'd once called me—a frightened virgin.

Edward St. Cyr, my boss who'd inspired me and irritated me in equal measure, who was way out of my league and didn't see me as anything more than someone he could casually flirt with, and perhaps casually sleep with, and casually forget, was naked beneath my hands. And I feared if I showed a moment of weakness, he might roll over and devour me. I pictured a lion devouring a gazelle in a documentary, the flashing jaws digging into the meat and sinew.

If he felt my hands shaking… All he had to do was turn

around on the table and pull me down hard against him
in a savage kiss.

Don't think about it, I told myself fiercely. Flexing
my fingers, I poured oil in one palm then rubbed my
hands together to warm them. Slowly, I lowered them
to his back.

Edward's skin was warm, like satin. I heard the soft
whir of the nearby space heater as I ran my hands down
the length of his spine, feeling the smoothness of his skin
over hard muscle.

I wondered what his naked body would feel like, pressed
against my own.

Muscles. I tried not to think of him as a dangerous man
I was longing to kiss, but focus instead on the individual
parts of his body, muscles, the tendons, the ligaments. I
tried to see him only as a patient.

Yes. A patient. Just a body, like a machine. Tissues connected to ligaments connected to muscles. Cells.

Not an amazing masculine body, rippled with muscles
and power, attached to the soul of the man who'd teased
and challenged me for the past seven-and-a-half weeks as
I lived in his castle. The man I thought of before I slept,
aware of his bedroom down the hall from mine.

As I ran my hands down the trapezius muscles of his
upper back, I tried to calm the rapid beat of my heart. I
looked across the room, past all the shiny, modern exercise
equipment and weights and yoga mats. Outside the windows, the noonday sun was peeking through the clouds,
a soft pink through the bare black trees, leaving patterns
and shadows across the winter-bare garden.

But as I stroked and rubbed Edward beneath my palms,
I felt hot as summer. I closed my eyes, trying *not* to imagine what it would be like if he were my lover. How it would
feel to sink into the pleasure I imagined he'd give me. Af-

terward my soul might be ash, but I'd finally know the exhilaration of the fire.

For all these years, I'd guarded both my body and my heart, afraid of ever again feeling the pain of losing someone or something I cared about. But it turned out I hadn't really managed to shield myself from pain. Could anyone?

Sadness and ash came into life anyway. People died. People broke your heart.

Edward sighed. "That feels great."

"I'm glad," I said hoarsely. Dripping more richly scented oil onto his skin, I rubbed the length of his back in silence, the long muscles of his legs, one at a time, to the soles of his feet. Then I lifted the towel a few inches above his body. "Roll over."

He didn't move. "It's, um, not necessary."

"Of course it is." It was difficult to stand there holding the towel away from his naked backside and not look. My tone was waspish. "I have to do your other side. Do you want your muscles to be lopsided? Your back relaxed, your front all stiff?"

"Um…"

"For heaven's sake, just turn over!"

So he did. Exhaling with relief, I gingerly tossed the towel over his front for modesty.

And I saw that his front side was, indeed, stiff. My eyes went wide.

Oh my God, was that—him?

I'd never seen any man naked before. I wasn't seeing him naked now, just the shape of him jutting from his body, almost pornographically explicit beneath the white terry cloth towel, cylindrical and huge. Were all men that large? My cheeks burned, but I stared down at him, fascinated, unable to look away.

Then I felt Edward's gaze. "I took you for a virgin, but you truly don't have any experience at all, do you?"

"I've had lots," I lied. Our eyes met, and my shoulders sagged. "If you mean work. With men—none."

"Not even with Jason?" he said incredulously. "No experience with sex, of any kind?"

The burn of my cheeks had turned radioactive now, and I couldn't meet his gaze. "I've been kissed once or twice."

"You're twenty-eight!"

"I know," I snapped. To hide my embarrassment, I turned away to grab the oil. He'd had a purely physical reaction, I told myself, the automatic response of his hungry male body to the touch of any female. It wasn't that he wanted *me*. Not in particular. It couldn't be.

Could it?

I did a quick comparison between his perfectly chiseled body, his power and wealth and his incredible masculine good looks—and what I had on offer.

Nope.

If you lose an inch of moral high ground, rush back to it as quick as you can, Mrs. Warreldy-Gribbley advised. Clearing my throat, I said reproachfully. "Keep this professional, please."

"You first," he said, sounding amused. Leaning his head back against his palms, he closed his eyes, and I remembered how he'd caught me staring.

Feeling foolish, I tentatively massaged the muscles of his chest, his arms, his shoulders. I was gentle with the injuries that still hadn't completely healed, but even those were starting to disappear. He was no longer wearing bandages of any kind. There was nothing to keep my hands off his skin as I traced over the twisted muscles, the jagged scars. He was powerful, virile, sexy. He'd nearly vanquished the accident that had devastated his body. Heaven only knew what gaping wound still remained in his heart.

I looked down at him on the massage table. His eyes were still closed, but there was a twist to his lips I couldn't read.

"What are you thinking?" I blurted out. I bit my lip, but there was no taking it back.

His dark blue eyes slit open infinitesimally.

"A dangerous question," he murmured. "Better perhaps for you not to know."

Was he thinking about the accident? The woman? Or something else entirely? "That's silly." I gave a stilted laugh. "Knowledge is never bad."

"In that case..." His lips curved sardonically. "I am thinking, Miss Maywood, that it would be amusing to seduce you."

A shiver ripped through my body. Wide-eyed, I stepped back from the massage table. "I work for you."

"So?"

"I'm—in love with someone else," I said weakly.

He abruptly sat up. "Not that it matters, but..." He lifted a dark eyebrow. "Are you sure?"

I stared at him. "Of course I'm sure."

"You saw their picture, two movie stars gleaming together on the red carpet, entwined, stupid with love. He cheated on you, left you months ago, you never even slept together—but after all this time, you still love him? You're still faithful? Why?"

Yes, why? My body echoed. Swallowing, I looked at the floor. "I don't know."

"It's true what they say," he said harshly. "The best way to get over someone is to get *under* someone else."

"Really?" I looked at him steadily. "And have all the women you've slept with burned the image of *her* from your brain—the woman you loved? The woman you almost died for?"

His lips curled, and a low growl came from the back of his throat. "Don't."

"Love doesn't just disappear. You know that as well I do."

"It can. It has. And you're stupid to let it do otherwise." Holding the towel around his hips with one hand, he rose to his feet. His eyes narrowed as he went on the attack. "How does it feel, knowing that your stepsister has everything—the career you want, the man you love?" He tilted his head. "And he probably wanted her from the beginning. He was likely using you, to get to her...."

"Shut up!"

"I feel sorry for you. How it must hurt to know they'll never be punished for hurting you. That while you suffer, they're making love in oblivious joy." He snorted, his lip curling. "You're so meaningless, they've forgotten you even exist."

His face was close to mine, his expression cruel. My heart pounded with grief and pain. Then looking at him, I suddenly understood.

"You're not talking about me," I breathed. "You're talking about yourself."

The air between us was suddenly cold in a way that had nothing to do with the wintery bluster rattling the leaded windows, and the weak afternoon sun falling behind the bare black trees. His lip curled. He turned away.

"We're done."

"No." Reckless of the danger, I grabbed his arm. "I'm trying to make you better," I said in a small voice. "How can I, if I don't understand the depths of your injury?"

Edward looked at me, his jaw tight. "You can see it. You've touched it with your hands."

"Some wounds can't be seen or touched," I whispered. I took a deep breath. "Some go deeper. Let me help you, Edward," I said pleadingly. "Tell me what you need."

His dark blue eyes stared down at me, haunted. Then they turned cold and cruel as the Arctic. Still holding the towel loosely over his hips with one hand, he wrapped the other around the back of my head.

"Here's how you can help me," he said huskily. "Here's what I need."

And he pulled me against him in a hard, hungry kiss.

I didn't have time to resist, or think; my body tightened, then melted against his. Edward's lips were like silk, hot and fiery with need, his tongue brushing against mine. He held me against him, towering over me, strong and powerful and nearly naked.

Then his towel fell to the floor, and there was no *nearly* about it.

I was wearing a zip-up cotton hoodie, a T-shirt and knit workout pants, as always. But his skin scorched right through my clothes.

His hand moved slowly down my back, as the other cradled the back of my head, his fingers moving through my hair. I felt a whoosh and realized he'd pulled out my ponytail. My hair tumbled down my shoulders. He murmured words against my lips, his voice low, almost a growl.

"I want you, Diana," he breathed, and claimed my lips savagely.

I'd never been kissed like this before. The pallid, tentative kisses of a brief college boyfriend had left me cold. Jason's kisses, as I said, were pleasant, nothing more. This?

This was like fire.

Edward St. Cyr wanted my body. Not my soul. Not my heart. There was no respect in his embrace, no concern for my feelings. There was no emotion at all—just physical need and reckless desire.

But my hunger matched his. He made me forget everything—the past, my broken heart, my pain. When he kissed me, I almost forgot my name. He brought me to life,

like a single hot ember from cold ash. He made my body
blaze like the sun.

I gripped his bare shoulders with an answering fervor
that belonged to some other bolder woman—someone fearless—and kissed him back. With everything I had.

I heard his low hiss of breath, then a rising growl at the
back of his throat as he pulled me tighter against his naked
body. His hands ran over me possessively. He kissed my
lips hard enough to bruise, then nibbled my lower lip. He
flicked his hot tongue in each corner of my mouth before
he slowly moved down, kissing my chin. Kissing my neck.

My head fell back, my hair tumbling down my shoulders. The cottage seemed to spin around me, as if I were
at the center of a tornado. My skin felt hot, burning like
the desert. I squeezed my eyes shut. I couldn't open my
eyes. If I did, I'd see Edward St. Cyr—my handsome, arrogant boss—kissing down my neck to my chest. If I saw
that, I was afraid my mind would explode—along with
my body....

His hands brushed roughly over my breasts, over hard,
aching nipples. He cupped them over my thin cotton shirt
and bra, stroking the sensitive tips with his fingers. My
breathing became ragged.

"Take it off," he murmured in my ear, and I felt the flick
of his tongue against my ear. Prickles of desire, flashing
cold then hot, raced up and down my body. Leaning forward to kiss me, he whispered, "Take it all off."

His hands were insistent against my naked belly as he
reached beneath my T-shirt. He reached higher still, toward my thin cotton bra that barely seemed to contain my
breasts, which felt strangely tight and heavy, heaving with
every gasp of breath. He kissed my lips hard, filling my
mouth with his tongue, as he reached to take a breast in
his hand. He squeezed an aching nipple.

Sensation ripped through me, and I gasped, gripping

his bare shoulders. Electricity coursed through my veins, and blind raging need that frightened me with its intensity.

"I'll help you," he whispered, and pulling on my sweatshirt, he started to push me down, back onto the massage table.

Abruptly, my eyes flew open.

I realized he intended to take me right here. In the gardener's cottage, surrounded by gym equipment and free weights. Against the massage table. He would ruthlessly help himself to my virginity without any more thought than that he had a hard-on, and I was conveniently available to slake it.

He didn't want *me*. He wanted a *woman*. He intended to make use of me, in the same way I'd scarfed a bag of chips, the times I'd come home from work too starving to wait for a proper meal.

When Edward had kissed me so passionately, when I'd felt his naked body hard and powerful against mine, I'd been overwhelmed with the intensity of sensation. I'd been lost in fantasy and need.

In another moment, I would have let him rip off all my clothes, or—if that was too much trouble—simply pull down my stretchy yoga pants and thrust inside me, like an animal grunting as he took his pleasure, until he left me thirty seconds later, sticky and used upon the table.

None of my romantic dreams had fantasized about *that*.

I pushed on his shoulders. "No."

Edward's heavy-lidded gaze suddenly looked confused. "What?"

My hands pressed harder against his shoulders. I stared up at him in the gray, slanted winter sunlight gleaming dully from the window. Outside, I heard the howl of the wind, the roar of the sea. The barking of a dog. I heard my own thin voice. "I said no."

Looking bewildered, Edward released me, and we stood

facing each other beside the table, my clothes disheveled, his entirely absent. I tried not to look down. Tried not to think about how I'd just nearly given him everything— my hungry body and bruised heart—for the sake of blind passion.

But oh, that passion…my body was still trembling with the pleasure of it, with the desperate need. My body hated me right now for stopping. I wanted him still, desperately.

But he had to want me.

Me, Diana, not just any random woman.

All right, so I wasn't exactly a beautiful movie star like Madison. That didn't mean I had to settle for being a stale bag of chips. Not to anyone.

Pulling away, I fisted my hands at my sides. "You are my patient. There are some lines I will never cross."

"Oh, for…" He gave a low curse. "Surely you've crossed lines before."

I shook my head stubbornly.

"Never broken a single rule?"

"No."

Reaching out, he brushed tendrils of hair from my face, tracing his fingertips down my temple, to my cheek, to my trembling lips. "Then," he whispered, "you've missed a lot of fun."

He towered over me, unselfconscious and proud, though utterly naked. While my own body was trembling. Blood rushed through my veins and I was breathing too fast. I didn't let myself look anywhere but his eyes. Just meeting his hot, hungry gaze was hard enough.

"Let me love you, Diana," he said in a low voice.

For a second, my heart stopped. Then…

"Love me? You said you'll never love anyone."

His breath exhaled on a hiss. "That kind of love is over-rated. Hearts and flowers and pledging fidelity forever." His lip curled. "As if you can make emotion permanent by mummifying it in a vow." He took a step closer. "I do like you, Diana. I respect you enough to treat you as my equal—"

"Gee, thanks." My voice was tart.

He placed a finger on my lips. "We both know what is going to happen between us. Pretend otherwise, if you like, but you're fooling no one. Not even yourself." He traced his fingertips along my cheek. "I felt how you just kissed me. You want me, as I want you."

I could hardly deny it. "That doesn't mean I have to act on it."

"Why not?"

I struggled to remember, and finally managed, "Jason—"

"Ah yes. Jason Black, the bright flame in your heart," Edward said mockingly. He shook his head. "Let him keep your heart. I will have your body." He ran his hand gently down my back. "Very soon. And we both know it."

His words shocked me. But I feared he was right. Even now, it was all I could do not to turn my face into his caress.

It would be so easy to surrender. Part of me wanted nothing more than to be bold—to be a rule breaker like he was. What had following the rules ever done for me, except leave me brokenhearted and alone?

If your employer's temptation grows too great, Mrs. Warreldy-Gribbley had warned, *run as if your life depended on it. It does.*

Trembling, I turned and fled.

"Diana—"

I didn't stop. Tripping over the yoga mat, I wrenched open the door and ran out into the cold garden.

The earlier snowflakes had changed into a chilly, sodden mist that threatened rain. I was nearly crying by the time I made it back to the main house. But the instant

I pushed open the heavy oak door, the thick gray walls started to close in on me.

Never broken a single rule?

No.

Then you've missed a lot of fun.

Caesar whined at my feet. Wiping my tears savagely, I looked down to see the sheepdog pacing in front of the door. I'd gotten in the habit of taking him for a walk, since his nominal owner, who was actually and surprisingly Mrs. MacWhirter, had little patience for giving him long walks or letting him sleep on the bed. Getting away suddenly felt absolutely necessary. Grabbing my raincoat and Caesar's leash, I went back out into the rain, the large sheepdog galloping happily beside me.

I walked the opposite direction of the gardener's cottage, heading for the path that led to the rocky edge of the cliffs. The mist had turned to drizzle, already melting down the thin layer of snow, which I knew overnight would harden into ice. Ice like Edward's heart.

Some wounds can't be seen or touched. Some go deeper. Let me help you, Edward. Tell me what you need.

Here's how you can help me. Here's what I need.

Oh. Oh, oh, oh. I abruptly stopped on the path, causing Caesar to jump beside me, before he ran ahead with a snuff.

That was the reason Edward had kissed me. Not because he wanted me. Not even just because he wanted a woman. Oh no.

He'd kissed me to shut me up. Because I'd been asking about his accident, probing with questions he didn't want to answer. He'd deflected me the easiest, simplest way he knew how. The way that always worked with any woman.

My cheeks were burning now, my throat aching with humiliation. Tears streaked down my face, leaving cold trails beneath the chill of the wind, as I looked out at the vast gray sea.

Edward St. Cyr was used to riding roughshod over people, especially women. He was used to twisting them all around his finger. I knew this. And I'd still let him do it to me.

I stared out at the ocean, watching the light's play of sparkle and shadows. My tangled hair flew around me in the chilly wind. Watching the seagulls fly away, I almost wished I could join them. To fly away and disappear and never be seen again.

Penryth Hall was supposed to be my place to hide. How did you hide from a hiding place?

Maybe there was nowhere to hide, I thought suddenly, when the person you were really trying to hide from was yourself.

Sooner or later, I'd have to go back to California. Face the scandal, the pity. Face the two people who'd ripped out my heart. And most of all: face myself.

Picking up a stick, I tossed it down the beach. With an eager yelp, Caesar ran after it. My mouth still felt seared from Edward's kiss. I touched my bruised lips. They still ached for him. For that one single moment, when I'd thought Edward wanted me—me, the invisible girl, completely unnoteworthy either in looks, intelligence or career—I'd felt like I was worth something. Like I *mattered*.

I writhed with shame to remember it now.

Caesar barked happily, dropping the stick at my feet. I picked it up and tossed it farther down the rocky shore. I stayed out there, procrastinating for as long as I could. But by the time we were both wet with rain and freezing cold, I'd made up my mind.

I was leaving Penryth Hall.

As the dog raced ahead on the return path, I realized

I'd finally found something that frightened me more than
going back to California.

Staying here.

Edward didn't really need me anyway. Not anymore.
I'd known that when I'd seen him running on the treadmill today.

"You don't need me," I said aloud.

Need me, need me, the wind sighed mournfully in return.

As Caesar hurried ahead of me on the wet path, his
tongue lolling out as he raced eagerly to get back home to
the castle of gray stone, my steps became slower. When I
finally reached the door, my feet turned to the left, and I
found myself walking around the house to the front door,
procrastinating the moment I'd have to go inside and tell
him I was leaving. Once I said it, I'd have to do it.

I stopped in shock.

Two expensive sedans were parked in front of Penryth
Hall. Standing next to them were my stepsister's two bodyguards, Damian and Luis.

I stared at them, goggle-eyed. "What are you…"

"Hello, Diana," Luis said, smiling. "Long time no see."

But next to him, Damian glowered down at me. "Miss
Lowe and Mr. Black are here to see you." Seven feet tall,
bald, and scowling, he shook his head at me. "And she's
really, really mad at you."

CHAPTER THREE

WATER DRIPPED NOISILY from my raincoat to the flagstones as I walked nervously into the shadowy foyer of the castle. The thought of facing them all at once scared me to death.

Edward, Madison and Jason.

All at once.

I couldn't do it. I stopped, clenched my hands at my sides.

Caesar loped up beside me in the foyer. With a sympathetic look, he shook his fur, splattering me with water and mud. I gasped as cold wet dirt hit my face, then gasped again as I looked down at my messed-up hair, my muddy raincoat and sneakers. I hadn't buttoned the raincoat so even the T-shirt beneath, which Edward had recently groped, now had a splatter of mud across the front.

If I thought I couldn't face them before...!

With a satisfied snort, Caesar trotted happily down the hall, no doubt intending to plunk himself in his nice spot on the rug in front of the fire. What did he have to fear? *He* wasn't facing the firing squad.

I heard voices down the hall, coming from the library. Madison's high-pitched voice, two lower masculine ones. Sharing tea, or lying in ambush for me?

Maybe I could make a run for it. If I tiptoed down the hall, I'd sneak by the library unseen. Then I'd pack my bag and flee for Tierra del Fuego.

"What are you doing?" Edward said quietly.

He was standing in the hallway, his face in silhouette. He'd showered and changed from his exercise clothes. His dark hair was still wet, slicked back against his head, and he was actually wearing a jacket and tie, button-up shirt and trousers. It was…sexy. I licked my lips. "Why are you dressed up?"

"We have company." Flickering firelight from the open doorway of the library cast shadows on his grim face. "Care to join us?"

He was so handsome and sophisticated. Everything I was not. It seemed incredible to me now that he'd kissed me, for any reason whatsoever. I put my hand to my hair. Yup. Just as I thought, it was damp with rain, tangled as a bird's nest. I put my hand down.

"Well?"

"I don't think I can do this," I whispered. My heart was pounding, my feet ready to take flight. "I thought about it on my walk. After all that's happened, I've realized you don't need me anymore and maybe it's time for me to just—"

"Is that you, Diana?" Madison's voice carried sharply from the library. "Get in here!"

Edward's eyebrow lifted. He came closer, and I shivered as he pulled my raincoat off my body. I felt the brush of his fingertips. I breathed in his scent, masculine and clean, like a Bavarian forest. Hanging up the wet coat, he turned back to me.

"You're going to have to face them sooner or later, Diana," he said quietly. His hand fell bracingly on my shoulder. "Might as well be now."

His camaraderie made me feel strangely comforted, even strengthened. That brief moment helped me square my shoulders, lift my chin and walk with my head held high into the library.

The firelit room was impossibly elegant, two stories high, with leatherbound books on all sides, a ladder to reach them and an enormous white marble fireplace at one end. Not to mention two movie stars sitting on the white leather sofa near the fire.

Madison looked beautiful as always. Her long blond hair was straight, her eyes huge beneath fake eyelashes, her cheekbones sharp enough to cut glass. Even casually dressed in a white cropped jacket of tousled fur, thousand-dollar silk blouse and size 0 toothpick jeans, no one could have mistaken her for anything but a movie star.

Jason sat beside her, his hand protectively on her knee. Handsome, broad shouldered and corn-fed like the Texas farm boy he'd once been, he looked different than he had just six months ago. The gloss of success covered him now, like his newly expensive clothes.

Looking at them, my body flashed hot, then cold. Jason started to rise to his feet, but Madison grabbed his hand, keeping him seated beside her.

"Diana," she said coolly. "It was rude of you to keep us waiting. But I don't blame you for being afraid to face me after what you did."

I would have staggered back, except Edward was behind me, his hand supportively on my lower back. I felt his strength and somehow my knees steadied themselves.

"What *I* did?" I queried dangerously.

"You left me when I needed you most!"

I gaped at her. "I went to California to give the reporter a tour of your house—as you asked me to!"

She waved her hand dismissively. "That? All that happened ages ago. I'm talking about my movie premiere last night. You should have been there for me!"

"Are you kidding?" I breathed.

"You know how nervous I get, being at public events. You promised you'd always be there...."

"Yeah, when I was your assistant." I swallowed looking between her and Jason. "Before I was completely humiliated in front of the whole world—"

"Are you still trying to punish me for that?" she demanded. "We didn't mean to fall in love. It was an accident. When it's right, you just know." She looked lovingly at Jason, then glared at me. "It's petty of you, Diana, it really is, and I'm disappointed. You and Jason didn't even sleep together."

"You told her that?" I breathed, staring down at him.

Rubbing the back of his blond head, Jason gave me the rueful smile I used to find so irresistible. "You and I were friends, Diana. We dated and yeah, there was a little flirting going on, but hell," he shook his head, "you never let me touch you. Said you wanted to wait for true love or some such…but this is the twenty-first century. I don't know what century you're living in, but as far as I'm concerned, if there's no sex, there's no relationship."

For a second I couldn't breathe. No relationship? As if I'd imagined it all in my mind? "You—"

And it was then I saw the sparkle on Madison's left hand.

A huge canary-yellow diamond ring.

On *that* finger.

With an intake of breath, I covered my mouth with my hand. For a moment, the only sound in the library was the crackle of the fire in counterpoint to the miserable drip-drip-drip of water from my hair as I stood like a mud-splattered, drowned rat in front of my beautiful stepsister, who had a ten-carat engagement ring on one hand, and the man I'd loved holding the other.

"You're—" I was horrified to feel tears burning the backs of my eyelids as I looked between them. "You're engaged?"

Madison put her hand over the ring. "Yes…" A smile

softened the sharp lines of her face as she looked at Jason. "He asked me last night, after the premiere."

Jason smiled back. Lifting her hand to his lips, he kissed it. "Best night of my life."

Their eyes glowed as they looked at each other. They were in love. Really, deeply in love. It was one thing to know it in my mind, and something else entirely to see it right in front of me. I not only felt sick, I felt invisible. An echo went through my mind.

I feel sorry for you. How it must hurt to know they'll never be punished for hurting you. That while you suffer, they're making love in oblivious joy. You're so meaningless, they've forgotten you even exist.

"Stop pouting and be happy for us." Madison turned back to me. "Come back and work for me. I need you. Someone will have to coordinate with the wedding planner…"

Wedding planner!

"And don't worry," Jason said to me kindly. "You'll find a real boyfriend someday, Di. Great girl like you. It's bound to happen, even if it takes a while…"

Violently, I held up a trembling hand, unable to bear another patronizing word. My heart was collapsing in my chest, squeezing into hard little pieces, about to fly out of my ribs like bullets. In another moment, I'd weep in front of them, and then I really would have to die.

"Darling." Edward purred behind me, suddenly wrapping his arms around me. Pulling me back protectively against his body, he murmured, "Didn't you tell them?"

I looked back at him blankly. "Tell them?"

He smiled down at me, his expression tender, his dark blue gaze caressing mine. "About us."

"Us?" I said.

"Us." Edward looked at me as if it were all he could do right now not to lift me up in his arms and carry me up-

stairs to bed. No man had looked at me like that before.
Not ever. The full seductive force of his gaze was a blast
of heat, an intoxicating drug that made every part of me
yearn to tremble and unfold like a flower. "Diana, why
didn't you tell them…" he stroked back a tendril of my
hair, "that we're lovers?"

What? My heart stopped beating.

"What?" Madison said.

"What?" Jason said.

Edward looked down at me with concern. "But darling,
you're chilled to the bone. Your clothes are wet. Were you
taking the dog on a walk?"

Teeth chattering—and not just from cold—I nodded
like a fool.

He gave me a slow, sensual smile. "Why don't you
go upstairs to our room—" *our* room? I thought dumbly
"—and change. We'll wait."

"I will *not* wait," Madison snapped. "Not until you
agree to come back and plan our wedding." Looking between Edward and me, no doubt comparing his perfect
gorgeousness to my slovenly mess, she added suspiciously,
"And I don't believe for a second that the two of you…"

Edward didn't even look her way. "Actually, Diana," he
whispered, twining a long muddy, tangled tendril of my
hair as if it were silken perfection, "I think I'll come upstairs. Help you out of these cold, wet clothes."

Any woman could get warm instantly, just by looking
up into Edward's hot dark gaze. Had I wandered into some
strange parallel universe, where I was the beautiful movie
star, instead of Madison? Had I fallen on my walk and hit
my head on a rock?

I felt my stepsister's gaze travel over us both, from the
way I was standing to the way that Edward supported my
arm. There was new doubt in her melodious voice as she
said, "You're really—together?"

"Only recently," Edward said, smiling down at me hungrily, cupping my cheek with his hand. As if he were already thinking about what he intended to do to me in bed. "I wanted Diana from the moment we met. But she tortured me," his eyes traced mine, "making me wait. And wait. The sexiest, most desirable woman in the world."

"She's just a physical therapist." Madison sounded grumpy.

Edward finally looked at her. "Yes. A healer. And what Diana knows about the human body—" He exhaled, looking at me in wonder. "No wonder she's the most amazing lover I've ever had."

My body flashed hot, then cold.

"The two of you are in love?" Jason said, dumbfounded.

"Love?" Edward snorted. "No." He looked down at me, stroking my cheek, and I felt his fingertips against my skin. "What we have is purely physical. Sex. And fire."

A little sound came from the back of Jason's throat as he stared between us, his eyes comically huge.

"I don't understand." Madison's beautiful face was bewildered, as if she was confused how any other woman could be the center of a man's attention when she herself was in the room. "It's only been a couple months."

"When it's right, you just know." He smiled as he echoed her earlier words. Wrapping both his strong arms around me, he pulled me back against his chest. "I'm sorry Diana's not available to be your assistant, Madison. But after your long trip from London, perhaps the two of you will join us for dinner?"

"Uh." Jason couldn't stop staring at me, as if he'd never quite seen me before. "I don't think…"

"Of course we will." Madison looked at Edward with new, almost proprietary interest. "I look forward to getting to know your new boyfriend, Diana."

"Good," Edward replied, as if he hadn't noticed her sudden pointed look, like a cat who'd just noticed a particularly appealing mouse. But I'd noticed it. And by the crease in his forehead, so had Jason. "Please excuse us while I take Diana upstairs." His voice lingered wickedly on the word *take*. "In the meantime help yourselves to tea, or there's drinks at the bar if you'd like something stronger."

Edward pulled me out into the hall.

"*I* need something stronger," I muttered.

"Hsst," he said beneath his breath. Holding my hand, he drew me down the echoing flagstones of the dark hallway and up the sweeping stairs. It wasn't until we were at my bedroom door that I stopped, looking at him with my brow creased.

"You made them think we were lovers."

"Yes."

"Why?"

"Because I felt like it."

I swallowed, shaking my head. "I don't understand."

Edward's eyes narrowed. "They were treating you so badly. Trying to guilt you into *planning their wedding. Don't worry, you'll find a real boyfriend someday,*" he mimicked Jason, then snorted with a flare of nostril. "Supercilious, condescending prats."

An unwilling laugh burbled to my lips, then faded. "But maybe they were right," I said softly, looking down. "I should have known he'd choose Madison over me. And I don't have a boyfriend. I'm starting to think I'll never—"

"Don't be an idiot." He put his hand against my cheek. "You could have any man you want, any time you want. If you don't have one at the moment, it's by your choice."

I swallowed, looking up at him. "You're being very kind, but…"

"I'm not kind." He paused. "I just didn't like them treating you as if you were invisible. As if you were nobody."

"I am nobody," I whispered.

Dropping his hand, he gave a low heartfelt curse. "For the last two months, you've matched me toe-to-toe, like a fighter. An equal. But the instant you walked into the library, you changed into a timid little mouse. What happened?"

"Why do you care?" I forced myself to meet his eyes. "You were *running* on the treadmill today, Edward. You don't even need a physical therapist anymore." I shook my head a little tearfully. "It's time for me to—"

"Oh, no, you don't," he said furiously. "Don't even *think* about using that as an excuse to run away. Why do I care? Because I don't like to see the woman who regularly brings me to my knees—that's you—falling apart at the feet of those vapid, self-absorbed idiots!"

"When did I bring you to your knees?" I said stupidly.

He looked down at me. "Have you already forgotten," he said softly, "how just two hours ago, I took you in my arms and begged you to make love to me? I was putty in your hands."

A shiver went over me, starting from my tingling, bruised lips. Tossing my head, I tried to laugh. "I don't remember any begging—"

My sentence cut off as he pulled me abruptly into his arms. His fingertips stroked down my cheek, skimming lightly down my jaw, my neck. I trembled beneath his touch, feeling the warm caress of his breath, the heat of his powerful body against mine.

"This is how I beg," he whispered, his lips close to mine, making me burn, making me lose my breath. Slowly, he kissed me, softly, so softly. "You're strong, Diana. And brave." His lips flickered like a whisper of breath against mine. "Why are you suddenly pretending not to be?" He moved back, and his expression changed, almost to a glare. "I want the woman I hired, the one who's constantly trying to kick my ass. Bring her back."

I licked my lips. "It's hard…"

"No. It's easy. Be your real self again, or get the hell out of my house."

My lips parted in shock. It was funny. I'd been planning to leave Penryth Hall, talking myself into it. But the thought of Edward kicking me out suddenly felt unbearable.

"You're firing me?" I said faintly. The way he looked at me made me shiver. My heart pounded, and my lips tingled in memory. "You don't understand. Madison and I have a history. And Jason—" My voice stopped.

"You still love him?" His eyes grew hard. "You're a fool. But that's what love does," he said grimly. "Makes us fools."

Thinking of Jason, sitting next to Madison on the couch as he said patronizingly, *If there's no sex, there's no relationship,* I shook my head. "I don't know what I feel anymore."

"Whatever. Doesn't matter. Pull yourself together. You're better than this, Diana. And I'm not interested in watching you let them wipe their feet on you." He glared at me. "Either stop acting like a doormat or you can ask them for a ride back to London."

I stared up at him, feeling faint, assaulted on all sides. How I wished I could be the woman he described—the one who was brave and strong. But the thought of facing them and telling them what I really thought…. Jason… and Madison…

"I don't think I can do it," I choked out.

"You have twenty minutes to decide." Edward's jaw tightened. Turning away, he stopped at the bedroom door. "Take a shower. Brush your hair. Get on dry clothes. When you come back downstairs for dinner, I'll see your answer."

My legs were shaking as I came downstairs a half hour later. I'd taken my time in the shower, closing my eyes beneath the hot steam. I combed out my wet hair, then started to reach in the closet for my typical wardrobe of casual T-shirt and cargo pants. Then I stopped.

Instead, I took out a skirt and blouse, and black high-heeled shoes. I put on red lipstick, which I'd almost forgotten I owned, and a headband. Then I looked at myself in the mirror. It looked like me, but not me. It looked like the me that I used to be, in high school. Before Mom had gotten sick. Before Madison had taken the dream I'd wanted.

You're strong, Diana. And brave. Why are you suddenly pretending not to be?

As I came downstairs, I could hear that the three of them had already started dinner without me in the medieval great hall. Well, Edward had told me twenty minutes. He was probably starting to wonder if I'd decided to pack for London.

I was still wondering myself.

I could play it safe, say nothing tonight and quietly leave with Madison, back to my old life. I could plan their wedding, be silently helpful and invisible.

Or—

Or I could be brave enough to be myself. And tell Jason and Madison how I really felt. Then I could remain at Penryth Hall—but I'd almost certainly end up in Edward's bed.

Let him keep your heart. I will have your body. Very soon. And we both know it.

Yes. I swallowed. If I stayed here, it would happen. Sooner or later. Probably sooner. I wouldn't be able to resist for much longer. I'd give my virginity to a playboy who wanted only a physical affair. It would be just sex, as he'd said.

Sex. And fire.

I felt dizzy just thinking of it.

So which would it be?

Remain invisible, mute and untouched?

Or risk everything, be honest and brave—but know that it would irrevocably change my life?

Standing outside the great hall, I still didn't know. I was caught between longing and fear. But I was already late. Clutching my hands into fists, I took a deep breath and walked in.

Madison had appropriated the place of honor at the long, candlelit dining table, with Jason on her right side and Edward on her left. Edward saw me, and his expression sharpened.

"You're here," he said, motioning toward the place to his left. Avoiding his gaze, I slid quietly into the chair beside him at the table.

Glancing at me dismissively, my stepsister didn't break stride in her story, which was mostly explaining the unbearable burdens of being young, rich, famous and beautiful. "You'd think I'd be used to press junkets by now," she finished with a sigh, moving her hands gracefully over the long, gleaming table, to make her enormous diamond ring sparkle in the candlelight. "But the one this morning was especially exhausting. They barely let me plug the movie. They just wanted to know about our engagement." She gave Jason a flirtatious sideways glance. "They wanted every detail. How he proposed, when the wedding will be…" Madison turned to me. "Why did you take so long, Diana? We're halfway through our dinner."

It was worth it, to miss most of your story, I thought. But I didn't have the nerve to say it.

"Sorry," I mumbled, and reaching for the silver tray at the center of the table, I pulled off the lid and served myself some rosemary lamb, herbed red potatoes and vegetables. Then I saw the basket, and gave a happy smile. "Mrs. MacWhirter made fresh rolls!"

"I asked her to, this morning," Edward said, smiling back. "I know they're your favorite."

"Bread makes you fat, you know," Madison said.

But skipping bread makes you mean, I thought. I said only, "Aren't Damian and Luis joining us?"

"They're eating in the kitchen with the staff."

"Smart," I mumbled.

"What?" Madison said.

"Nothing." I sighed. I felt Edward tighten up beside me. I could almost feel his glower.

I tried to eat, but sitting with Madison and Edward I could barely taste the food. Even the freshly baked white bun tasted ashy.

"Anyway," Madison continued, "sometimes I just get tired of all the attention." She yawned in a showy way, stretching her hands upward, showing off her figure to clear advantage. Then she flashed her beguiling smile, her trademark that no man could resist, first at Jason, then—at Edward. "Our engagement is news all over the world. My fans everywhere are thrilled… They're so sweet, sending congratulations and gifts." She gave a tinkly laugh that sounded like music. "Though I've had a few male fans threaten to throw themselves out windows unless I cancel the wedding. You know how it is, I'm sure." Reaching out, she patted Edward's hand. "How difficult it is, when people want you constantly."

My eyes went wide as I stared at Madison's perfectly manicured hand. Patting over Edward's. Slowly. Languorously. Like a dance.

Pat, pat, pat.

With the same hand that held the ten-carat diamond engagement ring given to her by another man.

She wanted Edward's attention now, too, I realized. Why was I surprised? It had happened all our lives. Madison always had to be the center of male approval. Even when we were teenagers, and my mother was dying, Madison had snuck away with the pool cleaner and smashed her father's car into a palm tree—effectively pulling Howard's attention away from my mom.

All our lives, I'd tried to look out for Madison. I'd tried to treat her like the sister I'd always wanted, back when I was a lonely only child. But she'd just taken from me, and taken more.

But as I watched her hand with the huge diamond ring pat Edward's on the table—*pat, pat, pat*—I suddenly couldn't stand it one second more.

"Are you seriously flirting with Edward now?" I said incredulously. "What the hell is *wrong* with you, Madison?"

She stared at me, her gorgeous pink mouth a round O. Then she ripped her hand off Edward's as if it had burned her. "I wasn't flirting with him! I'm an engaged woman!" She glared at me, then turned to give her fiancé a tender glance. "I'm in love with Jason."

"Are you? Are you really? Do you even know what it means?"

"Of course I do—we're engaged!"

"So what? You've been engaged five times!"

"Really?" Edward said, looking at me with growing joy.

"Five?" Jason gasped.

"You're crazy!" she said in outrage. Then, as the two men stared at her, she moderated her expression and said more calmly, "I haven't been engaged five times."

"No? Let's see." I tilted my head thoughtfully. "That punk rock musician you met on Hollywood Boulevard…"

"You call *that* an engagement?" Glancing at Jason and Edward, she trilled a little laugh. "I was fifteen! It lasted six days!"

"But Rhiannon never talked to you again."

Madison tossed her head. "He loved me, not her. She should have accepted that."

"Yes. He loved you. For six days, till his band left for Las Vegas. For that, you destroyed a friendship you'd had since kindergarten." I lifted an eyebrow and inquired coolly, "How many friends do you have left now, by the way, Maddy?"

She looked at me in wide-eyed fury. "I have plenty of friends, believe me!"

"*Friends.* People who suck up to you," I murmured. "People who need something from you. People who laugh at your jokes even when they're not funny. Are those really friends? Or are they employees?"

"Shut up!"

Picking up my fork, I idly traced it along my plate, crushing my potatoes against the gold-rimmed china, creating a pattern like tracks through snow. "Then when you were sixteen, there was the man who cleaned our pools..."

"A pool cleaner? That wasn't an engagement, it was a cry for help!"

"Right." I gave her a tight smile. "You were trying to get Howard's attention. He'd been neglecting you, spending so much time at my mom's deathbed. Drove you crazy."

She tossed me an irritated, petulant glance. "You make me sound selfish, but for months and months it dragged on. A girl needs her father!"

The casual cruelty of her words took my breath away. *For months and months it dragged on.* Yes. It had taken my mom months and months to die. Months of her fighting her illness with courage, long after hope was gone. Months of her fading away, so sweet and brave, still trying so hard to take care of everyone, even Madison. My jaw hardened.

"I know. I was there. Every day. All day." I ticked off another finger in a violent gesture. "Third engagement. My agent."

"*Your* agent?" Edward said in surprise.

"Yeah." I looked at him. "We met at Howard's wrap

party for a film. Lenny signed me when I was almost seventeen. I worked on a soap opera for about six months before Mom got sick."

"You were on a television show?" he said incredulously.

"I quit to stay home with her." And I'd quit without regret. I'd missed my friends, and the tutor was a poor replacement for school. I'd felt lonely. "I didn't try to act again until months later, when my agent sent me a script. He wanted to pitch me as a 'fresh new face' to star in a Disney show for preteens. My mom convinced me to go to the audition. But on my way there, I got a message from Howard that Mom had just had a seizure. He wasn't sure she'd make it…." My lips quivered at the edges. "She did. That time. But when I went back to do the audition two days later, the part was gone. The show had already hired someone else." I turned to look at Madison. "*Moxie McSocksie* made you a star."

Edward frowned. "*Moxie* what?"

"I'm surprised you haven't heard of it." I turned to him wearily. "Moxie. You know. Regular student by day, adventurous cub reporter by night. It was a huge hit."

"*Moxie Mc*—" Frowning, he looked at Madison, his eyes wide. "I remember. Your face was on the side of buses for months when the show came to London. It was your big break, wasn't it? Made you famous. Made you rich."

Wide-eyed, Madison looked from Edward, to Jason, to me. She abruptly slapped her hands hard against the table.

"I deserved the role, not you!" she cried in a shrill voice. "I'd been doing commercials since I was a baby! I was the actress, not you. And you were eighteen by then, Diana, way too old for the role!"

"Compared to you?"

"I was seventeen—the perfect age!"

"For getting engaged to my agent?" I said dryly. "The

second you heard about the role, you went for him. You knew he could get you that audition, and more. He could get you the career you wanted."

"You make it sound sordid," she gasped, putting her manicured hand against her chest in a fake laugh. "It wasn't like that!"

"Oh?" I said coolly. "So you didn't seduce him to get him to take you on as a client, and sell you to the show?"

"You're jealous! It's not my fault you gave up the audition and rushed home. The next day, when Lenny and I spent time together, he realized I was the perfect Moxie, not you. That's all!"

"He was fifty," I said.

"I loved him!"

"You dumped him fast enough, after he got you your first movie role, and you realized that dating a big Hollywood director would help you further up the ladder. You didn't mind that he had to break up with his *wife* to do it."

"Enough." Jason rose from the table, his face like granite. He looked at Madison. "So I'm number five, am I?"

"You're different," she whispered. "Special."

"I don't feel special." Jason looked at me. "I'm starting to think I chose the wrong sister."

Madison looked frightened. "Jason—"

"Here." Reaching into his pocket, he tossed a set of car keys onto the table. They skittered helter-skelter down the long polished wood. "I'm taking a car back to London. I'll leave the keys at the front desk of your hotel."

"Wait," she said desperately, rising to her feet. "You can't leave. I need you—"

He left without a backward glance.

Madison staggered back.

"Does this mean the wedding is off?" Edward inquired pleasantly.

Ignoring him, she slowly turned to face me. "Diana. I

know I've done a lot of stupid and selfish things. But I never thought you would be the one to list them out. Not you."

The injured fury in my heart deserted me, just when I needed it most. I rose to my feet.

"I never thought you would attack me like that." Her crystalline eyes glimmered in the candlelight. Her voice caught as she looked away. "You're not my big sister. You're just like all the rest."

My throat suddenly hurt as I remembered how we first met, virtual strangers to each other attending our parents' wedding as slightly-too-old flower girls, both feeling awkward, uncertain. My mom had told me Madison's mother died of a drug overdose when she was a toddler. *So be nice to her*, she'd chided.

Seeing her sad little face, I'd wanted to protect her. *We're family now*, I'd said at the wedding, hugging her over the flowers. *I'm gonna be your big sister, Maddy. So don't worry. I'll take care of you.*

"Maddy—" I whispered.

"Forget it," Madison choked out. "Just forget it."

She turned away in a cloud of grief and expensive perfume, stumbling out of Penryth Hall, calling Jason's name, then her bodyguards'.

The great hall was suddenly quiet, the only sound the whipping of the wind outside rattling the glass panes of the windows.

Edward looked at me.

"I wondered what it would be like, if you ever really let yourself go," he said quietly. "Now I know."

A sob lifted to my throat. My knees wobbled beneath me, and suddenly Edward was there, catching me before I could fall. I stared up at him in bewilderment, wondering how he'd moved so fast.

"I was horrible," I whispered.

"You were magnificent," he said softly, brushing hair from my face.

"Magnificent?" I gave a harsh laugh. "I was so determined to list all her faults. But what I've done is worse."

"What's that?"

"I told her I'd always take care of her," I whispered. "Then I hurt her like this...."

"Seems like she had it coming," he said softly, caressing my cheek.

I shuddered at his touch, longing for his comfort, fighting the desire to turn my cheek into his caress. "All these years I've blamed her for taking the role that might have made me a star. But it was never mine in the first place. She was right. I had the chance to audition. I went home."

"To be with your mother..."

"Whatever the reason. It was a choice I made." I wiped my eyes with the back of my hand. "After losing my parents, and the role of Moxie, I never wanted to have my heart crushed again. It's not Madison's fault I spent the next ten years hiding, not letting myself feel or want too much...."

"Until you fell for Jason," he said.

But was Jason the exception? Or had he just been one more example of me taking the safe path? The thought was new and troubling.

Swallowing, I looked up at Edward through shimmering tears.

"It wasn't Madison's fault," I whispered. "I did it to myself. I chose to be a coward." My voice caught as I turned away. "Playing it safe has ruined my life."

Edward said quietly, "Your life isn't over yet."

Our eyes locked in the shadowy great hall. An almost palpable electricity crackled between us.

"I have a private island in the Caribbean," he said huskily. "That's where I'd go if I needed to escape a broken heart. I stayed there after my accident. I needed to be alone." He gave a grim smile. "Well, alone with a doctor and two round-the-clock nurses." Reaching out, he gently twisted a long tendril of my hair. "No one can get at you there, Diana. There's no internet, no phones, no way to even get on the island except by my plane." He gave me a smile. "Want to go?"

Looking up at him, I tried to smile back, but couldn't quite manage. "Thanks, but it wouldn't help." I looked down at my hands. "Not when the person I want to escape from is myself."

Reaching out, Edward tilted up my chin, forcing me to meet his gaze. His dark blue eyes gleamed with silver and sapphire light, like the half-bright sky at dawn. "I understand," he said quietly. "Better than you might think."

"You do?" I whispered. Of its own will, my hand reached up to stroke his tousled black hair. It was so thick, and soft, just as I'd thought it would be. Five o'clock shadow traced the sharp edges of his jaw. Everything about him was masculine and foreign to me. I didn't understand him at all. "Why are you being so nice to me?"

He gave a sudden crooked smile. "Maybe it's just to lure you in my bed." His hand moved gently from my hair to my cheek. "Did you ever think of that?"

I gave a tearful, hiccupping laugh. "You don't have to try this hard for me."

"I don't?"

I looked up at him.

"No," I whispered.

His hand froze on my cheek. His expression changed as he looked down at me.

Cupping my face in his large, strong hands, Edward lowered his mouth to mine, slowly, deliberately. I could have pulled back from his embrace at any time. But I didn't move. I held my breath in anticipation as time suspended.

Then his lips finally touched mine, and I exhaled with a sigh. My breath comingled and joined with his. His lips were tantalizingly soft at first, sweet and warm. He lured me in, made me lean forward against his chest, reaching up to wrap my arms around his shoulders. Then he shifted me in his grip. As he held me more tightly, the world started to whirl around us.

He'd seen me at my worst, but he still wanted me....

His kiss deepened, became hungrier, more demanding. I clutched his hard, powerful body to my own, like a woman seeking shelter in a storm. Edward was solid, like a fortress in my arms. And if somewhere in the back of my mind, a voice shouted at me to stop, telling me this would destroy me, I pushed it away. I clutched Edward to me, kissing him with every cell in my body, my skin hot with need.

I was tired of being safe.

With a low growl, Edward lifted me up into his arms. Leaving the great hall, he carried me up the sweeping stairs.

Held against his chest, I looked up at him, dazed, lost in desire. I watched the play of shadows against his hard, handsome face as he carried me up the stairs. He carried my weight like a feather.

Edward St. Cyr was taking me to his bed. In just moments, my virginity would irrevocably be taken by this cold playboy, this breaker of hearts.

But he was so much more than that.

Lifting my hand to his cheek in wonder, I felt the roughness of his skin, the dark bristles along the hard edge of his jaw. He was so powerful. So masculine. So different from me in every way.

And yet somehow, tonight, I felt we were not so different. Out of anyone on earth, Edward understood me. He'd seen the scared girl I'd been, and the bold woman I wanted to be. He knew me....

Using his shoulder, Edward pushed open his bedroom door. I'd never been inside it before. The room was dark with shadows. Dark, Spartan furniture lined the edges of the walls.

A large white bed was at the center of the black-lacquered floor, illuminated by a pool of moonlight from the window like a spotlight.

Kicking the door closed behind us, Edward gently set me down on the moonswept, king-size bed. He hadn't said a word since we'd left the great hall. I looked up at him, shivering in my headband and simple skirt and blouse. I was twenty-eight years old, but felt as innocent as a schoolgirl.

Never taking his eyes off me, Edward slowly pulled off his tie. He dropped it to the lacquered floor. He moved toward the bed.

And I started to shake.

Moonlight glazed the bed around me as his strong hands tangled in my hair. "This is the first thing to go," he murmured, and he pulled my headband aside. Bracing his arms on the mattress around me, he leaned forward. Gently, he kissed me. His mouth seared mine, pushing my lips apart as he pushed me back against the bed.

My head fell back against the soft pillows, and he gave my cheeks little feather-soft kisses before returning to my mouth. His tongue flicked possessively between my lips before he trailed kisses down my throat. My head tilted back as I gave a soft gasp. Feeling lost. Feeling new.

"I don't love you," I breathed—speaking to him? Or myself?

"No." His dark blue eyes gleamed. "You want me. Say it."

My voice was almost too quiet to hear. "I want you."

"Louder."

I lifted my gaze. "I want you."

My voice had turned strong. Dangerous. Reckless.

He looked at me with such intensity I forgot to breathe. "And I want you."

Lowering his mouth hard against my own, Edward pushed me deeper into the soft white pillows. His hands stroked slowly down my body, light as a whisper, hot as a desert wind. His kiss deepened. Reaching down, he cupped my breasts that were aching beneath my prim white shirt.

I barely felt his fingertips move against my blouse. The buttons were just suddenly undone, and the unwilling thought crossed my mind that he'd had a lot of experience. He pulled my body up, and my blouse vanished into thin air, revealing my flimsy bra of blue silk.

What had made me wear my only truly pretty bra today, underneath my blouse? A coincidence? Or had I known, even before I came downstairs for dinner, that I intended to end my night this way?

"So beautiful," he whispered, his hands touching everywhere, sliding over my bare skin. "You've been driving me mad...."

"Me too..." I breathed. We'd been both alone, I realized, both wounded deep inside, in injuries we'd caused ourselves. But in this moment, it felt like loneliness no longer existed. My heart and my arms were both overflowing. We were together. We were the same....

I pulled him down hard against my body, wanting to feel his weight over mine. I heard the appreciative murmur from the back of his throat as I kissed him, hard, and tried to unbutton his shirt. My hands were trembling and clumsy.

"Stop," he said huskily, putting his hands over mine. For a moment, I was afraid he'd changed his mind. Then I realized he was unbuttoning his shirt for me, his expert fingers doing it three times as fast. Rising from the bed, he unbuttoned his cuffs and dropped his expensive tailored shirt to the dark floor. I gasped when I saw the muscles and planes of his naked chest, lit by the slanted moonlight. I'd seen his body before, during massage and occasionally when I'd taken him to swim at the local center. But never like this. Never with the full knowledge that I could run my hands over his skin, that I'd soon feel his naked body roughly take my own.

Edward's eyes never left mine as he deliberately undid his trousers and pulled them with his silk boxers down his thickly chiseled thighs. A choked noise came from the back of my throat as he stood naked in front of me. He'd been naked in the gym that morning, but I'd been afraid to look. I was still a little afraid now. Blushing, I started to look away.

His gaze locked with mine, challenging me. With a deep breath, I lifted my chin, and looked, really looked, at his naked body.

He was not ashamed, standing there with quiet pride and giving me time to look, to accept. His shoulders were broad, and a dusting of dark hair trailed like a V from his nipples and hard-muscled chest down to a taut, flat waist. His legs were powerful as a warrior's, and as he shifted his weight in front of me, he moved with an athlete's grace. His thighs were hard and huge. Which could also describe what I saw if I dared to look between his thighs... But there my nerve failed me.

He was powerful. He'd been healed. But the injuries had left scars that couldn't be denied. The raised scars across his torso, where his ribs had been broken, left white lines across perfect olive-toned skin. Similar lines slashed brutally across his right shoulder and arm, and his left leg, like cobwebs of his body's memory, forgiven but not forgotten.

Men prey on the tender weakness of the feminine heart, Mrs. Warreldy-Gribbley had warned. *He will lure you into bed by using your own heart against you.*

Turning away, I squeezed my eyes shut. The mattress moved beneath me. I felt Edward come closer, felt the warmth of his body as he said in a low voice, "What is it?"

"This is wrong," I whispered. "You are my patient."

"It's wrong," he agreed.

My eyes flew open.

He was looking down at me with a glint in his eye. "You're sacked, Miss Maywood. Effective immediately."

I gave an indignant squeak. "You're *firing* me?"

"You said it yourself." He quirked a dark eyebrow. "I don't need a physio anymore. What I need…" Reaching out, he slowly stroked down the valley of my breasts, "is a lover."

Lover. I shivered at the word. So erotic. So suggestive. Not just of sensual delights, but emotional ones.

"You want me to be your girlfriend?" I breathed.

"No." He gave a low laugh. "Not a *girlfriend.* Just my friend. And my lover. For as long as we enjoy it." Lowering his head, he kissed my naked belly, making me shiver at the sensation of his lips and rough chin and tiny flick of his tongue against my belly button. He looked up. "This isn't a *commitment.* I won't be asking you to the movies with a box of chocolates, asking to meet your family." His eyes narrowed. "I am not *nice,* Diana. I look out for myself. I expect you to do the same." His lips lifted at the edges. "For all I know, you'll soon go back to Jason Black."

"I—"

"It doesn't matter," he cut me off. "I don't expect you to stay with me forever. It's fine," he said lightly, searching my face. "I wouldn't want to get too accustomed to you."

I am not nice, *Diana. I look out for myself. I expect you to do the same.* When a man tells you something bad about himself, that is the time to listen. I stared up at him in the shadows of the bed, hearing only my own ragged breath, my own heartbeat, as I tried to focus on his words. But I was distracted, burning hot with his naked body over mine.

Don't lie to yourself about what the end will be, Mrs. Warreldy-Gribbley had warned. *If you forget yourself and let him lure you into his sensual designs—*

But I didn't want to think about her anymore. The woman had written the book in 1910, I thought irritably. What did she know? I shut the book in my mind, locking it away forever.

And I smiled up at Edward. "Good to know," I said, matching his light tone. "I wouldn't want to get too accustomed to you either. I have things to do in life."

"Do you?" he said, sounding amused. Then, moving closer, he looked at me. My heart pounded as his breathtakingly beautiful face, just inches from mine, was illuminated in moonlight, making him look like a dark angel. "Yes," he murmured. "I think you do. You're meant for great things in life, Diana."

My lips parted, and I felt suddenly tearful for no good reason, other than that no one had ever said such a thing to me. No one, not since my mother had died—

"Great things," Edward whispered again, lowering his head to mine. His lips curved wickedly. "Starting with tonight…"

He kissed me, his hands stroking down the length of my body, slowly removing the last of my clothes, my skirt, my cotton stockings. He ran his hand appreciatively along my hips, my thighs. My breasts. He unclasped my bra so easily, he practically just looked at it to make it spring open. Dropping the flimsy blue silk off my body, he cupped one of my breasts with both hands. I sucked in my breath, my whole body taut.

He pulled away with a low curse.

"I forgot you're a virgin." He shook his head with an irritated growl. "So let me make this really clear for you. One more time. For the sake of my own conscience."

"I thought you didn't have one," I said weakly.

"This is all I can give you." His eyes met mine. "No marriage. No children. All I can offer is—this." He kissed me, feather-light, running down my bare, trembling throat, to my clavicle. I felt his hands cup my naked breasts, felt his fingers lightly squeeze the full, heavy flesh. He lowered his mouth with agonizing slowness to an aching nipple, then stopped at the last moment. He looked up at me. "Do you agree?"

As he spoke, his lips and breath brushed my taut nipple, and I shook beneath him, lost in desire, lost in pleasure, *lost*.

He was offering cheap, no-strings sex. No marriage. No children. Not even love.

So? I thought suddenly. What had love ever done for me? Only broken my heart.

This was better than love.

"Yes." I whispered, reaching for him. "Yes…"

Then his lips came down on my skin, his tongue swirling my nipple as he suckled me, and I gasped, gripping the sheets.

CHAPTER FOUR

His tongue swirled hot and tight against my nipple, and I shivered beneath him. He nibbled with his teeth, drawing me more deeply into his mouth. My breast felt full and heavy and taut beneath his hands. I felt his hips grind against me.

Moving to my other breast, he squeezed the aching nipple, tasting the exquisitely sensitive nub with a flick of his tongue. He took it fully into his mouth, suckling me. And all the while, I felt the hard ridge of him between my legs.

Drawing back, he ran his hands down the sides of my body. I felt his heat and weight pressing me into the comforter and soft white pillows of the king-size bed. Unlike the soft stroke of his hands, his lips were hard, searing mine as he gave me a kiss that had no tenderness, only fierce demand.

His fingers tangled and twisted in my hair, tilting my head so he could plunder my mouth more deeply. All my memories, all my regrets, faded into the past as I dissolved into lust—so purely alive, so purely desired. I kissed him back with all the trembling pent-up desire of my whole life.

The bristles of dark hair that covered his chest and forearms and his legs—and everywhere between—brushed roughly against my naked skin. He held me with ruthless, raw masculine power.

I felt his enormous hardness between my legs, brushing against my lower belly as he moved against me. His tongue twirled around mine as he kissed me, flicking the edges of my bruised mouth before he moved lower, kissing along my throat, working his way downward. Pressing my breasts together with his hands, he thrust his tongue into the crevasse between them, and I gasped. His breath was hot against my skin as he continued to kiss downward... down my belly and then...

Abruptly, he moved up to suckle an earlobe. My nipples felt taut almost to the point of pain as I felt the brush of his muscled chest. He moved to the other earlobe, still moving his hips sensuously against mine.

"You're—teasing me," I panted accusingly. I felt his smile against my neck.

"Yes," he murmured against my skin. "I intend to make you weep."

Slowly, delicately, he lifted my palm. He kissed the hollow, then moved his head to suck each fingertip, one by one.

I'd never thought of fingers as erogenous zones but feeling the warmth of his mouth on each fingertip, the hot wet swirl of his tongue, the hard pull of his teeth, I shook beneath him. He repeated it on my other hand, delicately sucking on each finger until I was dizzy and gasping for breath.

Slowly, he moved down my body. I felt his hot lips and wet tongue against each taut, aching nipple. His tongue swirled, his hands cupping each full, heavy breast. With a gasp, I closed my eyes, gripping the comforter.

With deliberate, agonizing slowness, he again began to move down my naked body in a trail of hot kisses. My eyes flew open in the semidarkness of the bedroom when I felt his hands move low, over my hips, running lightly over my thighs. When he brushed feather-light over the hair between my legs, I audibly choked out a gasp.

He lifted his head up lazily. "Just wait."

Lowering his head to my belly button, he flicked it with his tongue, inside it, inside me. But even as I shivered, his mouth moved down farther.

And farther.

Running his hands over the swell of my hips, he lowered his head between my legs. I felt the warmth of his breath *right there* and gave a sharp gasp, gripping his shoulders as my head tossed back.

But he made me wait. Made me *want*. He just kept moving down my legs, all the way, down to my feet. Parting my knees, he stroked the hollow of each foot, gently massaging it, causing a different kind of pleasure to spiral up my body. He pushed my legs farther apart. Stroking up my calves, he kissed the hollow beneath my knee. I gripped his shoulders, my eyes squeezed shut.

Using his shoulders, he roughly spread my thighs all the way apart.

My breathing was ragged as I gripped the comforter, trembling beneath him. I felt the heat of his breath on the tender skin of my inner thighs. Shivering, I tried to scoot away, though I wanted it so badly. He held me down firmly. His hands pressed my legs wide. He lowered his head with agonizing slowness, making me hold my breath until I thought I might faint—

I felt the hot, wet stroke of his tongue against my slick core, and gave a muffled cry. He paused, then licked me again, this time lapping me with the full width of his tongue. As my hips twisted helplessly beneath him, he held me down, forcing me to accept the pleasure as I nearly writhed with agonized need.

"Please," I whimpered, hardly knowing what I was saying. Barely realizing that I was speaking at all. "*Please*."

He gave a low laugh.

Pushing me wider, he worked me with his tongue, lap-

ping me with the full width one moment, then using the tip
to swirl tighter, ever tighter, against the hard aching center.

He slowly pushed a fingertip inside me. Then two. As
I held my breath with pleasure, he stretched me wide with
his thick fingers, while licking and suckling me with his
tongue.

My body was on fire, my back arching from the bed.
I'd lost the ability to take a full breath. I twisted beneath
him, no longer trying to get away, merely to end the sweet
torment. I'd never imagined it could be like this—pleasure
to the point of pain— Higher—tighter—

I heard a building scream from a voice I'd never heard
before, a voice I would only later realize was mine. My
eyelids half closed as I left the earth and exploded past
the sun.

As I gasped for breath, Edward moved quickly, bracing himself with his hands on either side of my hips. Posi-
tioning himself between my legs, he thrust himself inside
me. His full length. All at once, thick and hard, ripping
through me with jarring pain.

With a choked gasp, I pushed on his hips, wanting the
pain to stop. He held still inside me. Then, as my grip
on his hips loosened, he slowly began to move again. He
pulled back, then slowly filled me again, giving me time to
grow accustomed to the size of him. He filled me, stretching me inch by inch, slowly, sensuously; and the red haze
of pain turned orange, then pink, then began to bubble and
fizz like champagne. My body, which had been briefly
limp on the bed, began to quicken again, to grow taut and
tense with new desire.

Gripping my hips with his large hands tight enough
to bruise, he thrust harder, until he was riding me rough
and fast. My back again began to arch off the bed as he
filled me deep and hard, stretching me to my limit, and
beyond....

With a curse, he abruptly pulled out. I opened my eyes, nearly hyperventilating with need.

Looking at him in the slanted moonlight on his enormous bed, I saw he'd opened a condom and was peeling it over his huge length.

"I forgot," he said grimly. "I never forget."

My mouth suddenly went dry. "Then is it possible—"

"It's fine," he growled. Leaning forward, he kissed me passionately, until I forgot to worry about anything, until I forgot my own name. "Look at me."

I did. Our eyes met as he pushed back inside me, inch by throbbing inch. I gasped. As the pleasure built, I started to close my eyes, to turn away.

"Look at me," he repeated harshly.

Against my will, I obeyed. Our eyes locked as he thrust inside me. I felt every inch of him as he filled me, then increased the rhythm, shoving harder and faster as he gripped my hips. Tension coiled low and deep inside me, building tighter and tighter.

It was shockingly intimate to watch his face. Almost more intimate, even, than having him inside me. I felt the muscles of his backside grow tense beneath my hands, tense with the strain of holding himself back so tightly. Why did he hold back? Why?

Then I knew.

For me.

He thrust roughly into me, swaying my breasts as our sweaty naked bodies slid and clung together. He thrust again, so deep he impaled me. And something inside me suddenly spiraled out of control, rising from ash like a burst of fire. I was consumed by it, then exploded like a phoenix. I screamed, and heard his answering growl, as he clutched my hips tight enough to bruise. With a hoarse cry, he filled me with one last brutal, savage thrust, then collapsed over me with a groan.

I held him in the moonlight on the bed, this powerful giant of a man who'd overwhelmed me with the sweet torment of pleasure, now weak as a kitten. Closing my eyes, I cuddled him to my body, my heart in my throat.

I'd never imagined sex was like this, never.

"See?" Still panting, Edward nuzzled my neck. His voice was filled with masculine self-satisfaction as he traced his fingertips down my cheek. "I told you."

"What?" I choked out, holding him closer, never wanting to let him go.

His dark blue eyes smiled sleepily into mine. "That I would make you weep."

Astonished, I touched my face and found he was right. He'd made me weep. It was the first time.

It wouldn't be the last.

Sunlight poured golden through the windows as Edward woke me with a kiss. "Good morning."

"Good morning," I said a little shyly, yawning. Our bodies were still naked, our limbs intertwined. I felt amazingly, blissfully sore in all the right places.

We'd made love three times last night. After the explosive first time, we'd slept in each other's arms until at midnight we'd decided we were hungry. Putting on robes, we'd gone down to the dark, empty kitchen to hunt for a snack, giggling like naughty teenagers.

Naughty indeed. One minute Edward's hand was reaching for the bread box, the next it was beneath my silk robe, and the minute after that he pushed me against the kitchen wall. The fact that we could have been discovered at any moment by Mrs. MacWhirter or the other servants just made it more dangerous. Ripping my belt loose, he'd taken me against the wall, wrapping my legs around his hips as he thrust hard and deep, until I gripped his shoulders in a silent cry. It was fast. It was rough.

It was delicious.

After a quick meal of sandwiches and cake in the dark kitchen, giggling and whispering, we'd gone back upstairs. We were both so sweaty, we decided to take a shower. I don't know how this happened, either. One minute he was shampooing my hair, and I was standing on my tiptoes, reaching up to shampoo his. He playfully flicked some lather on my nose, and in retaliation, I smacked his butt really hard. He grabbed me, and two seconds later, he was shoving me against the shower's steamy glass, murmuring words of desire against my hot, rosy skin as he made love to me beneath the scorching stream of shooting water.

I shivered, remembering. Even now, as he held me in the morning light, Edward was looking at me hungrily, and I felt my body respond.

Had he been watching me sleep, waiting for me to wake? I hoped not. I'd been dreaming about him. We'd been having a summer picnic in the garden. The sky was blue, the sun warm, and flowers were in bloom around us. He'd held me close on the blanket, and when I whispered that I loved him, his dark blue eyes had lit up. *I love you, Diana,* he'd said.

What if I'd been talking in my sleep? He would freak out if he knew. "I hope I didn't wake you up by snoring or, er…" I blushed. "…talking in my sleep."

"No," Edward growled, rolling me beneath him. It seemed he hadn't woken me to talk. "You slept like the dead. Another two seconds and you would have woken up with me inside you."

"It doesn't sound like the worst way to—" He covered my mouth with his own, thrusting smoothly inside me. He was as hard as if we hadn't made love three times already; I was as wet as if he hadn't brought me to aching, explosive climax again and again.

If the other times had been passionate or rough, now,

as he took me in the golden light of morning, he was tender, even gentle. How could we still be so unsatiated, so hungry for more? I grasped his shoulders tight, digging into his skin with my fingertips, holding my breath as he pushed deeper into me, until six thrusts later we were both sweaty and crying out and clutching each other.

He pulled me close, kissing my temple.

"What you do to me..." he whispered against my sweaty skin, and my soul expanded into every inch of my body. I sighed, closing my eyes and pressing my cheek against his warm, hard-muscled chest. It felt so right to be in his arms. For the first time in my life, I wasn't thinking about the past or the future. I was exactly where I wanted to be.

It was after noon by the time we woke again. "Good afternoon," he whispered now, smiling as he kissed me.

"Good afternoon." I sighed, then stretched across the bed. "I hate to get up."

"So don't."

"I'm hungry." I smiled, then my smile faltered. "And I have a lot to pack."

"Pack?" He frowned. "For what?"

"For home."

"You're leaving?"

He sounded indignant. An unwilling laugh lifted to my lips. "You fired me."

"Ah." Relaxing, Edward looked thoughtful. "*Fired* is such a strong word. *Made redundant* is more accurate. By your own hard work, I might add." He tilted his head. "Now, you're probably asking yourself, what kind of heartless bastard would cut someone out of a job right before Christmas?"

"Um, you?"

He laughed. "You've been paid in full. While you were on your walk yesterday, I had my secretary deposit your entire promised salary—the whole year's worth."

I stared at him. "What?"

He looked amused. "You really should pay more attention to your bank account."

"You're right," I said. Tell me something I didn't know. "Well. Um. Thanks. I guess I'll go pack…"

"Don't go." He grabbed my wrist. His voice was low. "I want you to stay with me. Through the New Year, at the very least. Not as my employee, but as my—"

"Yes," I blurted out.

Snorting, he lifted a dark eyebrow. "I could have said *slave*."

I gave him a crooked grin. "Then definitely yes."

"Thank God," he said softly, smoothing tendrils of hair off my face. "One last week of holiday," his lips turned downward, "before I go back to London."

My stomach growled. Standing up, I walked naked across the room and picked up my silk robe. I tied it around me. "What's in London?"

"My job."

"You really have to go?"

"I've been gone too long. My cousin Rupert is trying to convince the shareholders he should take my place."

"Sounds like a jerk."

"He's a St. Cyr."

"Then definitely a jerk," I said teasingly, but he didn't smile back. I hesitated. "But why does it matter?"

"What do you mean?"

I motioned around the bedroom. "You seem to have plenty of money. I figured being CEO of the family company was a sort of honorary title, you know…."

"Like a sinecure—getting paid for doing nothing?"

"I wasn't trying to insult you. But you don't seem keen to get back there. If you don't need the money, there's nothing forcing you to do it, is there?"

He scowled. "St. Cyr Global was started by my great-

grandfather. I'm the largest shareholder. I have a responsibility…."

"I get it," I said, but I didn't.

Edward looked away. "Come on. Let's see about breakfast."

Mrs. MacWhirter was making bread in the kitchen, and
it smelled heavenly. The housekeeper's eyebrows rose almost all the way to her white hair when she saw me still
in my robe, with Edward looking tousled in a T-shirt and
sweatpants that clung to his chiseled body. There could be
no doubt about what we'd been up to. But she recovered
quickly when Edward meekly asked if we'd missed any
chance of breakfast.

"Missed? I'll say not! With everything?"

"Black tea for me, if you please, Mrs. MacWhirter. And
extra tomatoes."

"Of course. And Miss Maywood?"

I found it impossible to return her gaze without blushing. "Everything, please. With extra toast and jam. Coffee with cream and sugar. Please, thank you, if you don't
mind, you're so very kind…."

Edward grabbed my hand, stopping me before I could
babble any further.

"We'll be in the tea room," he said firmly, and drew
me away. A moment later, we were in a bright room with
big windows facing the garden and beyond that, the sea. A
brisk fire was going. I blinked when I saw the rose-colored
carpet, the chintz pattern of the wallpaper.

"Whose room is this? You can't have designed this."

His jaw tightened. "It was my mother's."

He'd never mentioned her before. "Does she visit often?"

"She died last year," he said shortly.

"I'm so sorry—"

"Don't be. As far as I'm concerned, she died long ago.

She left when I was a child. Ran off with an Argentinian polo player when I was ten."

"Oh," I breathed.

It was a good reminder of the lesson I learned as a child, he'd said. *Never depend on anyone.*

He shrugged. "Dad worked all the time, and traveled overseas. Even when he was home, he had a mean streak a mile wide." He gave me a humorless smile. "The St. Cyr trait, as you said."

My heart ached for the ten-year-old boy who'd been abandoned by his mother. Even though both my parents had died, I never had any doubt of their love for me. My heart twisted. And then I suddenly felt furious. "Your parents were selfish."

His expression froze. Turning away, he threw himself into in an overstuffed chintz chair in front of the fire. "I was fine."

I sank into the matching chair on the other side of the tea table. "Fine? To run off and leave you? Abandon you with a mean, neglectful father?"

"Well." He gave me a wry smile. "I do wish Mum had told me the truth from the start. The day she left for Buenos Aires, she cried and said she was breaking up with Dad, not me. She promised she'd always be my mother and that the two of us would still be a family." He looked away. "But within a year, her letters and calls began to dwindle. She stopped asking me to Argentina for Christmas. Not that Dad would have let me...."

"He wanted to spend Christmas with you?"

Edward shook his head. "He went to Mustique at Christmas with his mistress du jour. He just hated Mum and didn't want to do anything nice for her. It wasn't just that. Antonio didn't want me at his house, really. He just wanted Mum."

"That must have been hard...."

He shrugged. "When I was fourteen, Mum had a new baby. She was so busy, and so far away. She quit phoning, or sending letters. It was easier just to leave me behind." He barked out a laugh. "It all happened long ago. But I wish Mum had told me from the beginning how it would be." He looked out toward the lead-paned windows, bright with afternoon sunlight. "Rather than letting me wait. Letting me hope."

"I'm so sorry," I whispered, despising all the selfish adults who'd hurt him as a child. "Who took care of you?"

"The household staff. Mrs. MacWhirter, mostly. The gardener, too. But not for long. At twelve I went to boarding school."

"Twelve?" I sputtered.

"It was good for me. Built character and all that." He sighed. "I used to get homesick for Cornwall. I'd daydream about hitchhiking back here so the old gardener could take me out fishing. He also taught me how to catch a ball, tie a reef knot. Old Gavin was great."

"You called him Old—to his face?"

"Everyone did. To distinguish him from his son. Young Gavin." He sighed. "But his children had grown and moved away to find jobs, and Old Gavin missed his grandchildren. I promised if he'd just wait, when I grew up I'd create a factory near Penryth Hall that built things for adventures, so there'd be plenty of jobs for everyone. All he had to do was stay."

"Things for adventures?" I queried.

"Blow darts and slingshots and canoes. Come on, I was ten."

"Did you ever do it? Create the factory?"

"No." He looked away. "Old Gavin emigrated to Canada, to be with his daughter. A few months after that, I was at boarding school. He didn't keep his promise. I don't have to keep mine."

"Oh, Edward…" I tried to reach for his hand. But he wouldn't accept either my hand or my sympathy.

"It's fine," he said roughly. "I was lucky. I've learned not to count on people. Or make promises I can't keep."

Mrs. MacWhirter came bustling noisily into the room, followed by a maid, both of them carrying trays. As they set down china cups and napkins and solid silver utensils, Edward smiled at the housekeeper. I realized that the older woman, gruff as she could be, was the closest to family he had. She poured Edward's black tea and my coffee, set down our plates and left us.

I looked down hungrily at my breakfast, with eggs, toast, beans and grilled tomato, and a type of bacon that tasted like ham. I loved it all. I slathered the buttered toast with marmalade, then took a delicious crunchy bite. We ate in silence, sitting together near the fire. Then our eyes met.

"I don't blame you for never wanting to depend on anyone," I said softly. "Why would you? People lie, or love someone else, or move to Canada. People leave you, even if they don't want to. Even if they love you." I paused. "People die."

For a moment, the only sound was the crackling of the fire. He stared at me. "You're not going to argue with me?"

I shook my head.

"I'm surprised," he said gruffly, watching me. "Most women accuse me of having no heart."

I thought of my kindhearted father, a professor, who'd died suddenly in an accident when I was in third grade, and my mother, who'd filled my life with roses and sunshine before her long, agonizing decline. They'd never have chosen to leave me, or each other. But they'd had no choice. In spite of their fervent promises. "Maybe you're right," I said in a small voice, looking down at my plate. "Maybe promises are worthless. All we have is today."

His hand took mine across the table.

"But if we live today right," he said quietly, "it's enough."

The air between us suddenly electrified, and my hand trembled beneath his. Slowly, he started to lean across the tea table....

Mrs. MacWhirter coughed from the doorway, and Edward and I pulled away, blushing like teenagers who'd just been caught kissing.

"I'm sorry to interrupt you, sir," she said, "but I wanted you to know I'm getting ready to leave. The rest of the staff has already gone."

"Fine." Edward cleared his throat. "Good. I hope you have a nice holiday."

"Yes, indeed, sir," Mrs. MacWhirter said warmly. "The staff wanted me to thank you for the extra large Christmas bonus this year. You're always so generous, but this one topped it all. I nearly fell over when I opened the card. Sophie said she's going to surprise her boyfriend and take him to the Seychelles for Christmas. I'm going to get my sister that new roof, and I'll still have some left to put by. Thank you."

"It's the least you all deserve for putting up with me," Edward said. "Especially over the last few months. I haven't always made it easy."

Her lips lifted into a smile. "You haven't been so very bad as all that. Considering all you've been through..." She hesitated. "I needn't go to Scotland for Christmas, you know. I could stay over the holiday, if you think you might need me."

"Don't be ridiculous," he said sharply. "You've been talking about visiting your sister for months. You get the week off, as always."

"But in your current state...who will take care of you?"

"Miss Maywood."

She eyed me dubiously. "What about in the kitchen?"

"In the kitchen," he said gravely, "as in all areas."

He didn't meet my eye, and a good thing too, since I could barely keep from laughing.

"In that case…I'm off." Mrs. MacWhirter looked relieved. "Happy Christmas, Mr. St. Cyr, Miss Maywood. Take good care of him," she added with a beady glint in her eye.

"I will," I murmured, feeling new appreciation for her, now that I knew she'd been caring for Edward since he was a child.

And I kept my promise, all right. I took very good care of Edward over Christmas week. Just as he took very good care of me. We huddled in the warmest rooms of Penryth Hall, lighting a fire with a Yule log, and watched the snow rise in the chilly wind outside.

We had sex for Christmas. Sex for Boxing Day. Sex for New Year's Eve. In between, we had champagne, opened Christmas crackers, wore paper crowns and gobbled up a Christmas goose we'd prepared ourselves—Edward actually knew how to cook, somewhat to my surprise—and a great deal of trifle.

I'm not going to lie. It was a very naked week. Alone just the two of us, we barely bothered with clothes. Edward said it was more efficient that way, plus he just liked the look of me. We lit fires in every room, in every possible way.

Christmas morning, we made love beneath the tree and it was so explosive that at the critical moment, ornaments and tinsel fell on Edward's head. Edward looked up with a mix of amusement and annoyance.

"I've heard about choirs of angels singing," he grumbled, looking at the angelic item that just had landed on his back from the very top of the tree, "but this is ridiculous."

With a laugh, I pulled him back over me, and we wrapped ourselves in tinsel.

But on New Year's Eve, as all the world looked with anticipation toward the bright, shiny new year, I felt building sadness, the sense that our time was running out. I tried to ignore the feeling, telling myself I should be grateful for the magical weeks we'd spent together. But all I could feel was misery, that soon Edward would return to London, to work long hours at a job he didn't particularly like, and I would go back to California, to face the scandal I'd left behind, and see if I had the courage to try acting again. Just thinking of it made me want to cover my head with a pillow. And as for the thought of never seeing Edward again, never ever....

"Stop sighing," Edward said across the table. "I don't believe it for a second. I'm not going to fall for it again."

We were sitting in the study, at a folding table we'd moved directly in front of the fire, where for the past hour we'd been playing strip poker. Caesar the sheepdog was stretched out on a rug beside us, ignoring us, clearly disgusted by the whole thing. I sat half-naked in my chair, wearing only panties, a bra, knee socks and Edward's tie. Which probably sounds grim, where strip poker is concerned. But Edward had only his silk boxers left. He was sweating.

"Where did you learn to play like this?" he demanded, staring down fiercely at his own cards.

"Madison taught me," I said sweetly. "We used to play all the time."

His scowl deepened. "I might have known Madison was at the bottom of this."

"Yeah." I looked down at my own cards. I didn't even have a particularly good hand, but due to my confidence—and the straight flush I'd had in the last round—he believed I might. Nothing except a miracle could save him now. Madison had taught me this much about acting—how to bluff.

Madison. I missed her, in spite of everything. I'd called my stepfather on Christmas, on set in New Mexico, where he was filming the latest season of his highly regarded cable TV zombie series. I would have tried to call Madison too, except Howard let me know she'd just left for some ashram in India, to cope with her explosively public breakup with Jason.

"She could use a friend, kiddo," Howard had told me quietly.

"She doesn't want to talk to me," I'd mumbled. "She hates me."

"No, sweetie, no. Well, maybe. But I think the person she hates most right now is herself."

Edward's cell phone rang, rattling violently across the table, drawing me out of my reverie.

"Saved by the bell," I murmured. "Don't think it will save you. Those boxers will be *mine*..."

But he was no longer listening. His jaw was tight as he answered the phone. "Rupert. What the hell do you want?"

Rising to his feet, he kept the phone to his ear as he stalked back and forth across the study, barking angry words into the phone—words I didn't understand, like EBITDA, proxy fight, flip-over and poison pill. Whatever it meant, it made Edward so angry that he utterly forgot me sitting half-naked in the chair, staring up at him, wearing his tie. He just paced back and forth in front of the fire. Caesar lifted his head and watched his master walk to and fro, as bewildered and alarmed as I was.

"And I'm telling *you*," Edward bit out, "if you don't pull this together the shareholders will never forgive...no, it was *not* my fault. I set it on target. It was fine in September." He paused, then strode five steps before turning. His pace was almost a stomp as he said acidly, "Oh, I'm sorry, was it *inconvenient* to the company that I had to take a few months off when I nearly died? Even half-dead, I'm twice the man you…" He halted, grinding his teeth. "No, *you* listen to me…." A curse came from his lips that made me flinch. "If the deal is falling apart, you're the one to blame, and the board of directors will see—" He stopped. His shoulders looked so tight that I was afraid of what he might be doing to the muscles of his shoulders and spine. He ground his teeth. "I know what you're doing, you bastard, and it won't work. St. Cyr Global belongs to me…."

I couldn't listen anymore. Sliding miserably off the chair, I grabbed my clothes that had been flung so eagerly to the floor. Shivering, though I was near the roaring fire, I pulled his tie off my throat. Edward's eye caught me, now standing in front of the enormous fireplace that was taller than me, and his expression briefly lightened as his eyes approvingly traced the scarlet lace bra and panties that had been a Christmas gift. From me to him. His forehead furrowed into a frown as, without answering his smile, I turned away and silently pulled on my long cotton sweater and black knit leggings.

"I'll be there tomorrow," he snapped, and clicked off the phone. Coming toward me, he said, "What are you doing?"

"That should be obvious," I said.

"Take your clothes back off," he said huskily, pulling me into his arms. "We're in the middle of a game. There's no reason for you to quit. You're winning."

Winning. The word made me shudder. Because when he was on the phone, talking to that man—his cousin?—Edward's voice had sounded different. Harsher. Like someone who cared about winning. At any cost.

I'd come to see another side of Edward over the past few months. Even Jason Black, the man I'd thought I'd loved, now seemed like a pale shadow of memory compared to the devilish, sexy, arrogant man who'd become the center of my life. Edward knew the best of me—and the worst. For weeks now, I'd tried not to think about how soon I'd be leaving this magical place and returning to California, to face the real world. But now…

I pulled away from his embrace, avoiding his gaze. "You're going back to London."

"That multibillion deal I told you about is falling apart," he said grimly. "I'm going first thing in the morning."

"On New Year's Day?"

"My *cousin,*" he spat out the word, "is trying to sabotage it. I've been gone too long. Once the deal's back on track, I'll get the stockholders together and see about eliminating him…."

"Eliminating?"

He snorted a laugh. "From the board of directors. What did you think I meant?"

I licked my lips. "Well…"

"You really do think the worst of me," he said, sounding amused rather than offended. "But Rupert has a wife and young children he barely sees. I'd like to free him from all the pesky duties of COO, so he could devote more time to his family."

"You could do that yourself," I pointed out.

"Ah, but I don't have a family," he said lightly. Leaning forward, he kissed my nose. "I couldn't be responsible for a houseplant."

"That's not true."

"Sadly, it is."

"What about Caesar?"

The dog lifted his head at hearing his name. Edward looked down at him affectionately. "This lazybones? You know he's technically Mrs. MacWhirter's dog, not mine. And she'll be back from Scotland tomorrow. There's no help for it." Edward stared down at me grimly. "I need to go back."

In spite of his words, as I looked at his body posture, I'd never seen any man less keen to do anything.

"I understand." I kept my voice even, squaring my shoulders and trying to look calm, though I wanted to cling to him and whimper. "I'll go pack my things."

"Good." He looked distracted. Geez. It's not like I expected Edward to say he was wretchedly heartbroken, and that he'd miss me desperately, but...

I suddenly realized that was exactly what I'd expected. We'd had a torrid ten day affair, months of friendship before that, and I'd actually thought I meant something to him. In spite of the fact that he'd warned me that I wouldn't. In spite of his warnings, in spite of my promise, I'd come to care for him. Really care.

I was so stupid!

Trembling, I tried to smile. "I'll go see about the next flight to L.A." I bit my lip. "It's good timing, really. I should be thanking that cousin of yours. My stepfather invited me to spend a week on his set as an extra. It'll be fun to be a zombie. And I've heard New Mexico is beautiful...."

Edward focused on me. "What are you talking about?"

"You're going to London tomorrow."

"Yes."

I licked my lips. "So there's no point in me staying here."

"None."

"Right." I set my shoulders and tried to arrange my face into a calm, pleasant, totally unfazed expression. "That means this is goodbye."

His dark eyebrows raised. "You're abandoning me?"

"You just said there's no reason for me to stay!"

"There's no reason for you to stay at Penryth Hall," he said with almost insulting patience, "because you're *coming with me to London.*"

I stared at him. In spite of his almost rude care in speaking the words, it seemed he hadn't said them carefully enough, because I still couldn't understand them.

"You want me to come with you?" I said dumbly. "To London?"

"Yes-s-s," he said, enunciating even more slowly. "To *London.*"

I tried to ignore the rush of relief that went through me, the pathetic joy in my heart that he wanted me, that the moment of separation could be avoided for a bit longer. "But what on earth would I do there?"

He lifted an eyebrow. "I could hire you back as my physio."

"Come on. You can *jog* now. You don't need a physical therapist anymore."

"Then," he said huskily, "come as my full-time lover."

"I'd live in London and just—spend time with you in bed?"

"Think of it as a vacation."

"*You* won't be on vacation. You'll be working all the time."

"Not at night." He gave me a wicked grin. "I'll be your toy boy then, what do you say?" He came closer. "You'll have me all night. Isn't that what you love about me?"

I love everything about you, I wanted to say. *The way you touch me. The sound of your voice. The way you make me laugh. Everything.*

But I knew it was the last thing that he wanted to hear. It was supposed to be a physical affair, nothing more. I looked at him in the flickering firelight of his study. He was still dressed only in silk boxers from our strip poker match, and my gaze lingered at his powerful torso, hard-muscled biceps and thickly hewn thighs. Sex was enough, I told myself. It had to be enough.

"Diana?" He was staring at me. I realized I'd taken too long to respond.

"Of course that's what I love best," I said, tossing my head. "What else is there about you to love?"

"Such a heartless woman," he sighed, then drew closer. Nuzzling me, he cupped my breast through my thin cotton sweater. My nipples turned instantly hard, pressing up through the red lace of my bra, thrusting visibly against the sweater. He whispered, "Allow me to serve you, then, milady...."

Falling to his knees in front of me, Edward suckled me, pressing his mouth over my nipple. I gasped as I felt his hot mouth through the thin cotton and fillip of red lace beneath. His free hand wrapped around my other breast, then a moment later, he moved to that side.

My sweater disappeared, then the red lace bra. With a growl of satisfaction, he lowered his mouth to my bare skin. My head fell back, my eyes closed. His lips were hot and soft, satin and steel. When he drew back, I was shivering with need, just like the first time he'd touched me. As though we hadn't been making love four times a day, every day, for the past ten days.

"So we're agreed," he murmured. Rising to his feet, he pulled me into his arms. "You'll come with me to London."

"I can't just go there as...as your sex toy," I said in a small voice, my stupid, traitorous heart yearning for him to argue with me, to tell me I meant more to him than that.

"I know." He suddenly smiled. "London has a thriving theater scene. You can live at my house as you audition for acting roles."

"Audition?" I said, trying to keep the fear from my voice.

"It's perfect." Running his hands down my back, he kissed my cheek, my neck. "By day, you pursue your dreams. At night...you'll belong to me."

Cupping my face, he kissed me, hot and demanding. I wrapped my arms around him, kissing him back recklessly, ignoring my troubled heart.

I couldn't give him up. Not yet. Not when I could still

live in his world of passion and color and desire for a little while longer. I wanted to be the bold woman who wore red lace panties for her lover, and paraded around nearly naked. I wasn't ready to go back and be that invisible girl again. Not yet. I needed to be in his arms. I needed to be with him, one moment teasing each other, playing like children, and the next bursting into flame in the most adult way possible. It reminded me of the old definition of love—*friendship on fire...*

No. My eyes flew open. I cared about Edward, sure. I liked him a lot. But that wasn't the same as being in love.

I couldn't let it be.

I like him, that's all, I told myself firmly. *We have fun together. It's not a crime.*

I pulled away. "All right," I said, keeping my voice casual. "I'll come to London."

"Good," he said, with a low, sensual smile that said he'd never doubted he could convince me. Leaning me back against the poker table, he got me swiftly naked beneath the bright heat of the fire and made love to me.

And so the next morning, under the weak pink light of the dawn, I was packed up in his expensive car, along with the rest of his possessions, and driven east across the moor. Toward civilization.

CHAPTER FIVE

"Wow. You're not looking so great."

The girl sitting beside me on one of the plastic chairs lining the hallway had a concerned look on her beautifully made-up face.

"I'm fine," I replied, trying to breathe slowly, fervently trying to believe it. It had been two months since we'd arrived in London, and I'd felt strangely queasy, almost from the day we'd arrived here. I'd thought it was from fear, and also the guilt of lying to Edward about how I actually spent my days. But today, I'd finally faced my fear. For the first time, I was actually forcing myself to stay through an audition, rather than chickening out and fleeing for Trafalgar Square like a safely anonymous tourist.

For an hour, I'd sat here in the hallway, practicing my lines in my head and waiting for them to call my name. Shouldn't the queasy feeling have gone away?

Instead, it had only increased as I waited backstage at a small, prestigious West End theater, surrounded by beautiful, professional-looking actors, who were loudly practicing their lines and doing elocution exercises, and taking no notice of me whatsoever. Except for the American girl sitting next to me.

"Are you feeling sick?" she asked now.

"Just nerves," I said weakly.

"You look like you ate a bad curry. Or else it's the flu."

Wrinkling her nose, she leaned away from me ever so slightly. "My sister looked like that the first three months she was pregnant…."

"I'm fine," I repeated sharply, then swallowed, my head falling back as another wave of nausea went through me.

So much for my acting skills. Clearly not fooled, the girl looked nervously from side to side. "Oh. Good. Well. Um… Please excuse me. I have to practice my lines… over there."

Getting up, she left in a hurry, as if she'd found herself sitting next to Typhoid Mary. I couldn't blame her, because I felt perilously close to throwing up. Leaning my head against the wall, I closed my eyes and tried to breathe. I was so close to auditioning now. In a moment, they would call my name. I would speak my lines on the stage.

Then the casting agents would tell me that I sucked. It would be hideous and soul-crushing but at least I could slink home afterward and no longer be lying when I told Edward that while he was working eighteen-hour days at his office in Canary Wharf, I'd spent the day pursuing my dreams.

Just a few minutes more, and it would be over. I tried to breathe. They would probably cut me off halfway through my lines, in fact, and tell me I was too fat/thin/old/young/ wrong, or just dismiss me with a curt *Thank you*. All I needed to do was speak a few lines and…

My lines. My eyes flew open as I slapped my hand on my forehead. What were my lines? I'd practiced them for two days, practiced them in the shower and as I walked through the barren garden behind Edward's lavish Kensington townhouse. I knew those lines by heart. But they'd fled completely out of my brain and…

Then I really did feel sick and I raced for the adjacent bathroom, reaching it just in time. Afterward, I splashed cold water on my face and looked at myself in the mirror. I looked pale and sweaty. My eyes looked big and afraid.

My sister looked like that the first three months she was pregnant.

Leaving the bathroom, I walked out to the hallway. Then I kept walking, straight out of the theater, until I was outside breathing fresh, cold air.

My nausea subsided a bit. The sky was dark and overcast, not cold enough to snow but threatening chilling rain.

It was the first of March, but spring still felt far away. I walked slowly for the underground station, my legs trembling.

My sister looked like that the first three months she was pregnant.

The possibility of pregnancy hadn't even occurred to me. I carefully hadn't let it occur to me. I couldn't be pregnant. It was impossible.

I stopped abruptly on the sidewalk, causing the tourists behind me to exclaim as they nearly walked into me.

Edward had gone out of his way to take precautions. But I hadn't even worried about it, because I assumed Edward knew what he was doing. He was the one who never wanted to commit to anyone, and what could be a greater commitment than a child?

But there had been a few near misses. A few times he didn't put on the condom until almost too late. And that one time in the shower…

Feeling dazed, I walked heavily to Charing Cross station nearby and barely managed to get on the right train. I stared at the map above the seats as the subway car swayed. My cycle was late. In fact, I realized with a sense of chill, I hadn't had a period since we'd arrived in London two months ago. There could be all kinds of reasons for that. I was stressed by my halfhearted attempts at breaking into the London theater scene. I was stressed by the fact that I was lying to Edward about it. And then there was the nausea. I'd told myself my body was still growing accustomed to Greenwich Mean Time, or as the girl had suggested, I'd eaten a bad fish vindaloo.

All right, so my breasts felt fuller, and they'd been heavy and a little sore. But—I blushed—I'd assumed that was just from all the sex. The rough play at night was almost the only time I ever saw Edward anymore.

Every morning, his driver collected him before dawn to take him to his building in Canary Wharf, gleaming and modern, with a private shower and futon in his private office suite, and four PAs to service his every whim. Battling to save the deal that his cousin was trying to sabotage, he'd worked eighteen hours a day, Sundays included, and usually didn't return until long after I was in bed. Some nights he never bothered to come home at all.

But on the rest, Edward woke me up in the dark to make love to me. A bright, hot fire in the night, when his powerful body took mine with hungry, insatiable demand. Sometime before dawn, I'd feel him kiss my temple, hear him whisper, *Good luck today. I'm proud of you.* Half-asleep, I'd sigh back, *Good luck,* and then he was gone. I'd awake in the morning with sunlight slanting through the windows, and his side of the bed empty. And I would be alone.

My days in London were lonely. I missed the life we'd had in Cornwall. I missed Penryth Hall.

Everything had changed.

Was it about to change more?

Distracted by my thoughts, I almost missed my stop at High Street Kensington. I exited the underground station and then, not daring to meet the pimply sales clerk's eyes, I bought a pregnancy test from the pharmacy on the corner.

Edward had offered his driver's services to take me to auditions, but I didn't think it would do me any favors to arrive via chauffeured car, like the kept woman I'd some-how become. Plus, then I would have had to actually go to the auditions. Easier to take the underground and keep my independence—and my secrets. I didn't want Edward to feel disappointed in me, as he would if he knew I hadn't made it to a single audition in two months, in spite of all my bravado.

I hadn't wanted a driver then, but now, as I trudged up the street with my pharmacy bag tucked into my purse, the cold gray drizzle turned to half-frozen rain, soaking through my light cotton jacket, and I suddenly wished I had *someone* to look after me. Someone who would take me in his arms and tell me everything was going to be all right. Because I was scared.

I reached Edward's beautiful Georgian townhouse, with its five bedrooms and private garden, in an elegant neigh-borhood a few blocks from Kensington Palace. Heavily, I walked up the steps and punched the security code, then opened the front door.

"Diana?" Mrs. Corrigan's voice called from the kitchen. "Is that you, dear?"

"Yes," I said dully. No need to panic, I told myself. I'd take the pregnancy test. Once it said negative, I'd relax, and have a good laugh at my fears, along with a calming glass of wine.

"Come back," she called. "I'm in the kitchen."

"Just a minute." I went to the front bathroom. Trem-bling, I took the test. I waited. And waited. *Be negative,* I willed, staring down at it. *Be negative.*

The test looked back at me.

Positive.

The test fell from my numb hand. Then I grabbed it and looked at it again. Still positive. I stuffed it at the bot-tom of the trash, hiding it beneath the empty bag. Which was ridiculous.

Soon there would be no hiding it.

Pregnant. My teeth chattered as I stumbled slowly down the hall to the large modern kitchen at the back. Pregnant.

I looked out the big windows by the kitchen, overlooking the private garden that would be beautiful in spring, but at the moment was bleak and bare and covered with shards of melting snow.

"There you are, dear." Mrs. Corrigan, his full-time London housekeeper, was making a lemon cake. "Mr. St. Cyr just phoned for you."

"He called here?" My heart unfolded like a flower. Edward had never called me from work before. Had he somehow known I needed him, felt it in his heart?

She looked up a little reproachfully from the bowl. "He was dismayed that he couldn't reach you on your mobile."

"Um…" The sleek new cell phone he'd bought for me last month was still sitting on the granite kitchen countertop, plugged in, exactly where I'd left it two days ago. "I'll phone him back now."

My hands shook as I walked down the hall to his study, closing the door behind me. Dialing his number, I listened to the phone ring, in that distinctly British sound, reminding me I was a long way from home. And so did the fact that I needed to navigate through two different secretaries before I finally heard Edward's voice.

"Why didn't you answer your mobile?" he demanded by way of greeting.

"I'm sorry, I forgot it. I was at an audition and…" My voice trembled.

"The deal just went through."

His voice sounded so flat, it took me a moment to realize that he was calling to share good news. "That's wonderful! Congratulations!" I said brightly. My heart was pounding in my throat. "But, um, we need to talk—"

"Yes, we do," he said shortly. "There's going to be a

party tonight hosted by Rupert's wife, at their house in Mayfair. Wear a cocktail dress. Be ready at eight."

Rupert's wife. Victoria. I'd met her a few times. She was mean. I took a deep breath. "I'll be ready. But something has happened today, Edward. Something really important you should know about." I paused, but he didn't say anything. "Edward?"

It took me several seconds to realize he'd already hung up. Incredulously, I stared down at my cell phone.

"Everything all right, dear?" Mrs. Corrigan said cheerily as I came out of the study.

This is all I can give you, Edward had said, the night he took my virginity. *No marriage. No children. All I can offer is—this.*

It was more true than I'd realized. Because sex was truly all he gave me now. Sex that felt almost anonymous in the dark shadows of our bed. Sex, and a beautiful house to live in while I attempted to create the acting career that was supposedly my Big Dream. Except it made me sick.

Or maybe it was the pregnancy doing that.

What would he say when he found out? Would he be furious? Indifferent? Would he think I'd somehow done it on purpose? Would he ask me to end the pregnancy?

No way. My hands unwillingly went to my slightly curved belly. Even in my shock, I already knew that I was keeping this baby. There was no other option for me.

But I was scared of his reaction.

I feared I already knew what it would be.

Mrs. Corrigan was whipping the frosting, humming merrily as I walked into the kitchen. Her plump cheeks were rosy. "Such an afternoon it is!" she sighed, looking out the windows. "Rain and more rain." She looked at me. "Would you care for some tea? Or maybe some food, you're looking skin and bone," she chided affectionately.

Skin and bone? I looked down at my full breasts, my

plump hips. At my belly, which would soon be enormous. I felt another strange twinge of queasiness that I now knew was morning sickness. "Um, thanks, but I'm not hungry. Edward's taking me to a party tonight, to celebrate that his deal just went through—"

"Wonderful!"

"Yes. It is." Not so wonderful that I'd be spending time with his friends. All those bankers and their wives, and the worst of them all, Rupert and his wife, Snooty McSnotty. A low buzz of anxiety rolled through me, heavy gray clouds through my soul with lightning and rain.

And at that thought, thunder really did boom outside, so loud it shook the china cup in its saucer as the housekeeper poured me tea.

"Ooh," said Mrs. Corrigan with a shiver, "that was a good one, wasn't it?"

The rain continued all afternoon and into the evening. I paced the floor, tried to read, had to reread every page six times as my mind wandered. I managed some bread and cheese for dinner, and a little bit of lemon cake. I went upstairs and showered and dressed. I blow-dried my hair, making it lustrous and straight. I put on makeup. I put on the designer cocktail dress he'd bought me. It was tighter and skimpier than anything I'd ever worn before. Especially now. For heaven's sake, how could I not have noticed my breasts were this big?

I was ready early, at seven forty-five. Going into the front room, I sat shivering on the sofa as I waited. Outside, the traffic had dissipated, and the street was dark. Beneath the rain, puddles shone dull silver against the street lights. I waited.

It wasn't until an hour later, almost nine, that I heard the front door slam. He ran upstairs, calling my name.

"I'm in here."

"Sitting in the dark?" he growled. Coming into the front

room, he clicked on a light, glowering at me. "What are you doing, Diana?"

I blinked, squinting in the light. "I just didn't notice."

"Didn't notice?" Edward looked handsome, British and rich, a million miles out of my league in his tailored suit and tie. A warrior tycoon ready to do battle by any means—with his fists, if necessary.

But his eyes looked tired. I suddenly yearned to take him in my arms, to make him feel better. But I doubted my news would do that.

"Edward." I swallowed. "We need to talk...."

"We're late," he said shortly. "I need to change."

Turning, he raced back up the stairs, his long legs taking the steps three at a time. He seemed in foul temper for a CEO that had just made a billion-dollar deal. In record time, he returned downstairs, wearing a designer tuxedo, and looking more devilishly handsome than any man should look. I felt a sudden ache in my heart. "You look very handsome."

"Thanks." He didn't return the compliment. Instead, his lips twisted down grimly as he held out my long black coat, wrapping it around my shoulders. His voice was cold. "Ready?"

"Yes," I said, although I'd never felt less ready in my life. We left the house, getting into the backseat of the waiting car.

"How was your audition today?" he asked abruptly as his driver closed the car door.

As the driver pulled the car smoothly from the curb, I looked at Edward, suddenly uneasy. I licked my lips. "It was...surprising, actually."

"You're lying," he said flatly. "You didn't even go."

"I did go," I said indignantly. "I just didn't stay, because... Wait." I frowned. "How do you know?"

"The director is a friend of mine. He was going to give

you *special consideration*." Edward glared at me. "He called me this afternoon to say you never even bothered to show. You lied to me." He tilted his head. "And this isn't the first time, is it?"

Lifting my chin, I looked him full in the face. "I haven't done a single audition since we got here."

He looked staggered. "Why?"

I tried to shrug, to act like it didn't matter. "I didn't feel like it."

His jaw tightened. "So you've lied to me for the last two months. And every morning before I left for work, I wished you good luck… I feel like a fool. Why did you lie?"

As the car wove through the Friday evening traffic on Kensington Road, I saw the Albert Memorial in Kensington Gardens, the ornate monument to Queen Victoria's young husband whom she'd mourned for forty years after he died. I took a deep breath. "I didn't want to disappoint you."

"Well, you have." His jaw went tight as he looked out at the passing lights of the city reflected in the rain. We turned north, toward Mayfair. "I didn't take you for a liar. Or a coward."

It was like being stabbed in the heart. I took a shuddering breath.

"I'm sorry," I whispered. "Why didn't you tell me the director was your friend?"

"I wanted you to think you'd gotten the part on your own."

"Because you think I can't?"

He shook his head grimly. "You hadn't gotten a single role. I thought I could help. I didn't tell you because…" He set his jaw. "It just feels better to be self-made."

"How would you know?" I cried.

I regretted the words the instant they were out of my mouth. Hurt pride had made me cruel. But as I opened my mouth to apologize, the car stopped. Our door opened.

Edward gave me a smile that didn't meet his eyes. "Time to party."

He held out his arm stiffly on the sidewalk. I took it, feeling wretched and angry and ashamed all at once. We walked into the party, past a uniformed doorman.

Rupert St. Cyr, Edward's cousin, had a lavish mansion, complete with an indoor pool, a five-thousand-bottle wine cellar, a huge gilded ballroom with enormous crystal chandeliers hanging from a forty-foot ceiling and very glamorous, wealthy people dancing to a jazz quartet.

"Congratulations!"

"You old devil, I don't know how you did it. Well done."

Edward smiled and nodded distantly as people came up to congratulate him on the business deal. I clutched his arm as we walked toward the coat room.

"I'm sorry," I whispered.

"I'm sorry I ever tried to help you," he said under his breath.

"I shouldn't have lied to you." I bit my lip. "But something happened at the audition today, something that you should..."

"Spare me the excuses," he bit out. He narrowed his eyes. "This is exactly why I usually end love affairs after a few weeks. Before all the lies can start!"

I stopped, feeling sick and dizzy. "You're threatening to break up with me? Just because I didn't go to auditions?"

"Because you lied to my face about it," he said in a low voice, his eyes shooting sparks of blue fire. "I don't give a damn what you do. If you don't want to act, be a ditch-digger, child minder, work in a shop. Stay at home and do nothing for all I care. Just be honest about it."

"Auditioning is so hard," I choked out. I knew I wasn't doing myself any favors trying to explain but I couldn't help it. "Facing brutal rejection, day after day. I have no friends here. No connections."

His eyes narrowed as he stared at me. "You wish you were back in L.A. Is that what you're saying?"

His expression looked so strange, I hardly knew what to say. "Yes. I mean, no...."

Beneath the gilded chandeliers of the ballroom, Edward's expression hardened. So did his voice. "If you want to go, then go."

I shriveled up inside.

Turning, he left the coat room, leaving me to trail behind him.

"Edward!" I heard a throaty coo, and looking up, I saw Victoria St. Cyr coming toward us. "And Diana. What a pleasant surprise." Insultingly, she looked me up and down, and my cheeks went hot. My cocktail dress that had seemed so daring and sexy suddenly felt like layers of tacky trash bags twisted tightly around my zaftig body, especially compared to the elegantly draped gray dress over her severely thin frame. She bared her teeth into a smile. "How very... charming that you're still with us. And surprising."

Things only went downhill from there.

I did not fit into Edward's world. I felt insecure and out of place. Clutching his arm, I clung to him pathetically as he walked through the party. Even as he drank short glasses of port with the other men, and traded verbal barbs with his cousin, I tried to be part of the conversation, to act as if I belonged. To act as if my heart weren't breaking.

And Edward acted as if I weren't there, holding his arm tightly. Finally, my pride couldn't take it.

"Excuse me," I murmured, forcing my hands off his arm. "I need a drink."

"I'll get it for you," Edward said politely, as if I were a stranger, some old lady on the subway.

"No." I held up my hand. "I, um, see someone I need to talk to. Excuse me."

Was that relief I saw in his eyes as I walked away?

Awkwardly, I glanced toward Victoria St. Cyr and her friends standing by the dance floor. Turning the other way, I headed toward the buffet table. At least here I knew what to do. Grabbing a plate, I helped myself to crackers, bread, cheese—anything that promised to settle this sick feeling in my belly.

Was there any point in telling Edward I was pregnant, when it was clear he was already thinking up excuses to end our relationship?

"It won't last."

Victoria stood behind me, with two of her friends.

I stared at her. "Excuse me?"

"Don't mind her," one of the friends said. "She's not used to seeing Edward with a girlfriend."

Girlfriend made it sound like we were exclusive. Which we weren't. Well, obviously I was not dating anyone else. Was he?

My breath caught in my throat as I suddenly looked at all his late nights in a brand new light. The nights he hadn't even come home, when I'd assumed he was at work...could he have been with someone else? He'd never promised me fidelity, after all. I hadn't received a single word of commitment or love. In fact, he'd promised me the opposite.

"I wouldn't say I'm his girlfriend," I said thickly.

Victoria pounced. "What are you then?"

"His, um, physical therapist."

They all stared at me, then burst out laughing.

"Oh, is that what they're calling it now," one said knowingly.

"It's true." At least it used to be true. "Edward was in a car accident in September..."

"That's right." Victoria St. Cyr looked at me thoughtfully. Diamond bangles clacked over the music of the nearby quartet as she held up her hand. "Doesn't that all make you worry?"

"What?"

"Edward's accident." She sighed. "He was so in love with that American maid who worked at a nearby house." She looked me over insultingly. "She looked rather like you, in fact. When she fell pregnant, he helped her leave London and flew her all over the world for a year. But when she had the chance to marry the father of her baby, she dropped Edward without a thought."

"The other man was a Spanish duke," her friend added, as if that explained everything.

"Edward actually tried to blackmail her into leaving her new husband—and her baby. Fortunately, the car flipped down the hill. But if the Duke and Duchess of Alzacar had pressed charges, Edward would be in jail." Shaking her head, she said coldly, "He *should* be in jail. Rupert should be CEO."

Did she think this new knowledge would devastate me? "I know all that," I said coldly, though I was shaking. "And you're wrong. Whatever mistakes Edward made in the past, he deserves to lead St. Cyr Global. He'd never sink a billion-pound deal like his cousin tried to do." I drew myself up. "He's twice the man your husband is."

Victoria stared at me dangerously.

"Your loyalty is adorable," she said softly. "But let me offer you a little friendly advice."

Friendly? Right. I said guardedly, "Yes?"

"I understand your attraction. Truly, I do. The night I met Edward, I wanted him so badly, I would have done anything to get into his bed. *Anything.*" Her lips pursed. "Luckily I met Rupert before any damage could be done."

"Your point?"

Her thin lips curled. "Edward is poison for women. You'll see. He keeps a lover just long enough to use her body and break her heart before he tosses her in the rubbish bin. How long have you two been together now? Two months? Three?" She shook her head with a pitying sound. "You're *long* past your sell-by date. Here." She pushed a card into my hands. "Call me when you need a shoulder to cry on."

And she swept past me grandly, her entourage trailing behind her.

Numbly, I looked down at the embossed card. It was like a business card, only gilded and elegant and clearly for society. It was the craziest thing I'd ever seen.

Crumpling the card into a ball, I shoved it in my purse. Even living among the sharks of the entertainment industry hadn't prepared me for this. Edward's family was *awful*. No wonder he'd been a sitting duck for the first reasonably kindhearted person he met—that American girl he hadn't wanted to let go. Because he loved her so much.

While he was ready to dump me for a white lie I'd told, just because I'd wanted so desperately for him to think the best of me.

Turning blindly from the buffet, I ran into a brick wall. Edward was standing behind me. I wondered how long he'd been there.

"Having a good time?" he asked, his face inscrutable.

"No," I choked out.

"It might be better with champagne."

"I don't want any." I looked up at his handsome face. Was he already trying to figure out how best to end our relationship? How to let me down easy, and without a fuss?

I wanted him to love me. I wanted him to hold me close and never let go. Everything he'd told me—from the beginning—would never happen. Stupid. So stupid!

My voice was nearly a sob. "I just want to go home."

For a long moment, Edward just looked at me. All around us in the ballroom, beautiful, glamorous people were laughing and talking, celebrating, and a few had started dancing to the music from the quartet. But as he looked into my tearful eyes, for a split second it was as if the two of us were alone again. Just like at Penryth Hall.

"All right," he said quietly. Taking my hand, he pulled me from the ballroom, stopping for my coat. His driver collected us at the curb.

The streets of London seemed darker than usual. The rain had stopped, and the clouds had lifted. The night was frosty and soundless.

We walked into his dark, silent house after he punched in the alarm code. I started to go up the stairs. He stopped me.

"I never told you," he said huskily, pulling me into his arms, "how beautiful you looked tonight."

My heart went faster. "I did?"

"The most beautiful woman there by far." Pulling me closer, he twirled a long tendril of my hair around his finger and murmured, "I was glad when you left to get a drink, because the other men were flirting with you so indecently I thought I'd have to punch them."

"They were flirting with me?" I said dumbly. I had no memory of any of this alleged flirting, or of any of the men who'd surrounded us. I just remembered clinging to Edward's arm like a silent idiot.

"Any man would want you." His hand traced up my shoulder, my neck. "You're the most desirable woman I've ever known."

"More than the woman you loved in Spain?" I heard myself blurt out.

His hand grew still. His ice-blue eyes met mine. "Why do you say that?"

I swallowed. But I couldn't back down now. "Victoria told me you took care of her for a year, helping her when she was pregnant. After she married someone else, you still loved her. You wouldn't let her go. You were willing to die for her." I stopped.

"So?" He spoke without apology, and without explanation. As if he owed me neither. It made my heart turn to glass.

I took a deep breath. "Is it true she looked like me?"

His dark eyebrows lowered. "Victoria said that?"

"Yes."

"She was guessing." His lips creased in a humorless smile. "She never met Lena. But it happens she's wrong. You look nothing alike."

I exhaled. Then I shivered. *Lena.* So that was the other woman's name. "What made you love her so much?"

His eyes narrowed. "Why do you keep pushing?"

"Because I…"

I froze.

Because I wanted to know what special quality this woman had had, that had made Edward love her so much, when he couldn't even love me a little. Had she been pretty? Had she been wise? Was it the sound of her voice or the scent of her perfume?

I wanted to know because at my deepest core, I yearned for him to love me the same way. I yearned for him to want to be with me. To stay with me. Raise a child with me.

I was in love with him, and wanted him to love me back.

My infatuation with Jason had been nothing, a schoolgirl crush, compared to what I felt for Edward, the man I'd healed, the man I'd shared a home with, the man who'd teased me and encouraged me and demanded I follow my dreams. The man who'd taken my virginity and shown me what physical love could be. The man whose child I now carried deep inside me.

I was in love with Edward.

Desperately.

Stupidly.

"Diana?"

I took a deep breath. "I was just curious, that's all." I

gave him a weak smile. "After hearing Victoria talk about her. What made Lena so different?"

"Different?" Moonlight from the window caught the edge of his face, leaving his eyes in shadow. "Lena wasn't different. She was ordinary, really. But she acted helpless, as if I were the only one who could save her. She made me think…I could be her hero." His cruel, sensual lips twisted up at the edges. "Me. Isn't that hilarious? But I almost believed it. I took care of her for months, asking nothing in return. Until she suddenly left me for the Spanish bastard who'd abandoned and betrayed her."

"That's it? She acted helpless?" *I could be helpless,* I thought wildly. I felt helpless right now, looking at him, fearing there was nothing I could do to make him love me or want our baby.

He shrugged. "I thought I deserved her. That I'd earned her."

I blinked. "You can't *earn* someone's love. That's not how it works."

He gave a harsh laugh. "I've heard the words *I love you* from so many women…"

"You have?" I whispered. No one had ever spoken those words to me, except for my family.

"…but words are meaningless. Cheap. Women have said it after they've only known me a few hours—in bed. They barely knew *me* at all. They were just trying to trap me, to make me do something I didn't want to do. To *own* me."

"You mean, make you commit?"

"Exactly." He gave me a crooked grin, then looked away. "But I always imagined love to be an action, not a word. If I loved someone, I wouldn't say it, I'd show it. I'd take care of her, putting her needs ahead of my own. I'd put my whole soul into making her happy…." He cut himself off with a harsh laugh, clawing back his hair. "But what the hell do I know? I've never found love like that. So I gave up on it. And I've been happier ever since."

"I don't believe that," I said softly, looking at the stark emotion in his eyes. "I'm sorry that woman hurt you, but you can't live the rest of your life closed off from love."

"You're wrong," he said flatly.

Clutching my hands into fists at my sides, I whispered, "Do you still love her?"

He choked out a laugh. "*Love* her? No. It all seems a million years ago. I was a different person then. I'm leaving them to it. The Duke and Duchess of Alzacar are happy together, with their fat, happy baby, happily married in their big castle in happy, happy Spain. I wish them every happiness."

His voice had an edge to it. A darkness. I searched his handsome face. "You're sorry you tried to kidnap her… Aren't you?"

"I'm sorry I ever let myself care in the first place," he said coldly. "I should have known better than to think I could be any woman's hero. It's not in my nature. Now…I know who I am. Selfish to the core. And glad. My life is completely within my control."

Looking up at him, my glass heart broke into a thousand shards, each of them sharp as ice. "So you'll never have a wife—no child—no family of any kind?"

"I told you from the beginning," he said harshly. "Those are things I do not want. Not now. Not ever." With a deep breath, he took a step toward me. Gently, he cupped my cheek with his hand. "But I do want this. *You.* We can enjoy each other. For as long as the pleasure lasts."

His palm was warm and rough against my cheek, and I suddenly felt like crying. "It could be more. You have to know—"

He was already shaking his head grimly. "Don't do this

to me, Diana. Let this be enough. Don't ask for more than I can give. Please. I'm not ready to let you go. Not yet—"

Pulling me tight against his hard-muscled body, he kissed me passionately in the shadowy stairwell of the Kensington townhouse.

I knew I should stop him, to force him to listen, to tell him the two things that were causing such anguish—joy, terror, desperate hope—in my heart.

I loved him.

I was pregnant with his baby.

But I was scared the moment I told him, our relationship would end. He'd see me and the child I carried both as unwanted entanglements. Because he'd already made up his mind about what he wanted. And what he didn't want.

He wasn't going to change.

Holding him tightly, I returned his kiss. Tears streaming unchecked down my cheeks, adding salt to the taste. His lips gentled as he pressed me back against the wall of the stairwell. My head fell back as he kissed down my throat. I gasped, trembling, caught between desire and the agony of a breaking heart. How could I realize I loved him, only to lose him the same night? Blood rushed in my ears like a rhythmic buzz.

Edward pulled away with a curse, and I realized the buzz was actually his phone ringing. But who would call him so late? A business emergency? A secretary?

A mistress?

No. Surely not. But we'd never promised fidelity. He'd promised only pleasure.

"It's not me," he said shortly, looking at his phone.

Frowning, I reached down for my tiny purse that had dropped to the floor, and saw it was actually my new phone ringing. But other than Edward, the only person who knew the number was my stepfather, who'd just wrapped up production in New Mexico.

I stared down at the caller ID.

"It's Jason," I breathed.

"Black?" Edward's scowl deepened. "Why is he calling you?"

"I have no idea."

"Has he done it before?" he bit out, almost unwillingly.

I shook my head. "Something must be wrong… Oh my God." Images of Howard or Madison hurt flashed in front of my terrified eyes. Turning away, I answered anxiously, "Jason?"

"Diana?"

"Why are you calling me?"

"I'm in California… I got the number from Howard."

"What's happened? Is someone hurt?"

"Yeah. Someone's hurt."

I held my breath.

"I am," he said quietly. "I made a horrible mistake."

I frowned. "What do you mean, you made a mistake?"

Edward had been glowering beside me. But at this, he turned on his heel without a word. I watched him stalk up the staircase. Was he mad at me for answering a call in the middle of our kiss? But that wasn't fair. He was the one who'd picked up his phone first.

"I shouldn't have cheated on you," Jason said on the phone. "I should have known we'd get caught. Even at night, there's always people around the Eiffel Tower. I have so many regrets. I should have…" His voice trailed off. "You know Madison and I broke up."

"I know," I said gently.

He exhaled. "Is there any way you can ever forgive me?"

"Sure."

He paused. "Really?"

I realized somewhat to my own surprise that I'd forgiven and forgotten long ago. The way I felt for Edward

now, all the angst over Jason seemed a million years ago.
It didn't matter. As Edward had said—I was a different
person then.

"I forgave you a long time ago…." I said quietly.

"Oh?" he said hopefully.

"Because I'm in love with Edward now."

"Oh," he sighed.

I changed the subject. "But is there any chance that you
and Madison…?"

"Nah. She disappeared to India when we broke up. Now
I heard she's in Mongolia doing some independent film,
out on some steppe in the middle of nowhere, no makeup
trailer, no catering, getting paid at scale."

"Seriously?" That didn't sound like her at all.

"Crazy, right? Must be a nervous breakdown or something. At least, that's what I suggested when I was inter-
viewed last week for *People* magazine."

He was giving interviews about Madison, suggesting
she'd had a nervous breakdown? I didn't approve of that
at all. I thought of Edward, waiting for me upstairs. "If
that's all you called about…"

"No. Here's why I called. I'm costarring on a web series. It's just a side project, a spin-off to promote my movie
sequel coming out next summer. But the lead actress just
ducked out an hour ago to go back to rehab." He paused.
"I thought of you."

"You…what?" I said faintly.

"Don't get too excited. The pay is next to nothing. But
the movie has a large cult following, and good visibility.
So even though it's just on the web, it could help you get
the attention of agents…."

As he continued to speak, I stood in the dark foyer,
swaying. I felt lightheaded.

"…and you wouldn't even have to audition. I have that
much pull, at least." He paused. "Diana? You still there?"

"I just can't believe it," I whispered. My hand tightened on the phone. "You're calling out of nowhere to offer me my dream job?"

"Dream job?" He laughed "Oh man. If a shoestring web series is your dream, you need bigger dreams." He added apologetically, "It's not glamorous, either. The character is pregnant. You'd need to wear padding…."

I put my hand against the wall to brace myself. "Are you kidding?" *Pregnant?* Was it fate telling me to go? I said almost tearfully, "Why are you doing this?"

"Well, I owe you, Diana," he said quietly. "After all I put you through, it seemed the least I could do. Plus," he added, "I'd rather work with you than some no-name nobody. Will you come?"

I thought again of Edward upstairs, waiting for me, and my heart twisted. "I'm not sure…."

"I understand," he said dryly. "Edward doesn't seem like the California type." He paused. "It's up to you. But if you can get here within two days, the role is yours."

When I hung up the phone, the house was silent and dark. Mrs. Corrigan had gone to bed long ago, before we even got home from the party. It was the first time I'd been downstairs like this, with Edward up in our bedroom. Usually I was the one to sleep alone.

California. The memory of home came back to me. Sunshine. The ocean. The scent of roses in my mother's garden. I could have my dream job there, with my friends and family around me, raising my baby….

Except this wasn't just my baby. It was *our* baby. And no matter how scared I was, I had to tell Edward about it. I had to at least give him the chance to be part of our lives. And tell him I loved him. Right now.

But as I slowly went up the stairs, my heart was in my throat.

A baby. I gripped the slender oak handrail as I climbed,

each shaking step echoing across the dark house. *A sweet, precious baby.* Would he be a little boy with Edward's eyes? An adorable little girl with his smile?

Then I remembered my promise.

This is all I can give you, he'd said. *No marriage. No children. All I can offer is—this. Do you agree?*

An ache lifted to my throat. I was kidding myself if I thought Edward would be happy about this. He didn't want my *love.* He didn't want my *child.* He wanted convenient sex, and to leave if it got complicated.

I covered my mouth with my hand. *Please let him be happy about my news. Give me the chance to show him how to love again....*

My legs shook as I walked down the dark hallway. I stopped at our bedroom door.

"You've kept me waiting." Edward's voice was accusing from the shadows. "Come to bed, Diana."

Come to bed. I swallowed. Clenching my trembling hands at my sides, I went forward.

As my eyes adjusted to the dim light of the bedroom, I saw the large shape of him, lying on the bed. His long legs were crossed, his arms folded beneath his head as he stared up at the ceiling. He was still fully clothed in his tuxedo, with only his tie loosened.

"How is Jason?" he said coldly, still staring up at the ceiling.

I stopped. The two men were not exactly close friends. More like rivals, really, though I had no idea what they might be rivals about. I said haltingly, "He's all right."

"I bet." With a low laugh, Edward sat up on the bed. He turned to face me. The hard lines of his body and face were in shadow, but I saw the glitter of his eyes. "So he made a big mistake, did he?"

"He felt bad about cheating on me," my voice stumbled awkwardly, "so he called me to offer me a role. It's nothing big, just a web series. But I can have the role without having to audition, as long as I'm there in two days."

"How perfect. For both of you." He rose to his feet, slowly, like a giant rising in front of me. "Do you want me to help you pack?"

My lips parted at the coldness of his tone. "I don't want to leave you—"

"It's exactly what you want," he said acidly. "Go back to California, with all your industry connections. Jason Black is dying to have you back, so much he's obligingly dug up an acting job for you. Everything you want has fallen into your lap. There's nothing left to do but give you a goodbye kiss."

Every woman Edward had trusted had abandoned him, lied to him. But I would not. "I don't want to go. Because—"

He lifted a dark eyebrow and said mockingly, "Because?"

My spine straightened, and I forced myself to say it, simply, clearly, with every syllable full of equal parts anguish and hope. "Because I'm in love with you, Edward."

The effect was immediate.

Dropping his hands, he staggered back. His eyes looked wild in the shadowy light. He took a step toward me. Then stopped.

"I want to stay," I whispered, almost begging. "Please give me a reason to stay. Tell me I have a chance with you."

I heard his intake of breath. "Diana…" He caught himself. His jaw grew tight. "No."

"You don't want me," I said miserably.

"Of course I want you," he said fiercely. Then he looked away. "I just know how this will end." With a low curse, he yanked off his loosened tuxedo tie. "I should have broken this off weeks ago. Before we left Cornwall. But I couldn't." He looked at me, and I thought I saw a sheen of bewilderment in his eyes, even grief. "And this is the result. Pain for us both."

"Don't you have any feelings for me at all?" I choked out.

He stepped back. The short distance between us suddenly became wide. "I care about you." I saw the smudges of shadows beneath his eyes. He took a breath. "In fact I'm afraid, if I let myself, I could fall in love with you, Diana."

Joy leapt in my heart. "Edward—"

"But I won't let it happen," he said flatly. "I won't let myself love you."

The cut was so sudden and savage that my breath choked off and a sound came from my lips like a whimper.

His eyes glittered. "Love is a suckers' game, Diana. I've told you that all along. The only way to win is not to play. I've learned it the hard way."

But beneath his rough voice, I thought I heard something else. Vulnerability. He was holding himself together by brute force.

"Please don't do this," I said tearfully. "Don't."

Edward looked down at me almost wistfully. "We both know you haven't been happy in London. It was just a matter of time."

I couldn't argue with that, no matter how much I wished I could. As I stood beside the enormous bed where he'd given me such pleasure in the darkness, every night for the past two months, I felt Edward's emotional and physical withdrawal, as plainly as if someone had pulled a coat off my body. I hadn't even realized it had been wrapped around my shoulders until it was suddenly gone and I felt the chill blast of winter.

Reaching into the closet, he pulled out my old suitcase. Tossing it on our bed, he calmly started dumping my clothes into it. As I watched him, aghast, he finished packing in just three minutes. "If I've missed anything, I'll have it sent to you in California."

"You're tossing me out."

His eyes held no expression. "I'm saying goodbye."

But I still hadn't told him my secret—our precious, precious secret, due in September. "Wait. We still have to talk." I took a deep breath and tried desperately, "There's something more I have to tell you—"

"We've talked," Edward said. "And now we're done." Going to the window, he opened the blinds and looked out at the elegant street, dark and quiet with all the expensive townhouses tucked in for the night, sleeping cheek by jowl in the moonlight. Pulling his phone from his pocket, Edward called his driver. Hanging up, he glanced back at me as if I were a stranger.

"Nathan will be here in five minutes to take you to the airport. My jet is at your disposal, and will take you back to where your dream career and dream man await." His lips twisted. "Thank you for your assistance with my recovery." Edward held out his hand. "I will be glad to recommend you to anyone who needs a physiotherapist in the future."

Bewildered, I took his hand. He shook it once, briskly, as if we'd only just been introduced. He started to pull away. Desperately, I tightened my hand. "Come with me to California."

His lips curved. "And what would I do there?"

"Whatever you want!"

He shook his head. "St. Cyr Global is headquartered in London. The company is my responsibility. I was born to it...."

"And you hate it," I said tearfully. "Every single minute."

He looked down at me, and an expression of pain crossed his eyes. "It was fun while it lasted, Diana," he said quietly. "But there is no reason for us to ever see each other again."

"No reason? Are you crazy? I just told you I loved you!"

His expression hardened. "Do you expect me to change my whole life for the sake of a few cheap words?"

"Cheap?" My knees trembled from the emptiness I felt inside. It suddenly threatened to devour me, with the help of its friends, grief and despair. "I want to be with you forever. I love you, Edward," I whispered. "We could build a home together, a future." I lifted my tearful gaze to his. "We could have a child—"

My throat closed when I saw him flinch.

"Sorry. What I want," he said quietly, "is a clean break." He closed my suitcase with a snap.

"But there can't be." To my horror, my voice came out in a whimper. I wiped my eyes hard. "There will always be a connection between us now. Because you have to know that I…"

"For God's sake, stop it!"

"But I…"

"Not another word! If you won't go, I will." I had a brief view of his pale, stricken face as he rushed past me. Then he was gone, disappearing through the door in a few strides of his long legs.

I stared after him in shock. I heard the echo of the front door slamming downstairs. I looked out the window, and numbly watched Edward disappear down the street, walking out of my life forever.

A sob came from the back of my throat. I leaned against the window, my hand outstretched across the cold glass. Edward hadn't even given me the chance to tell him about the baby. Just telling him I *loved* him had made him run.

Just as I'd always known it would. Though I'd tried so hard not to know.

Through the blur of my tears, I saw a black sedan silently pull up to the curb in front of the house. Nathan, coming to take me to the airport.

I finally understood why Edward had ended our relationship. Why he'd been so determined not to love me.

It was so he'd never have to feel like this.

"Are you ready, madam?" I heard the driver's voice at the door. "Shall I bring your suitcase down?"

My hand closed to a fist against the window. Turning slowly, I gave him a shake of my head. "I'll do it myself."

"Very good, madam."

Squaring my shoulders, I wiped my eyes. I'd thought I could teach Edward something about love. Instead, he'd taught me.

Love is a suckers' game. The only way to win is not to play.

With a deep breath, I picked up my suitcase. I'd never weep over Edward again, I vowed. All that mattered now was our baby. No.

My baby.

CHAPTER SIX

"OUT HERE AGAIN?"

Looking up, I smiled when I saw my stepfather in front of the pink bougainvillea of the garden.

"I had the morning off," I replied. "Jason's coming to pick me up in an hour."

"Always so busy." Howard gave a mock sigh. "I should have gotten you to work as a zombie when I had the chance."

"Sorry." My smile lifted to a grin. "You'll have to ask my agent now."

The web series had been as good a launch as Jason had thought it would be. In just four-and-a-half months, I'd started to have a real career. I wasn't a movie star like Madison—not even close—but it turned out I had lots of friends who were anxious to see me succeed for no other reason than that they liked me. I had already expanded into commercials, doing character roles and bit parts on television shows. It was enjoyable at times, at other times mind-numbingly boring. If it wasn't quite the ecstatic dream I'd thought it would be, it at least had given me something to do after I left my real dream behind in London.

Or to be more accurate, he'd left me.

"Must be hard to be so popular," Howard grumbled. Then, as he looked around, a smile spread across his tanned, wrinkled face. "You've made the garden come to life again. It's exactly how Hannah had it."

"Thanks." I leaned back on my haunches, brushing dirt off my gardening gloves as I surveyed the red and yellow roses. At nearly seven months' pregnant, my belly was so large now that I had to brace myself so I didn't lose balance and topple over.

For the past four-and-a-half months, since I returned to California, I'd lived in my childhood bedroom at Howard's house, a white colonial in Beverly Hills. Whenever I wasn't working, I spent time in my mother's old garden behind the house. In April, I'd enjoyed feeling the sunlight on my face, and now it was late July, I relished the cool shade.

I was home, I told myself. I didn't let myself think about Cornwall anymore, or how happy I'd been at Penryth Hall.

I looked up gratefully at my stepfather. "Thanks for letting me stay here so long. When I asked to visit, you had no idea I'd be moving in permanently," I added, only half joking.

"Listen." He reached out to pat my shoulder. "Every single day I have you here, with a grandbaby on the way, is a blessing." Howard looked wistfully at the roses. "You've started a new career, a new life," he said gruffly. "Your mother would have been so happy about the baby. And so proud of you, Diana."

I felt a lump rise to my throat. "Thanks, Howard."

Funny to think now that I hadn't always liked him. I hadn't wanted anyone to replace my dad, and the two men were so different. My dad had been quiet and studious, caring and careful. Howard Lowe was brash and loud, and never afraid to yell—especially at actors—or start a fight.

But beneath his bluster, Howard had loved my mother more than life, and he'd taken me under his wing from the beginning, when I was a sad eleven-year-old, bookish and quiet compared to his own daughter Madison, the result of his earlier short marriage to an actress.

Swallowing, I looked from the pinks and reds and yellows of the roses, to the more exotic flowers beneath wide cypress, pine and palm trees. "You've been so kind to me. I feel bad, with Madison giving you the silent treatment for it...."

He made a dismissive gesture. "Who's to say she is? She's busy in Mongolia. And if she's mad that I'm letting you stay here, she'll have to get over it. We're family."

I shook my head. "She'll never forgive me for ruining her relationship with Jason."

"Hush. If it was so easy to ruin, it wasn't much of a relationship." He patted my arm. "I'm glad you're here, Diana. Don't rush into leaving. Especially with Jason Black. I don't think much about a man who keeps changing his mind which sister he wants to marry."

"Howard, you know Jason and I are just friends!"

"Sure, I know that. I'm just not sure he does."

I sighed. After we'd wrapped the web series, Jason had taken me out often, whenever he had time off from the superhero movie he was filming in Century City. After the scandal of last year, the paparazzi had a field day with this latest development, and they'd followed us constantly, photographing us doing boring things like drinking lattes at a café. Last week we'd been on the cover of multiple celebrity gossip magazines. *Madison Lowe Love Triangle*, one headline screamed. *Madison's Pregnant Stepsister Strikes Back with Baby Daddy Jason Black!*

I'd writhed when I read it. So much for trying to avoid the paparazzi, and maintain a dignified silence.

"Just tell everyone it's mine," Jason had urged. "It will be, after we're married."

"We're not getting married, Jason," I'd said, rolling my eyes. "We're friends. Just friends."

But did he really accept that?

I sighed in irritation, remembering. "Love is a suckers' game," I grumbled to Howard.

I suddenly realized who I was quoting. I didn't love Edward anymore. Instead, I'd become him.

"Okay, okay." Howard held up his hands. "Whatever. I'm staying out of it. But look." His expression turned ferocious, his gray eyebrows bushy and fierce. "I don't know what the deal was with your baby's father, or why you decided it would be a mistake to tell him about the pregnancy...."

"I don't want to—"

"Yeah, I know you don't like to talk about it. But take it from an old man. Life is short. It passes by in a blink. Even if the guy's every kind of jerk, he at least deserves a shot at knowing his kid."

I wished I'd never told Howard so much. Edward had made me love him as I'd never loved anyone. He'd filled me with his child. He'd made me so happy.

But he hadn't wanted me. He hadn't wanted any of it. Love. Children. Happiness.

Bluebirds soared above my mother's garden, singing as they lifted higher into the cloudless blue sky. Something caught in my throat, and I looked away. "He told me he didn't ever want a child. I was doing him a favor."

"People can change. Sometimes for better than you can imagine. He deserved the chance." He looked at me and said softly, "Your mom would have said the same."

I gave a soft gasp. Bringing Mom into it was punching below the belt.

Not that I actually had a belt anymore. Unthinkingly, I put my hand over my swelling body. It was a good thing that long dresses were in style, because now I was in my third trimester, none of my regular clothes fit me anymore. Not even the stretchiest yoga pants.

"He had his chance." I slowly rose to my feet. "He threw my love back in my face. I'm not giving him the chance to do it to her."

"He hurt you. I get it." My stepfather's rheumy eyes met mine in the bright, unrelenting California sunshine. "But take advice from an old man who loves you. Grab your chance at love when you can. Because right now, you think there will be endless chances." His throat caught. "There won't. You used to know that, until he turned you hard and cynical. When I think of the sweet kid you were, I'd like to punch Edward St. Cyr in the jaw." His bushy gray eyebrows lowered ferociously. "If I ever meet him—"

The hinge of the garden gate squeaked. I looked up. "Jason—"

But it wasn't Jason. Looking across the dappled sunlight of the garden, my heart was suddenly in my throat.

Edward stood across the green grass, in front of the bright pink flowers. Sunlight illuminated his dark hair, and luminous, deep blue eyes.

"Is it true?" He lowered his gaze to my pregnant belly. "You're pregnant?"

My breath caught.

Edward took a step toward me, and another. His eyes devoured me, as if he'd been dreaming of me for months and could hardly believe I wasn't a dream now.

"Is it mine?" he said quietly. "Or Jason Black's?"

I trembled, my hands shaking.

"Yours," Howard said helpfully.

I turned on him in outrage. "Howard!"

"Oh, c'mon." He rolled his eyes. "It's not as if you were going to lie. At least not for long," he amended, looking at me more closely.

"You're meddling," I accused.

"I'm saving you some trouble. You can thank me later. Excuse me." My stepfather walked toward the garden gate. He stopped in front of Edward. "About time you showed up." He rubbed his jowly chin thoughtfully. "I actually owe you a punch in the jaw—"

"Howard!" I cried.

"Later," he said hastily, glancing back at me, and he let himself out the gate. Leaving us alone.

Edward and I stared at each other across the soft green grass. He had a five-o'clock shadow on the hard edge of his jawline, and shadows beneath his eyes, as if he hadn't slept in days. And he'd never looked so beautiful to me. Never, ever.

Except I didn't care about him anymore. I didn't. And I wouldn't. I took a deep breath. "What are you doing here?"

"I'm here…" Edward seemed uncharacteristically uncertain. His gaze lowered to my belly, the shape of which was clearly visible beneath my cotton maxi dress. "I saw a picture of you online. The article said Jason Black was your boyfriend but…"

"I'm due in September."

He did the math quickly in his head, then his lips twisted downward. "So I'm the father."

I looked down at the grass, the color of emeralds, lush and spikey. "Sorry. Yes."

He shook his head. "How is it possible? We were so careful—"

"Not careful enough, apparently."

"You knew you were pregnant when you left London, didn't you?" His voice was deceptively quiet. "You knew, and you didn't tell me."

"I did you a favor."

"A favor?"

"You didn't want a child. You were very clear." My teeth chattered with emotion. I wrapped my arms around my body, which was suddenly shivering in the bright July sunlight. "You didn't want a child, and you didn't want me."

He came closer to me. "So you took your revenge?"

I shook my head fiercely. "I wanted to tell you about

the baby. I tried! But the moment I told you I loved you, you ran out of the house in terror!"

He gritted his teeth. "Don't you *dare* try to—"

"You said you wanted a clean break!" In spite of my best efforts to stay calm, my voice was shrill. "You said you never wanted to see me again! I tried to tell you, but you ran out of the house rather than listen to me! Don't you remember?"

Edward sucked in his breath. Then he came closer in the dappled sunlight, until he stood inches away from me. "Is that why you turned to Jason—because I wouldn't listen?" He moved closer. "Or was he the one you really wanted all along?"

"I wanted you." My voice was flat. "I told you. I was in love with you. I loved you as I'll never love anyone again."

He blinked.

"Loved?"

"Past tense." I shook my head. "Loving you nearly killed me. You rejected me. Abandoned me," I whispered. "I couldn't bear for you to reject her, too."

He exhaled, as if he were breathing toxic fumes. Then his eyes flew open. "*Her?*"

I nodded. "I'm having a little girl."

His face filled with wonder and he reached towards me. "We're having a girl…."

I jerked back before he could touch me. "*We're* not. I am. I can support us now." My eyes hardened. "We don't need you."

Pain flashed across his handsome face, then the lines of his cheekbones and dark jawline tightened. "You're not even giving me a chance."

"I tried that already."

He gritted his teeth. "I didn't know you were pregnant."

"You told me straight out you never wanted a child. Never. Never ever."

"People can change."

"What are you trying to say, Edward?" I clenched my hands at my sides. "Are you saying now I don't need you, now I don't even *want* you, you suddenly want to be part of our lives?" I tossed my head. "Forget it!"

His expression hardened. "Because you now have what you really wanted all along—an acting career, and Jason Black?"

"Leave him out of this!"

He set his jaw. "Has he asked you to marry him?"

I looked away.

"He has, hasn't he?" Edward's voice hit me like a blow. "So you could forgive him for sleeping with your stepsister? But not me for letting you go?"

"Look," I said acidly, glaring at him. "I don't know what kind of spiritual breakdown you're going through— seems a little early for a midlife crisis, isn't it? But keep us out of it."

"She's my daughter."

"Just biologically."

"*Just?*" he said incredulously.

"You can't be responsible for a houseplant. You said so yourself!"

"I could change."

"Don't."

My single cold word hung in the air between us. He took a deep breath, looking down at me.

"What happened to you, Diana?" he said softly.

I lifted my head. "Don't you know? Can't you tell? The naive woman you knew died in London."

"Oh my God…" he whispered, reaching towards me. Wild-eyed, I backed away. He straightened, setting down his hands at his sides. "All right, Diana," he said quietly. "All right."

Blinking fast, willing myself not to cry, I walked away

from him. My knees felt weak. I sank into a marble bench hidden amid a cool, shadowy copse of trees. But he followed, standing a few yards away.

I looked at him in the sunshine, in front of the brilliant colors of my mother's roses.

"You were right all along," I said. "I should have listened to you when you tried to tell me. Love is a suckers' game." I looked away. "The only way to win is not to play."

He took a single staggering step back from me. Then, with a deep breath, he held himself still. As if he were trying to hold himself back from—from what?

Clenching his hands at his sides, Edward came and sat beside me, on the other end of the bench, careful not to touch me.

"I'm sorry," he said quietly. "I never wanted you to learn that from me."

"You helped me out. Made me grow up."

"Let me tell you something else now." Sunlight brushed his dark blue eyes, and I saw the depths, like a brilliant sparkling light illuminating the deepest, darkest ocean. "I never should have let you go."

My lips parted. I stared up at him in shock.

He gave me a sudden crooked smile. "From the moment you left, I knew I'd made the greatest mistake of my life. In fact," he said in a low voice, "it was no life at all." He leaned forward. "I came to California to try to win you back."

I stared at him, stricken.

I could hardly believe Edward was sitting in my mother's garden in Beverly Hills. Sitting beside me on the marble bench Howard had given her one year for Mother's Day.

"You want me back?" I breathed.

He nodded. "More than anything."

We all create our own garden, Mom used to say. Gardening was a lot like life, in her opinion. Sure, plants depended on sun and soil, but the most important thing was the gardener. What choices did she make? Did she hack off roses with a dull blade? Did she overwater the ivy? Did she let wisteria grow wild, until it overran the walls, blocking all light in an insurmountable thicket of twisted vine? The garden you had showed the choices you'd made. What you'd done with the hand nature dealt you.

Now, Edward was offering me a choice I never imagined I'd have. He wanted me back?

I thought of the months of anguish I'd endured after London. He'd nearly destroyed me. I couldn't live through another broken heart. I couldn't.

My shoulders tightened. No. I lifted my chin. I'd finally stopped loving him. It was going to stay that way.

"We all make choices we have to live with," I said quietly. My eyes glittered as I looked at him. "I've moved on. So should you."

"Have you?" He straightened on the bench. And his jaw tightened. "You seem to forget one thing. I'm the baby's father. I have rights."

I stiffened. He was threatening me now?

"So it's like that, is it?"

He took a deep breath. "I don't want to fight you, Diana. It's the last thing I want. I came here to tell you I was wrong."

"Funny." Turning away, I gave a hard laugh. "Because I've decided you were right, ending our affair like you did. A long-term relationship just brings pain. Friends with benefits—that's the only way to go."

"Is that what you have with Jason?" he said roughly.

I shrugged. "More or less."

"Well, which is it? More—or less?"

"More friendship, less benefits."

"How much less?"

Gritting my teeth, I grudgingly admitted, "None."

He relaxed slightly. He leaned forward. "Diana, don't you want our child to have what you had—two parents? A real home?"

"Sure." I shrugged. "In a perfect world…"

"She can have it. All you have to do is say yes."

I lifted my chin. "What are you asking me, exactly?"

"I'm asking you, you little fool," his eyes glittered, "to marry me."

I was dreaming. I sat in shock beside him on the cool marble bench. Above the palm trees, I heard the birds singing as they crossed the blue sky. A soft summer wind blew through the flowers, causing the scent of roses to waft over me like an embrace. The only sound was the bluebirds, and a hummingbird and the lazy buzzing of the bees in the dappled sunlight.

"What did you say?" I whispered.

Edward stared down at me, his dark eyes intense. "I want to marry you."

I drew back.

"I don't understand." I put a hand to my head, feeling dizzy. "Everything you said in London—you swore you'd never want a wife or child—"

"It's all changed."

"Why?"

"You're pregnant with my child." He looked at me. "And I want you, Diana. I've never stopped wanting you. From the moment you left, I've hungered only for you."

I gave an awkward laugh. "You've had other lovers…."

"No."

My jaw dropped. "It's been four months!"

"I only want you," he said simply.

My heart was pounding. I tried desperately to bring it under control. "You didn't come to California because you wanted me." I lifted my chin. "You only came when you found out I was pregnant."

He clawed back his hair. "I was waiting for you to call me. I thought you would."

I looked at him in disbelief. "You thought I would call you—after what you said to me?"

"Women always try to win me back." A rueful smile curved his lips. "But not you."

I took a deep breath, remembering what it had cost me. I'd felt so alone and heartsick when I'd returned to California. For weeks, I'd cried myself to sleep—then was tormented in dreams, as hot memories of our nights together forced themselves upon me when I was sleeping and helpless to fight them.

"Your pregnancy just gave me the reason to come find you. It forced me to do what I'd been afraid to do. To ask you," he said, lifting his gaze to mine, "to come back to me."

Against my will, a shiver rose from deep inside me. A shiver deeper than fury and stronger than pride.

I stubbornly shook my head.

"I want you," Edward said, his handsome face intent on mine, making me tremble with sensual memories. His gaze fell to my lips. "I need you, Diana."

"Just missing sex…" My voice came out a croak. I cleared my throat. "That isn't a good enough reason to marry someone."

"I don't want to marry you for sex." He sat up straight on the park bench, and I was reminded of how powerful his body was, how much larger than mine. "I want us to be wed. So our child can have a childhood like yours. Not a childhood like mine."

I swallowed, remembering his loneliness then, how his mother had abandoned him when he was ten, and his father had ignored him, except when he could be used as a weapon against his ex-wife. Even the beloved gardener who'd taught him to fish had abruptly left. Boarding school at twelve. A horrible cousin. An empty castle. With only a paid housekeeper to care. That was Edward's childhood.

"You don't need to worry." I briefly touched his shoulder. "Our baby will always be safe and loved." I cradled my hands over my belly. "I promise you."

"I know." His eyes met mine. "Because I'll be there."

I glared at him. "Edward—"

Reaching out, he deliberately put his larger hand over mine, gently on the swell of my belly. I gasped when I felt him touch my hand for the first time, felt the weight of it resting protectively over the child we'd created. "I'm not going to let her go." He looked at my belly with a trace of a smile on his lips. Then he looked up at me. "Or you."

My mouth went dry.

"But I don't love you," I choked out, as if those magic words were a talisman that could make him disappear. "I'll never love you again."

The words seemed suspended in the air between us. Then he smiled. Moving closer to me, he cupped my cheek.

"Friends with benefits, then."

"And marriage?"

"And definitely that."

"I won't let you do this," I said, trembling beneath his touch. His fingertips stroked softly down my cheek, tracing my full lower lip. My breasts, now lush and full with pregnancy, felt heavy, my nipples hard and aching. I breathed, "You can't just come back, after the way you broke my heart, and force yourself into my life!"

"You mean I have to earn it."

"Well—yes—what are you smiling about?"

"Nothing." He lifted his chin. "I'm not afraid. I know exactly what to do."

"You do?"

"Yes." He slid down the bench until he was right against me. I felt him close to me, so close, and I shivered with heat in the cool shade of the garden. "I'll do whatever it takes to earn back what I've lost."

"You can't." I swallowed. "Yes, you're my baby's father. There's nothing I can do about that. But that's all. I'll never open my heart—or my body—to you again. I won't be your friend. I won't sleep with you. And I definitely won't marry you."

He pulled me into his arms. "We'll see...."

My heart beat fast as he held me against the warmth of his body. I heard the intake of his breath, and realized he was trembling, too. That was my last thought before he turned me to face him. And he lowered his mouth to mine.

He kissed me hungrily, and when his lips touched mine, in spite of my cold anger, I could not fight it. When he kissed me, the colors of the garden whirled around us, pink bougainvillea and green leaves and palm leaves glowing with sun, flying wild into the sky. And against my will, I kissed him back.

Just a kiss. One last kiss of farewell, I told myself. Before I sent him away forever.

CHAPTER SEVEN

THE COOL OCEAN BREEZE came in through open sliding glass doors on the other side of the cottage, oscillating white translucent curtains as I peeked inside the front door.

"Edward?" I called hesitantly, stepping inside the tiny house he had rented on Malibu Beach. "Are you in here?"

No answer. It took several seconds for my eyes to adjust to the light. The old grandfather clock on the other side of the floral sofa said nine o'clock. The tiny galley kitchen was empty and dark.

Edward had asked me so particularly to come over tonight, as soon as I was done filming a commercial on the other side of town. Where was he? Surely he couldn't have forgotten?

For the past month, since he'd arrived in California, he'd gone out of his way to take care of me, putting me first in anything. The only thing he'd flatly refused was to stay away from me.

"Give me a chance to change your mind about me," he said.

I'd told myself it didn't matter. He could pursue me as much as he wanted. I wasn't going to marry him. And after that first amazing kiss in the garden, I stuck to my vow and never let him kiss me again. I think I was afraid what would happen if I did.

The time we'd spent together over the past month had

been almost like Cornwall again—only far sunnier, of course, with summery blue skies and bright blue Pacific. And no sex. That was a big change. But that didn't stop Edward from spending every moment with me, taking me out for dinner, giving me foot rubs, helping me shop for baby gear. I continued to sleep in my childhood bedroom at my stepfather's house. One night, when I'd moaned about my cravings for watermelon and caramel pretzel ice cream, he'd showed up at the house with groceries. He'd had to throw a pebble against my window. Because it was three in the morning.

No man was this good. No man could work this hard for long. I couldn't let myself fall for it, because there was no way it would last.

He'd made it clear what he wanted. Marriage. A shared home for our daughter. And me. In his bed.

But it wouldn't last. Soon, his emotional breakdown— or whatever it was—would clear up, and he'd rush back to his selfish playboy workaholic life. As long as I never forgot that, or let down my guard, I told myself I'd be fine. But still…

"When are you going back to London?" I'd demanded yesterday. "How is St. Cyr Global managing without their CEO?"

Edward gave me a crooked grin. "They'll just have to cope."

He'd started accompanying me to OB-GYN visits. When he saw the first ultrasound images of our daughter, and heard her heartbeat, his eyes glistened suspiciously.

"Were those tears?" I asked as we left.

"Don't be ridiculous," he said gruffly, wiping his eyes with the back of his hand. "Dust in my eyes." And to change the subject he offered to take me to dinner at a famous restaurant which cost around four hundred dollars a plate.

I shook my head. "Nah. I want a burger, fries, frozen yogurt. How about a beachside café?"

He smiled at me. "Sure."

"You don't mind?" I asked later, as we sat on a casual wooden patio in Malibu, overlooking parked expensive motorcycles, the Pacific Coast Highway and the wide ocean beyond.

"Nope." Edward shook his head, smiling as he helped himself to one of my fries. "If you're happy, I'm happy."

For the past month, his only apparent job in California had been to take care of me. He treated me as if I were not only the mother of his child, and object of all his desire, but was in fact Queen of the World.

It was pretty hard to resist. In spite of my best efforts, he was slowly wearing me down. I found myself spending every minute with him that I wasn't working.

It irritated Jason to no end. "You never have time for me anymore," he grumbled when we ran into each other last week on a studio lot. "You're falling for him again."

"I'm not," I protested.

But now, I felt so oddly bereft as I walked through Edward's dark, empty beach cottage, I wasn't so sure.

Could he have suddenly decided he was bored with me and the baby, and flown off to London in his private jet, forgetting that he'd begged me to come over tonight?

Remembering the glow in his eyes as we'd had breakfast that morning, waffles and strawberries at an old diner near the set where I'd filmed a commercial today, I couldn't quite believe it. A low curse lifted to my lips.

Jason was right.

I was starting to trust Edward again.

Starting to let myself care.

Setting my jaw, I walked across the cottage and pushed past the white translucent curtains to the pool area in the back, with its view of the beach. "Edward?"

No answer. For a moment, I closed my eyes, relishing the cool ocean breeze against my overheated skin. It was August now, and the weather was hot, and at my advanced stage of pregnancy, so was I. As I turned back to go inside, my belly jutted so far ahead of me it seemed to be in its own time zone. Sliding the screen door closed behind me, I crossed the living room, my flip-flops thwacking softly against the hardwood floor.

I should have been here hours ago. But the shoot had gone over, and then I'd gotten a call from my agent on the way here. He'd had news so momentous I'd had to pull over my car.

"This is your big break, Diana," my agent had almost shouted. "You just got offered the girlfriend role in the biggest summer blockbuster. It'll make your career. Another actress fell through at the last minute, and she suggested you…"

"Who suggested me?" I'd said, confused.

"Someone with good taste, that's who. Movie will start shooting a few weeks after your due date," he said, cackling with glee. "How's that for perfect timing? You'll have three whole weeks to lose the baby weight before you need to report to Romania…that won't be a problem, will it, kiddo?"

Lose thirty pounds in three weeks? "Um…" Then I was distracted by the other thing he'd said. "Romania?"

"For three months. Romania is lovely in the fall."

I was dumbfounded. "But I'll have a newborn."

"So? Bring the baby with you. You'll have a nice trailer. Get a nanny." When I didn't answer, he said hastily, "Or leave the kid here with its dad. Whatever you want. But you can't turn this role down, Diana. Don't you get it? It's a starring role. Your name will be above the title. This is your big chance."

"Yeah," I'd said, wondering why I didn't feel more

thrilled. Of course I would say yes. I had no choice. Wasn't this what I'd wanted, what I'd dreamed of and strived for? This kind of luck didn't happen every day. But as I imagined losing thirty pounds in three weeks then taking my newborn off to live in a Romanian trailer, all I felt was exhausted. "I…have to think about it."

"Are you kidding?" He'd been stunned. "If you'd turn this down, I'm not sure how much I can help you in the future," he'd said warningly. "I need to feel like we're on the same team."

"I understand."

"I'll call you for your answer first thing tomorrow. Make it the right one."

I didn't know what to do. I was tempted to talk it over with Edward, but I had the feeling he'd just tell me he supported whatever I wanted to do. Heck, for all I knew, he'd come to Romania with me. So much had changed.

So where was Edward now? I was two hours late. Had he given up waiting for me and left, to walk off his irritation with a stroll on the beach? Malibu was a beautiful place. I should know. I was the one who'd talked him into renting this place.

The very first day he'd come to Beverly Hills, he'd recklessly told me he planned to buy a nearby house, on sale for twenty million dollars. "I want to be close to you." Privately, I'd thought he was out of his mind; even more privately, I thought if he lived forty minutes away, it would be a case of *out of sight, out of mind* and he'd stop pursuing me. So I'd convinced him he should instead rent a beach house getaway.

"You have to help me pick out the house," Edward had agreed. Backed into a corner, I'd consented. The estate agent had taken us to ritzy McMansions all over town, but I hadn't loved any of the newly built palaces, all of them the same with their seven bedrooms and ten bathrooms, with their tennis courts and home theaters and wine cellars. When Edward saw I wasn't interested in them, he wasn't either. Finally, in an act of pure desperation, the estate agent had brought us here.

Built in the 1940s on Malibu Beach, this cottage was squat and ugly compared to the three-story glass mansions around it. When Edward saw it, he almost told her to drive on.

"Wait," I'd said, putting my hand on his arm. Something about the tiny, rickety house had reminded me of my family home in Pasadena, where I'd lived when I was a very young child, before my father had died.

When he saw my face, Edward was suddenly willing to overlook the house's flaws. Good thing, because there were so many. No air conditioning. The kitchen was ridiculously tiny and last remodeled in 1972. The wooden floorboards creaked, the dust was thick and the furniture was covered with white sheets. When I pulled the sheet off the baby grand piano, a dust cloud kicked up and made us all cough, even the estate agent.

"I shouldn't have brought you here," she said apologetically.

"No," I'd whispered. "I love it."

"We'll take it," Edward said.

But where was he now? I went heavily up the creaking stairs to the second floor. I'd been up here only once before, when we'd toured the house with the estate agent. It was just a small attic bedroom with slanted ceilings, and a tiny balcony overlooking the ocean.

As I reached the top of the stairs, the bedroom was in shadow. I saw only the brilliant slash of orange and persimmon to the west as the red ball of the sun fell like fire into the sea.

Then I saw Edward, sitting on the bed.

And then…

I sucked in my breath.

Hundreds of rose petals in a multitude of colors had been scattered across the bed and floor, illuminated by tapered white candles on the nightstands and handmade shelves. When Edward saw me standing in the doorway, in my sundress and casual ponytail, he rose from the bed. His chest and feet were bare. He wore only snug jeans that showed off his tanned skin, and the shape of his well-muscled legs. Stepping toward me, he smiled.

"I've been waiting for you."

"I can see that," I whispered, knowing I was in trouble. Knowing I should *run*.

He lifted a long-stemmed red rose from a nearby vase. Leaning forward, he stroked the softest part of the rose against my cheek. "I know your secret."

I blinked. "My...my secret?"

Leaning back, he gave me a lazily sensual smile. "How you tried to resist me. And failed."

"I haven't. I haven't agreed to marriage or fallen into bed with you. Not yet," I choked out. Then blushed when I realized the insinuation was that I soon would.

His smile lifted to a grin. He nodded toward a pile of books in a box in a corner of the room. "I just got that box this afternoon from Mrs. MacWhirter. It seems you left something, buried in your bedroom closet at Penryth Hall.

I looked down at the open box. Sitting on top was the faded dust jacket of the fine manual written by Mrs. Warreldy-Gribbley, *Private Nursing: How to Care for a Patient in His Home Whilst Maintaining Professional Distance and Avoiding Immoral Advances from Your Employer.*

"Oh," I said lamely, looking back at Edward with my cheeks on fire.

He gave a low laugh. "Didn't do you much good, did it?"

Biting my lip, I shook my head.

Tilting his head, he looked at me wickedly. "What do you think Mrs. Warreldy-Gribbley would say if she saw you now?"

I looked down at my hugely pregnant belly, which strained the knit fabric of my sundress. "I'm not sure she'd have the words."

"I think…" He ran his fingertips lightly over my bare shoulder, turning me to face him. "She'd tell you to marry me."

A tremble went through my body. My bare shoulder pulsed heat from the place when he touched me.

Scowling, I glared at him. "Do you always get your own way?"

Lifting his hand, he cupped my cheek.

"Ask me tomorrow," he said softly.

And Edward fell to one knee before me.

I stared down at him, my mouth wide with shock. "What are you doing?"

"What I should have done long ago." He looked up at me in the small, shadowy attic bedroom. "You know I want to marry you, Diana. I'm asking you one last time. With everything I've got," he said quietly. "All I want is to make you happy." He drew a black velvet box from his jeans pocket and held it up in the flickering candlelight. "Will you give me the chance?"

Looking down at him, I couldn't move or breathe. I suddenly knew that whatever happiness or misery came to me—and my daughter—would all stem from the choice I made in this moment.

"Diana…" Edward opened the black velvet box. "Will you marry me?"

I saw the enormous diamond ring and covered my mouth with my hands. I blinked hard, unable to believe my eyes. "Is that thing real?" I breathed. "It's the size of an iceberg—"

"You deserve the best," he said quietly.

I'd spent years in Hollywood. So I'd seen big diamonds before. Madison had worn lots of big diamonds to awards shows—gorgeous borrowed jewels to go with her gorgeous borrowed gowns. But even in Hollywood, the million-dollar jewelry was an illusion. When the event was over, the jewelry had to be returned. Faster than you can say *glass slipper.*

But this wasn't borrowed. This was meant to last.

Edward meant this to last.

"Don't do this to me," I whispered, stricken. "We don't need to get married. We can live apart, but still raise her together...."

"That's not what I want," he said quietly, still on one knee. "What is your answer?"

I looked down at him. Looked at the rose petals, the candlelight. I took a deep breath. "You'll change your mind...."

"I won't." He hesitated. "But if you love someone else..."

I shook my head.

"Then what?" he asked gently.

I took a deep breath, and met his eyes.

"I'm scared. I loved you once, and it nearly destroyed me."

His hand seemed to tighten on the black velvet box. His voice was low. "You don't have to love me."

Marriage without love? The thought was a jarring one. I licked my lips. "I'm afraid if I say yes, you'll soon regret it. You'll wish you could be single again, and date all those women...."

"I'll only regret it," he said, "if you say no."

"Where would we live?" A hysterical laugh bubbled to my lips. "You don't want to spend your life waiting for me, as I film commercials... Sooner or later you'll have to get back to work."

He looked up at me, his dark eyes inscrutable in the fading twilight. "You're right."

"I won't live in London. We were so unhappy there. Both of us."

"There are other choices," he said quietly.

"Like what?"

"The whole world." Rising to his feet, he pulled my left hand against his chest, over his heart. "Just let me give it to you."

I could feel his heart pounding beneath my hand. The strong rapid beat matched my own. My fingers curled against his warm skin.

"I won't let you break my heart again," I choked out.

"I'll never hurt you, Diana. Ever." Dropping the rose and the black velvet box to the end table, Edward pulled me into his arms. His hands stroked back my hair, down my bare back that was only covered with the crisscross lines of my sundress. "Let me show you...."

Lowering his head to mine, he kissed me.

And this time, I could not resist.

His lips were tender. They enticed me, lured me, soft and sensual as the whisper of a sigh. I exhaled. There could be no fighting this. It didn't just feel as if he were embracing my body. It felt like he was caressing my soul.

"Marry me, Diana," he whispered, his lips brushing against mine.

All the reasons I couldn't marry him rose to my mind, but as he kissed me they dissipated into thin air like mist.

What was fear, against the incessant pull of his body against mine? His muscles were solid beneath my hands, his body powerful and strong. Something to cling to. Someone to believe in. And oh, how I wanted to believe.

I'd been keeping the secret for so long. Even from myself. But it had been right there all along. The real secret in my heart.

I loved Edward.

I'd never stopped loving him.

And all I'd ever wanted was for him to love me back....

"Say yes." Edward kissed my cheeks, my lips, my eyelids. "Say it—"

"Yes," I breathed.

He drew back. His handsome face looked vulnerable, his blue eyes caught between hope and doubt. "Do you mean it?"

Please let this be right. Please let this not be a mistake.

Unable to speak, I nodded.

Grabbing the black velvet box, Edward slid the obscenely huge diamond ring onto the fourth finger of my left hand. I felt its heavy weight for just a moment before he lifted my hand to his lips, kissing my palm.

In the candlelit bedroom, with the open window overlooking the twilight sea, the reverence of his gesture, like a private unspoken vow, lacerated my heart.

"You said yes," he said in wonder. He shook his head. "I was starting to think..."

His voice trailed off. With an intake of breath, he lifted me in his arms, as if I weighed nothing at all. Gently setting me down on his bed, he pulled off my sandals one by one, kissing the tender hollow of each foot.

Leaning forward, he pulled off my sundress, leaving me stretched across the bed in only my white cotton panties and a bra that seemed barely adequate, trapped between my overflowing breasts and full pregnant belly. The enormous diamond ring on my left hand felt heavy as a shackle, making me suddenly afraid. After everything I knew about Edward's soul, was agreeing to marry him, giving him not just body and soul but offering up all my future, all my life, and my child's in the bargain—an act of insanity?

Edward cupped my face in his hands. His expression

was tender, his eyes shining. "All I want is to take care of you forever…."

"I want to do the same for you." I was in so deep now. I wanted desperately to believe the fantasy was true. Wrapping my arms around his shoulders, I kissed him with trembling lips. Twining his hands in my hair, he kissed me back, matching my passion, exceeding it. A fire roared through me, and I gasped.

Drawing back, he pulled off his clothes and gently lay me back against the bed. My hair tumbled over the pillows. I shivered, closing my eyes as he kissed down my neck. His lips were warm beneath the cool ocean breeze blowing through the window. I breathed in the scent of him, clean and masculine, with the sea air and the rose petals scattered around us.

He unhooked my bra. I gasped as I felt his lips nuzzle my breast before he drew my full nipple gently into his mouth. Pregnancy had made my breasts so big, he had to hold each with both hands in its turn. I gripped his shoulders tightly.

Pulling back, he looked down at me. "You're in your third trimester," he murmured wickedly. "The doctor said you shouldn't spend too long on your back…."

Before I knew what was happening, he rolled me over, so I was on top of him. He pulled my knees apart, so I straddled his hips. My belly was huge between us, my breasts hanging almost to his face as I leaned forward to kiss him. I felt the size of him, hard and huge between my legs and the pregnancy hormones I'd tried to ignore for months suddenly rocketed uncontrollably through me, leaving me weak with lust. Pulling up, I came down hard, impaling myself, drawing him deep and thick inside me. He gasped, putting his hands on my hips. Not stopping, not waiting, I rocked back and forth, riding him with increasing speed until he was stretching me to the limit, filling me to the core, and with a loud cry, I exploded, and so did he. We both soared amid the fading purple shadows of the night.

Afterward, he drew me close, holding me in his arms. He kissed my sweaty temple. "I never want to let you go."

"So don't," I whispered. My body felt illuminated, glowing with happiness. I pressed my cheek against the warmth of his bare skin, glorying in the feel of his arm wrapped snugly around me in bed.

"Let's go to Las Vegas," he said suddenly.

Blinking, I lifted my head to look at him. "You want to elope?"

I thought I saw a shadow cross his eyes. Then he gave me a lazy smile. "I don't want to give you the chance to change your mind."

"I won't." I looked down at my engagement ring. "Though this thing is so heavy, I feel lopsided. What is it, ten carats?"

He grinned. "Twenty."

"What! I think you might have overdone it!"

"I'll get you a ring for your other hand. Then it won't be a problem." He stroked my cheek. "Just say you'll run away with me tomorrow."

It sounded like a dream. But… I bit my lip. "Without my family?"

He gave a low laugh. "I should have known you wouldn't like that thought. Bring Howard with us, then. And whomever else you want. Plenty of room on the jet." He stroked his jaw ruefully. "Though I'm still waiting for him to hit me on the jaw."

I snorted. "Howard would never go through with it. He loves you too much now." Then my smile faded. "Madison is coming home tonight…."

"From Mongolia? Is it the first time you've seen her since Penryth Hall?"

"Yeah. I need to try to work things out." I sighed. Rising to my feet, I started to pull on my clothes.

"Don't go." He held out his arm. "Stay with me tonight."

I looked at him longingly, then shook my head. "I need to talk to Madison. But then…" I looked at him. "If she forgives me for breaking up her engagement, and Howard can come, then…"

"Then?" he said, his voice filled with rising hope.

I smiled at him. I felt so happy, there were tears in my eyes. "Then I'll elope with you in the morning."

With an intake of breath, he rose to his feet. Taking me in his arms, he kissed me softly. "Go home. See your family tonight." He gave me a smile that was brighter than the sun. "And I'll see you tomorrow."

It felt so good in his arms, so warm, so right. It felt— like home. I bit my lip, suddenly reluctant to leave. "On second thought, maybe I could stay here tonight. I'll see Madison tomorrow…."

With a low laugh, he shook his head. "No. Go. Talk to them. Then we can start our new lives tomorrow." Drawing back, Edward looked thoughtful. "Anyway, I think there's something else I need to do tonight."

I frowned. "What?"

"Just something," he said evasively.

"Bachelor party?" I half joked. He didn't even crack a smile.

"It's nothing." Turning away, he pulled on his jeans. His face was hidden in shadow. "Just one last thing I want to do before I say my marriage vows."

"Oh?" I stared at him, waiting for him to explain.

He suddenly wouldn't meet my gaze. "I'll walk you out."

A moment later, I backed my car down the small driveway of the Malibu cottage, and soon eased onto the Pacific Coast Highway. As I looked out at the moonlight flickering over the Pacific, in the flashes of flat beach between the tightly packed million-dollar houses clinging to the strip of shore, I'd suddenly felt I'd never been so happy. Or so terrified.

Because I loved him.

He'd never once said he loved me.

I gripped the steering wheel. *It'll be fine,* I told myself. Edward didn't need to love me. We could still be happy together. Friends. Parents. Lovers. Partners.

But what was he so anxious to do tonight, "before we spoke our vows"?

It didn't matter. He'd promised he'd never break my heart again. It couldn't be another woman or anything like that. He was probably just planning a surprise for me. Like a wedding gift. When I saw it in the morning, I'd have a good laugh at my own fears. Getting married should mean that I could trust him. I never needed to feel insecure again. Right?

It's nothing. Just one last thing I want to do before I say my marriage vows.

Oh, this was ridiculous. I was only four blocks away from my stepfather's house in Beverly Hills when I banged on the steering wheel in irritation, then yelped as the big diamond cut sharply into my hand. Sucking my finger, I pulled over.

Forget this. I was going back to Malibu to find out what he was hiding from me. If it was some awesome wedding gift, I'd hate myself later for wrecking the surprise.

I flipped my car around, heading back west, toward Malibu.

Thirty minutes later, I was turning down Edward's small street, when I saw an expensive SUV pull ahead of me. It was going way too fast down the lane. Idiot, I thought. Then to my shock, it pulled haphazardly into Edward's driveway. A woman leapt out of the driver's seat. But not just any woman.

It was Victoria. The beautiful, vicious wife of Edward's cousin, Rupert. Dressed in a tight, sexy red cocktail dress and six-inch high heels.

I forced myself to keep driving slowly, past the cottage without stopping. But in my rearview mirror, I saw the cottage door open. Edward welcomed her swiftly inside.

Then the door closed behind them.

A horn honked ahead of me, and I swerved just in time to avoid crashing into opposing traffic. Cold sweat covered my body. This was what he wanted to do before he spoke marriage vows?

A bachelor party for two?

I remembered Victoria's earlier words: *I wanted him so badly, I would have done anything to get into his bed. Anything.*

Numbly, I turned back on the highway, back toward Los Angeles.

There had to be some rational reason for Victoria to be with Edward tonight. Something beyond the obvious. But as I tried to come up with a reason, all I could think about was that Edward had never claimed to love me. Not in all this time. He'd said he wanted us to marry for the baby's sake. And that he wanted me in his bed.

He hadn't yet promised fidelity. So it wasn't like he'd broken any vows. No. The only promise he'd broken was when he'd said he would never break my heart.

Why was Victoria there, alone with him in the house? Why would she visit him so late at night, wearing a skin-tight red dress? Why was she even in California at all?

I wiped my eyes savagely.

Traffic was light, late as it was, and I soon pulled past the gate of Howard's white colonial house. I saw Madison's expensive red convertible parked in the driveway. A car as red and wicked and expensive as Victoria St. Cyr's dress as she'd snuck in for a private tête-à-tête with the man I was supposed to marry tomorrow.

My legs trembled as I walked inside the house. Inside the large, lavish kitchen, I saw Howard and Madison sitting at the table, smiling and talking. But in this moment, I couldn't deal with it. I started to walk past the kitchen, but she saw me. She rose to her feet, her face serious.

"Diana," she said quietly. "It's good to see you again."

I stopped, clenching my hands at my sides. Madison looked tanner, a little weathered, her cheeks a little fuller. No makeup. No false eyelashes. Her blond hair was lightened by sun. She was wearing a white cotton T-shirt, jeans and flip-flops.

"You look—different," I said slowly.

"And you look pregnant." She smiled. "Dad told me you and Edward are back together...."

Tears rose to my eyes. "I'm tired," I choked out. "Excuse me. I have to go—to bed...."

I made it to my bedroom just in time, before the sobs started. Even with the air conditioning, the air felt oppressively hot. I stripped down to a tank top and tiny shorts and collapsed on the bed. Posters on the walls that I'd put up as a hopeful teenager, of places I'd hoped to see and the life I'd hoped to live, stared down at me mournfully. It felt like the walls were closing in.

As my head hit the pillow, I wept, covering my face, wept with choked sobs until there were no tears left, and I slept.

The phone woke me up. I flung my arm to answer it.

"What is your answer?" My agent's voice pleaded.

Slowly, I sat up in bed. My hair felt smashed against the side of my face, and the tank top I'd been sleeping in barely covered my breasts properly. I felt sore, too. For a moment I smiled, remembering how Edward had made love to me last night.

Then I remembered what had happened afterward. How I'd seen Victoria sneaking into his house for one last fling.

It's nothing. Just one last thing I want to do before I say my marriage vows

Cold despair seeped through me, and I pulled up my comforter almost to my neck.

"Well, Diana?" My agent said with desperate good cheer. "Do you want to be a star?"

I felt awful. Outside, the morning light was clear, the sky a pale blue. It almost never rained in California. Not like Cornwall. I missed the fog and bluster and wild gray storms. They suited me better.

"Diana? The blockbuster in Romania? Are you in?"

"Sure," I said dully. "Why not?"

His congratulations were so loud I had to pull the phone away from my ear. Then he started talking about terms and conditions and other contract stuff I didn't care about. Hanging up, I pulled on a robe and went downstairs.

"Rough night?" Madison looked up from the kitchen table, where she was now eating a bowl of cornflakes. Then her eyes widened. "Nice ring."

I looked down at my left hand. "Yeah," I said dully. "Want it?"

She laughed. "Good one. So you're engaged? I'm so happy for—"

"Edward's cheating on me."

Madison's mouth fell open. Then she looked dubious. "Are you sure? He seemed so in love with you last December. I mean, I even flirted with him," she blushed a little, "and he totally froze me out."

"I'm sure. I saw a woman he knows, his cousin's wife, going into his place late last night. Wearing a sexy dress."

"There could be all kinds of reasons for that. Geez. Maybe, um…" She frowned, scratching her head. "Hmm."

"I don't want to talk about it," I said, grabbing the milk and a bowl.

Madison pressed her lips together. "All right," she said finally. "Whatever you need. I'm here for you."

I stared at her incredulously. "What happened to you in Mongolia?"

"What do you mean?"

"You seem so—different."

"I grew up, I guess," she said quietly. "I decided to stop taking other people's stuff. Their careers. Their lovers. It never made me happy. It only made me feel bad about myself." Her eyes met mine as she whispered, "I'm so sorry for what I did to you."

I stared at her in shock, trying not to cry.

Then Madison's mouth fell open as she looked past me. In slow motion, I turned around.

Edward stood in the kitchen doorway behind me, dressed in a tuxedo that was molded to his perfect body. He smiled, looking from Madison to me. "Looks like all is forgiven." His blue eyes glowed with joy. "How soon can you be ready to go?"

My lips parted in a silent gasp. Then snapped shut.

How *dare* he act like this—look at me as if he loved me—when he'd been with another woman last night? And *Victoria,* of all the women on earth! Did he truly have no soul? I couldn't bear to even look him in the face.

Reaching down, I pulled off the enormous diamond ring. My fingers were swollen, so I had to yank hard. I held it out to him coldly.

"I've changed my mind," I said. "I can't marry you."

His broad shoulders seemed to flinch. There was a small sound from the back of his throat. He took a single step forward. I heard his low demand of a single word.

"Why."

He was looking at me as if I'd betrayed him. As if

I'd broken his heart. My throat hurt. How could Edward look at me like that, when he was the one who had never loved me?

Lifting my chin, I looked at him, my fists clenched almost violently. "I thought I could marry you without love," I whispered. Shuddering, I shook my head. "I can't." It was tantamount to admitting my own love for him. I felt like a pathetic fool. "I want the real thing."

My arm shook as I continued to hold out the ring.

He stared down at the twenty-carat diamond ring as if it were poison. He seemed to shudder. "Keep it."

"I can't." I pushed the ring into his hands. My heart hurt so much I could hardly keep from crying. "It's better this way. You can go back to London, and I'll be going to Romania to star in a movie...." The movie? Who cared about that? What was I even saying? I shook my head desperately. "We'll work out custody. You can visit our baby whenever you want."

He looked down at the enormous diamond ring, gleaming in his hand.

"Visit?" he said dully.

"Yes, of course, you..." My throat constricted. "I just want you to be free."

"Free." He lifted expressionless eyes to mine.

Unable to speak, I nodded.

"I thought I could make you happy." His voice was like a sigh, the last breath of a dying man. He tried to smile even as I saw a suspicious sheen in his eyes. "But I can't force you to marry me. Of course you deserve love. You deserve everything."

My heart twisted. I felt as if I were drowning in the haunted sea of his eyes, seeing right through his armor to the anguished soul within. Was it possible I was wrong? Was there any other explanation for what I'd seen?

"What did you do last night?" I cried out.

Staring down at me, he sucked in his breath. Then he grimly shook his head. "It doesn't matter."

"Tell me," I begged. I knew I was making a fool of myself, but I couldn't stop. If there was any chance, any chance at all that I was wrong... "What did you do when I left you last night?"

He stared down at me for a moment in the kitchen. Then he slowly shook his head.

"It's better you don't know," he said quietly. Leaning forward, he cupped my cheek. "I will always provide for you and the baby, Diana." Leaning down, he kissed me softly, one last time. "Take care of her. Be happy."

And he was gone.

I stared after him, gazing at the empty doorway, standing on the cold tile floor wearing a robe, a tank top that didn't quite cover my belly, skimpy sleep shorts and a dumb expression.

My stepfather's lavish, enormous kitchen turned blurry around me and I realized I was crying. I couldn't even feel the tears. All I could think was that I'd been so stupid. I'd let Edward St. Cyr break my heart not once, but twice....

"You are *so stupid*," Madison said aloud, as if she'd read my mind and agreed wholeheartedly. Wiping my cheeks, I looked down at her sitting at the table. I'd forgotten she was there.

She was shaking her head in disgust. "You gave him up for a movie? No career can ever fill the place in your heart where love should be." She gave a harsh laugh. "I should know."

"He doesn't love me," I whispered.

"Are you insane?" She looked as if she thought I was. "Did you see the way he looked at you? And from everything Dad told me about how he's been waiting on you hand and foot..." She snorted. "No man does that for a woman, unless he's desperately in love. Especially a man like Edward St. Cyr."

"He doesn't love me," I repeated, but my voice had turned uncertain. "He just said he didn't."

My stepsister looked at me incredulously. "You said you deserved a marriage based on love, and he agreed with you. It sounded like you didn't love *him*."

"What?" I put my hand to my forehead. A tremble was coming up through my body like an earthquake, rising from my feet to my legs to my heart. "Edward knows I love him. He has to know."

"Did you tell him? Recently, I mean?"

"No, I..." I bit my lip. I'd told him in London, before he'd sent me away. But never since then. Desperately, I shook my head. "He doesn't love me. He wanted to marry me for the baby's sake, that's all." I looked down at my huge baby bump. "If he'd loved me..."

I sucked in my breath, covering my mouth with my hand.

If Edward had loved me, he would have devoted himself to me, night and day, waiting for me to finish work, letting me choose restaurants, taking me to the doctor, rubbing my feet. Driving watermelon and ice cream to my house at three in the morning. He would have let me choose the house we'd live in. I would have been more important than his career.

His friends.

His country.

I always imagined love to be an action, not a word. His words in London came back to haunt me. *If I loved someone, I wouldn't say it, I'd show it. I'd take care of her, putting her needs ahead of my own. I'd put my whole soul into making her happy....*

A choked sound came from the back of my throat.

What kind of man would do so much for a woman, unless he loved her?

And worse—what kind of woman would not even notice, until it was too late?

"He loves you," Madison said quietly behind me. "And you threw it away for some stupid role in a movie." Her lips curled as she shook her head. "When I suggested you to the movie producer, I thought I was making amends for *Moxie McSocksie*...."

"You're the one who suggested me for the part?" I breathed.

"Yeah." She looked at me accusingly. "I didn't know you'd use the movie as an excuse to ruin your life!"

"You're one to talk," I said weakly.

"I know." She held her hands wide. "Look at me, Diana. Totally alone. With the hole in my heart. If a man ever loved me like that, if he saw all my flaws and could love me anyway..." She looked away. "I'd never let him go."

"He cheated on me," I whispered.

She lifted an eyebrow. "Are you still so sure?"

I stared at her. Then I turned and ran up to my bedroom. I dug through my purse until I found an old ratty card. My heart pounded as I dialed a number on my phone.

"Hello?" the woman's voice said.

"Victoria," I said desperately. "What were you doing with Edward last night?"

"Who's that?" She paused. "Diana?"

"Why were you at his house? Why are you even in California?"

Victoria laughed. "As if you didn't know. But I'm glad you called. I wanted to thank you. I misjudged you, Diana. You are a wonderful, wonderful person. Rupert and I will never forget...."

I gripped the phone. "*What are you talking about?*"

"The shares." She paused. "Do you really not know?"

"Shares?"

She gave a tinkly laugh. "For weeks, Edward hinted he might sell his shares of St. Cyr Global. Yesterday Rupert finally had to go back to London, but I stayed here with the children. Edward suddenly called my mobile last night, while I was at a friend's party in Santa Monica. I rushed over to sign the contract, before he could change his mind!"

Whatever I'd expected, that hadn't been it.

"What?"

"Oh, dear. Have I let the cat out of the bag? Edward did say he was doing it as a sort of wedding present, to both of you. New life, new career, all that. I gather you're eloping? Let me know where you're registered and I'll send something. We owe you. I promise you're leaving the company in good hands. And Diana?"

"Yes?" I repeated, my voice a gaspy wheeze.

"Welcome to the family!" she said heartily, and hung up.

My legs trembled. I slowly walked down the stairs, feeling like an old woman. Grief and heartache were building inside me, going radioactive, making my body weak, destroying me cell by cell.

"What?" Madison demanded when I stumbled into the kitchen.

"Edward sold all his shares in his family's company," I choked out. "That was why Victoria was there. That was Edward's big secret. He knew how miserable I was in London. This was his surprise." My throat caught. "It really was a wedding present."

"That's good—isn't it?"

I slowly turned to face her.

"He should have told me," I whispered.

Madison put her arm over my shoulders, as she'd done when we were kids. "He didn't want you to feel guilty."

Guilty? Edward had just sold his birthright for my sake. He could have manipulated me, pointed out everything he'd sacrificed for me. Instead, he'd set me free. Even though I saw now it was the last thing he'd wanted to do. What did it mean?

I wrapped my arms around my body, trying to stop my ice-cold limbs from shaking.

It meant Edward loved me.

"He loves me," I whispered, and I burst into tears. Awful sobs racked my body, almost doubling me over. My stepsister hugged me close.

"It'll be all right," she murmured.

I shook my head. I'd been so determined to never feel heartbreak again, that I'd raced for the exit at the very first scare. Instead of forcing him to tell me the truth about Victoria, I'd thrown his ring back in his face. I thought pride made me do it. It wasn't pride.

It was fear.

"What are you going to do?" Madison said.

I looked up, my heart pounding.

You only have one life, sweetheart, my mom said before she died. *And it goes faster than you ever imagine. So make it count. Be brave. Follow your heart.*

I took a deep breath. "I'm going to be brave," I whispered. "And follow my heart."

Madison's face lifted in a smile. "That's what I was hoping you'd say." Reaching into the pocket of her cutoffs, she tossed me her keys. "Take my car." Her smile turned to a grin. "It's faster."

CHAPTER EIGHT

THE SKY WAS sunny and blue, the air languorous with the scent of lilacs and roses.

Pushing my sunglasses up the bridge of my nose, I clutched my purse and ran toward Madison's red convertible, sandals flapping hard against the driveway, my sundress flying.

I'd tried to call Edward's phone, but there'd been no answer. I'd called the line at the Malibu cottage but there'd been no answer there, either. Why would Edward stay in California now? He wouldn't. Then I'd suddenly had a sick feeling.

I have a private island in the Caribbean. That's where I'd go if I needed to escape a broken heart.... No one can get at you there, Diana. There's no internet, no phones, no way to even get on the island except by my plane.

I'd wanted to run out of the house in my robe and sleeping shorts. Madison had talked me into getting dressed first, in the closest clean thing that still fit me. Twisting my hair into a knot, I jumped into the sports car and drove down the road like a race car driver.

Now, as I drove west toward the coast, the low-lying mist was growing thicker, the air cooler near the ocean. The wind felt fresh and cold against my skin as it blew over the convertible, pulling my hair out of the knot and flying it around me. I pressed on the gas.

I had to reach Edward in time. I had to. Because if his plane took off, I feared it would be a long time before I saw him again....

Red lights glimmered on the cars ahead of me on the highway, forcing me to push on my brakes.

"Come on, come on," I begged aloud, but the cars ahead just grew slower and slower until they stopped altogether. Was there an accident ahead? Someone filming a movie? A visiting political dignitary? Or was it just fate pulling Edward away from me, just when I'd finally realized what I'd lose?

What was the point in having a fast car just to be stopped in L.A. traffic?

I thought I could make you happy. But I can't force you to marry me. Of course you deserve love. You deserve everything.

Every time Edward had loved anyone, they'd abandoned him. His mother. His father. The woman in Spain. He'd learned not to trust. He'd learned words were cheap. So he'd tried to show me he loved me, in a way more real than words.

How had he found the courage to come to California and humbly tell me he wanted me back? What had it cost him, to try to earn back my love?

Everything, I realized. His heart. His pride. Even his birthright.

All of that—and he'd still let me make the decision. He'd loved me enough to let me go.

Traffic finally picked up speed again. The sun was growing warmer, but I still felt cold, my teeth chattering as I finally arrived at the small nonpublic airport where Edward kept his private jet. He'd been here a month, I realized, and he hadn't used it once. He'd been too busy taking care of me.

Would I be in time?

Driving past the gate, I parked the car helter-skelter in the tiny parking lot, leaving the convertible door open as I ran into the hangar.

No one was there, except for a lone airplane technician looking into the engine of a small Cessna. He straightened. "Can I help you?"

On the other side of the hangar, I heard a loud engine. Through the open garage door, I saw a jet that looked like Edward's accelerating away, headed down the small landing strip.

"Whose plane is that?" I begged.

The mechanic tilted back his baseball cap. "Well now, I'm not rightly allowed to say…."

"Edward St. Cyr," I choked out. "It's his plane, isn't it? Is he headed to the Caribbean?"

The man frowned. "How the heck did you…"

But I was no longer listening. I took off running, as fast as a heavily pregnant woman could run, across the hangar, straight through the garage door and out onto the tarmac.

"Wait!" I screamed, waving my arms wildly as I ran down the runway, following the plane, trying to catch it though I knew I had no hope. "Edward! Wait!"

The roar of the engine and wind from the propellers swallowed my words, whirling the air around me, pushing me back, making me cough. I felt a sudden pain in my belly and hunched over, at the same moment that the mechanic caught up with me.

"Are you crazy?"

"Edward!" I cried helplessly.

"Are you trying to get yourself killed? Get off the runway!" The man, who must have thought I was having some kind of pregnancy-related breakdown, half pulled, half carried me back to the hangar. Winded and weak and grief-stricken, I let him.

Edward was gone. I'd lost him forever, because I'd been

too much of a coward to fight for him, believe in him, when it counted. I'd let him believe that he could never earn my love, no matter how hard he tried....

Choking out a sob, I covered my face with my hands.

"I love you," I whispered brokenly, sinking to the concrete floor as I said the words I'd been too scared to say to his face. "I love you, Edward...."

"Diana?"

Hardly daring to believe, I looked up.

Edward stood outside the open garage door. Bright California sunshine burnished his dark hair. His face was in shadow, his posture uncertain. He'd changed from his tuxedo to a T-shirt and jeans, and his hands were in his pockets.

On the airstrip behind him, I saw his jet, with the propellers still slowing down. The engine was loud, a blast of white noise. Was he a miracle? A dream? I wiped my eyes, but he was still there.

"You came back...." I gasped. Rising to my feet, I stumbled across the hangar.

"I saw you," he breathed, his eyes hungry on mine. "And I was crazy enough to hope...."

Hiccupping a sob, I threw my arms around his shoulders. "You came back!"

"Of course I did." He held me close, caressing my back. I felt the warmth and strength of his body, smelled the woodsy scent of his cologne. He touched my cheek with a fingertip and said in a voice so tender and raw it twisted my heart, "But you're crying."

Taking his hand in my own, I pressed it against my cheek, looking up at him with eyes swimming in tears. "I thought I'd lost you."

I could feel him tremble. Then he exhaled.

"It's all right, Diana," he said quietly. "You can tell me the truth. If you're trying to be loyal to me for our baby's sake..."

"No!"

"I need you to be happy." He looked away, dropping his hand to his side. "I told myself I could marry you even if you didn't love me. That I could earn you back, and make you love and trust me again, over time."

"Edward…"

"But I can't be the man who takes away the light that's inside you. I can't. I can't condemn you to being my wife when you don't love me. When you might love someone else." Looking away, his jaw tightened as he said, in a voice almost too low for me to hear, "I love you too much for that."

"You love me," I breathed.

Edward gave a low, choked laugh. "And for the first time in my life I know what that means." He looked down at me. "I would do anything for you, Diana. Anything."

"Even sell your shares of St. Cyr Global to your cousin."

He looked started. "How did you know?"

"I called Victoria."

"Why?— How?"

"I saw her going into your house last night."

"You did?"

I hung my head. "You were acting so weird and secretive. I went back to ask you what was going on. Then I saw her going into your house so late, wearing that dress, and I thought the two of you…"

"What!" He blinked in astonishment. "You thought me and *Victoria*…"

"I was so scared of getting hurt again," I whispered, feeling ashamed, "I took the first excuse to run. I'm sorry."

His expression darkened. "When I think of how I treated you in London, I don't blame you." He stroked my cheek. "I didn't want you to feel guilty, or feel like you were under obligation, because I'd made some kind of sacrifice…. Because you were right. I hated that job. I hated the man it made me. Now I'm free." He gave me a sudden grin. "In fact, there's nothing to stop me from coming with you to Romania, as I'm currently unemployed...."

Reaching up, I put my hands over his. "I don't want to go."

He frowned. "What?"

"I thought being an actress was my big dream. But I never wanted to audition." The corners of my mouth quirked. "There was a reason. Whatever my brain tried to tell me I wanted, my heart stubbornly knew it wanted something else entirely."

He pulled me closer, running his hands over my face, my hair, my back. "What?"

I thought of my mother, and the life she'd lived. Hannah Maywood Lowe had never been famous or celebrated. People who didn't know her would have thought her quite ordinary, in fact, not special at all. But she'd had a talent for loving people. Her whole life had been about taking care of her friends, her home, her community, and most of all, her family.

"You're my dream," I whispered. "You and our baby. I want to go home with you. Be with you. Raise our family." I lifted my gaze to his. "I love you, Edward."

He breathed in wonder, "You do?"

"I have just one question left to ask you," I said, smiling through my tears. I took a deep breath. "Will you marry me?"

Edward staggered back. Then he gave a low shout. "*Will* I?"

As he took me in his arms, his handsome face no longer looked thuggish or brooding or dark. Joy made him look like the boy he'd once been, like the man I'd always known he could be.

"I love you, Diana Maywood," he whispered, cradling my cheek. "I'm going to love you for the rest of my life. Starting now...."

Pulling me against his body, he kissed me hard, until I was gasping with joy and need, clutching him to me.

"Um," I heard the mechanic's awkward mumble across the hangar, "you guys still know I'm here, right?"

We were married two weeks later in my mother's rose garden. All the people we loved were there, Mrs. MacWhirter and the rest of our closest family and friends. Our wedding was nothing fancy, just a white cake, a simple dress and a minister. No twenty-carat diamond ring this time, either. Seriously, I was afraid I'd put my eye out with that thing. Instead, we gave each other plain gold bands in the double ring ceremony.

It helps to have friends in the entertainment business. A musician friend of mine played the guitar, and a photographer friend took pictures. Madison was my bridesmaid, and Howard walked me down the aisle. As I held a simple bouquet of my mother's favorite roses, in her garden on that beautiful, bright California morning, it was almost as if she were there, too.

It was all perfect. The only guests were people we really loved. Rupert and Victoria sent their congratulations and a very nice blender.

After the ceremony, when we were officially husband and wife, we held an outdoor dinner reception beneath fairy lights. Howard and Madison openly wept, throwing rose petals as Edward and I roared off in a vintage car, before jetting off to Las Vegas for our honeymoon. We spent two lovely nights at the Hermitage, a luxurious casino resort owned by Nikos Stavrakis, a friend of Edward's, happily married himself with six children.

Our luxurious, glamorous hotel suite overlooked all the lights of the Strip, which we mostly ignored because we were too busy discovering the joys of married sex. Holy cow. I had no idea how different it would be. How it feels to possess someone's body when you also possess their heart and soul and name—and they have yours. There's nothing in the world like it.

"I'm just sorry the honeymoon has to end," I murmured as we left Las Vegas.

Edward looked at me. "Who says it does?"

"What do you mean?"

"We're both unemployed now." He lifted a dark eyebrow. "We can go anywhere you want. Rio. Tokyo. Venice. Istanbul. After all," he gave a wicked grin, lifting a dark eyebrow as he said, "we *do* have a jet...."

But there was only one place I wanted to go.

"Take me home," I said.

"Home?"

I smiled. "Where we first began."

Hannah Maywood St. Cyr was born a few weeks later in Cornwall, at a modern hospital near Penryth Hall. We named her after my mom. She's the sweetest baby, with dark hair and beautiful blue eyes, just like her father's.

The three of us like to visit California in the winter. We even bought the Malibu cottage as a vacation house. But now we've been married a year, we're already starting to outgrow it.

It's summer again, and Hannah is starting to walk. Cornwall is a sight to behold, all brilliant blue skies and fields of wildflowers. I've started a small theater company in a nearby town, just to be creative and have fun with new friends—because who doesn't love a play? But most of my time has been spent on my project of remodeling Penryth Hall, to let the light in. A dangerous endeavor. Yesterday I smashed my thumb with a hammer. I have no idea what I'm doing. But that's part of the fun.

Edward opened his new business a few months ago, manufacturing athletic gear for adventure sports like skydiving and mountain climbing, renting a old factory in

Truro. It's a small company, but rapidly growing, and he loves every day of it. We live a mostly simple life. We got rid of the jet, sold the townhouse in London. Honestly, we didn't need that stuff. We took most of the payout from his St. Cyr Global shares to create a foundation to help children all over the world, whether they need families or homes, water or school or shoes. I think my mom would approve.

We aren't filthy rich anymore, but we have enough, and we're rich in the things that matter most. Love. Hope. Most of all, family.

Madison was nominated for a prestigious award for that little movie she did in Mongolia, which left her unrecognizable as a gaunt slave of Genghis Khan riding bareback across the steppes. She was thrilled, but she's even happier now she's found true love with someone totally outside the industry—a hunky fireman. "He actually *saves lives,* Diana. And he's so funny and makes this amazing lasagna…." My stepsister is a loving aunt to Hannah and often sends pictures and toys. Madison is happy, even with all the minor annoyances of being a movie star.

Annoyances I'll never have to worry about, since my agent fired me, as threatened, when I told him I was turning down that movie after all. I called Jason next, to tell him I was leaving Hollywood to marry Edward. He got choked up, telling me in his Texas drawl that he'd never get over me, never. Then he replaced me with a beautiful blonde starlet in the five seconds it took you to read this sentence.

Howard visits our little family in England when he can, on breaks from his zombie series; or else we visit him on set, as we did recently in Louisiana where he was directing his upcoming TV Christmas movie, *Werewolves Vs. Santa.* (In case you're wondering, Santa wins.) He's just started dating a gorgeous sixty-year-old makeup artist named Deondra. After almost a decade alone, he's giddy as a teenager.

He's also the proudest grandpa alive, and the love is mutual. At just eleven months old, Hannah is already showing a scary amount of interest in covering her face in gray makeup and making "ooh—ooh" noises, just like all the zombie "friends" of her Grandpa Howard. Maybe she'll go into that particular family business. Who knows?

But here in Cornwall, it's August and the world is in bloom. As our little family sits together on a blanket, having a picnic amid the newly-tended garden behind Penryth Hall, I look down at Hannah playing next to me on the blanket, building a bridge out of blocks. Nearby, our sheepdog Caesar is rolling in the grass, snuffing with satisfaction before going back to chew a juicy bone. In the distance below the cliffs, the sun is sparkling over the Atlantic. The ocean stretches out toward the west, toward the new world, as far as the eye can see.

Our own new world is limitless and new.

I look behind me, at the gray stone hall I've come to love. The first time I saw it, it looked like a ghost castle in twilight. I thought then that it was a place to hide.

Instead, it was the place I came alive. The place where my body and soul blazed into fire. Where Edward and I each sought sanctuary when we were hurt, and Penryth Hall healed us.

It was the place our family began.

"I love you, Diana," Edward whispers now behind me. I lean back against his chest, against his legs that are wrapped around mine, as one of his large hands rests protectively over the swell of my belly. Yes, I'm pregnant again. A boy this time.

Life is more complicated than the movies, that's for sure. But it's also better than I ever dared dream. Real life, the one I'm living right now, is better than any fantasy. Smashed thumbs and all.

I've finally found the place I belong.

Mrs. Warreldy-Gribbley never wrote a "how-to" manual about how to fall in love, or raise a child, or discover what you really want in life. Because there are no guide books for that, really. There are no surefire, guaranteed instructions. Each one of us can only wake up each morning and make the best choices we can, hundreds of choices each day, big ones and little ones we don't even think about.

Sometimes bad things happen. But sometimes we get lucky. Sometimes we're brave. And sometimes, when we least expect it, we're loved more than we deserve.

It turned out I didn't need to be a movie star. I didn't need to be famous or rich. I just needed to be loved, and to be brave enough to love back with all my heart.

People can change, Howard told me once. *Sometimes for better than you can imagine.*

He was right. Real life can be better than any dream. And it's happening, right now, all around us.

* * * * *

A DEAL WITH BENEFITS

SUSANNA CARR

To my editor, Carly Byrne, with thanks.

Susanna Carr has been an avid romance reader since she read her first Mills & Boon book at the age of ten. Although romance novels were not allowed in her home, she had always managed to sneak one in from the local library or from her twin sister's secret stash.

After attending college and receiving a degree in English Literature, Susanna pursued a romance writing career. She has written sexy contemporary romances for several publishers and her work has been honoured with awards for contemporary and sensual romance.

Susanna Carr lives in the Pacific Northwest with her family. When she isn't writing, Susanna enjoys reading romance and connecting with readers online. Visit her website at susannacarr.com.

PROLOGUE

"OUR GUEST IS early, Miss Ashley. Ooh, that boat is sweet," Clea, the housekeeper, said and gave a squeal of laughter that rang through the hall. "You should see Louis running down the dock to get a closer look."

"It must be quite a boat," Ashley said. Clea's husband didn't move fast. No one did on Inez Key. Their families had been here for generations and they followed the gentle rhythm of island life.

Ashley took a step outside and stared at the scarlet red boat. The sharp and dramatic lines seemed obscenely aggressive against the lazy waves of the ocean. The boat said a lot about the owner. Loud and attention seeking. She squinted and noticed that there was only one person on the boat. "Damn," she muttered. "He's single."

Clea patted Ashley's bare arm. "I'm sure he won't require that much work."

Ashley rolled her eyes. "Single guests are the worst. They expect to be entertained."

"I can meet him while you change into a dress," Clea said as she headed down the hill to the dock.

Ashley followed her. "No, thanks. I'm not dressing up for paying guests anymore. Not after that basketball player thought I was included in the weekend package."

Clea gestured at Ashley. "And what is this man going to think when he sees you dressed like that?"

Ashley looked down at the bright yellow tank top that didn't quite reach the frayed cutoff shorts. Her worn sandals were so old they clung lovingly to her feet and her long hair was gathered up in a messy ponytail. She only wore makeup or jewelry for a special occasion. A man did not fall into that category. "That we aren't formal around here."

Clea clucked her tongue and stared at Ashley's long brown legs. "You don't know much about men, do you?"

"I've learned more than I ever wish to know," Ashley said. She'd got her education whenever her father had been around during the tennis off-season. What she didn't discover from Donald Jones, she had learned from his entourage.

She had finally used all that knowledge to secure a generous loan from Raymond Casillas. It had been a huge risk. She didn't trust the aging playboy and knew he was going to find a way to have her repay him with sex. That wasn't going to happen.

Unfortunately, she was behind on her loan payment and she couldn't miss another month. Ashley shuddered, the icy-cold fear trickling down her spine as she considered the consequences. Just a few more rich celebrities seeking privacy on her island—okay, quite a few more—and she would be free of the threat.

Ashley walked down the hill with renewed determination. She strode along the sturdy wood dock, blocking the bright sun with her hand as she took a closer look at her guest, Sebastian Esteban.

The man stood on the deck like a conquering hero waiting to be swarmed by the grateful natives. Her heart started to pound against her chest. She noticed the thick dark hair ruffling slightly in the wind and the T-shirt stretched against his broad chest. His powerful legs were encased in faded jeans. She felt an unfamiliar pull low in her belly as she stared at the gorgeous stranger.

"Huh," Clea said as she walked alongside Ashley. "There's something familiar about that man."

"Is he famous? An actor?" Ashley immediately dismissed that idea. While his stunning good looks would make Hollywood lay down the red carpet for him, she sensed Sebastian Esteban wasn't the kind who would trade on his harsh, masculine features. The blade of his nose and the slash of his mouth suggested aristocracy, but the high, slanted cheekbones and the thrust of his angular jaw indicated that he fought for every inch of his territory.

"Can't say for sure," Clea muttered. "I feel like I've seen him before."

It didn't matter what he did for a living, she decided. She wasn't going to be starstruck. Ashley had intentionally cut herself off from the world when her parents died five years ago. She would probably recognize a few superstars, but she didn't keep up with the current celebrities. Yet she didn't think she could tolerate another famous person who thought basic manners applied to everyone else and not them.

"Mr. Esteban?" Ashley asked as she reached out her hand. She looked up and their gazes clashed and held. Her safe little existence went completely still as the beat of her heart pounded in her ears. Anticipation rushed through her as Sebastian touched her hand. When his large fingers enclosed hers, her world shifted. She saw the glow of interest in his dark eyes as the energy, wild and violent, ripped through her.

Ashley wanted to jerk back, but the stranger held her fingers captive. Her muscles clenched as every instinct told her to hide. But she couldn't move. She was frozen as the dark, swirling emotions threatened to pull her under.

"Please, call me Sebastian."

She shivered at the sound of his rough, deep voice. "I'm Ashley," she said. It was difficult to push the words out of her tight throat. "Welcome to Inez Key. I hope you will enjoy your visit."

Something hot and wicked flickered in his eyes before he released her hand. "Thank you, I will."

As she stiffly introduced Clea and Louis, she reluctantly noticed how Sebastian towered over her, his broad shoulders blocking out the sun. She could feel his masculine power coming off him in waves.

She covertly watched him as he refused Louis's assistance and tossed his backpack over his shoulder. Who was this man? He was wealthy enough to own that boat, but he didn't wear designer clothes. He had no entourage or tower of luggage, but he could afford to stay at her home for an exclusive weekend.

"You'll stay here in the main house," Clea said as they escorted him up the hill toward the white mansion.

Sebastian stood for a moment as he studied the plantation home. His expression was blank and his eyes were hooded, but she felt an explosive tension emanating from him.

Ashley wondered what he thought about her home. The guests were always in awe of the antebellum architecture. They saw the clean lines and graceful symmetry, the massive columns that stretched from the ground to the black rooftop and surrounded every side of the house. The balconies hinted of an elegant world long forgotten and one could almost ignore that the large black window shutters were for protection from the elements instead of decoration.

But no one noticed that her home was falling apart. There was only so much that a slap of paint, a carefully angled table or a fresh bouquet of flowers could hide. The antique furniture, the artwork, anything of value, had been sold years ago.

As they walked into the grand hall, she dimly heard Clea offer refreshments. Ashley glanced around and hoped she had not overlooked anything. She wanted Sebastian Esteban to notice the curving staircase and how the sunlight caught the crystal chandelier instead of the faded wallpaper. Yet the way he quietly studied the room, she sensed that he saw everything.

Ashley stifled a gasp when she felt Clea jab her bony elbow in her ribs. "Miss Ashley, why don't you show Mr. Sebastian his room while I get the drinks?"

She gritted her teeth. "Of course. This way, please."

Ashley bent her head as she approached the stairs. She didn't want to be alone with this man. She wasn't afraid of Sebastian Esteban, but she was uncomfortable with her reaction. This wasn't like her.

Ashley's skin tingled as she climbed the stairs ahead of Sebastian. Her cutoff shorts felt small as she felt his heated gaze on her bare legs. She should have listened to Clea and worn a dress that covered every inch of skin.

But she immediately dismissed that idea. She wanted to hide, but at the same time she wanted Sebastian to notice her. Her chest rose and fell as she quickened her step. Ashley wished she could ignore the fast and furious attraction. So what if she found Sebastian sexy? Any woman would find him desirable.

Ashley didn't look at Sebastian as she flung open the door to the master suite and gestured for him to enter. "This is your room," she announced. "The walk-in closet and bathroom is through that door."

He strode to the center of the room and Ashley knew he wouldn't find fault in his accommodations here. It was the largest room and offered a magnificent view. She had placed the best furniture in the sitting area. The four-poster bed was carved mahogany and was big enough for him to lie in the center with his arms stretched out.

Ashley closed her eyes as the unwelcoming heat flushed through her skin. Why did she have to think of that? She wanted to purge the idea of him on the bed, as he lay on the rumpled sheets, naked and gleaming with sweat. She imagined his lean and muscular arms extended as if he was waiting for her. Welcoming her.

"Am I kicking you out of your bed?" Sebastian asked.

"What?" she asked hoarsely. The vision of her curled up next to him on the four-poster bed bloomed in her mind. She shook her head to dispel it. "No, I don't stay here."

"Why not?" he asked as he tossed his backpack on the bed. The bag looked out of place against the vintage handmade quilt. "It's the master suite, isn't it?"

"Yes." She nervously darted the tip of her tongue along her dry lips. She couldn't explain it to him. That this room, this bed, had been the center stage for her parents' destructive relationship. The affair between her father, Donald Jones, and her mother, his longtime mistress Linda Valdez had been fueled with jealousy, infidelities and sexual obsession. She didn't want the added reminder. "Well, if you need anything, please let me know," she said as she slowly made her way to the door.

He tore his gaze away from the ocean view and Ashley saw the shadows in his eyes. It was more than sadness. It was grief. Loss. Anger. Sebastian blinked and the shadows suddenly disappeared.

Sebastian silently nodded and walked to the door with her. He guided her through the threshold by placing his hand on the small of her back. His fingers brushed her bare skin and her muscles clenched as her skin tightened. He dropped his hand, but she still felt the blood strumming through her veins.

Ashley took a deep breath and hurried away from Sebastian, refusing to look back. She was scared to explore these feelings. She was not used to being tempted while she stayed on Inez Key and this was going to be a challenge. She had hidden away for years, purposely disconnected from the world and was quiet and contained. None of the guests who came to her house interested her, but this man…this man reminded her of what she was missing.

And she wasn't sure she wanted to hide anymore.…

CHAPTER ONE

One month later

"SIR? THERE'S A woman here who wishes to speak with you."

Sebastian Cruz didn't look up as he continued to sign papers. "Send her away." He didn't tolerate any kind of interruption while he was at work. It was probably a former lover who mistakenly thought the element of surprise and drama would gain his attention. His employees were experienced in handling the situation and he wondered how the woman had managed to get into the executive suite in the first place.

"She insists on seeing you and hasn't left the reception area all day," his assistant continued, this time with a hint of sympathy for the uninvited guest. "She says it's urgent."

They all said that, Sebastian decided as he scanned another letter before he signed it. It annoyed him rather than made him feel curious or flattered. He didn't understand why these sophisticated women would stage public tantrums when the relationship was clearly over. "Have security remove her from the premises."

The younger man cleared his throat and nervously adjusted his tie. "I had considered that, but she says you have something of hers. She wouldn't tell me what it was because it was a private matter. She's here to get it back."

That was impossible. Sebastian frowned as he scrawled his name on another document. He wasn't sentimental. He didn't keep mementos or trophies. "Did you find out her name?"

His assistant squirmed from the censure of his icy tone. "Jones," he said hurriedly. "Ashley Jones."

Sebastian went still as he held the pen in midair. He stared at the heavy paper, the words a blur, as memories of Ashley Jones crashed through him. He remembered her soft brown hair cascading down her bare shoulders. Her wild energy and her earthy laugh. His body clenched, excitement pulsing through his veins, as he thought about her sun-kissed skin and wide pink mouth.

That woman had haunted his dreams for the past month. He had tried to purge Ashley from his mind, distracting himself with work and women, but he couldn't forget her uninhibited response. Or her haughty rejection.

Sebastian remembered that morning vividly. She had still been naked in bed when she had told him she wasn't interested in anything more than a one-night stand. She had shared more than her body that night, but now he wasn't good enough to breathe her rarefied air. Her lips had been reddened from his kisses, but she wouldn't deign to look him in the eye.

Ashley had no idea that he was the most sought-after

bachelor in Miami. A billionaire with incredible influence. Women of power, wealth and royalty chased after him. He had shed the stench of the ghetto years ago and now belonged to the glittery world of high society. But she had dismissed him as if she was a princess that belonged in an ivory-white tower and he still belonged in the filthy streets. Who did she think she was? Ashley had never lifted a finger for the lifestyle she enjoyed, while he continued to fight for the empire he'd created with his bare hands.

"I think she's the daughter of that tennis legend," his assistant continued in a scandalized whisper. "You know, the murder-suicide. It was big news a few years ago."

Donald Jones. Sebastian's nostrils flared as he forced back the rising hot anger. He knew all about the tennis player and his family. He had made a point of learning everything about Ashley.

There had been a few surprises when he had met her, but his first impression had been correct. She was a spoiled heiress who lived in paradise. She didn't know the meaning of scraping by, suffering or surviving. For a woman like Ashley Jones, the world catered to her.

Until now. Sebastian narrowed his eyes as an idea formed. Anticipation beat hard in his chest as he considered the possibilities. He knew why she was here. She wanted to find out how he'd got her precious island and how she could get it back.

His mouth twisted as he imagined his revenge. She wouldn't be so quick to dismiss him now that he had something she wanted. Now was his chance to watch her bow down and lose that superior tone. Sebastian wanted to turn the tables and strip this woman of her pride and status. Take her to bed for one night, indulge in the exquisite pleasure that would make the most cynical lover believe in destiny, and then discard her.

"Please send her in," Sebastian said coldly as the call of the hunt roared in his blood, "and then you may leave for the day."

Ashley sat on the edge of the pearl-white leather chair as she watched the sun set over the Miami skyline. She felt a pang of homesickness as she saw how the tall buildings pierced the coral and dusky pink streaks in the sky. She felt uncomfortable surrounded by steel and glass, noise and people. She missed sitting alone in her favorite spot in the cove of her island and watching the sun dip past the endless turquoise ocean.

She may never see it again. Fear squeezed her heart, and her fingers pinched her white clutch purse. Bile churned in her stomach as she remembered the eviction letter. She still felt the same agonizing horror when she had discovered a Sebastian Cruz had bought her loan and now owned her family island because she'd missed two payments.

Ashley pressed her lips together and prayed that she could meet Mr. Cruz and come to an understanding. Get her island back immediately. What was she going to do if she couldn't get the man to see reason?

She couldn't think this way. Ashley exhaled slowly, wishing the panic that banded her chest would dissolve.

Defeat was not an option. This was her last chance, but she was going to find a way to get back her family home.

Ashley glanced around the waiting room, noticing that it was quieter now that most of the office workers had gone for the day. It didn't make the space any less intimidating. She almost hadn't stepped into the building when she noticed the towering height and the aggressive sleek lines. It had taken more courage than she'd care to admit to stay seated on the chair throughout the day, feeling small and invisible, as she watched the employees attack the day with ruthless energy.

Her head jerked when she heard purposeful footsteps echo against the polished black floor. The tall man in the designer suit and prestigious school tie she'd spoken with earlier approached her. "Miss Jones? Mr. Cruz can see you now."

Ashley nodded as her throat tightened with anxiety. Her hands went suddenly cold as she rose from the seat. She felt uncoordinated, her legs stiff and her borrowed heels heavy, as she followed the man in the suit.

You can fix this, she reminded herself fiercely as she nervously smoothed her hand over her hair. It had taken ages to coax her wild mane into a tight bun and she felt as if the waves were threatening to break free.

As she tried to keep up with the man who was undoubtedly an assistant, she tried not to notice the imposing features of the stark and colorless corridor. She didn't know how this Sebastian Cruz had got Inez Key, but she knew it had to be a mistake. She couldn't imagine why someone with this amount of wealth would want a run-down island.

Ashley glanced at the assistant. She was tempted to ask about Sebastian Cruz, but she sensed the man wouldn't reveal much. She regretted not researching the man who owned Cruz Conglomerate. If the executive suite indicated anything, she suspected Sebastian Cruz was an older, formal gentleman who valued propriety and status.

Ashley tugged at the vintage white dress that had once belonged to her mother. She was glad she'd made the choice to wear it. It was outdated and restricting but she knew she looked sweet and demure.

Now, if only she could remember to speak like a lady. Ashley paused at the grand black doors to Mr. Cruz's office. Everything went into slow motion as she watched the assistant knock and open the door. *Just watch your mouth.* Ashley swiped the tip of her tongue along her dry lips. She knew more than anyone how one reckless word could ruin everything....

Ashley barely heard the assistant's introduction over the sound of her heart pounding in her ears. She sensed the magnitude of the room but controlled the impulse of looking around. She placed a polite smile on her lips, stretched out her hand and froze when she saw Sebastian Cruz.

"You!" she blurted out as she instinctively snatched her hand back. Standing before her was the one man she'd hoped she'd never meet again. *This* was Sebastian Cruz? The man had turned her world upside down a month ago, had torn down all of her defenses and introduced her to a world of pleasure and promise.

Ashley gasped for her next breath as her body went rigid, primed to flee. What was going on? This could not be Sebastian Cruz. It was Sebastian *Esteban*. The name was burned into her mind forever. A woman never forgot her first lover.

But this man didn't look anything like the mysterious guest who had arrived for a weekend getaway on Inez Key a month ago. The faded jeans and knowing smile were replaced with a severe suit and a stern mouth. Her gaze traveled from his short black hair to his large brown eyes and the hard thrust of his chin. He was attractive but forbidding. Menacing.

Sebastian's raw power was barely concealed underneath the tailored lines of his black suit. His lean and muscular build hinted that he was sleek, swift and that he moved with stealth. This man could fight hard and dirty.

He smiled and a sense of unease trickled down Ashley's spine. This time his smile didn't make her heart give a slow tumble. His sharp white teeth made her think of a cold-blooded animal tearing apart his quarry.

Feeling a little shaky, Ashley took a step back. Sebastian was stunning, but her memories had muted the brutal power and raw masculinity he possessed.

"Ashley," he said silkily and gestured at the chair in front of his desk. He didn't look surprised to see her. "Please sit down."

"What are you doing here?" she asked as conflicting

emotions swirled ferociously inside her. She felt dizzy. Vulnerable. She wanted to sit down and curl into a protective ball but she couldn't give the man any advantage. "I don't understand. He called you Mr. Cruz."

"That is my name," he said as he sat down behind his desk.

"Since when?" She winced when her voice rose. Ashley tried desperately to hold back. "You introduced yourself to me as Sebastian Esteban."

"That is part of my name. Esteban is my mother's family name." His dark eyes were intent as he watched her closely. As if that name should mean something to her. "I am Sebastian Esteban Cruz."

That was his excuse? She stared at him, waiting for more. Instead, he sat in his chair that was as big as a throne and watched her with an air of impatience. He wasn't going to apologize for anything.

"Why did you lie to me? Is that part of your routine?" A woman only had to look at Sebastian Cruz and know he was a heartbreaker. She thought she could remain unscathed by limiting their encounter to a one-night stand. She had been wrong.

But she hadn't been thinking during that sensual weekend, she thought as regret pricked at her. Instead, she had followed a primal call and fallen into Sebastian's bed.

She had known better. Expected more from herself. After being raised by a philandering father, Ashley had recognized the signs of Sebastian's tried-and-true routine. She should have remembered the devastation that immediately followed the promise of paradise.

"When a wealthy person is interested in buying property, it's in their best interest not to reveal who they are," he said unrepentantly. "Otherwise the sale price goes up."

"Inez Key wasn't for sale," she said hoarsely as the anger whipped through her. Now she understood why he'd chosen to visit her island. He had intended to steal her family home from the beginning!

"So you kept saying." He gave a dismissive shrug. "I had approached you through several of my representatives, but I kept getting the same answer. The offered price was extremely generous. I made a personal visit in the hopes that I could convince you to sell."

She had thought it was strange that a man like Sebastian had arrived at her island for rest and relaxation. He was the kind of man who thrived on challenges and conquering uncharted territory. "Instead, you stole it from me," she whispered as her stomach churned. "This is all making sense."

"I didn't steal it," he corrected her. "You missed the deadline to repay the loan. Inez Key is mine."

Ashley didn't like the triumph she heard in his voice. She clenched her purse tighter as she choked back the fury. "That loan is none of your business! It was a private agreement between Raymond Casillas and me."

"And I bought the loan from Casillas. You shouldn't have put up your island as collateral." He mockingly clucked his tongue and shook his head at her poor judgment.

"It not like I had a lot of choices," she pointed out fiercely. How dare this man question her decision? Her father's finances had been a shambles when he died. Sebastian had no idea what she'd had to do, what she'd had to sacrifice, to keep Inez Key. "It was the only thing I have of value."

He tilted his head and captured her gaze. "Was it?" he asked softly.

Ashley stiffened as she sensed the danger lurking beneath that question. How much did this man know? She needed to take control of this meeting. Her legs shook and she felt jittery, but she forced herself to remain standing. "Inez Key suffered a lot of damage during the hurricane, and the insurance wouldn't pay for all of it."

He shrugged. "I don't care how you got into debt."

She wanted to claw at his bored expression. Ashley curled her fingers into her palms as she felt her temper flare dangerously. "I didn't make an agreement with you," she said roughly. "I had a payment plan with Raymond."

"Which you couldn't pay," he said. "You took a gamble and you lost."

Ashley gritted her teeth. It was true and she couldn't deny it. She had taken many risks when she'd accepted the loan. She'd had difficulty finding the money to repay, but she couldn't let it end here. She had to get Inez Key back.

"Raymond understood why I was having trouble making the payments," she said, her voice shaking as emotions ran wild inside her. "He was giving me more time since he had been best friends with my father."

"I'm sure he was the epitome of understanding and compassion. But it was smart of you to keep it out of the banking system." He wagged his finger at her. "I would have found out about it earlier."

Did he think this was funny? That this was a game? Her future was at stake here. "And then you wouldn't have had to sleep with me to get that kind of information," she retorted.

Sebastian's gaze slowly traveled down her tense body, resting briefly on her gentle curves. "That isn't why I took you to bed."

Her skin burned. She couldn't stop the fragmented memories flooding her mind. She remembered his hot masculine scent and the taste of his golden skin. Her dress felt tight as she recalled the sharp hiss between his teeth and the bite of pain when his strong fingers had tangled in her hair.

Ashley abruptly looked away. She had a tendency to remember that night at the most inconvenient moments. Her heart was pounding against her chest and her body was flushed. "You didn't have seduction in mind the moment you stepped on Inez Key," she mumbled. "I find that highly unlikely."

"I didn't know that you would indulge in pillow talk after sex," he drawled as he leaned back in his chair and steepled his long fingers together. "I certainly didn't expect you to reveal your agreement with Casillas. That was a bonus and it was impossible for me not to use that information for my benefit."

Ashley stared at Sebastian as her chest twisted painfully. How could he be so callous about that intimate moment? Didn't he realize that she never confided in anyone? But she had felt close and safe enough to tell

him her worries. She had been interested in his opinion and valued his advice. It was only in the light of
day that she realized she had been lulled into a false
sense of security.

She somehow knew that rare slip of the tongue would
come back and haunt her. He had used that moment of
weakness to his advantage. "I will not allow you to take
this island from me!"

Sebastian was unmoved by her heated declaration.
"It's too late."

"Why are you being so unreasonable?" Her voice
echoed in her ears. She lowered her hands firmly against
her sides and tried again. "Why can't you give me a second chance?"

He seemed genuinely surprised by her question. As if
she was more naive than he had given her credit. "Why
should I? Have you done anything that would suggest
you deserve a second chance?"

She saw the way his eyes darkened. There was something about his choice of words. Suspicion slithered
and coiled around her weary mind as she crossed her
arms. "Is this because I kicked you out of bed the next
morning?"

Ashley wanted to bite her tongue the moment she
spoke without thinking. She knew she had to be careful with her words. She cringed as she heard his husky
chuckle.

Sebastian's smile was a slash of white against his
dark skin. "Don't flatter yourself."

She knew she had caught him off guard when she'd

refused his offer to continue the relationship. Sebastian would never know how much the idea had both delighted and scared her. If he had seen her resolve weaken, he would have gone in for the kill. Her answer came across cold and unfeeling and she knew the rejection had stung.

To think she had felt bad about it! She had spent hours reviewing that moment and wishing she had refused more gracefully. And more than once she wished she had the courage to have accepted his offer.

But she realized that even after one glorious night, she was in danger of becoming the kind of woman she hated. A sexual creature. A woman who was driven by her emotions and needs. She had pulled away to protect herself.

"I can't help but think this is all personal," she said, glaring at him.

He arched a dark eyebrow. "How is that possible when we had not met until I arrived on Inez Key?" he murmured.

Ashley felt as if she was missing something. She knew they'd never met. One would never forget the briefest encounter with Sebastian Cruz. "You lied to me about your name, you had a hidden agenda and you seduced me. I was right to follow my instincts and get rid of you."

"And I'm right to follow my instincts and remove you from the island immediately," Sebastian said, clicking his computer keyboard as if the discussion was over.

Immediately? Panic gripped her chest. Before she'd walked in here she'd had two weeks to leave the island.

She was making this worse. "Inez Key is all I have," she said in a rush. "Without it, I have no home, no money…"

He didn't glance away from the computer screen. "That is not my concern."

She marched over to his desk and braced her hands on the edge. She would demand his attention if she had to reach over and grab him by the throat. "How can you be so cruel?" she asked in a low growl.

He lifted his gaze and held hers. "Cruel? You don't know the meaning."

She leaned forward. "I can't lose Inez Key. That is my home and my livelihood."

"Livelihood?" He scoffed at the word. "You haven't worked a day in your life. You rent out your home to wealthy people for the occasional weekend."

She let that criticism slide. She may not have a traditional job, but that didn't mean she didn't work hard to hold on to everything that was dear to her. "They pay good money for privacy. You did. What makes you think others won't?"

He reached for his pen and uncapped it. "There aren't enough rich celebrities looking for privacy to pay back your loan."

"I haven't been doing it long enough," she insisted. She needed to buy a little time. "Raymond understood that."

Sebastian shook his head. "Raymond Casillas wanted you to dig a deeper hole. He knew you were never going to be able to pay back the loan. Why do you think he offered in the first place?"

Ashley straightened and took a step away from the desk. "I don't know," she muttered. She didn't want to talk about it. Her skin felt prickly as the nausea swept through her.

"He hoped you would pay back in another way. And I think you knew that. Which is why you had requested a contract. Under most circumstances, it would have been a smart move."

"A lot of good it did me," she said under her breath. That contract now put her right in the hands of the ruthless Sebastian Cruz.

"You didn't want there to be any misunderstanding. You would offer Inez Key as your collateral, not your body." Sebastian paused. "Or your virginity."

She flushed bright red and refused to meet his gaze. "You knew?" Ashley whispered. She had done everything to conceal her inexperience. Out of pride, out of protection. She couldn't allow Sebastian to know how much advantage he had in that moment. But how did he know? How did she give herself away?

He set down the pen. "You should have told me." His tone was almost soft. Kind.

Ashley took another step back. She felt exposed. She wished she could walk right out of the office, but her unfamiliar heels felt like shackles. "I had already told you too much. And how did you know that Raymond wanted…" She swallowed roughly as her voice trailed away.

"Casillas has a reputation for liking innocent girls," he said with distaste as he leaned back in his chair. "And once he found out that you and I had been together, he was no longer interested in helping you out."

She closed her eyes as mortification weighed heavily on her shoulders. Sebastian had discussed their private moment with Raymond? He was just like her womanizing father and his raucous drinking buddies. A wave of disappointment crashed through her. She had expected better of Sebastian. "You're disgusting," she whispered.

"I do what is necessary to win."

He was a worthy opponent. She didn't care if his indiscretion helped her escape Raymond. He was still a dangerous enemy and she needed to remember that. "This isn't over. I will see you in court," she declared as she headed for the door.

"Good luck with that," he called out after her. "You can't afford legal advice and any good lawyer will tell you that you don't have a case."

"Don't underestimate me." She tossed the warning over her shoulder.

"How badly do you want Inez Key?" he asked lazily as she grabbed the door handle.

She dipped her head as she considered the question. How could she explain? Inez Key was more than her home. It was the only thing left of her family yet it was also a constant and unwelcome reminder. It was her sanctuary but it was also her dungeon. She was both caretaker and captive. She was determined to live there until she exorcised her demons. "Probably as much as you did."

His chuckle sent a shiver down her spine. "You shouldn't have told me that."

She turned around and narrowed her eyes. He looked so calm and in control as he lounged in his chair and watched her with barely concealed amusement. "What do you want, Cruz?"

His smile sent a shiver down her spine. "You."

CHAPTER TWO

SEBASTIAN SAW ASHLEY flinch from his answer. He knew she wasn't surprised by his admission. He saw the flare of interest in her eyes and the flush in her cheeks before she tried to shield her reaction. She was trying to hold back her response, but her body was betraying her. She couldn't hide the hectic pulse beating at the base of her neck. Ashley still wanted him, but she wasn't going to admit it.

"You've made it very obvious," Ashley said in a withering tone.

"I'm not ashamed of it." He didn't consider his desire for Ashley a weakness. It was more of a problem, a distraction and a growing obsession. She, on the other hand, was ashamed by the attraction they shared. She acted as if it went against everything she believed in.

"I'm not for sale," she declared.

The corner of his mouth slanted up. "You said the same about Inez Key and look at how that worked out."

Her jaw clenched. "I'm serious, Cruz," she said in a growl.

If she'd been serious, she would have tossed back his

indecent proposal. Used a few choice words and punctuated her indignation with a slap. Instead, she held the door handle in a death grip. She was wavering. Horrified but enthralled. If he played this right he could have Ashley back in his bed for more than a night.

"I'm sure we can work out an arrangement," he said smoothly as the excitement burned inside him. He had ached for her for weeks and the sensation intensified now that he knew the wait was almost over.

"You are no better than Raymond," she said in a hiss.

Sebastian smirked. Her comment just proved how innocent and unworldly she really was. Hadn't she realized by now that he was much, much worse?

"On the contrary, Casillas had set a trap. I'm being extremely honest about what I want." And he wanted Ashley more than anything. It didn't make sense. She wasn't like the other women in his life. She was untamed and inexperienced. Trouble. An inconvenience.

He should cut her loose. After all, he was lying about what he was willing to offer in exchange. He wasn't letting her back on that island. He wasn't going to break a promise just so he could please this spoiled little princess. But he was intrigued to see what her price would be.

"Honest?" she asked, the word exploding from her pink lips. "How can you say that when you introduced yourself under a different name with the intent of seducing the island from me?"

He rose from his seat and approached her. This time she was too angry to be cautious. She didn't catch the scent of danger. Her brown eyes glittered and she thrust out her chin.

Sebastian wondered why she attempted to hide behind the shapeless white dress. Her beauty was too bold, her personality too brash, to be restrained. His palms itched to pull her hair free and watch it tumble past her shoulders. He wanted to smear the pale makeup from her face and reveal the island girl he knew.

"You're the one who isn't being honest," Sebastian said as he stood before her, noticing how her chest rose and fell with agitation. "You knew what Casillas was really after and you didn't disabuse him of that idea because you needed the money."

"I tried the banks but—"

"Casillas makes your skin crawl. Don't you think he knew that? Did you realize that made you even more desirable to him?" Sebastian asked. "You tried to play the game and got in too deep."

Ashley raised an eyebrow. "Did *you* consider that I fell into bed with you because I wanted to get rid of my virginity? That I needed to so I could escape Raymond?"

Sebastian jerked his head back. He had *not* considered that. The possibility ate away at him like acid. He was not going to be used by a pampered princess.

Sebastian gripped her chin with his fingers and held her still. He felt the fight beneath her smooth, silky skin. "Did you?" he asked in a low, angry tone that would send his employees scurrying for safety.

Her eyes gleamed with reckless defiance. "Not so sure anymore, are you?"

He watched her closely as the unfamiliar emotions squeezed his chest. With her natural beauty and independent spirit, Ashley Jones could have had any man. He didn't know why she'd waited for her first sexual experience, but if she needed to get rid of her virginity, she would have picked an uncomplicated man whom she could control.

He stroked the pad of his thumb against her chin as he held his fiery emotions in check. "I think you slept with me because you couldn't help it," he said in a husky voice. She wanted him even though it meant yielding. Surrendering. "Casillas had nothing to do with it. You forgot all about him when you were with me."

She tried to slap his hand away. "Dream on."

He couldn't help but dream about Ashley and the night they had shared. He remembered every touch and kiss. Every gasp and moan. Ashley hadn't been faking it. "You want me so much that it scares you. And that's why you tried to push me away."

"I pushed you away because I didn't want to continue the fling," she argued. "You served your purpose and I was done. I have no interest in playboys."

He dropped his hand. *Served his purpose*? He knew she said that to hide the fact that he would always be a significant part in her love life, but she was going to pay for those words. "I'm not a playboy."

"Ha!" she said bitterly. "You tried to hide it when you were at Inez Key, but I grew up around womanizers. I know what kind of man you are. You would dangle a woman's home as bait, but we both know you will not give it back."

Sebastian bit back a smile. Ashley Jones thought very highly of herself. Did she really believe he would give up his treasure for another taste of what they'd shared? "I never said I'd give back your home."

She went still and frowned. "I don't understand. You asked me—"

"How much you wanted Inez Key," he clarified as he stepped closer, inhaling her citrusy scent. "The ownership of the island is not up for grabs. I keep what is mine and I will not let it slip through my fingers."

Ashley paled and she leaned against the door. "I've taken care of the island for years," she said in a whisper. "I have given it my love, sweat and tears. I've sacrificed everything for it."

"Why?" There was nothing remarkable about the island. It had no natural resources or historical significance. It was in an undesirable location and he had been the only prospective buyer interested in the island.

"Why?" she repeated dully. "It's my home."

Sebastian saw the guarded look in her eyes and knew she wasn't giving the whole answer. He also knew she wouldn't share it with him. She'd learned her lesson and didn't trust him anymore.

There had been moments during that weekend when Ashley had been unguarded and spontaneous. Now she was wary. He ignored the surprising pang of regret. It was time she learned how the real world worked and he had given her a very valuable lesson. "Your attachment to Inez Key doesn't make any sense."

"What about you?" she countered. "Not that many

people would go to such lengths to steal someone's home."

"I didn't steal it," he said with a hint of impatience. "You couldn't pay back the loan so the island is now mine."

"What are your plans for it?" she asked as if it hurt to think of the changes he was going to make. "I can't imagine you want to live there. I'm sure you have many homes. Inez Key is practically roughing it in comparison."

"Don't worry about it," he said as he reached for the door. It was time to force her into making a decision. "Inez Key is now my concern."

Ashley bit her bottom lip as she stared at the open door. The beat of silence stretched until her shoulders slumped. "Cruz."

"The name is Sebastian," he reminded her. She had said his name repeatedly during that one night. She'd said it with wonder and excitement. With longing and satisfaction. And tonight it would be the last thing she said before she fell asleep.

Sebastian. No, she wouldn't call him that. Sebastian had been a mysterious stranger on the island. His intensity and raw masculinity had unleashed a fierce sexual hunger that she hadn't known was in her. She would never be the same again.

This arrogant man was calculating and intimidating. He was breathtaking and she couldn't take her eyes off him. But he was not the fantasy lover she remembered.

Maybe that was the problem. Had she built up that

one magical night in her head? Everything had been so new. Almost foreign. She wouldn't feel overwhelmed from the wild sensations if she had sex with him again. Yet the memory of sharing a bed with Sebastian still made her weak in the knees.

"If you have no intention of giving me back my home," she asked carefully as her heart pounded against her ribs, "what are you offering?"

"You'll be the caretaker and stay in the cottage behind the main house."

She held back the flash of anger. She had been the mistress of the house. She had free rein of the island. Now he was offering the role as caretaker as if it was a gift? "Not good enough."

He placed his finger against her lips. "Careful, *mi vida*," he said softly as his eyes glittered with warning. "I don't have to let you on the island at all. I don't have to let anyone who is living there stay."

She gasped at his thinly veiled threat. "*No*. This has nothing to do with the other families on the island. They've been there for generations."

"You are going to champion the others?" he mocked. "How adorable."

She thought of the five families that lived on the small island. They had been there for her during her darkest moments. Since then, she had provided for them and protected them. She wasn't going to let them down. "Don't interfere with their lives," she said. "This is between you and me."

"Yes, it is," he drawled as he closed the door. Sebastian rested his hand above her head. He was too close. She felt trapped. Cornered.

It was a struggle to remain still and meet his gaze. "What do you want from me?"

"Two weeks in my bed."

Her skin went hot and her mouth dropped open. "I wouldn't stay in your bed for two more minutes, let alone—"

"Make it three," he said coldly.

Her eyes widened. "You bastard." She bit out the words.

"And now it's four," he said with no emotion. "Do you want to make it five weeks?"

A month with Sebastian? The wall she had painstakingly built around herself had shattered after one night with him. What would happen to her after four weeks in his bed?

Now if only she could silence the dark excitement building inside her, threatening to break free. She didn't like this side of her. She was not going to let this sexual hunger govern her thoughts and decisions. She was nothing like her parents.

"Ashley, one month won't be enough for you," he promised.

She pressed her lips together as she struggled to remain silent. She shouldn't have allowed him to rattle her. Her angry words always had consequences.

"It may not even last that long," he said. "I have a short attention span when it comes to women, but you'll beg me to stay."

That was what she was afraid of. She prided herself

on not being a sexual woman, until she met Sebastian Cruz. One look at him and the dormant sensations had sprung violently to life. Her response to his touch had frightened her. She hadn't recognized herself. This man had wielded a power over her like no other.

She was going to break this spell he'd woven. She'd figure out how he lowered her defenses so easily, and kill the craving she had for Sebastian Cruz. And when this month was over, she would never let a man have this kind of hold on her again.

"I want to make sure I understand this," she said shakily. "I will have a home on the island if I share a bed with you for a month?"

"Correct," he said as his eyes held a devilish gleam.

There had to be a catch. Why would he kick her out of the main house only to give her a smaller one on the island? It was convenient for him to have a caretaker who already knew Inez Key, but did he think this arrangement would continue for as long as he wished? "How do I know that you won't fire me?"

"You'll have a contract just like my other employees," he murmured as his attention focused on her mouth.

Her lips stung with awareness. They felt fuller. Softer. She tried not to nervously lick them. "How long do I have before I give you my decision?"

He moved closer, his mouth above hers. She felt his warm breath waft over her skin. "You have to give it to me now."

Alarm jolted through her veins. "Now? That's not

fair!" What was she saying? Sebastian didn't play fair. He played to win.

"Take it or leave it," he said.

She wanted to look away. Find another option. As much as she wanted to stay on Inez Key, she didn't think she was strong enough to fight the desire she had for Sebastian. But she couldn't walk away from this. "I'll take it," she whispered.

Sebastian captured her mouth with his. His kiss was bold, rough and possessive. She wanted to resist. Was determined to give no response. Yet she parted her lips and leaned into him as he deepened the kiss. Their tongues parried as he pulled her closer. She tasted his lust and it thrilled her. She yielded as he conquered her mouth.

Ashley jerked away. *What was wrong with her?* Her heart was racing and she fought the urge to place her fingers on her tingling lips. She couldn't look at Sebastian. She was confused. Aroused. Her emotions had been ambushed.

How could she have responded so eagerly? For him? Sebastian Cruz represented everything she despised in a man. "I need to leave," she said as she clumsily reached for the door handle. "I have a few things I need to deal with back home."

"You're not going home." Sebastian wrapped his hand around her wrist and pulled her hand away from the door. "You will return to Inez Key on my terms."

She stared at him as his calmly delivered words filtered into her jumbled mind. He wasn't allowing her to go home? How dare he? But then, it wasn't her home anymore. Technically, it was his. "I said I would share a bed with you. There was nothing—"

"You are now my mistress," he said as he raised her hand and pressed his lips against the skittering pulse on her wrist. "You live where I live. Sleep where I sleep."

Mistress? Her knees threatened to give out. She hated that word. Her dad had kept many mistresses. Vulgar women who didn't care who they hurt as long as they got the attention they felt they deserved. "I didn't agree to that."

"I didn't say that I would share my nights with you," he reminded her. "I am sharing a bed. That could happen at any time of day. Or all day."

All day. The wicked excitement pulled low in her belly. No, this was bad. This was really bad. What had she gotten herself into?

"Backing out already?" he said in a purr.

This was her chance. She could extract herself from this agreement and run back to her safe little world. But that world no longer existed. He owned it. Now she had to fight for a little piece of it. Ashley swallowed roughly. "No."

"Good." Sebastian's satisfaction vibrated in his deep voice as he pulled the door open and led her out of his office.

"Where are we going?" she asked, stumbling in her heels as she tried to keep up with him.

"To get you out of that dress."

She went rigid. He wanted to seal the deal *now?* She wasn't ready. Her mind froze yet her nipples tightened in anticipation as her legs went limp.

"I'm calling a stylist," Sebastian announced. "The dress you're wearing hides your body and ages you about two decades."

She didn't care. She didn't like dressing up or bringing attention to her body. Her clothes were meant to fade into the background. "Why do I need another dress?"

"I have an event I must attend and you are coming with me," he said as they reached his private elevator.

An event? No doubt it was glamorous and luxurious. There would be the Miami elite attending. Many of them would be the friends and former lovers of her parents. It was going to be a nightmare. "I don't want to go."

"You don't know much about being a mistress, do you?" he asked as he wrapped his arm around her waist and dragged her against him. "You really don't have a say in the matter."

Ashley was very aware of his hand spanning the small of her back. She felt delicate, almost fragile, next to him. She didn't like it. "Are you aware that there's a difference between mistress and sex slave?"

"Try not to put ideas into my head," he murmured.

The last thing she wanted was to be seen in public on the arm of the most unapologetic playboy. After years of shielding herself from the tabloids that had been fascinated with her parents' escapades, she didn't want the world to see how far she had fallen.

No one would be surprised, though. She was, after all, the daughter of Linda Valdez and Donald Jones. "I thought men hid their mistresses," she complained under her breath, "not showed them off."

"You have a lot to learn, Ashley," he said as his hold tightened on her waist. "I'm looking forward to teaching you everything."

CHAPTER THREE

How HAD SHE got to this point? Ashley stared at her reflection in the full-length mirror. Sebastian had brought in a stylist and hairdresser to his penthouse apartment at the top of his office building and they had spent the past few hours getting her ready for the night. Most women would have found it fun and relaxing. She thought it had been pure torture.

Her eyes were wide and her hands were clenched at her sides. The sumptuous walk-in closet faded in the background as she focused on her wild mane of hair. Her gaze traveled from her red lips to her stiletto heels. There was something familiar about the look.

Was this how all of Sebastian's women dressed? She couldn't live up to this sexual promise. This outfit, this look, was for a woman whose only goal was to please a man. Who placed her worth on whom she could attract and how long she could keep the man interested. She had seen plenty of women like that while she was growing up.

Ashley frowned and studied the orange dress a little closer. Why would Sebastian want a woman who didn't make any demands? He didn't seem to be the type who would surround himself with vapid women who didn't challenge his intellect. But then, she didn't know much about his love life.

Love? She snorted at the word. Sex, she mentally corrected herself. His sex life. If she asked him, would he remember all his lovers or were his women indistinguishable, one from the other?

The possibility pricked sharply at her. She didn't want to be grouped with those women. Nameless and forgettable. She couldn't go out looking like this. Like one of his mistresses. The dress wasn't as revealing as she'd feared, but the daring attitude carried more than a promise of sex. It suggested her status and her price.

She abruptly turned her head and a memory collided with the movement she saw in the mirror. She froze. *No, no, no!* Slowly looking back, Ashley stared at her reflection with a mix of panic and horror. Big hair. Little dress. Bold color.

For a moment, she resembled her mother.

Linda Valdez had always worn bright and daring colors. She had wanted Donald Jones to notice her whether she was watching his tennis match from the players' box or whether she was in a room filled with nubile women. When that didn't work, Linda's dresses started to get shorter and more revealing. She had been afraid to change her hairstyle in case it displeased Donald.

Everything her mother had done was to keep Donald's interest. If his eyes strayed on to another woman, Linda would become desperate for his attention. Ashley knew her father never cared about her mother's interests or opinions; his only concern was that Linda was beautiful, sexually available to him, and that everyone knew it. He would dress Linda in cheap and tasteless clothes and publicly discuss their relationship in the crudest language.

Ashley squeezed her eyes shut as she remembered one dress her mother had refused to wear. The bright red dress had been unforgiving. The corset bodice had painfully thrust Linda's breasts out while the tight skirt had puckered and stretched around her bottom.

Her mother had been extraordinarily beautiful, but that unflattering outfit had exaggerated her curves and made her appear almost cartoonish. Yet what Ashley remembered most was, despite the epic argument about the dress, her mother had reluctantly worn it. That dress represented the inequality in her parents' relationship. Ashley remembered clearly how Linda had hunched her shoulders and bent her head in shame when she wore that dress, defeated and humiliated.

Ashley's nails bit into her palms and she choked back the panic. She fought the urge to kick off the delicate heels and rip off the dress. She wanted to get them off before they tainted her.

It was too late. The clothes weren't the problem. Ashley flattened her hand on the mirror and bent her head as she exhaled shakily. For years she had been determined not to follow in her mother's footsteps. She didn't dress up for a man or try to gain his attention. She didn't barter with her looks. And yet, here she was, a rich man's plaything.

The only difference was that her mother had worked

hard to gain Donald Jones's attention. It had taken strategy to become his mistress. She had tried to bump up
her status to become a trophy wife with an "unplanned"
pregnancy. Unfortunately, Linda Valdez had not been
Donald's favorite trophy.

"You are nothing like Mom," Ashley whispered
to herself. She made sure of it. Once she thought her
mother had been as perfect as a fairy-tale princess and
she wanted to be like her. But as Linda got older, and
Donald refused to marry her or give her his name, she
became more insecure. She felt her beauty fading and
knew she was losing the battle with her younger com-
petitors.

Linda Valdez had been beautiful but fragile. Jealous
and tempestuous. Ashley had seen the dark side of love
and passion even before her mother had killed Donald
before turning the gun on herself.

Ashley had been eighteen when that happened. Before that fateful moment she had been wary of men and
kept her distance. As she struggled with the aftermath
and scandal of the murder-suicide, she knew she would
never allow love or sex to influence her life. Ashley had
suppressed her passionate nature and hid on Inez Key.
She didn't mind being celibate. She had believed sex
wasn't worth the tears and heartache.

There were times when the isolation was almost too
much to bear. But it was better than what she had witnessed in her parents' relationship. She was ready to
spend her life that way until Sebastian showed up on
her island.

She had relaxed her guard under his charm and attention. One night with him and her quiet, contained life had spun wildly out of control. Even now, a month later, she found it difficult to hold back. She was too aware of him. Too needy for his touch.

Sebastian had proven her deepest fear. Ashley knew that she was very much her mother's daughter. She was stronger and more disciplined, but she had been wild in Sebastian's arms. The desire had been primal. Almost uncontrollable. She hadn't been the same since. She didn't want to feel the heights of passion because she knew the crash and burn was inevitable. If she wasn't careful, she would succumb to the same torment as her mother.

Sebastian glanced at his watch and strode to the door leading to the walk-in closet. He was not used to waiting for a woman. They followed his schedule and didn't cause any inconvenience. Ashley needed to learn that she was no different. He would not give her any special treatment. "Ashley, I'm not a patient man. It's time to leave."

As much as he would like to stay in and reacquaint himself with Ashley's curves, this was one party he couldn't miss. Wouldn't. The opening of his newest club would bring in hundreds of thousands for charity. His old neighborhood needed that money. And yet, even now, he was tempted to strip off his gray suit, knock down the door and reclaim Ashley. He went hard as he imagined sinking into her welcoming body.

"Ashley?" he snapped.

"Have fun without me," she said through the door.

Sebastian closed his eyes and inhaled sharply. He should have known that she would pout and sulk. Heiresses. It didn't matter if they lived in stilettos or sandals. Each of them knew how to throw a tantrum.

"You're coming with me," he said in a low voice. "That's the agreement."

"Actually, I didn't agree to it," she said, her voice loud and clear. "I said I'd share your bed. I didn't say anything about dressing up like a whore and being put on display to stroke your ego."

Whore? Sebastian shook his head. The dress and shoes were bought at one of the most exclusive boutiques in South Beach. He had paid the hairstylist and makeup artist an exorbitant fee to give Ashley a natural look.

Even if Ashley rolled out of bed and only wore a wrinkled sheet, she couldn't look like a whore. There was something in the way she carried herself. She acted like a queen. Like she was too good for the rest of the world. Too good for him.

"Fine," Sebastian said as he walked away from the door. He could find another woman in a matter of minutes. Someone who was so grateful to be on his arm that she wouldn't challenge him every step of the way. "You don't want Inez Key that much. Understandable. It really isn't much of an island."

"Wait," she called out.

Sebastian hesitated. He didn't wait for anyone. That was one benefit he discovered after making his first million. The powerful people who used to ignore and instantly dismiss him would now wait endlessly for a minute of his time. Why should he treat Ashley any differently?

And yet he was compelled to turn around. Because he wanted Ashley. No other woman would do. She had already invaded his dreams and captured his imagination. When Ashley wrenched the door open and stood defiantly in the threshold, his breath caught in his throat.

Her long brown hair fell past her shoulders in thick waves. He bunched his hands as he remembered how soft and heavy it felt. His gaze drifted down to her face. Only the scowl marred her exquisite beauty.

He couldn't stop staring. The thin leather dress was perfect for Ashley. The casual design made him think of the oversize T-shirts she favored, yet the burnt-orange color reminded him of the sunset they'd shared on Inez Key.

"Perfect," he said gruffly.

She skimmed her hands uncertainly against the metallic embellishments that gave the simple dress an edge. "Did you choose this?"

Sebastian shook his head. "I told the stylist what I expected." He'd wanted something that had symbolized the weekend they'd shared in Inez Key. He didn't know that the dress would cling to her curves and accentuate her sun-kissed skin. His gaze gravitated to her long, toned legs. He remembered how they felt wrapped tightly around his waist. Sebastian swallowed roughly as his mouth felt dry.

"It's too short." She tugged at the hem that barely skimmed the top of her thighs. "Too revealing. Too—"

"Sexy as hell," he said in a growl.

Ashley's breath lodged painfully in her lungs as she watched Sebastian advance. She took a step back and bumped against the door frame. The man moved quietly, like a jungle cat ready to pounce, and she stood before him like helpless prey. Her heart was already beating hard when she saw him. Now it wanted to explode out of her chest.

Ashley wasn't sure how she was going to get out of this situation. She wasn't sure if she *wanted* to. She liked how he looked at her. Liked this tension that coiled around them, excluding everything else. She felt beautiful, powerful and vibrantly alive. Only Sebastian made her feel this way.

But how many other women had felt like this with Sebastian? Her pulse skipped hard as the question bloomed in her mind. Just as he was about to reach her, Ashley held up her hand to stop him. She hoped he didn't see how her fingers trembled. "Not so fast."

"Don't worry, *mi vida*," he said, his voice husky and seductive. "It will be slow and steady."

"That's not what I meant." She felt the heat flood her face as she imagined Sebastian exploring her body, taking his time while she begged for completion. Begged for more. "First, some ground rules."

He raised an eyebrow. "You can't be serious."

Were mistresses not allowed to negotiate? She found that hard to believe. What they had was a business deal. "Do not tell anyone about this arrangement," Ashley demanded as she crossed her arms, forming a barrier. She knew how men bragged. She remembered hearing her father discuss his conquests to any man who'd listen. Each story got bolder and raunchier as the men tried to one-up each other. "This is a private matter."

Sebastian watched her carefully. She couldn't tell if he was offended by her request or if he didn't know why it was worth mentioning. "I don't discuss my private life," he confided in a low voice. "And I won't let anyone talk about you."

Ashley blinked. She wasn't expecting that answer or the sincerity in his dark eyes. Sebastian Cruz was a good liar. He knew what she wanted to hear. If she didn't know that he would say or do anything to get his way, she'd almost believe him.

"Anything else?" he drawled as he moved closer, towering over her.

Ashley felt the pulse fluttering at the base of her throat. His scent, his heat, excited her. But she had one demand that wasn't negotiable. If he denied her this, she would walk out immediately. "You will have to use protection."

He reached out and brushed his knuckle along the line of her jaw. She shivered with anticipation at the gentle touch. "I always do."

"Always?" she taunted. Womanizers didn't think much about the future. They focused on instant gratification. It was the women who had to protect themselves and deal with the consequences alone.

"Always," he repeated as his fingertips grazed her throat and shoulder. "I take care of my lovers."

Sure. That had to be the real reason. It had nothing

to do with giving up control. "And you wouldn't want a gold digger to get pregnant and live off your money."

Sebastian's eyes flashed with agreement. "Any more rules?"

Ashley nervously licked her lips with the tip of her tongue. She wanted to create a list of rules, but her mind was blank. "No…"

"Good." Sebastian wrapped his fingers around her wrists. His hold was firm and commanding. She gasped when he held her hands high above her head. He leaned into her and Ashley hated how her body yielded to him. Her soft breasts were thrust against his hard chest and her pelvis cradled his erection. Sebastian surrounded her.

His powerful thigh wedged between her shaky legs. "Now, for my ground rules."

Ashley swallowed hard. She should have expected he would have rules of his own. She was ready to refuse them all, but she was secretly intrigued. She wanted to know what he demanded from a woman.

"First," he said as he pressed his mouth against her cheekbone, "you are available to me twenty-four hours a day."

"You don't ask for much, do you?" she asked sarcastically as the excitement clawed up her chest.

"And you have no claim on me," Sebastian said as he kissed his way down the curve of her throat. She couldn't refrain from arching her neck and encouraging more. "When I want you, I will call for you."

Now, *that* she had expected from Sebastian. He would decide when and where. Any affair would meet his schedule and the woman would have to learn how to adapt.

"Maybe you don't understand," Ashley said, closing her eyes as his hot breath warmed her skin. "I'm not the kind of woman who sits around and waits."

"You will be with me." His mouth hovered against her wildly beating pulse point at the base of her throat. He circled it with the tip of his tongue, silently showing that he knew how he made her feel. "It will be worth the wait."

She took in a ragged gulp of air. "You talk big—"

He cupped her cheeks with his large hands and kissed her. She was ready to counterattack, but he disarmed her immediately. His lips were demanding as he drew her tongue inside his mouth. She was out of control, mindlessly following his lead as the desire bled inside her.

When he withdrew, Ashley saw the stain of lipstick on his firm mouth and the way his eyes glittered knowingly. "I know how much you want this. Want *me*."

She was embarrassed at her response. Humiliated that he stopped the kiss. She felt scorched. Boneless. Ashley remembered feeling like this. Sebastian knew exactly how to touch her. She wanted more and yet she wanted it to stop. She needed to take control but at the same time she wanted to throw caution to the wind and see where she landed.

"Anything else?" she asked hoarsely.

His hand grazed her breast and he drew lazy circles around her hard nipple with his fingertip. "I expect total obedience from my women."

She flinched. She wasn't sure which part of his rule bothered her. The fact that she was lumped into a group known as "his women"? Or the obedience part? She wasn't going to let this man—or any man—master her. She wasn't a plaything. "Following the rules has never been my strength," she said.

"You'll learn. All you need is the right motivation." Sebastian smiled as he trailed his fingertips down her rib cage. His touch was as light as a feather and yet her skin tingled with awareness.

"I can't promise you obedience," she said between pants. "In fact, I won't."

Her words made him smile. "I can make you promise anything."

She wanted to give a bitter laugh. Slap his hand away. Tell him he was only fooling himself. But deep down she knew Sebastian could have that power, and she didn't want to test it. "You are very sure of yourself."

He didn't reply. Instead, he splayed his hand between her thighs. Sebastian's eyes held an unholy gleam when he realized she wore nothing underneath her dress. He murmured his approval in Spanish as he began to stroke the folds of her sex.

Ashley immediately clamped her legs together but it was too late. Sebastian wasn't going to let that deter him. He gave a husky laugh of triumph as she responded. She looked away as the liquid heat flooded her body.

"Look at me," he said roughly.

Ashley shook her head. She couldn't look in his eyes and show him how she felt. How he made her feel. From his expert touch, it was obvious that he already knew. The humiliation burned and yet she bucked against his hand.

She wouldn't look at him. And yet she couldn't tell him to stop. She didn't want to push him away. She felt the white heat whipping through her, catching fire. Her fear was that he would stop unless she followed his command.

Sebastian growled. "Look at me," he repeated.

She squeezed her eyes shut and shook her head again. A guttural moan escaped from deep in her chest as Sebastian dipped his finger into her clenching core. Ashley felt his hot gaze. She knew he saw everything. He knew what she wanted. What if he held back? Oh, God…what if he didn't stop until she revealed her deepest need and darkest fantasy?

"Ashley." His voice was raw and urgent.

She was compelled to open her eyes. Ashley met his intense gaze just as the climax rippled through her. Her mouth sagged open and her muscles locked as she chased the pleasure. Sebastian saw everything and she couldn't hide. How was he going to use this to his advantage?

He slowly, almost reluctantly, withdrew from her. Ashley ached from the loss and she sagged against the wall. Her body trembled. She wanted to hold on to him, but she wouldn't dare.

"Total obedience," he reminded her quietly.

His words were like a slap. Was this a display of his dominance? Did he want to prove that he could make her do whatever he wished?

Ashley pushed away from him and smoothed her dress with clumsy hands. She would not submit to his will. "No, Cruz," she said as she fought to stand straight on wobbly legs. "That will never happen."

"Haven't you learned by now, Ashley?" he asked as the challenge glinted in his eyes. "I always get what I want."

CHAPTER FOUR

As ASHLEY STOOD in the VIP section of Sebastian's dance club, she couldn't help but feel as if she had fallen into the looking glass. The flashing lights were hypnotic and the dancers moved to the music as if they were in a trance. She had never seen a place like this before. It was fantastical. Otherworldly and a little frightening.

And this was just part of Sebastian's kingdom. The moment they entered, she had felt the ripple of interest and awe. At first she had been uncomfortable being in the spotlight, but as Sebastian spoke to members of the Miami elite, she realized she was invisible to the guests. They lobbied for Sebastian's attention and saw no need to speak to her. She was arm candy. An expensive accessory.

She should feel grateful that no one noticed or cared about her. She recognized a few of her parents' friends, but they didn't seem to remember her. She felt small and powerless in the cavernous club. More than once, Ashley wondered how much of the club reflected Sebastian's personality. It was darkly sensual and seductive. The music pulsated from the floor and she tried to ignore the carnal rhythm, but her heartbeat matched the tempo.

The wild laughter punctuating the air made her flinch. She didn't want to be here, around these people who had enjoyed her parents' downfall. Ashley wished she was back on Inez Key. It was quiet and relaxing. Calm and predictable. That was where she belonged. It had been *her* kingdom.

But there had been a time when she'd needed to get away from her island. Sebastian must have known that. She remembered the unexpected fun she'd had with Sebastian on that weekend when he let her take his boat out for a spin.

The offer had been too tantalizing to resist. She loved being out on the water and had wanted to try his speedboat. At the time, she had thought her acceptance had nothing to do with the promise of having Sebastian's undivided attention.

Ashley had known the boat would slice through the choppy waves and reach incredible speed. She had wanted to go on a fast-and-hard ride, determined to forget Inez Key and her financial problems for a few hours.

She remembered Sebastian's warm smile as he had teased her, suggesting she was trying to tip him out of the boat. Perhaps she had been trying to test his courage. She had to find out if his restraint had just been a guise. Ashley had wanted to know how long it would take before he grabbed the wheel.

He never did. Sebastian had been lazily sprawled on the chair next to her, arms outstretched, his dark glasses perched on his bold nose. Sexual heat had bubbled underneath their banter, but she had enjoyed his companionship.

Sebastian had been relaxed and unconcerned while she made hairpin turns and the boat flew over the waves, but he had been alert. He had noticed every move she made, offering the occasional direction only when she hesitated.

Ashley had to wonder if any of that rapport had been real or part of the seduction. Had he done that to lower her guard or had he enjoyed those moments, too? Looking around this nightclub, she sensed the simple joy of a sunny afternoon would have been lost on him.

She glanced up, her heart lurching to a stop as she watched gorgeous couples dance with unbridled enthusiasm on the mezzanine. Their movements were bold and suggestive. Her skin flushed and she shifted uncomfortably. She was already painfully aware of Sebastian and primed for his touch. She didn't need anything else to encourage her imagination.

Her grip tightened on her small clutch purse and she fought the urge to retreat. The club was mysterious and spellbinding. Dangerous. Much like it's owner. If she lowered her guard, the music would pull her in. The atmosphere would seduce her into releasing her inhibitions. That could ruin her. Take her to a point of no return.

Ashley studied the DJ booth and the small VIP areas that circled the dance floor. She recognized a few movie stars and professional athletes lounging on the big white couches with other celebrities and models. All of the party girls were glamorous creatures with wild hair and generous curves.

"And how is your mother doing?"

Ashley turned sharply as she caught the question. A trio of beautiful women were standing in front of Sebastian. She didn't know which one asked the question. They all looked similar with their smooth hair, flawless makeup and colorful dresses that wrapped around them like skimpy bath towels.

"She's recuperating well," Sebastian replied before he smoothly changed the subject. Within moments he had the group of women giggling and fawning all over him.

Ashley wondered if she was the only one who noticed the way his features softened at the mention of his mother. Or the flash of worry in his eyes before he banked it. She wished she hadn't seen it. She didn't want to know anything about him. The less she knew about his private life, the better.

What they shared was a business agreement and she needed to keep an emotional distance. She was having a short-term sexual relationship with Sebastian and she wasn't required to love, respect or even *like* the man.

So what if he had been the most fascinating and exciting man when they first met? Sebastian had been playing a role. Or had he? She thought she had seen glimpses of the real Sebastian during the quieter moments on Inez Key. It was as if the island life had pulled away the harsh mask and revealed his romantic nature.

That was not his true character, she reminded herself fiercely as disappointment rested heavily in her chest.

She wasn't going to be like her mother, who clung to her benefactor's rare thoughtful gestures and created a fairy-tale love story out of it. There was nothing Sebastian could do to make her think he was anything other than a cold-hearted and ruthless womanizer.

"Sebastian!"

Ashley lifted her head when she heard a booming male voice over the music. She saw a large, muscular man approach Sebastian with his arms outstretched. The stranger was about the same age as Sebastian but was built like a giant. The curvy blonde woman at his side looked tiny in comparison.

"Omar," Sebastian greeted. Ashley was startled by Sebastian's wide smile and the way his face lit up before he embraced his friend.

She was more surprised that Sebastian *had* friends. Sebastian could be charming and a scintillating conversationalist, but for some reason, she assumed he was a loner. An outsider.

"And who is this?" Omar asked, gesturing at Ashley while Sebastian gave the other woman a kiss on the cheek.

Ashley felt a twinge of fear. Omar was obviously a good friend. Would Sebastian lie to spare her embarrassment? Why would he do that? Yes, he'd made her a promise, but his friend was going to be more important than a temporary mistress.

She didn't trust Sebastian. She had to get in front of this before he showed just how little power she had in this arrangement. Ashley thrust out her hand to Omar. "I'm Ashley."

Sebastian wrapped a proprietary arm around her waist as his friend shook her hand. "Omar and I grew up in the same neighborhood before he became a football star."

Ashley nodded as she tried to fit this new information in with what she knew about Sebastian. She didn't expect him to value friendships from his old world. She had seen a few self-made men who had discarded old friends while in pursuit of making strategic alliances. Sebastian wasn't as ruthless or driven as she thought.

"And this is my wife, Crystal," Omar introduced the blonde.

"It's a pleasure to meet you," Ashley said as she greeted Omar's wife. The woman was beautiful, but Ashley recognized the subtle signs of multiple cosmetic surgeries. Most of the women she knew while growing up had the same unlined forehead, puffy lips and enhanced breasts.

"I like your dress," Crystal said as the two men started speaking to each other in Spanish.

"Thank you," Ashley said as she pulled at the short hem. She was still uncomfortable in it, but it wasn't as revealing as Crystal's. Most of the women in the club wore dresses that were staying on their bodies with little more than double-sided tape and a prayer.

Crystal gave a cursory glance over her outfit as if she was adding up the price. "Who are you wearing?"

Who? Oh, right. She remembered this part of the social world that she used to belong to. It was all about getting the designer bag or dress that no one else had.

She had once been like that until her world came crashing down. "I forgot to ask about the designer."

Crystal shook her head as if she couldn't believe Ashley would forget such an important detail. "So how did you two meet?"

Ashley glanced at Sebastian, but he was involved in an animated conversation with his friend. She hadn't come up with a cover story but she knew she had to be very careful. It was best to keep it as close to the truth as possible. "I met him a month ago. We immediately hit it off."

"I'm surprised," Crystal said as she studied Ashley, as if she was cataloging all of her flaws and shortcomings. "You're not really his type."

"What is his type?" Ashley asked reluctantly, not entirely sure if she wanted the answer.

Crystal gave a laugh of disbelief. "You don't know?"

She shrugged. "I didn't know who Sebastian truly was until it was too late."

"How is that possible? He's in the news all the time. From the financial page to the gossip column. Have you been living under a rock?"

"More like a deserted island."

Crystal frowned as if she wasn't sure Ashley's comments was a joke or the truth. "Well, I would say Sebastian's women are more…"

"Blonde?" Ashley supplied wearily. "Curvaceous? Vacuous?"

"Accomplished," Crystal corrected her.

Ashley's muscles stiffened. That hurt. She wasn't proud of where she was in her life. She had fallen in status and wealth. Her world had become smaller and she was no match for Sebastian. But she had achieved more than she thought was possible. She had taken care of the families on Inez Key. She maintained her island home with nothing more than ingenuity and hard work. Her most important accomplishment had been becoming a woman who was nothing like her mother.

Ashley was proud that she hadn't broken under the heavy burden placed on her five years ago, but she wasn't going to share that. Not with Crystal or anyone at the nightclub. They would belittle it. Dismiss it. Sneer at her. She remembered this world. All the guests cared about was being noticed. They would never understand that her greatest achievement was creating a peaceful life hidden from the spotlight.

"Accomplished? You mean famous," Ashley corrected.

Crystal shrugged. "They are the best in their fields or famous for their philanthropy and humanitarian efforts. He's dated CEOs and pro athletes. Politicians and princesses."

"I guess he doesn't feel threatened by a woman's achievements," she said with a fixed smile. If this was true, what was he doing with her? She had struggled in school and dropped out of college in her first semester. She had no skills or special talents. No ambitions other than to build the strong and happy family life she'd never had.

"Don't get me wrong," Crystal continued, as if her words hadn't pierced Ashley's thin guard, "he's had his share of supermodels and movie stars. He's just not interested in a woman whose goal is to be a wife or a girlfriend."

What about a mistress? Not that she strived for that job. She had been blackmailed into bed because she had no power or influential friends. Ashley bit the tip of her tongue in case she blurted out her thoughts.

Crystal tilted her head. "I feel like I've seen you before."

Ashley stiffened. She remembered comments like that. It only took a few moments before they connected her with one of her father's scandals. "I haven't been in Miami for years."

"Have you been in the news lately? I have to admit, I'm a bit of a news junkie," Crystal said as she pressed her bejeweled hand over her impressive cleavage. "TV, newspapers, blogs, tabloids. I get my news anywhere and everywhere."

"No, I haven't done anything newsworthy."

"Crystal, they are playing our song," Omar said as he wrapped his large hand over his wife's wrist. "It's time to hit the dance floor."

Sebastian watched Ashley as her frown deepened. She hadn't spoken much. She had stood at his side, but he knew she wasn't paying attention to her surroundings.

Was she was thinking about tonight? How she would lose control in his arms? She had no idea that he also couldn't stop thinking about the magical night that lay ahead. Or that he would make sure she lost control before he did.

He didn't know how much longer his restraint would

last. Having her close to him, touching him, was a test. He was careful not to stroke her skin or allow his hand to linger on the curve of her hip. Once he started, he wouldn't stop.

He tightened his hold on her waist. "Smile, Ashley."

Ashley gave a start and then glared at him. "I am smiling."

"No, you're not." He dipped his head and pressed his mouth against her ear. She shivered with awareness and his body clenched in response. "But I know one way I can put a smile on your face."

She yanked her head back and bared her teeth. "I'm smiling, I'm smiling. See?"

"Can you look less bloodthirsty and more adoring?"

"Why? The only people who looked at me were Omar and Crystal." She tugged at her short hem again. "Don't get me wrong, Cruz. I'm grateful that I'm un-recognizable. I can only assume I look like all your other mistresses."

He'd never had a mistress, but she didn't need to know that. He didn't want her to get any ideas that she was different or special. He'd had many lovers, but he'd never had to pay for the exclusive rights of a woman.

"And how much longer do we have to stay here?" she asked.

"Eager for bed, *mi vida*?" He certainly was. He hadn't felt this desperate since he was a teenager. It was difficult to circulate among the crowd when he wanted to drag Ashley to his bedroom.

She clenched her jaw. "No, I'm tired of acting like I know what's going on. Your guests talk about people

I don't know and places I haven't been. I wasn't aware that you were raising money for a charity until you talked that socialite into giving double. Where is the money going?"

"To my old neighborhood," he said tersely. He briefly closed his eyes as he tried to banish the memory of graffiti-stained walls and the stench of rotted garbage.

She sighed. "Can you be a little more specific?"

"You wouldn't recognize the address. It's the ghetto," he said with a hint of defiance and anger. He should have had the idyllic childhood that Ashley had enjoyed. While her life had been luxurious and carefree, his days had been difficult and unsafe. He'd had to fend for himself and his family and there were many early days when he had failed.

He'd left the ghetto years ago, but he had honed his survival instincts in his old neighborhood. Stay alert, know how to fight and shut down any potential threat before it gained power. Those rules helped him in the streets and in building his empire.

Her eyelashes flickered. "You're right. I don't know where that is, but only because I don't get out much. And the money is for…?"

"The medical clinic," he said slowly as he watched her expression. She showed no pity or fear. No disdain about his background. Just polite interest. Considering her sheltered and privileged life, Sebastian wondered if she understood living in the ghetto was like a prison term.

He grabbed her hand, ignoring how it fit perfectly in his, and led her out of the VIP section. "Let's dance."

He couldn't wait anymore. He needed to feel her curves flush against his body.

Ashley froze and dug her heels in. "I don't dance."

Sebastian stopped and turned around. "You don't dance. You don't drink. You don't party." He didn't believe any of it. He knew many heiresses and socialites. They lived to be seen at the right places with the right people. "What do you do?"

Ashley shrugged and looked away. "Nothing that would interest you."

It shouldn't interest him. He didn't care what women did when they weren't with him. Sebastian didn't want to know about their jobs, hobbies or passions. Yet he was intensely curious about Ashley. "You don't date."

She looked at him cautiously from the corner of her eye. "I never said that."

She didn't have to. "I was your first," he reminded her. And for some reason that was important to him. Was it because she was his first virgin? He didn't like the possessive streak that heated his blood and made him want to keep her close.

"I've been busy," she declared as she tried to slip from his grasp.

"Busy doing what?" he asked as he pulled her closer. How did she fill her day? "You live in a tropical paradise. You don't have a job or obligations. Most people would kill for that kind of life."

"Is that what you think?" She abruptly stopped and pressed her lips together. "Okay, sure. My life is perfect. And that's why I will go to great lengths to keep it."

Sebastian narrowed his eyes as he watched Ashley's guarded expression. What was she hiding? He was about to go in for the kill when he felt a feminine hand on his sleeve.

"Sebastian?"

He recognized the cultured voice before he turned around and saw the cool blonde standing next to him. He dropped his hold on Ashley as he greeted his former flame with a kiss on the cheek. "Hello, Melanie," he said.

"And who is this?" she asked with false brightness.

Sebastian swallowed back a sigh. This always seemed to happen when an ex-lover met the current one. He found the territorial attitude tiresome. "Melanie, this is Ashley Jones. Ashley, this is Dr. Melanie Guerra. She works at the medical clinic."

"And I'm also your predecessor," Melanie said bitterly as she shook Ashley's hand. "I believe you stole him from me."

"Would you like him back?" Ashley asked hopefully.

Melanie was momentarily surprised before she gave a shrill of laughter. Sebastian wrapped his hand around Ashley's arm and shot her a warning look. He wasn't sure what Ashley was going to do next. It was a rare feeling.

"No, thanks," Melanie said as she gave Ashley a thorough look. "Our fling was very brief and he dumped me after he came back from some island off the Florida coast. I got a bouquet of flowers, a bracelet from Tiffany and no explanation. Now I understand why."

Ashley went rigid under Sebastian's grasp. To his surprise, Ashley didn't respond to Melanie's statement.

Her expression was blank, but he sensed her slow burn of anger.

"She's not really an upgrade, is she, Sebastian?" Melanie said. She smiled, knowing she had dropped a bomb, and strolled away with her head held high.

"I apologize for her, Ashley," he said roughly. "Melanie isn't known for her tact or manners."

"I'm sure that wasn't what drew you to her in the first place," Ashley replied, her eyes flashing with anger. "You were dating her when you slept with me. Are you with someone now?"

"I'm with you." He didn't want anyone else. No woman compared to her and he didn't know why.

"Is there anyone else?" she asked insistently as she tugged away from his grasp.

"What if there was?" he asked. She had no claim, no power over him, and he would remind her of that every moment of this agreement. "What would you do about it? What *could* you do about it?"

She thrust her chin out with pride. "I'd leave."

He scoffed at her declaration. "No, you wouldn't." She wouldn't walk away from him. She'd entered this agreement because she wanted to explore the pleasure they shared.

"Inez Key means everything to me, but—"

"It has nothing to do with the island," he said. He wasn't going to let her hide behind that reason. "You got a taste of what it's like between us and you crave it."

She crossed her arms and glared at him. "No, I don't."

"It's okay, *mi vida,*" he said in a confidential tone. "I crave it, too."

"Of course you do. You're insatiable," she argued. "It doesn't matter who you are sleeping with as long as you have a woman in your bed. You're like all men who are ruled by lust and—"

"I'm not an animal," he replied as the anger roughed his voice. "I don't sleep with every woman who flirts with me. I can control my baser instincts. You, I'm not so sure about."

She gasped and took a step back. He saw the surprise and guilt flicker in her dark brown eyes. "What are you talking about?" she asked, her eyes wide.

"You can't wait to go to bed with me," he said with a satisfied smile as the desire swirled inside him. When they finally got to be alone, he knew she was going to go wild. The anticipation kicked harder in his veins.

"I can't wait to get this agreement over with, if that's what you're talking about," she said. "And you didn't answer my question. Are you with another woman right now?"

Ashley was tenacious. "You have no right to ask me that question."

She tossed back her hair and raised an eyebrow. "Because I'm your mistress?"

"Exactly." He splayed his arms out with exasperation. "You really don't have an understanding on how this arrangement works."

"And you don't seem to understand how I function," she retorted. "If you're in a relationship with someone,

I'm going to leave. Play any mind games with me and you will regret it."

He knew she was bluffing, but her voice held a hardened edge. As if she was talking from a past experience. "You'll lose the island."

Ashley leaned forward. "And you won't get another night with me," she said with false sweetness. "Those cravings you have will just get stronger and there will be nothing you can do about it."

Their gazes clashed and held. It was time to teach Ashley a lesson. She suspected just how much he wanted her and was testing her power over him. He wasn't going to let her get away with it.

He heard a feminine squeal of delight next to him. "Sebastian!"

Sebastian reluctantly turned as a woman wrapped her arms around his shoulders and clung to him. He barely recognized the model who had flirted with him a few weeks ago and he couldn't remember her name. She was an exotic creature, but she didn't capture his imagination like Ashley.

"It's been forever since I've seen you," the model declared before she brazenly kissed him on the mouth.

Knowing that Ashley was watching, Sebastian didn't pull away. He wasn't going to allow Ashley to make any demands on him.

Ashley hunched her shoulders as the bile-green jealousy rolled through her. The conflicting emotions were ripping her in shreds. She wanted to pull the other woman away and yet she felt the need to hurt Sebastian the way he was hurting her.

She looked away, unable to see Sebastian in the arms of another woman. She hated this feeling. The ferocity scared her. She didn't know if she could contain it. Ashley jerkily turned away. She refused to live this way for even a moment. She wouldn't tolerate this, even if it meant losing her family home forever.

Ashley pushed her way through the dance floor. She was dragged in and then thrust from side to side as she bumped against dancers. She gritted her teeth and placed a shaky hand on her churning stomach. She had to get out of here.

Forcing herself not to look back, Ashley wasn't even going to think about where she could go next. She didn't have money for a taxi or a hotel room. It didn't matter. She just needed to get away.

She stepped out of the club and took a deep breath, inhaling the hot and humid air. A crowd of people was waiting to get into the club and the flashing lights from the sea of paparazzi cameras blinded her. She felt lightheaded as the emotions battled inside her. Her legs wobbled just as she felt Sebastian's hand wrap around her waist.

"Make me run after you again," he whispered against her ear, "and you will not like the consequences."

"That wasn't my plan," she said quietly. "And you will not like the consequences if you make me angry again."

"I believe the term is jealous," Sebastian said as he escorted her to his black limousine.

"I'm not jealous." Jealousy would mean that her emotions were involved. That it wasn't just sex between them. "I simply don't share."

"Neither do I," he warned.

"Where to, Mr. Cruz?" the chauffeur in the dark suit asked as he opened the door for them to enter the car.

"Home," Sebastian said.

Ashley shook her head. "I'm not getting in there with you." She sensed the chauffeur's surprise, but she didn't look at him. She knew it was a bold statement, when Sebastian could easily pick her up and toss her in the backseat. Considering the dark mood he was in, he might choose the trunk.

His hand flexed on her waist. "I'm not in the mood for a scene."

She felt the attention of the crowd and the flashing lights from the cameras were going fast and furious. She didn't want an audience, but she had to tell Sebastian exactly how she felt. "I told you that I don't play games," she said in a low voice, hoping no one could hear their conversation. "If you are going to spend the next month trying to make me jealous, we are going to end it here."

There was a long beat of tense silence before Sebastian spoke. "You're right. I shouldn't have done that and I'm not proud of it," he said begrudgingly. "I was trying to prove a point and it backfired."

Ashley didn't move or look at him. She knew this was as close as she was going to get to an apology but she needed more. He wasn't going to give it to her. It was best to end this now.

"It won't happen again," he said. "I promise."

She glanced up. She hadn't expected that from Sebastian. She stared into his eyes and saw the sincerity and regret. She didn't know if she should trust it. He could be lying. This could be a game to him. The man was a seducer. A womanizer.

But she wanted to believe him. And that's what scared her. She was willing to believe he would honor his promise when there was no proof that he would.

It was because she wanted to stay, she realized dazedly. Her body yearned for his touch and she knew she would regret it if she left. Sebastian had been correct; this agreement wasn't just about Inez Key. She wanted another chance to experience the exquisite and intense pleasure one more time.

Ashley gave a sharp nod and saw the sexual hunger flare in Sebastian's eyes. Excitement gripped her as she stepped into the limousine. She found it hard to breathe as her heart pounded in her ears. She was ready for whatever the night may bring.

But she would not surrender.

CHAPTER FIVE

ASHLEY SAT NEXT to Sebastian as the limousine slowly drove through the busy streets of Miami. The bright, colorful lights streamed through the dark windows. She stared at the tinted divider that separated them from the driver. She knew the chauffeur couldn't see or hear them. No one could. They were alone in a luxurious cocoon and the wait was agony.

The air crackled between them. The silence clawed at her. This was no longer lust. This was chemistry. Ashley knew Sebastian felt this dark magic between them.

She turned her head and greedily looked at Sebastian. She noticed every harsh angle in his face and the powerful lines of his gray suit. Her heart stopped for one painful moment when she saw his face tighten with desire.

"Ashley," Sebastian said huskily.

She rubbed her bare legs together and shivered when he said her name. It was a plea and a warning. He didn't want to wait any longer. Couldn't.

"Cruz," she said breathlessly. She blushed as she fought the overwhelming need to touch Sebastian and hold on to him. She took a sharp intake of breath and inhaled his clean, masculine scent. She felt the heat invade her body. She wanted to get closer and burrow her face into his skin.

"Call me Sebastian," he reminded her. He spoke softly, but she saw the glint in his eyes. He was the hunter and she was the prey. Ashley went very still, every instinct telling her he was about to pounce.

Instead, he reached for her hand. She felt a tremor in him as he raised her fingers to his mouth. A sense of power flooded her body. She was an average woman, young and with very little experience, but she could make the great Sebastian Cruz tremble.

"I want you right now." Sebastian brushed his mouth against her knuckles and her skin tingled from his touch. "But I know you're not ready. You need something more private before you lose control. Feel safe before you say exactly what you want."

He knew. He knew exactly how she felt. In his bed, she would go wild. It would be just the two of them. No interruption. No confined spaces. But here...in this limousine, on the crowded streets, she would be careful. She would be constantly aware of her surroundings.

Sebastian cupped her jaw with his hands. She felt surprisingly delicate under his large fingers. "You don't need to hold back with me."

"I'm not," she lied. She was cautious with everyone. She usually didn't act unless she knew the outcome. She didn't speak until she considered the consequences.

"I'll take care of you, *mi vida,*" he said in a low, clear voice.

Her heart gave a twist. She wanted to believe him. She wanted to believe that he cared more than this moment, more than the thrill of the hunt. That he cared about her. She would like to think he was the kind of man who viewed sex as something more than a sport.

But that wasn't a fairy tale she could afford to believe. "Do you tell that to all your women?" She tried to say it lightly, but she couldn't hide the cynical edge in her voice.

"I'm telling it to you," he said as he covered her mouth with his.

He kissed her and she immediately melted into him. She had dreamed about this moment every night since he had left Inez Key. She didn't realize how much she had yearned for his touch until now. But it wasn't enough. She needed more.

Sebastian's kiss was slow and tender. That wasn't what she wanted. She wanted to feel the heat and the passion from their first night. Ashley kissed Sebastian with abandon.

She poured everything she felt into the kiss and it was like touching a lit match to a firecracker. Something inside him broke free and Ashley tasted the wildness in his kiss. It excited her and she deepened the kiss, craving more.

"If you don't want this," he said roughly against her lips, "tell me now. This is your last chance to walk away."

Ashley was surprised that Sebastian was giving her an escape. Thanks to their agreement, he no longer had to seduce or romance her. She thought he would grab and take—and some part of her wished he would take the decision away from her. Then she couldn't blame herself for wanting this or enjoying his touch.

She wouldn't completely shatter here, in the back of a limo. No matter what he did, she wouldn't lose her inhibitions. Not when she felt as if they could get caught any moment.

Sebastian, however, didn't seem to be aware of their surroundings. Or he simply didn't care. This time, she could seduce him while he got lost in the sensations.

She was in full control and she was almost dizzy with the power. She knew she could ask for anything and he would give it to her. But she wanted something more. Ashley wanted—needed—Sebastian to surrender. She needed to see that he would do anything, give up control, just for the taste of her.

But how did one seduce a seducer? Could a man like Sebastian be seduced if he knew all the techniques and tricks? She knew she had to be daring. No fear. No hesitation.

Ashley deepened the kiss. She yanked off his tie and hastily unbuttoned his shirt. She stopped midway and flattened her hands against his warm skin. Sebastian moaned against her mouth as her fingertips tugged the dusting of dark curls on his chest.

She wanted more and shoved his jacket off and pulled his shirt down his arms. Tearing her mouth away from his, she kissed a trail down his chin and neck. She felt the choppy beat of his pulse and smiled as it matched hers.

Sebastian bunched her dress in his hands. She couldn't

strip bare for him. Not now. Not here. She stopped him, her hands firm against his. "Not yet," she mumbled against his chest.

"Are you telling me what to do?" he teased.

By the end of the night, he wouldn't notice that he was following her directions. He wouldn't care that she was in charge. Sebastian would only notice how she made him go wild. He would find out just how much power she had over him.

"I'm telling you to be patient," she corrected him as she grabbed his belt and pulled him closer. "Good things happen to those who wait."

"I have never found that to be true," he drawled.

She held his gaze steadily. "Trust me." The agreement didn't make them equals, but she needed his trust as much as she needed his touch.

Ashley was pleased when Sebastian reluctantly pulled his hands away from her dress and continued caressing her legs. Her fingers shook as they skimmed along his waist. Without taking her eyes off him, she slowly unbuckled his belt and pressed her hand against his erection. Her breath fizzled in her lungs when she realized how large and powerful he was. Her memory had not exaggerated.

"I'm not that patient," he warned as she rubbed her palm against him.

"Good to know." Her seduction was working. She had admired the restraint and patience he had displayed on Inez Key. It set him apart from the playboys she knew. Ashley knew he wasn't reckless or impulsive, but now she knew he had a limit.

But knowing his limit didn't make him any less dangerous. And right now *she* was feeling dangerous. She wasn't ready to stop this. She didn't think she could if she wanted to.

Ashley slowly unzipped his trousers and shoved them past his hips and down his legs. His hooded eyes glittered as he was sprawled half-naked before her. She couldn't stop staring at his masculine beauty.

"Now you." His voice was thick with desire as he reached for her.

She held up her hands. "Not yet." Ashley wasn't ready to give up the power that was rolling through her. She wanted to set the pace or he would take over. This would be the most brazen move she'd ever made.

She met his gaze as she wrapped her fingers around his thick penis. Sebastian hissed as she stroked him. She watched with fascination as he responded to her quickening pace. She felt his power underneath her skin and she wanted more of it.

Ashley knelt down in front of Sebastian and took him in her mouth. His deep moan echoed in the interior of the car as he clenched his hands into her hair. She loved the taste of him, loved driving him wild. She enjoyed the bite of pain as he twisted her hair in his fists and she welcomed his thrusts.

Just when she thought she was going to take him over the edge, Sebastian pulled away. She murmured her protest when he lifted her. She wasn't going to let him take this away from her. Not now, not when she found the courage to take charge.

Ashley pushed Sebastian back in the seat and

climbed on top of him. She straddled his hips and met his hot gaze. He didn't look smug or arrogant anymore. He looked wild, almost savage.

She felt beautiful. Confident. She had the man who had invaded her dreams and taken over every waking moment underneath her. He was at her mercy.

"Wait," he said in a growl as he reached for his wallet and retrieved a condom. As he tossed his wallet aside and slid on the condom with quick, efficient moves, Ashley realized he was nowhere near to losing control. He had the sense to remember protection and it had slipped her mind. Was she fooling herself, believing she was in charge?

Ashley placed her palms on his broad shoulders just as he clenched his hands on her hips and guided her down. The heat washed over her. She tossed back her head and moaned as he filled her.

The sensations were almost too intense. She rocked her hips as the pleasure rippled through her. Sebastian leaned forward and captured her breast with his mouth. She begged for more, her words broken and jumbled, as the heat flared deep in her pelvis.

He cupped her bottom and squeezed as he murmured his encouragement in Spanish. She didn't catch all the words. She rocked harder, chasing the pleasure that she didn't quite understand. Couldn't quite curb. But she wasn't scared because she knew Sebastian would take care of her. He wouldn't let her go too close to the fire and burn.

Sebastian grabbed her hips and controlled the rhythm. She could barely catch her breath. She saw the muscle bunching in his clenched jaw. She saw the lust glittering in his dark eyes. He was desperate to hold on to the remnants of his control. He wanted to be the last to let go.

Ashley wasn't going to let that happen. She was in charge. She would make him beg for release and she would decide if she would give it to him.

Sebastian slid his hand to where they were joined. He pressed his fingertip on her clitoris and Ashley stilled. She arched back and groaned as the climax ripped through her body. Her mind went blank as she surrendered to the white heat.

"Sebastian!" His name ripped from her throat. Ashley slumped against him, her muscles weak and pulsating, as she heard his short cry of release.

So this is how it feels to be a rich man's plaything, Ashley thought as she lay in bed hours later, naked and spent. Sebastian was curled next to her, his arm wrapped around her waist. Even in his sleep, he made his claim known.

She was now a mistress. A sigh staggered from Ashley's throat as she looked at the moon through the windows. The one thing she swore she'd never become.

Ashley knew she should be filled with shame and self-hatred. She should feel as if a piece of her soul had been stolen. Instead, she felt protected. Taken care of. Cherished.

Was this how her mother felt when she had been a mistress? Was this why Linda designed her life around

Donald? Why she suddenly came alive every time he stepped into the room?

No, her mother had it much worse, Ashley realized. Linda made the mistake of falling in love with her benefactor.

Ashley turned and looked at Sebastian while he slept. She wouldn't make that mistake. She may desire Sebastian, she may even be infatuated with him, but she would not fall in love. If she did that, she'd never recover.

Hours later Ashley dived into the crystal-blue infinity pool that was on the rooftop of Sebastian's penthouse apartment. The water felt cold and refreshing against her skin. The pool was designed for lazy afternoons under the hot sun, but Ashley swam down the length as hard and as fast as she could.

She loved the water. Whenever she was upset or worried, she found peace watching the waves or swimming laps. But today, nothing could calm her.

Ashley tried to exhaust herself as she thought about what had happened in the limousine. And the wild, fierce sex they'd had when Sebastian carried her to bed. And this morning...

She felt her skin flush. Reaching the edge of the pool, Ashley did a turn and kept swimming. She was becoming a sexual creature and there were no signs that she could pull back. She needed to return to Inez Key before she got to the point of no return.

Ashley paused when she heard a splash. She stopped

swimming and started to tread water. Looking around, she saw Sebastian swimming toward her.

Her stomach tightened as she watched his clean, powerful strokes. She couldn't deny his strength and masculinity. Ashley couldn't stop staring. She was tempted to jump out of the pool before she wrapped her body around his.

Instead, she remained treading water, refusing to give an inch, watching him approach with a mix of dread and excitement. When he surfaced, she immediately thought that he was too close. She saw the amused gleam in his dark eyes.

"I thought you were at work," she said. She had been grateful for the time alone. She was used to solitude and thought the time away from Sebastian would help break this sexual hold he had over her. No such luck. She only had to look at him and she was right back where she started. Her pulse kicked with excitement as she savored the heat sizzling through her veins.

"I came back because I wanted to see you," he replied as his gaze settled on her skimpy bikini top.

Knowing that she had the ability to distract him from work gave her more joy than it should. He probably tossed these meaningless comments to every woman in his sight. "I found this swimsuit in the cabana," she said as she slicked back her wet hair. "There were quite a few of them."

"They are there for guests," he said, moving even closer. "They are not from my ex-lovers, if that's what you're thinking."

Her insecurity was pathetically obvious. She hated

what she was becoming. "If you say so." She realized he had moved in even closer. Ashley couldn't take it anymore and slowly moved to the corner of the pool.

"Where are you going?" With one smooth move, Sebastian cornered her. She felt the edge of the pool against her back and Sebastian's strong legs bumping against hers.

Her hands grazed his defined chest as she tried to tread. "My God, you are insatiable."

Sebastian rested his hands on the pool ledge, trapping her. "You were the one who woke me up this morning. Not that I minded..."

She didn't want to think about that. How she acted before she thought. She couldn't even use the excuse that she had been dreaming. That would make Sebastian more arrogant than he already was.

Ashley treaded hard and fast with her legs but she was getting tangled with Sebastian's. She was very aware of his body. His solid chest and golden-brown skin. The strong column of his throat and his sensual mouth.

Sebastian bent his head and kissed her. She arched her back as his hand slid down the curve of her breast. Ashley moaned as he rubbed his thumb against her hard nipple.

"I have a favor to ask," she said breathlessly.

"I can't wait to hear it." He dipped his head and whispered in her ear, "You don't have to be shy with me."

"I need to visit Inez Key," she said in a rush.

"No." His quiet, authoritative tone bothered her almost as much as his words.

She reared back her head. "What do you mean, no? Aren't you the least bit curious of why I need to go?"

He shrugged. "You have no authority on or responsibility to the island. It's mine."

"Shouldn't I at least get bonus points for asking?" She realized what she'd said and shook her head. Why was she asking for permission? If she wanted to go, she would. Thanks to a very informative phone conversation with Clea, Ashley knew Sebastian had added security on Inez Key. But she knew all the best hiding spots.

Sebastian's mouth formed into a grim line. "Don't even think about it."

"You don't know what I'm thinking," she said as she hoisted herself out of the pool.

"I'll arrest you for trespassing."

All right, he did know what she was thinking. Was her face that expressive? Or was she just predictable? "You'll have to catch me first," Ashley said as she strolled away. She refused to show how much she believed he would follow through on his threat.

"You won't get far," Sebastian said as he watched her from the pool.

Yes, she would. Ashley grabbed her towel and walked as regally as she could back to the penthouse. She was painfully aware of Sebastian watching her. Her skin felt hot and tight and her hips seemed fuller as they swayed with each step. She waited until she was out of sight before she wrapped her towel tightly around her body and ran down the steps as if she was being pursued.

CHAPTER SIX

A WEEK LATER, Ashley strolled from one guest to another at Sebastian's glamorous cocktail party. They were on the rooftop of the Cruz hotel in Jamaica. The breeze carried the scent of the ocean and the tropical-fruit appetizers the waiters offered.

Ashley wasn't sure why she'd quietly assumed the role as hostess. She could say that she was bored or that she rebelled from Sebastian's attempts to keep her away from the party. The truth was she wanted to show him that she was more than just decoration. She had some skills that weren't marketable but still valued in certain circles.

If Sebastian suspected that she would sabotage him, she hoped he realized he had no cause for concern. She knew how to act, what to provide and how to dress. Ashley's skin was bare of jewels, but her simple white dress made her stand out from the dark suits and frilly and colorful dresses.

More important, she made sure everyone felt comfortable and welcome. She knew this party changed the way Sebastian saw her. She saw the admiration and pride in his eyes.

"I thought you didn't like parties," Sebastian said as she made her way to him.

"When did I say that?" Ashley asked. She tilted her head as she tried to remember. "No, I said I didn't party. No late nights. No club hopping. Nothing like that."

Sebastian didn't try to hide his skepticism. "Not even in college? You had only been there for one semester."

"And you think I got kicked out of school?" What made him think that? She had done some dumb things when she was a teenager, but she wasn't a troublemaker. "No, I was struggling at school. I always had trouble with my grades. I dropped out after my parents died. I didn't see the point in staying."

She'd never wanted to go to school. Her parents forced her for their selfish reasons, but she had to admit that college offered her a respite from the tension at home.

"If you were such a poor student, how did you get into college?"

"My father pulled some strings and gave a big donation to the school," she admitted with the twist of her lips.

Sebastian raised his eyebrows. "Must have been nice to have rich parents," he said coldly. "They opened a lot of doors and gave you many opportunities."

"That wasn't why they did it," Ashley said as she tightly gripped the stem of her champagne flute tightly. "They wanted me out of the way. But I know what you're saying. I was given a lot. I had the resources to make something of myself. And where did I wind up? Broke, homeless and a rich man's sexual plaything."

Sebastian's eyes narrowed. "You twist my words."

She knew what he was saying. Really saying. That he could have conquered the world by now with that kind of financial support. "You may have had to crawl out of the ghetto but I'm sure someone helped you," Ashley said roughly. "Teachers, neighbors, relatives. Maybe the kindness of strangers."

"Then you would be wrong."

Ashley felt her heart pinch. Sebastian had had a grueling and lonely journey to the top. She couldn't imagine the strength and sacrifice it took to get to where he was. The more she learned about him, the more she admired and respected him. It made it difficult keeping her distance from Sebastian.

"And what about now?" she asked, deciding to take a different tack. "I'm sure that you would do exactly what my father did. If one of your sisters needed to get into a school, get a job or even a place to live, you would throw all of your money and influence to get it for her."

Something flickered in his eyes, but his face showed no expression. She watched Sebastian take a healthy gulp of champagne. "Yes, I would."

"And she would accept that help," Ashley predicted. "That doesn't make her spoiled."

"Of course not. I expect my sisters to come to me whenever they need help."

"But I'm a spoiled brat because I lived off my parents' money?" she asked. "You think I haven't worked a day in my life. That I'm just hanging around, working on my tan, until I land a rich husband."

"Are you trying to tell me that you aren't an heiress who enjoyed the good life," he asked.

"I once enjoyed being a socialite when I didn't have to worry about money or the future," she admitted. The amount of money she had wasted in those years still made her sick to her stomach. "But that disappeared the moment my mother pulled a gun on my father. My friends used their connection with me to sell the most salacious and untrue stories about my family. My father's money was gone and I inherited a mess. It has been a struggle for five years to keep what I had left."

"You could have gotten a job," he drawled.

She should have expected that she would receive no sympathy from Sebastian. "I couldn't leave Inez Key. Everyone thinks I've been living in paradise. No one wants to look past the island and notice that I've been living hand to mouth for years. Any money I had went to taxes or to the islanders who relied on me."

"If your home has been such a headache, why are you so desperate to go back?"

Ashley pressed her lips together. She had been trying to prove a point, but Sebastian only noticed the one thing she had been trying to hide. "You wouldn't understand," she muttered.

"Try me."

She looked away as she struggled with the urge to tell him everything. Why did she start this? Why was it so important for Sebastian to see her as something more than a pampered heiress? His opinion shouldn't matter so much.

"Inez Key is the only place where I feel safe." She

knew she'd told him that before but she wasn't willing to explain why. That she wasn't destructive or cruel when she was on the island. That she didn't have the ability to destroy people's lives and families if she disconnected with the world.

Sebastian's face darkened. "Do you feel unsafe now?" he asked hoarsely as his eyes glittered. "Here, with me?"

She didn't feel unsafe. She was scared. Worried of how addicted she was to Sebastian's touch. Afraid of the emotions whipping through her. Frightened of what she was becoming. A sexual woman. Emotional. Falling in love.

"You've enjoyed yourself the past couple of weeks," Sebastian stated. "And why not? Private planes, designer clothes and state-of-the-art spa services. We've been to the Bahamas, the Cayman Islands and now Jamaica. You've stayed at the most luxurious resorts that would put Inez Key to shame."

And he thought it was all because of the money he spent? Let him think that. If he knew she enjoyed his company, his attention and his touch, it would give him far too much power over her.

She had been amazed that Sebastian had taken time out of his busy schedule to show her the sights. He had taken her everyplace she had underlined in her travel guide, but he had also taken her to his favorite spots. She had cherished those moments as they offered her a deeper understanding about Sebastian Cruz.

"Is that why you dragged me along on your business

trip?" she asked coolly. "So I would see what the world outside Inez Key had to offer?"

"You don't seem to mind. Your every need has been catered to."

She had made the most of what he had to offer. It reminded her of what she used to take for granted. No wonder he thought she was a spoiled socialite. Little did he know that she'd had a makeover and subjected herself to the most painful spa services for his approval.

It was only later when she realized that she was following her mother's pattern. She could tell herself that she chose bright colors because it reflected her mood. That the mane of hair was easier to deal with and the short dresses were needed in the tropical heat. It wasn't true. It was all to please Sebastian.

Not that it mattered. He didn't seem to notice her haircut or her smooth skin. The lingerie she wore was for his pleasure as much as it was for hers, but he managed to get it off her before he gave it an appreciative look.

"And your needs are catered to especially in bed," he murmured.

Ashley blushed. She wasn't quiet about what she wanted in bed. The nights they shared had been mindblowing. She had never expected that it would become more magical. She clung to Sebastian all night, eager and greedy for his touch.

"I have no complaints," she replied stiffly. She wondered how amazing it would be if Sebastian had any emotion behind every caress and kiss. Her knees weakened at the thought.

"Nor do I," he whispered as he leaned forward. "You are a very generous lover."

Her face felt incredibly hot from his compliment and the noise from the cocktail party seemed louder. She never refused Sebastian and it had nothing to do with her role as his mistress. She was always ready for him at the most inconvenient times. Even now her breasts felt heavy, her nipples tight, as her skin tingled for his caress.

But she didn't have that power over him. Sebastian wanted her but only on his terms. His timetable.

"If you will excuse me," she said as she forced herself to step away. They were not equals and they never would be. "I'm not being a good hostess. I should circulate with your guests."

Impatience gleamed in his eyes. "Running away again, *mi vida?*"

She didn't answer and she walked away. Ashley felt his gaze on her. She knew she couldn't hide from Sebastian Cruz. He saw everything.

Sebastian fought the impulse to grab Ashley and pull her closer. To find a dark corner and reacquaint himself with her scent and taste. Instead, he restrained himself as he watched the haughty tilt of her head as she glided through the crowd.

Ashley may think she was an island girl but she was meant for the glittery world of high society. She had nothing in common with the guests, but she worked the room with effortless grace. The businessmen were dazzled by her friendly smile and their wives gravitated to her sunny personality.

"Who's the girl?"

Sebastian's hand tightened on his champagne glass when he heard the gravelly voice. He turned to see Oscar Salazar, one of his fiercest rivals.

"Salazar." He gave the man a brief handshake. "I didn't see you come in."

"Your attention was elsewhere. I can see why." A streak of red highlighted Salazar's blunt cheekbones as he stared at Ashley. "You always had good taste in property."

"Don't let her hear you say that," Sebastian warned. Not that he was going to allow Salazar that close to Ashley. He was territorial, but he knew better than to show it around Salazar. The man liked to compete. The more Sebastian wanted something, the more determined Salazar was in wrestling it free from him.

The possessive feeling was so strong that Sebastian almost vibrated with it. He couldn't remember the last time he'd felt this way. The women in his bed had always been interchangeable and temporary. If any of them tried to make him jealous, Sebastian didn't hesitate to cut them loose. He never second-guessed or regretted his actions. He knew he could replace his lover with someone who was willing to follow his rules.

But it was different with Ashley. The woman didn't understand the word *obey*. She was exasperating, difficult and never boring. Why did he allow her to act that way? Was it because she was his mistress? Was it because he was her first? Or did it have anything to do with sex?

He wanted to share his day with Ashley. It didn't matter if they were exploring the waterfalls of Jamaica, falling asleep in each other's arms or enjoying a cup of coffee in a busy sidewalk café. He yearned for her. So much that he found himself calling her when he was at the office just to hear her voice.

"Who did you say she was?" Salazar asked as his gaze narrowed on Ashley's slender body.

Sebastian gritted his teeth. He had to play this carefully. "Her name is Ashley."

"She looks familiar."

He doubted Salazar socialized with Donald Jones. He was too young and had only made his fortune a few years ago. "You probably saw her in Miami," Sebastian said. He tossed back the champagne but didn't taste it.

Salazar dragged his gaze away from Ashley. "She's different from your other women."

And that automatically made her an intriguing challenge. The ultimate prize. The man understood what made Sebastian tick. "I don't have a type."

Salazar smiled. "This one looks more innocent. Untamed."

Sebastian curled his hand into a fist. "You don't know anything about her." *And you're not going to.*

"But I know you," Salazar said. "You'll tire of her very soon."

No, he wouldn't. He wanted more than a month with Ashley. Craved for something more. "And you'll swoop in and catch her?"

Salazar shrugged. "I wouldn't normally take your hand-me-downs..."

Sebastian wanted to punch his rival. No one talked about Ashley that way. *No one*. Instead, Sebastian stepped in front of Salazar and stared him down. "Stay away from Ashley," he said in growl.

Salazar looked very pleased that he'd riled him. "Worried that you don't have that much of a hold on her?" he taunted.

He *was* worried about that. The only way he got Ashley back in his bed was through blackmail. He wasn't proud of it. She wanted him but not enough to make the first move or accept his original offer.

"She's mine," Sebastian warned in a low voice. Most people would scatter from the threat in his tone, but Oscar Salazar's smile only widened.

"Not for long." Salazar returned his gaze on Ashley. "I could steal her away if I wanted to."

"No, you couldn't." Sebastian's heart pounded against his ribs as the need to defend his territory coursed through his veins. "You have nothing she wants. No extra incentive."

"Incentive?" Salazar's eyes glowed as he pondered the new information. "She has a price?"

"One you couldn't afford," Sebastian snapped.

"I'm sure I could get a bargain," he murmured.

"You've been warned, Salazar." He didn't like this side of him, but he couldn't stop it. He was ready to unleash all of his power and weapons on Salazar. If he had fangs, he would have bared them. "Go anywhere near her and you're dead."

"Understood." Salazar took a sip of his champagne and casually strolled away. Sebastian wanted to follow, but one of his Jamaican business partners chose that moment to approach.

Sebastian ruthlessly pushed aside any thought of Salazar. His blood roared in his ears and his hands shook with the need to land his fist into Salazar's jaw. He had nothing to worry about. He didn't trust the man, but he knew Ashley wouldn't be interested in Salazar's questionable charms.

Yet he kept an eye on Ashley during the cocktail party. Sebastian was always aware of where she stood. Even when he was in a deep conversation with his executive assistant, Sebastian heard Ashley's earthy laugh from across the room.

He wasn't sure what made him look up a few minutes later and actively seek her out in the party. His mother would have called it a premonition. Sebastian knew it had more to do with the fact that he was attuned to her.

He found her next to the door on the rooftop. The ocean breeze tugged at her white dress and her long brown hair. His voice trailed off as he noticed that Ashley stood ramrod straight. Her tension was palpable. Her polite smile was slipping and he saw the caution in her eyes.

It took him a moment to realize Oscar Salazar had his back to the party and was talking to her. A red haze filled Sebastian's vision as the anger flared inside him. He strode through the crowd, determined to keep Salazar away. He didn't notice the guests as he bumped shoulders and cut through small groups. A few guests saw the murderous rage in his expression and immediately got out of the line of fire.

He didn't know what Salazar was saying to Ashley, but it didn't matter. Ashley was *his*. Body and soul.

He saw Ashley's face whiten. The color leached from her sun-kissed skin as if she was going to be sick. She turned her head and Sebastian knew she was searching for him. Their gazes clashed. Her brown eyes shimmered with hurt. Pain. Betrayal.

Ashley flinched and jerked her attention back at Salazar. Ashley's mouth parted in shock a moment before she slung her champagne in Salazar's face. She dropped the flute on the ground and marched away before Salazar could react.

Sebastian wanted to chase after his woman. Comfort and protect her. But first he had to take care of Salazar. He turned and glared at Salazar's proud face. That man needed to learn that if he slighted Ashley, the wrath of hell was upon him.

Ashley brushed away the last tear as she gathered up her T-shirt and jeans and dumped them in the smallest suitcase she could find. Her hands shook as she zipped up the case. How could Sebastian do this to her?

Why was she so surprised? She meant nothing to him. She was just the mistress. A very temporary one. Hadn't she seen enough on how men treated their mistresses? Why did she think Sebastian would have been any different?

Ashley jumped when she heard the door of their bedroom swing open and bang against the wall. She refused to look at Sebastian. She knew he filled the doorway with his hands clutching the frame. He was barring her exit and she felt his anger pouring through him.

"What happened between you and Salazar?" he asked with lethal softness.

"Bastard," she muttered as she lifted the suitcase off the bed.

"He's been called much worse, but what did he say to you?" Sebastian asked impatiently. "I couldn't get a word out of him."

"No, you are the bastard," Ashley said as she thrust a finger at him. He looked like a dark angel. He had discarded his jacket and tie, but that didn't diminish his raw masculinity. There was something angry and volatile about him. Dangerous and powerful. "I trusted you. I thought we had an agreement."

"We do," he said as he stepped into the room. "You are my mistress for a month."

"Which you told Oscar Salazar." Her voice shook as she remembered the way that man had looked at her. As if he wanted to sample the goods before he made a bid.

"I didn't say you were my mistress." Sebastian's voice was as stinging as the flick of a whip. "I warned him off."

Then how did Oscar know? She didn't act like a mistress. She didn't dress like one, either. The only way he would have known was if Sebastian said something. "You broke your promise and you broke our agreement. I'm leaving."

"Like hell you are." Sebastian rushed forward. He

grabbed the case and tossed it on the floor. "You're not going anywhere until I say so."

She'd never seen Sebastian like this. His movements were rough and clumsy. His sophisticated veneer was slipping. It was as if he was upset that she was leaving. But that was ridiculous. Sebastian Cruz didn't care enough to panic.

Ashley thrust out her chin and met his gaze. "You can't tell me what to do. I'm not your mistress anymore."

A muscle bunched in his jaw. "Then you will never see Inez Key again."

"Fine," she retorted. She pressed her lips together as the horror snaked through her. She wanted to take those words back.

His eyes widened with surprise. He was silent for a moment, his breathing hard, as a strange urgency pulsed around them. "Fine? You are ready to walk away from the home you fought to hold on to?" he asked as he stepped closer. "The home you took care of and made sacrifices for? The one where you lowered yourself and slept with me so you could stay on the island?"

"This isn't about Inez Key. It's about you," she replied. "You don't care about what is important to me and you certainly don't care about my feelings."

He rocked back on his feet as he looked at her with such intensity that she felt she was going to burst. "How are you going to get back?" he asked. "You have no money."

Ashley closed her eyes as the pain ricocheted inside her. He didn't deny her accusation. He didn't care about her feelings. "I don't know," she whispered. "I'll hock this dress. I'll swim all the way home. Maybe I'll trade my body for favors. That's what everyone thinks I do anyway."

He snatched her wrist. She felt the tremor in his hand. "Don't even joke about it."

"Why not, Sebastian?" She tried to yank her arm away from him but he tightened his hold. "You made me a joke. You made me a mistress."

"And you accepted," he said. "You had other choices. You could have walked away but you didn't."

"You dangled my home as bait," she cried out.

"Like you said, Inez Key had nothing to do with it," he reminded her coldly. "You wanted to be with me but you were afraid to go after it. And now you're upset because you like being a mistress."

Her gasp echoed in the room as she went still. "No, I don't," she said in a scandalized whisper. "Take that back."

"I stand corrected." Sebastian let go of her wrist. "You like being *my* mistress."

She wanted to slap him. Push him away. But it was true. She liked sharing his bed and enjoyed seeing the desire in his eyes when she walked into the room. She treasured their private moments and was proud to be at his side in public. She ached for his touch and she was greedy for his undivided attention. She would accept whatever role he chose for her if it meant she could share a part of his life.

And he knew it. He knew that she would take the

measly crumbs that he offered. He knew he had that much power over her. "Get out of my way."

He crossed his arms and braced his feet. Any concern he felt a moment ago had disappeared. Sebastian was calm and in charge again. "Make me."

And now he was going to prove how she had no power over him. Ashley curled her hands into fists and dug her nails into her palms as she tried to hold back the rioting emotions. "I'm warning you, Sebastian. I'm about to lose control."

Sebastian wasn't worried. "I can handle it. Give me your best shot."

"Oh, my God." She thrust her hands in her wavy hair. "You *want* me out of control? Are you insane?"

"I want you to stop hiding. Stop running away."

That was all she wanted to do. Run. Hide. Regain control of her temper before she broke into a million pieces. "You have no say in what I do."

"I'm sorry about Salazar," he said grimly. "I warned him off but I revealed more than I should."

"Did you tell him I had a price?" she asked wildly. "That he could talk me down from my asking price because I was damaged goods? That I should accept his offer because you would kick me out of your bed soon?"

"I'm going to kill him," Sebastian said through clenched teeth.

"You'll have to get in line," she declared as she strode to the door. "I knew I shouldn't have trusted you, Sebastian. I respected your wishes but you didn't respect mine."

Sebastian was at the threshold before she could get there and slammed the door shut. "You are not leaving."

She reached for the doorknob. "I see no reason to stay."

"What about this?" he asked as his hands covered her shoulders.

It was the only warning she had before Sebastian turned her around and covered his mouth with hers. His kiss crushed her lips. Ashley pressed her hands against his chest, determined to push him away. He ignored her attempts as he settled her against the door.

Excitement burned through her. She shouldn't want this. Shouldn't encourage it. Yet she did want it, had waited for this moment. Ashley wanted to feel his hands shake with barely restrained emotion. She wanted the last of his control to snap and show exactly what was going through his mind.

Sebastian shoved her lace panties down her hips before he lifted her up. She wrapped her legs around his waist when he yanked her dress up her thighs. As he deepened the kiss, Ashley tore at his shirt, wanting to strip it from his body.

Sebastian groaned against her swollen lips. "Tell me you don't want this."

She wished she could. She wished she didn't come alive under his touch or that she was always waiting, yearning, for his kiss. Ashley bucked her hips, silently demanding more.

Sebastian whispered something in Spanish as he shucked his trousers off. She couldn't tell if it was a prayer or a curse. She clung to his shoulders, yielding to his fierce kisses, unable to deny him anything. Desire and anger coiled deep in her belly, hot and tight. It was a potent combination. A dangerous mix.

Ashley tensed when she felt the crown of his penis pressing against her. She hated herself for wanting this. Hated that she made it so easy for him. She tilted her hips as he drove into her welcoming heat.

She turned her head and moaned as he filled her. Ashley held on to Sebastian tightly as he thrust deep. His rhythm was ferocious and wild. She couldn't get enough. The sounds of their uneven breaths and the creaking door were harsh to her ears. The scent of hot, aroused male electrified the air. She clutched to his fine cotton shirt as she rocked her hips against him.

"Walk away and you'll never feel like this again," he declared gruffly as he burrowed his head against the base of her throat. His teeth nipped her skin as if he was leaving his brand.

Ashley knew he was right. Only Sebastian had this power over her. The sexual hunger clawed inside her. It was unbearable, pressing against her, demanding to break free.

"You will always be mine."

Ashley's sobs caught in her throat as the violent climax ripped through her. She sagged against him as he continued to thrust. She couldn't fight the truth anymore. When he discarded her and moved on to another woman, she would still long for his touch.

She surrendered to the knowledge that she would always be his.

* * *

Sebastian woke up to the sound of his cell phone. He reached for the bedside table, his hands fumbling, but he couldn't find it. Blinking his eyes open, he immediately noticed two things: it was daylight and Ashley wasn't curled against him.

The silence in the hotel suite indicated that he was alone. Ashley was probably sulking. Angry that he'd proved his claim on her once and for all. He rolled out of bed and stalked naked to where he had shed his clothes the night before. He grabbed his cell phone from the pile of clothes and saw that his assistant was calling him.

"What is it?" he asked abruptly.

"I just found out that Ashley left Jamaica."

He hunched his shoulders as the news slammed against him. He'd made his claim and it had scared her off. She'd waited until he'd fallen asleep before she'd sneaked out of his bed. "How?" His voice was raspy and low.

"I heard a rumor," his assistant said nervously. "I don't have verification at the moment."

Sebastian closed his eyes as he got a bad feeling. He knew Ashley was angry with him, but she wouldn't betray him. Not like this. "Where is she?"

"With Oscar Salazar," his assistant whispered. "She's on his private plane back to Miami."

CHAPTER SEVEN

THE SUN STREAKED across the morning sky as Ashley saw a glimpse of Inez Key. The wind was cold and all she wore was a T-shirt, jeans and boat shoes. She didn't care. Her bottom lip quivered and the emotions crashed through her. She was home.

Home. She studied the antebellum mansion as she considered the word. It didn't feel like home anymore. Was it because it was time for her to move on or because she knew Sebastian owned it?

She knew she didn't belong here. Not because she was trespassing, and not because she'd ruined any chance of staying on as caretaker. There was no way Sebastian would allow her back now that she'd broken her promise.

But she didn't use Inez Key as just a home. It had been her hideaway. She had stayed here after her parents' murder-suicide because it was a safe place. She could evade prying eyes and evade living life.

Ashley knew she had been a lot like her mother and that scared her. She had an all-or-nothing attitude like Linda Valdez. Passionate about her causes, extremely loyal to her friends, and a hot temper that took years for her to control. Ashley knew how to hold on to a grudge and her friend's enemies were her enemies. It was only a matter of time before she followed in her mother's footsteps. To love completely and unwisely. To destroy and self-destruct.

Ashley thought she had escaped from that future when she hid away on Inez Key. It was paradise and yet solitary confinement. Her wild temper disappeared and her passions quieted. She was still fiercely loyal, but she wasn't consumed by love. She thought she'd broken the cycle and become the woman she wanted to be. But one night with Sebastian and Ashley realized she had only been fooling herself.

Ashley closed her eyes as the bleakness swirled inside her. She didn't want to think about that. Not now. First, she needed to step onto the beach and let the sand trickle between her toes. Then she needed to lie down and let the quiet wash over her. She would watch the view of the Atlantic Ocean and find the familiar landmarks. It could take hours before she felt whole and strong again. Days. But it would happen and then she would figure out what to do next.

Ashley struggled with exhaustion as she stepped out of the water taxi and paid the captain. It took effort to smile and give her thanks. She walked along the wooden dock, but she didn't feel like her old self. Everything felt new and different. She was different and she would never recapture the old Ashley Jones again.

She heard the boat speed away, but she didn't look back. The changes on the island had her attention. She noticed the repairs on the house and the fresh coat of paint. The wild vegetation was tamed. Inez Key was slowly returning to its former glory.

Unlike her. She was breaking down. Breaking apart. Even though she was finally back on Inez Key, she had to keep it together. She sensed that this island could no longer contain her.

Ashley walked to the front door of the main house and tried to open it. To her surprise, it was locked. She frowned and jiggled the doorknob. That was odd. Inez Key was a quiet and safe place with just a few homes and buildings. No one locked their doors. She couldn't remember the last time she'd used the key or where she had left it.

"Ashley, is that you?" Clea asked as she walked from around the house. She gave a squeal and ran to Ashley, welcoming her with a big hug. "What are you doing back?"

"I was going to get my things and leave," Ashley said as she gestured to the door. "But the main house is locked."

"I know, isn't that strange? Who locks their doors?" Clea asked. She planted her fists on her hips and shook her head. "I haven't been in there since they started renovating."

"A lot has changed." She gave a nod at the tropical flowers and plants near the white columns. At first glance the landscaping looked natural, but she knew it had been meticulously planned. How did Sebastian manage all of the changes when the island had only recently been in possession? "I wasn't gone that long."

"The new owners have been busy," Clea said as she guided Ashley away from the front door. "And there are a lot of new security features. It won't be long before the guards find you."

"They haven't torn anything down," Ashley murmured as she gave the main house one last look.

"It's more like adding and updating," Clea said. "I'm glad to see they have respect for the history of the island, but I think the way of life on Inez Key won't be the same."

The gentle rhythm of the island life would change if there were bodyguards and security features. "Have you heard from the new owners?"

"We received letters from Cruz Conglomerate," the housekeeper said as they walked along a dusty path. "I thought it was going to be an eviction letter like yours, but they promised nothing has changed for us."

At least Sebastian didn't break that promise. She had suspected it was a threat to keep her in line, but she couldn't be sure. "What else did the letter say? Anything about turning the island into a resort or a hotel?" Or worse, razing it and destroying it inch by inch. Ashley shuddered at the thought.

She didn't think Sebastian would do that, but she obviously couldn't predict his every move. She suspected he wanted Inez Key for an exclusive getaway. He had undoubtedly posed as a paying guest to see if buying the island was worth his time.

And after spending a few weeks with the man, she noticed his interests focused on travel and leisure. She had stayed at some extraordinary hotels and exclusive resorts. All of them were part of his global business. Her home was definitely going to be part of that. The crowning jewel of his empire.

"No, I haven't heard what they plan to do with Inez Key," Clea said without a hint of concern. "We're expecting to see the new owner next month after the renovations are complete."

"You've already met the new owner," Ashley said bitterly. She hated how her voice caught in her throat. "You know him as Sebastian Esteban."

Clea halted and stared at Ashley. "That man took your island from you? The man you fell in love with?"

She shifted her lower jaw as she fought back the spurt of anger. "I did not fall in love with Sebastian Cruz."

"Honey, I saw how you were with him," Clea argued with a knowing smile. "You were in full bloom every time he looked at you."

Ashley closed her eyes as her skin heated. She couldn't be in love with Sebastian. She had more pride than that! The man had kicked her out of her home, made her his mistress and ruined her life.

But she couldn't hide from the truth anymore. She had been enthralled by Sebastian Cruz. It was more than the sizzling sexual hunger. Ashley didn't want to admire his hard-earned accomplishments or value his opinions. She tried not to help him or smile at his humor. She hid the longing for Sebastian's company and the way her heart leaped every time he entered the room.

None of it worked. No matter how hard she had tried, she had fallen for a man who had no respect for her. He only wanted her for sex.

It was official. She had inherited the same self-destructive tendencies as her mother.

"I'll get over it," Ashley muttered.

Clea patted Ashley's arm. "What are you going to do to get the island back?"

The question caught her by surprise. She had given up that plan weeks ago. "Nothing. I've done everything in my power." And discovered she was no match for Sebastian. "The most I could get out of Sebastian was the caretaker position, but I managed to mess that up."

"Caretaker? The owner of the island becoming a hired hand? I don't think so! Just as well you didn't get that job," Clea said with the cluck of her tongue. "You'll think of something. In the meantime, stay with Louis and me. Just for a couple of days."

The offer was tempting but Ashley hesitated. "I don't want to get you in trouble. He made it very clear I had to have his permission to stay on Inez Key. If he knew I was staying with you…"

Clea curled her arm around Ashley's. "Don't worry about him," she said in a conspiring tone. "He'll never know you were here."

Where was she? Icy anger swirled inside Sebastian as he strode across the beach on Inez Key the next evening. He curled his shoulders as the cold ocean breeze pulled at his jeans and hoodie. He didn't notice the colorful birds flitting from one flower to the next. The sound of rolling waves faded in the background. There was only one thing on his mind: finding Ashley.

He couldn't believe she would have pulled a stunt

like that. It was bad enough she had left his bed in the middle of the night, but to escape with Salazar? His anger flared white-hot. She was going to pay for that.

Didn't she know that he would follow her? Or was that the plan all along? Was Ashley determined to prove her sexual power? Her hold on him had been obvious on their last night in Jamaica.

He had chased her back to Miami and invaded Salazar's kingdom only to discover she wasn't there. Salazar had had great fun at his expense. Sebastian's anger had been a slow burn until the other man made one too many innuendos. The guy was no longer laughing and Sebastian hoped he'd left a scar. It would be a daily reminder to Salazar not to come near his woman.

Sebastian hated the fact that he had been compelled to chase Ashley. She made this decision. She chose to give up her last chance to stay on this island.

But he couldn't turn back now. When he first heard she'd left, he had been numb. It took a split second for the fury to crack through his frozen shell and drive him into action. The need to follow had been instinctive and strong. He seized upon it, not caring what his colleagues thought.

He had no strategy. He wasn't looking ahead. That wasn't how he operated, but Sebastian was working on pure rage. His anger had festered as he spent hours searching for her in Miami.

Sebastian let the anger swell inside him, ready to burst through his skin. Ashley Jones was a spoiled princess and he was going to teach her a lesson.

But where was she?

She had to be here. Sebastian ignored the panic squeezing his chest. If she wasn't in Inez Key, he had no idea where she would be.

Sebastian stopped and looked around. The island was quiet and sleepy, but it did nothing to cool his temper. He heard the rustle of palm trees and the incessant chirping of birds. Inez Key looked idyllic, but that was an illusion. Who knew such a small piece of land would cause him so much grief?

He looked over his shoulder and glared at the black roof of the main house. It may have been a dream home for some, but an image of the antebellum mansion had been in his nightmares since his childhood. He didn't see the gracious beauty but instead the cold emptiness. It was better suited as a museum than a family home. If he could, he would burn it down.

He would destroy the whole island if he had the chance, Sebastian thought grimly. He wanted to erase this particular ocean view. Get rid of the briny scent that still triggered bad memories. Wipe away the sunset that had been the backdrop of the night he had lost his innocent childhood.

No, he would keep the sunsets, Sebastian decided as he glanced at the cloudless sky. For the past month he had associated Ashley with sunsets. The orange-and-pink streaks were no longer ominous but instead held promise. He remembered every detail of the night Ashley had sat next to him on the veranda as they had watched the sun set.

Her warmth and soft femininity had cast a spell on him. He'd had trouble following their desultory conversation; Sebastian knew Ashley had been nervous that evening. It was as if she had known they would wind up in bed together. He had felt as if he could hear her heart pound against her ribs as a flush had crept into her cheeks.

Excitement had coiled around his chest when the stars blanketed the night sky. The thick and heavy air between them had crackled. She had teased his senses and a dangerous thrill had zipped through his veins.

Wild sensations had sparked inside him, pressing just under his skin when he had kissed her. That moment had been magical. Sebastian had meant to gently explore her lips, but the passion between them had exploded into something hot and urgent.

He'd keep the sunset, Sebastian decided. And the island, too. It was, after all, where he had first met Ashley. He didn't want to erase those moments he had shared with her, so the house must stay as well. It wouldn't be that great a hardship. Since he had stayed in the mansion with Ashley, Inez Key no longer had power over him.

He walked swiftly along the beach, following a bend that led to a cove. Sebastian paused and looked around, wondering where Ashley would hide. It would be somewhere that made her feel safe and protected. That could be anywhere on this small island. He had heard so many stories about Inez Key. As a kid who was raised on the dangerous streets, he had thought they were fairy tales.

His heart clenched when he saw Ashley curled in a tight ball next to a large piece of driftwood. Her damp jeans were caked with sand and she was almost dwarfed in her sweatshirt. Her hair was pulled up into a messy ponytail, but what he noticed the most was her tear-streaked face.

The anger slowly weakened as he stared at her. Ashley was suffering and he was to blame. When he first started this journey, he wanted to take away her safe little world. He got what he wanted and now he felt like a monster.

Sebastian had to fix this and get Ashley back. He needed her. Somehow he had been aware of it from the moment they met. He always knew this woman would be his redemption and his downfall. She would tame him and at the same time drive him wild.

He knew the moment Ashley saw him. Her body went rigid and she jumped up. Even from a distance, he could see Ashley was considering her options to pounce or make a run for it.

She wouldn't get far, he decided. He was ready to chase her, the thrill of the hunt in his blood. Ashley must have known that hiding was futile. Her shoulders sagged in defeat but she held her ground.

"What are you doing here?" she asked as she looked around the cove. "I didn't hear your speedboat."

"Which is why I took a different boat," he said as he walked toward her. He had known the only way he would find her was using the element of surprise. "Don't worry. I dismissed the security, so you don't have to hide."

Her eyes narrowed with suspicion and that annoyed him. Did she really think he'd lie about that? About everything? Did she think he lied with such fluency that he was incapable of speaking the truth?

"How'd you know I would be here?" she asked. "Did your security guards call you?"

"No, you managed to get past them. But then, you know all of the hiding places. It had been a lucky guess," he said as he stood in front of her. He wanted to grab her arms and shake her for making him worry. For making him chase her from country to country. And yet, he wanted to hold her close and not let her go.

"And it just happened to be your first guess?" Ashley clenched her jaw. "Am I that predictable?"

"It wasn't my first guess. I hunted down Salazar." He shoved his fists in the pockets of his hoodie. "He enjoyed that."

If he had hoped Ashley would show a hint of discomfort or remorse, he would have been greatly disappointed. "Good," she taunted. "Why should I be the only one embarrassed?"

"I'm very territorial and you know that," His low voice held an edge. "That's why you went off with him. It was a bad move."

"Is that what you think?" She raised her eyebrows with disbelief. "I don't base every decision on you. I had to get out of there and I took the first flight I could find. Salazar offered. Normally I would keep my distance from someone like him, but I was desperate."

"How desperate?" Sebastian asked. Ashley wasn't the kind of woman who would sleep with any interested man, but he knew how she responded when she was desperate and cornered. "How did you repay him for the favor?"

"What are you suggesting?" she snapped. "Do you think that I would sleep with him? Of course you do. After all, I'm sleeping with you for a chance to stay on this island."

"I don't think you had sex with Salazar," Sebastian said. Ashley was wild and sexy with him and *only* him. He had seen how she recoiled from Salazar's touch. She may have played on Salazar's twisted desires to get a ride home, but Ashley wouldn't touch another man. "I do, however, believe you went with him to hurt me."

She covered her face with her hands. "You're right. I did. I'm ashamed of what I did. I swore I would never act that way, and what happened? I allowed my emotions to take over. Oh, God. I'm just like her."

Her? Sebastian frowned. Who was Ashley comparing herself to?

"It doesn't matter how much I tried to…" She took a deep breath and lowered her hands. She squared back her shoulders and struggled to meet his gaze. "I'm sorry, Sebastian. I felt I had to leave but I didn't need to go with Salazar. There were other options. Better options. I can tell myself that I was desperate to get back here, but the truth is I wanted to swing back at you."

She'd succeeded. It was as if Ashley knew exactly where to strike. He must have lowered his guard or revealed how he felt when they were in bed. He was addicted to Ashley. He couldn't stop thinking about her, couldn't refrain from touching her. She was his weakness and she exploited it. Just as he knew Inez Key was her weak spot.

"Why is this place so important to you?" he asked. "Why are you willing to fight for just a piece of it?" He watched as she swallowed roughly. For a moment he didn't think she would answer.

"It's where I grew up," she said unevenly, as if she had to pull out the words. "It was a special place for me and my mother."

"That's it?" He sensed there was more. This island had a pull on Ashley that she couldn't break. What would cause that?

"No, it's more than that," she admitted. "Whenever the tabloids found out about my dad, my mom would bring me here. There was no TV, no internet and no paparazzi. We could stay here and heal."

"You're lucky you had this place," he said harshly. "I would have killed for this island when I was a child."

"I'm not so sure." She held her arms close to her body. "Sometimes I felt like my mom used this place to hide from reality. The lack of distractions should have given her some clarity. Instead, it became a cocoon that blocked out all the facts. It gave my dad a chance to hide the worst of his sins. He would beg for forgiveness, swear it was all lies, and we would head back to the mainland until the cycle started all over again."

Inez Key wasn't quite the haven he thought it was for Ashley. It was connected to good memories and bad. It was part of her childhood and the loss of her innocence.

"And there is no need to escort me off the premises.

I'm going." Ashley announced. She bent down to brush the sand off her jeans.

"You'll leave with me and return to Miami."

"Our deal is off," she said as she straightened and dusted off her hands. "From the moment you broke your promise."

"Which one?" he muttered.

She narrowed her eyes. "I'm confused. What are you saying?"

"About last night…" He took a deep breath. This was going to be difficult but it couldn't be ignored. "We didn't use protection."

Ashley went pale as she stared at him. She didn't say a word. He wasn't sure how she was going to handle the news. From the way she interacted with the young islanders, he knew she liked children. Sebastian could easily imagine that she would be a fierce and protective mother. But that didn't mean she liked the idea of having *his* children.

"I apologize," Sebastian said as he raked his hand through his hair. "I don't know what happened. I always remember to use protection."

His claim seemed to wake her up. "Of course you do," she said in a withering tone.

"I'm serious." He watched her stalk past him. "I don't take any unnecessary risks."

"I'm sure you believe that," she said over her shoulder.

"But you don't." He had been careful about protection every time. It hadn't been easy. He almost forgot on more than one occasion, so caught up in the moment that nothing else seemed to matter. It had never been like that with any other woman.

But why didn't she take his word for it? Why was she that determined to see the worst in him? "It doesn't matter what you believe," he decided. "It was my responsibility and I failed you."

Ashley turned around. "Sebastian, I don't need you to take care of me. I can take care of myself. I've been doing that since I can remember."

"There's no chance of you being on the Pill?" he asked hopefully.

Ashley glared at him. "What do you think? You were my first." Her voice rose with every word. "I never had a need until I met you and I wasn't planning a repeat performance."

"We've been together for weeks and you still haven't considered protecting yourself from pregnancy. Why is that? You know, there are a lot of women who live well because they had a rich man's baby." He didn't think Ashley was one of those women, but he also knew his judgment was impaired when she was around.

Ashley rubbed her hands over her face and blew out an exasperated puff of air. "I have no interest in getting pregnant, no interest in having your baby, and I no longer have any interest in this conversation."

He ignored the sting from her words. "You have to admit that this is a concern." He needed to be more careful next time. He needed her to trust him so that there *would* be a next time.

She looked away and stared at the water. As if seeing the ocean would calm her and give her a sense of peace. "Is this how you respond whenever you have a pregnancy scare?" she asked.

He clenched his teeth. "I've never had one because I always use protection."

She pressed her lips together. "I find it hard to believe that a man with your—" she paused "—legendary sex life has not had any paternity suits, payoffs or baby drama."

"Believe it," he said in a growl.

"Every time I think I'm wrong about you, I am slapped with the truth. You remind me a lot of my father. He was something of a playboy." Her lip curled in a sneer when she said the word. "He was supposed to be a tennis legend, but he's known more for his sexual escapades and paternity suits."

"I am not a playboy," he insisted. He hated the word. It diminished everything that he had achieved. "And I'm nothing like your father."

"Right. Right." She raised her hand to stop him. "Because you're smarter. You use protection. Sometimes."

"Ashley, I give you my word." He grabbed her arm and held her still, but she looked the other way. "If you become pregnant, I will take care of you and the baby."

She whipped her head around and stared at him. "You would? Why?"

He was offended by her surprise. "You and the child would be my responsibility."

She tilted her head as she studied him with open suspicion. "What do you mean by taking care?"

"I would take care of you financially and I would be involved in the child's life." He would want a lot more, but he would wait to discuss it if there was a child. There was no reason to tell Ashley every sacrifice he would make for his family.

"Really?" She pulled away from his grasp. "You wouldn't ask for a termination or take legal action against me and swear I'm lying about the paternity?"

"What kind of man do you think I am? No, don't answer that." He was already feeling volatile and he knew he wasn't going to like what Ashley had to say.

"It's what my father did," she said with disgust. "It's what most men do."

"You don't know much about men. Or me." Sebastian took a step forward until they were almost touching. He noticed Ashley didn't back down. Most people would. "I take care of my family. That would include you and the baby."

She frowned and studied his face. "This doesn't make any sense."

"Let me make it clear to you," he said through gritted teeth. "If you are pregnant with my child, I will give him my last name. I will let everyone know that he is mine and that I take care of what is mine. I will protect and provide for him."

She stared at him as if in a daze.

"And if I need to marry his mother," he forced the words out, "I will do so."

Her mouth dropped open. "Are you serious?"

"But don't take that as a marriage proposal," he warned. "The only reason I would marry any woman is if she was carrying my child."

CHAPTER EIGHT

"COME ON, ASHLEY, we'll discuss this later. We need to leave," Sebastian said as he stuffed his hands in his hoodie pocket. He was never comfortable with the topic of marriage. The idea of sacrificing his freedom usually made him break into a cold sweat. Right now, he felt the hope and longing swirl inside him as he imagined Ashley's belly swollen with his child.

"Already?" she said with a sigh.

He heard the longing in her voice and hated how it affected him. Sebastian wanted to make her happy. He wanted to give her everything she wanted and be the reason there was a smile on her face. He glanced at his watch. "You can show me around the island before we leave."

Ashley's eyes lit up, but she gave him a suspicious look. "Really?" she asked uncertainly. As if she knew he was trying to make up for the argument they'd just had.

"Show me everything about Inez Key," he said. He knew a lot about this island, but he wanted to see it through her eyes.

Ashley grabbed his hand. "First, I'll show where the best place is to scuba dive. Oh, and surf. Did I tell you about the time I got stung by an eagle ray? It was an extremely painful experience, but not as much as when I broke my ankle when I fell from climbing a palm tree. I'll have to show you which ones are best to climb."

"I can't wait," Sebastian said with a small smile. He was curious to know what Ashley was like as a child and wanted to hear every story and anecdote.

They had explored the island for an hour, hand in hand, as Ashley pointed out her favorite spots. Some were connected to happy memories while others were breathtaking views.

"Do you know how the island got the name Inez Key?" Sebastian asked as he walked beside Ashley.

"It's called a key because it's a small island on coral," she explained.

"And Inez?"

"I assume the first settler on this island named it after a loved one." She stared at the main house as she slowed her pace. Her tour was almost done and then she would have to leave Inez Key.

"Assume?" he asked sharply.

"Okay, I'm not an expert on everything about this island. You should ask Clea. Her family has been on this island for generations," Ashley said as her smile dipped. Once she thought her descendants would live here for generations. She had imagined having a big family and the island being their safe haven. "Now that you mention it, I'm surprised my father didn't change the name. Make it Jones Key or something like that. Are you going to change the name?"

"Never."

His gruff response surprised her. "Why not? The name doesn't have any meaning to you."

Sebastian's hand flexed against hers. "How long have you lived here?" he asked.

"This wasn't our primary residence," she replied as she focused her attention on the main house. "I spent my summers on this island. My mother brought me here when she needed a getaway."

"So it wasn't used very often," he murmured. "It was almost forgotten."

"I'm sure it wasn't always like that. It's been in my family's care since before I was born. My father got it—"

"Got it?"

Ashley bit her tongue. Funny how he caught her choice of words. The man noticed everything. She had to be more careful. "My father's story about this island changed constantly," she admitted.

"What did you hear?" he asked as he slipped his hand away from hers.

She felt the tension emanating from Sebastian and hesitated. She didn't like revealing her family history. It offered people a chance to question her heritage and judge her. "It's difficult to extract the truth from the legend. Some say my father won it in a poker game. Others suggested it was a gift from a woman. I once heard a politician bought it for him in exchange for silence."

"What do you think happened?"

I think he stole it. She didn't know how her father had got the island, but she knew what kind of man he was. He cheated on and off the tennis court, but that wasn't her only clue. She remembered the sly look in his eyes when he spoke of Inez Key. She knew something bad happened and she had been too hesitant to dig deeper.

Ashley forced herself to give a casual shrug as she marched to the main house. "It's hard to say."

"I'm sure you have a theory." Sebastian watched her carefully.

"Not really," she said in a rush as they stood by the columns in the back of the main house. "Well, that's it of Inez Key."

"Don't you have more stories to tell?"

Ashley returned his smile. She had talked endlessly about her childhood adventures on Inez Key, but Sebastian hadn't seemed bored. He had been genuinely interested. "That's for another day," she promised.

"Thank you for sharing your stories," he said gently. "And for showing me your island."

She suddenly felt shy, as if she had shared a secret part of her. Ashley felt the warmth rush through her. "What's your favorite part of Inez Key?"

"The cove," he said. "It's the perfect hideout. No wonder the sea turtles nest there."

Ashley frowned. She didn't remember telling him about the nests that are laid during springtime. "How did you know we have sea turtles?"

Sebastian paused. "Uh, I think Clea said something about it."

"We usually get the loggerhead turtle to nest on our

island. Two months later, all of these hatchlings find their way to the water. It's an amazing sight."

"I'm sure it is," he murmured.

"I think the sea turtles pick this place because there aren't that many predators. The island is a good hide-away for people, too. The paparazzi never bothers us." Not even when her father was caught up in one scandal after another. She didn't know if it was because it was hard to find the remote island or because no journal-ist found it worthwhile to follow the betrayed mother and child.

Sebastian saw the shadows in her eyes. Was she re-calling a bad memory from her childhood or was she reluctant to leave. "It's time to go, *mi vida*."

Ashley bit her lip. "Can't we stay just for the night?"

"Impossible." He didn't want Ashley to stay any lon-ger. It was Cruz property now and the last thing he needed was the previous owner hanging around caus-ing trouble. "I need to be at my mother's tomorrow morning."

"I'm sure she didn't extend the invitation to me," she said. "I can stay here until you return."

Sebastian hated that idea. He didn't want to spend another night away from Ashley. He hadn't been able to sleep and he ached all night to have her in his arms. The idea of finding a replacement hadn't even occurred to him. He only wanted Ashley.

"You forget our agreement," he said silkily. "You are supposed to be with me every day for a month. You missed a few days when you skipped out on me in Ja-maica. That's going to cost you."

"Cost me?" Her face paled as she looked around her beloved Inez Key. "What do you mean?"

"You have not been with me for a consecutive thirty days," he explained. He smiled as he realized this gave him the chance to keep Ashley at his side for a little bit longer. "I'm adding those missing days at the end of your month."

Her lips parted in surprise. "That was not agreed upon."

He didn't care. He had torn through Miami looking for this woman and he wasn't ready to give her up. "Would you rather we start over and make this day one?"

Something hot and wild flared in her eyes. Ashley dipped her head as she dug her foot in the sand. "I thought you'd be bored staying with one woman for a month."

Sebastian frowned. That had been true, but not with Ashley. Now he was trying to find ways to keep her in his bed.

"Wait a second." Ashley lifted her head and stared at him with something close to horror. "Does this mean I'm meeting your mother? No. No way."

"I don't have much of a choice. Anyway, she's expecting you."

Ashley closed her eyes and slowly shook her head. "Do you usually introduce your mistress to your mother?" she asked huskily.

"I've never had a mistress," he admitted.

Ashley opened her eyes and stared at him.

Sebastian scowled. He hadn't planned to tell her that,

but for some reason it was suddenly important for her to understand that he wasn't that kind of man. Yet now he felt exposed under her gaze. As if he'd revealed too much of himself. "Don't think that makes you special."

Ashley glared at him. "Why should I? You had pushed me in a corner so efficiently. It was only natural to assume you blackmailed women in your bed on a regular basis."

He stepped closer. "You wanted to be in my bed," he declared. "I only had to give you an extra incentive."

She gave a haughty tilt to her chin. "Think that if it makes you feel better."

He curled a finger under her chin and brushed his thumb against her wide pink mouth. "You will need to curb your tongue before you meet my family," he warned her softly.

She tried to nip his thumb with her teeth, but he had anticipated that response. He removed his hand before she could catch him.

"I can't make any promises," she said and paused. "Did you say I'm meeting your family? I thought it was just your mother."

"My sisters will be there. That means their husbands, fiancés and children will also be around."

"Why? Is there a special occasion?"

"No, my family has these get-togethers all the time." And he worked hard to be there for his family. He didn't just write a check for his relatives—he was present for every important moment of their lives.

"Is there anything I should know about your family?" she asked.

"Do not introduce yourself as my mistress," he ordered.

She clucked her tongue. "Do you think I wear that label as a badge of honor?"

"You made it clear in Jamaica that you are my woman." He reached for her hand and laced his fingers with hers. "I didn't have to make a claim. You wore that status with pride."

"That was before you introduced me as your mistress," she said as the anger tightened her soft features. "I thought we actually made a good team until you warned off Salazar. Then you had to mark your territory. So how am I supposed to define this relationship?"

He was not going to introduce Ashley as his lover or girlfriend. That gave her privileges she didn't deserve. The reason he made Ashley his mistress was to knock down the status she never worked hard to earn. "You won't need to."

"Are you serious?" She tugged at his hand but he didn't let go. "Didn't you tell me you had sisters?"

"Yes, four of them."

"And how often have you brought a woman home to meet the family?" she asked brightly.

He exhaled sharply. "I haven't."

"You are in for an inquisition." Ashley smiled broadly as she imagined the treatment he would receive.

Or she was dreaming up ways to make his life miserable. He could send Ashley back to his penthouse apartment while he went to visit his family, but he didn't like that idea. He wanted Ashley there with him, but it was a risk. "Cause any trouble and you will regret it."

She flattened her hand against her chest. "Me? I won't have to say a word. I'll just cling to your arm and bat my lashes like a good little mistress."

"Ashley," he warned.

"At least tell me why we need to visit your family. Isn't your mother recuperating?"

He gave her an assessing glance. "How do you know about that?"

"What? Was it a secret? You said something about it at the opening of your club. I've often heard you talk to your mother on the phone."

Sebastian's eyes narrowed. "I didn't realize you knew Spanish." How much had she heard in his conversations? Did she also catch the endearments he whispered when they were in bed? He had to be more careful.

"I'm not fluent," she said. "I don't know anything about your mother's condition."

"She's recovering from heart surgery," he explained. "There had been a point when we didn't think she was going to make it. My mother made a dying request and we called the priest."

Ashley squeezed his hand in silent sympathy. "I won't do anything to upset her. I promise."

"Thank you." Sebastian realized how he was gripping her hand as if it was a lifeline. He reluctantly let go. "I don't want you to discuss our relationship with anyone in my family. Don't mention Inez Key. In fact, don't give any personal information."

"Should I pick an assumed name?" she asked wryly.

"Ashley Jones should be fine." It was a common name. His family wouldn't make the connection.

"Okay," she said with a shrug. "If that's what you want."

Her quick agreement made him suspicious. "What are you up to?"

"Nothing. I'll just keep the conversation all about you." She rubbed her hands with exaggerated glee. "I can't wait to learn all your secrets."

Dread seized his lungs until he remembered that there was an unspoken agreement with his family on some topics that were forbidden to discuss. "Good luck with that," he said with icy calm. "I don't have any."

Ashley made a face. "Everyone has secrets."

"You don't anymore," he said. "I uncovered them all when I took you to bed."

"You are so hung up on being my first," she muttered. Ashley looked flustered and shy. "If I knew that my virginity would have been so important to you..."

Sebastian stepped in front of her, blocking her from turning away. "What would you have done?" he asked. She had not been above using her virginity with Raymond Casillas to get what she wanted. "Keep away from me until I begged? Waited for a wedding ring on your finger?"

"No!" she said, staring at him with wide eyes. "I would have told you."

Would it have been that simple? Could their first night have been about two people giving in to a fiery attraction? "Why didn't you?"

"I didn't want you to know how inexperienced I was," she confessed as a ruddy color streaked her high cheekbones. "It would have given you the upper hand."

He always had the advantage even with the most experienced women. Although there had been some nights with Ashley when he wasn't sure who was seducing whom. She had gradually begun to realize the depths of his excitement when she made the first move. She was beginning to tap into the sexual power she held over him. He should hide his responses, or at least take over when she became too daring, but he didn't want to.

"You had nothing to worry about, *mi vida*. You're a very sensual woman." He noticed how his compliment horrified her. "I'm surprised you abstained for as long as you did. Why did you wait?"

"Lack of opportunity?" she hazarded a guess.

She was not telling him the truth. Not the whole truth. "That's not it at all," he said gently. "Men would subject themselves to Herculean tasks if it meant a chance for one night with you."

"Every man but you," she muttered. "You just had to snap your fingers and I was there."

"Why did you wait?" he repeated. What he really wanted to ask was, *Why did you choose me?*

"If you saw the house I was raised in you would understand." She crossed her arms and looked at the ocean, unable to meet his eyes. "My mother was a mistress. A sexual plaything for my father. My father was a womanizer. He was worse than his friends. The things I saw…heard. I didn't want to be a part of that."

Sebastian felt a sharp arrow of guilt. Shame. He was beginning to think he had made a mistake when he'd claimed Ashley as his mistress. He thought she didn't like the drop in status. Instead, he had made her the one thing she swore she would never be.

"And yet you slept with me." It didn't add up. Did she sleep with him so she could stop Raymond Casillas from calling in her debt? "According to you, I'm just like your father."

"I thought you were," she said quietly before she walked away. "I'm not so sure anymore."

The next evening, Ashley was on a luxurious patio that overlooked a private beach as she watched the sunset with Sebastian's mother. A group of children were playing in the sand. Music drifted from the open windows of the Cruz mansion and Ashley heard Sebastian's sisters bicker while they prepared the dinner table.

"Why is this the first I've heard of you?" Patricia Cruz asked as she intently studied Ashley.

Ashley hid her smile. She had a feeling that Sebastian took from his mother's side in temperament. "I don't know what to tell you, Mrs. Cruz. Perhaps you should ask Sebastian."

She gave a throaty chuckle. "He's not very forthcoming."

Neither was his mother. The older woman wasn't a tiny and weathered woman who favored housedresses and heavy shawls. This woman was tall and regal. Her elegant gray shift dress highlighted her short silver hair and tanned skin.

Patricia Esteban Cruz was polite but wary. She had expected Sebastian's family and home to be just as guarded. When Ashley had seen the iron gates open to

the Cruz's beachfront mansion, panic had curled around
her chest. She had looked out the window and saw a forest of palm trees flanking the long driveway.

Ashley had tried not to gasp when she spotted the
villa at the end of the winding lane. The home was
unlike anything she had seen. She had expected the
Cruz mansion to be a dramatic and modern house. A
fortress. But this was gracious and traditional with its
terra-cotta rooftops and soft white exterior. Ashley was
used to high society but this was another level. It was a
reminder of Sebastian's power and influence.

"His sisters, however, are very warm and open,"
Ashley said. They had easily welcomed her. Sebastian's
siblings were boisterous and inquisitive, but they had
made Ashley feel as if she belonged.

And they had no reservations talking about Sebastian. At first it had been a trickle of information and
it quickly became a flood of memories. The anecdotes
and stories all described Sebastian as curious, volatile
and too smart for his own good. He had been a lot of
trouble, but everyone spoke about him with pride, love
and exasperation.

"Yes, they didn't have as hard of a time as Sebastian," she said with a heavy sigh. "When my husband
died, Sebastian became the head of the family. He was
only a boy. Not even fifteen."

There was a fine tremor in the woman's fingers and
Ashley noticed the gray pallor underneath the woman's
skin. It was clear Patricia was still fragile from her surgery. "Sebastian doesn't talk about that time in his life.
Or his father."

"He lives with the constant reminder," the older woman said. "He looks just like his father. My husband was very much a traditional man. Proud and artistic."

"Your husband was an artist?" Ashley asked.

She nodded. "He was a painter. Watercolors. He wasn't famous, but he was very respected in the art world. Some of his landscapes can be found here in my home." Patricia's eyes grew sad. "He stopped painting when we moved to the ghetto. He was working two jobs and feeding a growing family."

This was why Sebastian scoffed at the way she made a living. She may repair and maintain Inez Key, but she never had to do hard labor. She didn't know the strain of having a family depend on her.

"Which of your children inherited your husband's artistic talent?" From what she could tell, all of the Cruz daughters were brilliant, successful and creative.

"Mmm, that would be Sebastian."

"Really?" Sebastian thrived in the cutthroat business world. She hadn't seen any indication that he had an artistic side.

"You should have seen the work he did at school," Patricia said with a hint of pride. "His teachers encouraged him to find classes outside of school. If only we had the money. But Sebastian told he me didn't have the inclination to pursue it."

Ashley imagined Sebastian saying that with a dismissive wave of his hand. But she wondered if Sebastian didn't choose the arts because he had to be sensible. He would have known it would have been a financial strain for the family and he acted disinterested to protect his mother's feelings.

"Well, if there's one thing I've noticed about Sebastian," Ashley said brightly, "he can do anything he puts his mind to. If he had wanted to be an artist, he would have been."

"And what is it that you do, Ashley?" Sebastian's mother asked. "You're twenty-three? I'm sure you have found your passion by now."

Ashley knew it was another attempt to learn about her past. She wasn't willing to share, and not just because of Sebastian's request. It was unlikely that she would meet Patricia Esteban Cruz again, but she didn't want to be judged by her parentage.

"I'm still trying to figure that out," Ashley carefully replied. "What did you want to be when you were twenty-three?"

"Home." Patricia had a faraway look in her eyes. "I wanted to be home, safe and sound with my babies while my husband was happily painting pictures of sunsets and nighthawks."

Nighthawks? Ashley frowned. Those birds were indigenous to the keys. She hadn't realized they were up here on the mainland.

Ashley turned sharply when she heard the piercing squeal of a child's laughter. She saw Sebastian, sexy and casual in a T-shirt and jeans, at the edge of the beach. The water lapped at his bare feet as he held one of his nephews in his strong hands.

"More, Tio Sebastian! More!" the little boy shrieked as Sebastian tossed him high in the air before catching him. One of his nieces clung to Sebastian's legs with her thumb firmly planted in her mouth. Ashley noticed the toddler had attached herself to her tio Sebastian the moment they had arrived.

"Ah, my grandchildren are precious to me, but they wear me out," Patricia confessed as she watched the trio on the beach. "Sebastian is so patient with them. Gives each of his nieces and nephews extra attention. If only he was so patient with his sisters."

"He's very good with children." She remembered how gentle he had been with Clea's granddaughters on Inez Key. Ashley had been concerned Sebastian would be like most of her paying guests who didn't want to hear or see children on the island. She recalled how he had found them playing on the beach one day and when he had approached them, Ashley's first thought had been to protect them. Ashley thought the girls would have been scared or intimidated by Sebastian. But he had surprised her when he had crouched down in front of the curious children and got down to their level.

A smile tugged on Ashley's mouth as she remembered that hot and humid morning. The scene had been so incongruous with Sebastian's dark head next to Lizet and Matil, who wore silly hats to protect them from the sun. He had given the girls his full attention, speaking in a low voice as he praised their efforts in building a sand castle.

The children immediately adored him, with Lizet shyly offering her battered pink bucket while Matil danced excitedly around them. Ashley had quietly watched as Sebastian had played with the children.

She had been amazed by the gentleness and patience he had displayed.

"He would make a good father," Patricia declared.

Ashley wanted to reject that idea. Sebastian was a playboy. A good father would be sweet and tender. A family man. He wouldn't be someone like her father who would destroy a family in his pursuit to have sex with many women.

But Sebastian wasn't like Donald Jones, Ashley realized with a start. Sebastian cared about his family. Family was his haven, not his burden. He honored his commitments and was willing to put his family's needs before his. And he would protect his loved ones instead of overpowering them.

Ashley knew she would be included if she was carrying his baby. She closed her eyes and imagined Sebastian holding her close as his fingers splayed against her swollen stomach. His touch would be gentle and possessive. He would not allow anything to happen to them as a family. As a couple.

"Do you think differently?" Patricia asked, jarring Ashley from her musings. "Do you think Sebastian would make a bad father?"

"He would be the father any child would hope for," Ashley said slowly as she thought about how Sebastian embodied everything she hoped for in a man, a husband, and yet he was also everything she feared. "But I don't think he has the inclination to become one."

"That's what I'm worried about. Sebastian had to look after his sisters at such a young age. He may not want to do it again. But that man should have a wife. Children of his own."

"Carry on the Cruz name?" Ashley added as she absently rubbed her flat stomach. She wanted Sebastian's child. More than one. She wanted to create a large family filled with sons and daughters that had the same dark hair, stubbornness and strength as their father. Most of all, she wanted to see those children bring out Sebastian's fierce paternal side.

"Exactly." Patricia smacked her armrest with her hand like a judge would bang a gavel. "He should marry."

Don't look at me. Ashley gritted her teeth before the words tumbled off her tongue. Men didn't marry their mistresses. She had it on good authority. Her mother had tried every trick for twenty years to make Donald her husband.

Donald and Linda may have shared a past and a child, but they never shared a family name. Donald had given his surname to Ashley, but she had never understood why. Why had she been considered good enough for the Jones name and not her mother?

But Sebastian was different, Ashley thought as she watched him set down his nephew and hoist his small niece into his arms. He would marry her if she was carrying his child. She longed for a traditional family but not like this. If she was pregnant with his baby, she would have some tough decisions to make. She had been tolerated in her father's home, part of a package deal. Ashley wasn't going to go through that again.

* * *

Later that night, Sebastian stepped out of the bathroom and into the guest bedroom. The steam from his shower curled around him as he slung a towel low around his waist. His heart beat against his ribs as he anticipated having Ashley all to himself.

He stopped in the middle of the room when he noticed Ashley wasn't in the large bed waiting for him. She wasn't in the sitting area or at the desk. Sebastian turned and saw Ashley standing at the long open window, the gauzy curtains billowing against her.

Desire slammed through him as he noticed how the silk slip skimmed against her gentle curves. The dark pink accentuated her sun-kissed skin and the short hem barely reached her thighs. He was tempted to pull the delicate shoulder straps until they broke and watch the silk tumble to the floor.

It took him a moment to notice that Ashley was waving at someone outside. "Who are you waving to?" he asked gruffly. As much as he enjoyed the sight, he was prepared to cloak her with something heavy. He should be the only one who saw her like this.

"Your sister Ana Sofia and her husband," she responded without looking at him. "Apparently, they take a moonlight stroll along the beach every night."

"I'm sure that's real romantic when it's pouring down rain." He refused to hear the catch in her throat. "You and Ana Sofia were thick as thieves tonight."

She turned away from the window and he saw her smile. "She wanted to tell me all of the mean things you did to her while you were growing up. I have to say, none of it surprised me."

"I had to be strict with her," he said as he approached her. "I'm her big brother and our father had died."

She nodded. "I understand, but you're lucky you had your sisters."

"It didn't feel so lucky," he muttered.

"Well, I was an only child. I would have loved a sister or two."

He noticed Ashley had watched how his family interacted with a mix of amusement and bewilderment. "They were in full force today. You didn't find them overwhelming?"

"It took some time to get used to it," she admitted. "Your sisters got a little vocal at the dinner table."

"That?" He rested his hand against the wall and he leaned into her. "That was nothing."

She gave him a look of disbelief. "You were arguing about a vase that broke almost twenty years ago."

"I was blamed for that because I was supposed to be looking after my sisters." He hadn't been surprised that Ashley didn't side with him during the argument. Did she still see him as the opposition? The enemy? "Ana Sofia was the one who actually broke it."

"Twenty years ago," she reminded him. "You can certainly hold a grudge."

"You have no idea." He gritted his teeth and took a step back. Sebastian wasn't going to reveal just how much a grudge motivated him. Dominated his thoughts. "I'm sure this happened in your house, too. Who were you able to blame when you broke something? The family dog?"

"It never happened, but I don't think my parents would have noticed. Quite a few breakables were thrown against the wall during an argument in my house," she said matter-of-factly. "And I can't count how much damage occurred during one of my father's famous house parties."

Was this why Ashley didn't drink or party? Why she didn't enjoy dancing and preferred her solitude? He wouldn't blame her. Ashley's home life was more of a war zone than a wonderland. "How did you escape? Did you spend a lot of time at a friend's house?"

"Not really. Once their parents found out that I was a mistress's love child I wasn't invited over. Something about being a bad influence." She grimaced as if she had tasted something unpleasant. "Love child. It sounds like I was born out of love, but I wasn't. I hate that label."

And she hated the label of mistress. He didn't know that it would hurt her so much. He didn't know she had been an outcast because of the stigma. He had made a power play without considering Ashley's past. But how could he fix it now?

Ashley raked her hand over her hair and rolled back her shoulders. Sebastian had seen that movement before. He knew this was a sign that she was finished with the conversation.

"I've been meaning to ask," she said as she walked away. "Did your father paint this watercolor?"

His gaze flew to the framed picture that hung on the wall. He'd forgotten about the picture of the sunset. "Yes."

"It's very good," she said as she walked to the bedside table and gave the picture a closer look. "It reminds me a lot of the sunsets I see on Inez Key. It kind of makes me homesick."

The longing in her quiet tone scored at him. He wasn't going to fall for this guilt trip. He had to be strict with Ashley or she would soon discover that he was willing to give her almost anything she wanted.

"Is this another attempt to go back to the island?" he asked as he followed her.

She jerked her head in surprise and turned to face him. "No. I'm a mistress for a month and I have to be at your beck and call for a little over two weeks. I can wait."

The pang of guilt intensified. He should honor his word and allow her to become the caretaker for Inez Key. But he didn't want her on the island. She didn't belong there. Ashley Jones belonged in his bed and at his side.

"What if we renegotiated?" he asked.

Ashley frowned and she studied his expression, as if trying to determine whether he was reneging. "What are you talking about?"

"The time frame remains the same but we drop the mistress part," he suggested as he reached for her. "Forget the rules I set in place."

She pressed her hand against his bare chest. Her fingers curled in the damp mat of his dark hair. "What's the catch?"

"No catch," he said as he moved closer.

"Is this renegotiation because you don't want your mistress in your family home," she asked, "or because you can't tolerate the idea that your mistress might be having your baby?"

"You know, I should have walked away when you broke your promise," he said. "You were supposed to be available to me at all times, but you went off with Salazar for a few days."

Ashley gave an exasperated sigh. "You make that sound much more scandalous that it was. And may I remind you that you broke both of my rules?"

"Do you want to drop the mistress label or not?" he asked roughly as he gathered her tightly until her body was flush with his.

She swiped her tongue along her bottom lip. "What would I be known as instead?" she whispered.

"Mine."

He saw the flare of heat in her dark eyes. She dipped her head and looked away. "I'm serious."

"As Ashley." *My Ashley. My woman. Mi vida. Mine.* And the next man who tried to take her away from him would deeply regret it.

Ashley frowned and lifted her head to meet his gaze. "Do you still expect total obedience?"

"If it hasn't happened yet, it's not going to," he said as he pressed his mouth against the fluttering pulse point at the base of her throat. He liked how trusting and wild she was in his arms. That was all he needed.

"I can make my own decisions on which events to attend with you?" Ashley asked, her breath hitching as he shoved the delicate strap down her shoulder. "And what I'm going to wear?"

Sebastian cupped her breast with his large hand. He

felt her tight nipple against his palm. "Yes," he said almost in a daze.

"And tonight I could get my own bedroom?"

He stilled as something close to fear forked through him. "No," he said with a growl. He should have known that if he gave her an inch, she'd take a mile. The only hold he had left on Ashley was the sexual chemistry they shared. She couldn't hide her emotions, her needs, when they were in bed. He wasn't going to allow any distance between them.

"Why not?" she teased. "Is it really that important to you? I—"

"You are not kicking me out of your bed again. You don't want sex tonight? Fine," he snapped. "But we're sharing the same bed. Always."

"It's a deal," she said with a seductive smile. "And Sebastian?"

"What?" His tone was harsh as the relief poured through him.

"I want you tonight," she said as she reached for the towel wrapped around his waist. "All night and every night."

"I've noticed," he drawled as his heart pounded in his ears. Sebastian lifted Ashley and she wrapped her legs around his waist. He had wondered when she was going to admit that she couldn't keep her hands off him. He knew she wouldn't have made the confession as a mistress.

This impetuous renegotiation was going to give him everything he wanted.

CHAPTER NINE

THE ELEGANT SOUTH BEACH restaurant offered a spectacular view and an award-winning menu, but Sebastian barely noticed. He didn't care that he had a mountain of work waiting for him at the office or that some of the most powerful people in Miami were sitting nearby, hoping to catch his eye. Nothing mattered except the exquisite brunette at his side.

Sebastian leaned back in his chair and smiled as he heard Ashley's earthy laugh. It made him tingle as if a spray of fireworks lit under his skin. Ashley's laugh was one of his most favorite sounds. It was right up there with her moan of pleasure and the way her breath hitched in her throat when he knew just how to touch her.

He watched Ashley as his friend Omar told her about one of their ill-conceived childhood antics. Omar embellished the story, making it sound as if he'd saved Sebastian from a gruesome death instead of the daily violence they had faced. His friend's wife shook her head as she listened to the story with a mix of horror and amusement.

Sebastian wished he could freeze this moment. It was rare for him to feel content. Satisfied. Hopeful. He didn't allow himself a lot of downtime. He couldn't remember the last time he'd spent the evening with his friends. Sebastian didn't feel the need to relax and have a drink. He was always pursuing the next challenge, creating the next strategy.

All that changed once he had Ashley at his side. His body tightened with lust as he studied her. She wore her hair piled high on her head. He was tempted to reach over, pull the pins and watch the heavy waves fall past her bare shoulders. He suspected she chose the style to tease him all evening.

Her dress was another matter. Short, strapless and scarlet, Ashley had worn it to please him. She knew how to showcase her curves and she was aware that his favorite color was red. The bold cleavage made him grit his teeth, but he was secretly touched that she dressed with him in mind.

He was glad she chose to be at his side tonight and every night. Not as his mistress, but as... As what? His lover? His girlfriend? Possibly the mother of his child? He was reluctant to give her that kind of power or accept her claim in his life. He wasn't sure what Ashley was, but she was important to him.

But their month was almost up. If she wasn't pregnant, he had to let her go. Unless he followed through and allowed her to become the caretaker of Inez Key. It wasn't an ideal choice since he wasn't going to live on the island. But he planned to visit frequently....

Ashley tilted her head back and laughed. "I can just

picture it," she said between gasps as she flattened her hands against her chest. "You two were trouble."

"Wait a second!" Crystal's eyes lit up as she pointed her finger at Ashley. "Now I know why you look familiar."

Sebastian saw Ashley stiffen. He wanted to silence Omar's wife. Protect Ashley. It was unfair for Ashley. She had lowered her guard only to be confronted with her family history.

"You are the daughter of that tennis legend," Crystal exclaimed.

"Yes, I am," Ashley confirmed quietly as she reached for her water glass. "How did you know?"

"Like I said, I am a news junkie," Crystal said proudly. "There was something about the way the light hit your face. You look exactly like your mother."

"Thank you," Ashley said. Was it only Sebastian who noticed the pain that flashed in her eyes? Linda Valdez had been a beautiful woman, but Ashley didn't like being compared to her mother.

"Who are you talking about?" Omar asked his wife.

"Ashley's father was Donald Jones. The tennis star," Crystal explained.

Sebastian admired Ashley's calm. He knew what she was thinking. That his friends were going to see her differently because she was a love child and her mother was a mistress. Because her parents died in a murder-suicide.

She would soon learn that his friends—his true friends—didn't judge. After surviving the ghetto and witnessing the darker side of humanity, nothing shocked them.

"Donald...Jones?" Omar repeated slowly and gave Sebastian a quick glance.

Damn. Sebastian's gut twisted with alarm. He'd forgotten that Omar knew how his past was intertwined with Donald Jones. Sebastian gave the slightest shake of his head and Omar immediately went quiet. He hoped Ashley didn't notice the silent exchange.

"Oh, I'm sure I have mascara streaming down my face," Ashley murmured as she pressed her fingertips underneath her eyes. She grabbed for her purse and stood up. "I'll have to fix my makeup."

Sebastian quietly rose from the table. He knew Ashley wanted to hide. Just for a moment so she could firmly fix the cool mask she displayed to the public. The one that made people think she lived a quiet and uneventful life on a private island.

"I'll come with you," Crystal offered as she scrambled out of her seat.

Ashley didn't say anything, but Sebastian noticed the tension in her polite smile. He wanted to intervene and protect her from the intrusive questions Crystal would undoubtedly ask. He couldn't. His guarded response would create more questions.

He reached for her and pressed his lips against her temple. He felt Ashley lean against him briefly before she stepped away. He wanted to block Crystal, but Ashley was experienced in facing this kind of attention with grace.

He sat down once the women left the table and immediately faced Omar's disapproving glare. "Donald

Jones?" his friend asked angrily. "It can't be a coincidence."

He wasn't going to insult his friend with a lie. "It's not."

Omar rubbed his forehead and exhaled sharply. "What have you done, Sebastian?"

He jutted out his chin. "I settled an old score. Karma was taking too long."

"I thought you put all this behind you," Omar said. He looked around to make sure no one could hear the conversation. "You've become richer and more powerful than Jones."

That didn't mean he'd won. "It doesn't erase what he did."

Omar shook his head. "I don't get it. Why now? Why, after all this time?"

There had been a time when Sebastian had been consumed by the injustice. It ate away at him, making him feel weak and empty. He had been an angry boy. He had been a kid who'd lost his innocence too soon and his childhood the moment he had been thrown into a cruel world. He wanted to get what was stolen from him and pushed himself every day to the brink of exhaustion to become rich and powerful.

He had suffered setbacks and bad luck, but by the time he had made his first million, Sebastian wasn't thinking about Donald Jones. His goal had been to protect his family from losing everything. They would never be at the mercy of the Donald Joneses of the world.

But then his mother had heart surgery, and everything changed. He realized he was still the angry little boy who couldn't allow the injustice to go untouched.

"When we thought my mother was dying, she had only one request." Sebastian remembered his mother lying on the hospital bed, pale and fragile. She had struggled to speak and he knew this favor meant everything to her, even after all these years. "How could I deny her?"

"I know your mother," Omar said with a frown. "She didn't ask for revenge."

"What I'm doing is righting some wrongs," Sebastian argued. "Finding justice."

"Then I have to ask you this." Omar rested his arms on the table and leaned forward. "What threats did you make to Ashley? What did you take from her? And what will she have left when all this is done?"

"You don't have to worry about Ashley. Spoiled heiresses always land on their feet." Sebastian winced. He shouldn't have called her that. Ashley had once lived in a world of excess and privilege, but if she were really a pampered princess, she wouldn't have survived on her own for this long.

"She's no spoiled heiress," Omar insisted. "Believe me, I'm married to one. Ashley is innocent. She's going to be collateral damage. Just like you were."

Sebastian glared at his friend. Ashley wasn't getting the same treatment that he had received. She lived in luxury and under his protection. "Omar, you don't know what you're talking about."

"I hope not," Omar's eyes were dull with disappointment. "Because I never thought I'd see the day when you became just like Donald Jones."

"I am nothing like that man," he hissed.

"Time will tell," Omar murmured. "Sooner than you think."

It was hours later when Ashley returned to the penthouse apartment with Sebastian. Despite Crystal's inquisitive nature and the painful memories that were dredged up with her pointed questions, Ashley had been determined to end the night on a lighthearted note. She didn't want anyone to know how much her family's action still hurt after all these years.

Sebastian excused himself and went to his office to return a few phone calls. She knew he would be there for a while and she was grateful to have a moment alone. Kicking off her heels, Ashley headed to the swimming pool.

She was too tired to swim. The cold water wasn't going to take away the chill that had seeped into her bones. Ashley paced around the pool as she tried to purge her memories.

"Ashley?" Sebastian's voice cut through her troubled thoughts. "What are you doing here?"

She shrugged. "Just thinking. Don't you have some calls to return?"

"That was hours ago," he said as he strolled toward her.

"Oh." She stopped and stared at the Miami skyline. She had no idea that much time and passed.

"What did Crystal say when you two were alone? Did she upset you?"

Ashley shook her head. "Crystal kept asking the same questions everyone else does. It's nothing I can't handle."

"Her questions stirred up something?"

"I still can't forgive what my parents did to each other," she muttered. "Most of all, I can't forgive myself."

Sebastian frowned. "Why do you need forgiveness?"

Ashley crossed her arms tightly against her. She wanted to remain quiet, but the confession pressed upon her chest. "When I was eighteen I'd had enough of my father's infidelities. I couldn't stand the fact that my mother was unable to see what was going on right under her nose."

"What did you do?" Sebastian asked.

"I told my mother the unvarnished truth." She closed her eyes and remembered her mother's expression. It had been a gradual transformation from disbelief to shock. The pain had etched into her mother's face and Ashley didn't think it would ever disappear. "I had been harsh and I didn't spare her feelings. I was the one who told my mother about his long-standing affair with her best friend."

Sebastian showed no reaction. He wasn't scandalized by her parents' choices or her actions. Most people were and couldn't wait to hear all the dirty details. Instead, he said, "That had to have been the most difficult moment in your life."

"No," she admitted for the first time. "It had been a

relief. I felt we could have a new start. I wanted to end the drama and the fear. I never felt safe while I was growing up. I never knew when another fight would happen."

She wasn't sure why she was telling Sebastian this. Ashley had never shared this secret. She had destroyed her family and no matter how much she stayed on Inez Key and barred herself from the world, she would never find redemption.

But Ashley didn't feel the need to hide this from Sebastian. If anything, she was compelled to share it with him. Her instincts told her that he would understand.

"I didn't care that I betrayed my father," Ashley said, rubbing her hands over her cold arms. "I felt like he had betrayed us a long time ago."

"I take it that your father found out."

"Yes, he shipped me off to college. I should have been grateful to get out of that toxic environment, but instead I retaliated." She had been hurt and out of control. She didn't think she had done anything wrong and her father should have been the one who was punished. "I should have stopped, but instead I told my mother about his other…transgressions. The ones that the tabloids hadn't uncovered. My mother responded by shutting me out of her life."

"Both your parents punished you for telling the truth."

"A month later they were dead," she said as the old grief hit her like a big wave. "Instead of protecting my family, I destroyed it. I caused so much pain."

"You didn't know that would be the end result."

"I knew it wouldn't end quietly. That wasn't their style." She walked past Sebastian, no longer able to face him. She had to get away and find somewhere she could grieve and suffer alone. "People always want to know what triggered the murder-suicide. No one has figured out that I'm the one who set everything into motion."

"Ashley?" he called after her.

She reluctantly turned around, prepared to see the condemnation and disgust in Sebastian's eyes. "What?"

"Whatever happened to the best friend?" he asked. She realized he had already figured out but was looking for confirmation. "The one who had an affair with your father?"

Only he would ask her that. He knew how her mind worked. It should scare her, but she felt he empathized. He knew she wasn't as innocent as she appeared. What he didn't know was that it was the last time she'd confronted and took action instead of running away and hiding.

"I wanted vengeance," she said. "It was wrong of me. I should have let it go, but I couldn't let her get away unscathed. She had pretended to be a loyal friend, but I made sure everyone discovered her true nature. She lost everything that was important to her—her status, her social connections and her husband."

"We're not so different," Sebastian said quietly. "I would have done the same."

Ashley silently walked to Sebastian and rested her head against his shoulder. She sighed as he wrapped his arms around her. She wasn't sure if it had been smart to reveal her darkest secret to Sebastian. He had used her confessions in the past. He had broken his promises.

If he wanted to destroy her completely, nothing could stop him from using this information.

The next morning Sebastian covertly watched Ashley at the breakfast table. Her tousled hair fell over her face like a veil and she wore his bathrobe that overwhelmed her feminine frame. She grasped her mug with both hands and stared into the coffee as if it held all the answers of life.

He knew she loved her morning coffee to the point that it was a sacred ritual, but this was ridiculous. She was hiding from him. Distancing herself.

And Ashley was too quiet for his liking. In the past he would assume the lack of conversation meant she was plotting his demise. Today he suspected she was uncomfortable about sharing her secret with him.

He was offended but he also knew she had a right to feel this way. He didn't have a great track record when it came to Ashley Jones. When she told him about the loan with Raymond Casillas, he had used that information for his benefit. He had also used her sexual attraction to make her his mistress. A broken promise or two, and the possibility that he accidentally got her pregnant....

Sebastian swallowed back an oath. She was probably counting down the minutes until this agreement ended. He needed to show Ashley that he could take care of her in and out of bed. He had to honor his agreement and have her stay on Inez Key.

But would she still want to be with him? Or was she

already distancing herself because there were only a few more days of their arrangement? Was it too late to prove to Ashley that he could be the man she wanted?

Sebastian hated this uncertainty. Most women were content with his attention and his lifestyle. That wasn't enough to hold on to Ashley. For a moment he wished she were pregnant with his child. He had a blistering need to create a lasting connection with this woman.

There was one place he could start. "I have to go on another trip today," Sebastian announced. "I want you to come with me."

Ashley pushed back her hair. "Where are you going this time?"

"Inez Key."

Ashley jerked with surprise. Her fingers shook as she set the coffee mug down with a thud. "You want *me* to go to Inez Key? Why?"

Because he wanted to make her happy. Give her everything she wanted. Find some kind of compromise that could even assuage the guilt that pressed against his chest. "The renovations are almost complete," he said as if that explained everything.

"That was fast," she said with a frown. "How did you manage that?"

"You can accomplish anything when you have money." And he had thrown a great deal of money on the project. Everything had to be perfect in the main house. The grounds had to be exactly as they were twenty-five years ago. Nothing else would do.

"Why do you want me along?"

"You're going to be the caretaker of the island," he said as he took the last sip of his coffee.

Ashley dipped her head. "About that…"

His hand stilled as he listened to her hesitant tone. He thought she would be pleased. Excited to remain on the island. Grateful for the chance to stay.

"I have to decline the offer."

"Why?" She had stayed with him for a month to gain the right to be on the island. Now she was throwing back his offer. "Isn't that what you wanted all along?"

"I needed the island five years ago. It was my haven." Ashley glanced up and met his gaze. "But I'm a different person now and I can't put my life on hold anymore. It's time for me to move on. I can't do that if I'm at Inez Key."

Sebastian struggled with the temptation to argue. He wanted to convince her that the island was the best place for her to stay, but deep down he knew it wasn't true. It was the best thing for *him* if she stayed. She would remain on an isolated island with no single men and always available to him. He liked that idea far too much.

"What are you going to do instead?" he asked gruffly.

Ashley looked away. "I don't know. I'll think of something."

She didn't seem excited about this change in her life. She simply accepted it. But if she didn't want Inez Key anymore, he had no hold on her. Unless he asked her to live with him.

Sebastian's heart pounded hard against his chest. He wanted to extend the invitation, but he wasn't sure what her answer would be. She had rejected him before, and that was before she discovered how he'd double-crossed her. Ashley knew what kind of man he was and she would not willingly choose to share her life with him.

"You should still visit Inez Key with me," he decided. "It would be a good time to collect your things and say goodbye to your friends."

"You're right," Ashley said softly. "I should have one last look and then move on."

Ashley didn't like staying in the antebellum mansion at night. There were too many memories and too many shadows to face in the lonely and quiet house. But tonight was different. The islanders had decorated the beach with torches and flower garlands for her. They danced to the beat of a makeshift drum, sang old pirate songs and drank rum.

The gathering felt more of a coming-of-age celebration than a going-away party. She felt the love and understanding from everyone. She was going to miss them, but she knew they would be thinking of her as she started this new journey.

"Thanks for inviting me to Inez Key," Ashley said to Sebastian as she curled against him while they took the winding staircase to the master suite. "I'm glad I came."

"The islanders are really going to miss you."

"Try not to sound so surprised," she said with an exasperated smile. "Everyone on Inez Key has been like family to me. Clea treated me as an honorary daughter. I'm not sure what she thinks of you." Ashley's smile dipped as she remembered how the older woman had stared intently at Sebastian for most of the party.

"She's angry with me because I'm the reason you're leaving," Sebastian said as he opened the door to the master suite. "She may always see me as the enemy."

Ashley stepped out of Sebastian's arms as she stepped into the master bedroom. She blinked when she noticed the change. The heavy furniture and the four-poster bed that once dominated the room had been replaced. The colorful and modern furniture changed the feel of the room. Erased the oppressive feeling she had whenever she had stepped inside.

"I forgot," Sebastian muttered. "This room had too many memories."

"No, it's okay. I'm right where I want to be." She cupped Sebastian's face with her hands and kissed him. This might be the last chance she had to touch him and lay with him. After her month was up, she no longer had a claim to him.

She broke the kiss and reached for his hand before she silently walked to the bed. She crawled onto the sumptuous bedding and reached for him.

Sebastian didn't seem to be in any rush. He cradled her face and brushed his mouth against hers. His gentleness made Ashley's breath catch in her throat.

He continued to kiss her slowly. Sebastian pressed his mouth against her forehead and her cheeks. His lips grazed the line of her jaw and the curve of her ear. It was as if he was committing her features to memory.

"This is how I would have made love to you the first time," he said as he dragged the thin shoulder straps of her dress down her arms. "If I had known you were a virgin."

"Our first night was special. Perfect," she insisted as she tilted her head back and arched her neck, silently encouraging him to continue. "I don't need a do-over."

"I scared you off," he reminded her as he kissed a trail down her throat.

"I scared myself," she corrected breathlessly as her pulse skipped a beat. "It was too much, too intense. I'd never felt that way before."

"You wanted to hide," he said as he reverently peeled her flirty sundress from her body. "That's why you had rejected my offer."

"It was stupid of me," she admitted as she dragged the buttons free from his shirt. She leaned forward and pressed her mouth against the warm, golden-brown skin she had just revealed. "I didn't mean to come across as a coldhearted bitch."

"What if I made that offer now?" Sebastian's tone was casual, but she sensed he was not asking lightly. "How would you respond?"

Her heart lurched. "That depends," she said huskily. "What is the offer?"

Sebastian shrugged off his shirt and lowered her onto the mattress. He stood before her, proud and male. "Come back to Miami with me."

For how long? And in what role? The questions burned on her tongue but she remained silent. Would she be his occasional hostess or his arm candy? Would she be his hostess or his baby mama?

Ashley wanted to accept his offer immediately and

not look too closely. Refuse to negotiate and dismiss any reservations. She loved him with a ferocity that bordered on obsession. She now understood why her mother had risked everything to be with the man that she loved. The only difference was that Ashley had chosen a good man. A man who would treat her with respect and adoration.

"Well?" Sebastian asked impatiently.

Ashley bit her lip. She wasn't sure whether he was suggesting this because he thought she was pregnant. He had asked her every morning and it didn't help that her period was late. Was he making a strategic move or was this invitation from the heart?

She stretched slowly against the mattress and watched Sebastian's features tighten with lust. "No incentives this time, Sebastian?" she teased.

"I don't have anything you need," he said as he hooked his large fingers underneath the trim of her panties and slowly dragged the scrap of silk down her trembling legs.

She swiped her tongue along her bottom lip. "Don't be too sure about that."

"Tell me what you want," he encouraged softly. "Ask for anything and I will give it to you."

She wanted his love. Ashley knew she should look away before her eyes revealed the truth, but she was ensnared by his hot gaze. She wanted more than his attention or his heart. She wanted everything Sebastian Cruz had to offer. She wished to be part of his life, his future and his very soul.

"You." Her voice croaked as the emotions gripped her chest. "I want you and don't hold anything back."

"And you shall have it," Sebastian said as he crawled onto the bed and hovered above her. His strong arms on either side of her head as his hands pinned her wavy hair. She couldn't move if she'd wanted to.

Sebastian crushed her lips with his mouth before he licked and kissed his way down her chest. He captured her tight nipple with his teeth and teased her with his tongue until the sensations rippled under her skin.

Ashley twisted underneath him as he caressed and laved his tongue against her flat stomach. She bunched the bedsheets in her fists. Her legs shook with anticipation when he cupped her sex with a possessive hand.

Sebastian held her gaze as he stroked the folds of her sex. Her skin grew flush and her breathing deserted her as he rocked her hips. He placed his mouth against the heart of her. Ashley moaned as her core clenched. She went wild under his tongue as he savored the taste of her.

Her climax was swift and brutal. Ashley went limp as her heart raced. She heard Sebastian remove his clothes and she slowly opened her eyes. Sebastian stood at the side of the bed, gloriously naked as he rolled on a condom.

He didn't say anything as he parted her legs with forceful hands before he settled between her thighs. She watched the primitive emotions flickering across his harsh face as he surged into her.

Ashley's gasp mingled with Sebastian's low groan. She rolled her hips as he began to thrust. It was a slow and steady rhythm that was designed to make her lose her mind.

Her flesh gripped him tightly as he surged in deeper. Ashley wanted more. Wanted this to last forever. She wanted Sebastian forever.

"I love you." The words tumbled out of her mouth in an agonized whisper.

Sebastian went still. Ashley closed her eyes and turned her head away. She hadn't planned to reveal her final secret to him.

Sebastian drove into her. His rhythm grew faster. Harder. She didn't dare look at him. Did he feel triumphant or annoyed? Was he amused or irritated by her spontaneous words?

The bed shook with each demanding thrust. It was as if he was branding her with his touch and making the most intimate claim. Another climax—harder and hotter—took her by surprise. She cried out just as Sebastian found his release.

He collapsed on top of her and she welcomed the weight of his sweat-slick body. There was no doubt anymore, she decided as she gulped in air. She belonged to Sebastian Cruz forever.

CHAPTER TEN

THE NEXT MORNING Ashley stood by the double doors that led to the balcony. It was a perfect day at Inez Key; hot with very little humidity. The ocean was calm and a vivid blue. The tropical flowers were opening under the brilliant sun.

But her troubled thoughts didn't allow her to enjoy the view. Ashley glanced at the bed behind her. The sheets were rumpled and the pillows had been thrown on the floor at some time during the night. Yet this morning she had woken up alone.

Sebastian was avoiding her because she had told him she was in love with him. Ashley bit her lip as she recalled that moment. What had gotten into her? She was good at hiding her feelings, but she'd lowered her guard last night. She had been compelled to share how she felt.

And Sebastian didn't say anything in return. In fact, he didn't say anything at all.

Ashley rubbed her forehead and leaned against the door frame. It didn't matter. She had said it in the heat of the moment. He wasn't going to take her words seriously.

She saw a movement on the beach and leaned forward. Sebastian was walking on the dock as he spoke on his cell phone. She couldn't hear his conversation but she knew from the smile and the way he dipped his head that he was speaking to his mother.

Sebastian Cruz was an arrogant and powerful playboy, but he was also a family man. She admired how he took care of his family. She thought that kind of man was only found on unrealistic television shows. But she also noticed how Sebastian treated his mother and sisters.

Unlike the playboys she knew, Sebastian respected women. No matter how exasperated he was with his sisters, Sebastian saw them as successful women who brought a valuable contribution to their fields, community and to the family. He listened to his mother's opinions and sought out her advice. He was ready to help the women in his family if they asked, but he never saw them as useless, porcelain dolls.

Ashley watched from her vantage point, knowing he couldn't see her on the shaded balcony. She could study him and memorize his hard angles and wide shoulders. The man was raw male and sexuality even in his wrinkled cotton shirt and low-slung jeans. It was a shame she wasn't carrying his child.

She'd discovered that this morning, and instead of feeling relieved, Ashley had struggled with her disappointment. She hadn't realized how much she'd wanted Sebastian's baby until that moment. Now there was nothing to keep him at her side.

Ashley saw Sebastian disconnect his call as he

walked to the front door. She couldn't see him but she heard him greet Clea.

"Good morning, Mr. Sebastian," the housekeeper said. Her tone was friendly as usual, but Ashley recognized a bubbling excitement underneath the words. "I've been meaning to ask you, but I haven't had a chance to speak to you alone."

"What do you want to know?" Sebastian's voice was low and rough.

"Did you use to live in this house? I would say about twenty-five years ago?"

Ashley jerked back as her heart stopped. What was Clea saying? That the Cruz family had once owned Inez Key? That was ridiculous, surely.

"Yes," Sebastian said with eerie calm, "this used to be my home until Donald Jones stole it from my family."

Ashley's skin went hot and then cold as the bile churned in her stomach. Her father had taken this island from the Cruz family. Ruined them. And for what? He'd had no interest in Inez Key.

"And you stole it back," Clea said dazedly.

The housekeeper's words echoed in her head. Ashley leaned against the wall as her shaky legs threatened to buckle. That was why Sebastian had been so interested in this island. Why he'd refused to accept Inez Key wasn't for sale.

A collage of images slammed through her mind. Sebastian standing at the dock like a conquering leader. The watercolors Sebastian's father had painted. The shadows in his eyes when he looked at the main house.

He'd set out to seduce and steal Inez Key from her

because her father had stolen it first. It was an eye for an eye.

Ashley inhaled sharply as the fury and pain whipped through her. She tried to breathe, but her chest was constricted. This was why he didn't respond to her declaration of love. Because he had no feelings for her. She was just a pawn in his game of revenge.

How had she got it so wrong?

She had made herself believe that Sebastian was nothing like the men she knew. That he could love and respect a woman. That he was a good man. A man she could trust and share her life with. Because she believed her happiness and safety was his priority. That he wanted what was best for her.

She had ignored her first instinct. Was it his incredible good looks or his overwhelming sexuality that had distracted her? He used her without compunction. She had been a pawn he could easily sacrifice. She had believed what she wanted to believe.

Ashley closed her eyes and turned her head. She wanted to block out the world around her. Pretend that this wasn't happening. Run and never look back.

But there was a simple truth she couldn't ignore: She was no better than her mother.

Linda Valdez wasn't the only woman in this family who made stupid decisions over the men they loved. Donald Jones had not been worthy of her mother's time or tears, but Linda didn't want to see it. Her mother had built a fantasy world, a place where she had finally felt loved and special.

Ashley slowly opened her eyes. She had done the same.

Ashley couldn't speak. It took all of her strength to stand still when her instincts urged her to escape before she lashed out. The walls were closing in on her. The anger—the howling pain—bubbled underneath the surface, threatening to break free. It was going to be ugly and violent.

No, she wouldn't let it. She was not going down the same path as her mother. Ashley curled her hands into fists and dug her nails in her palms. She welcomed the bite, but it didn't take the edge off her fury. Now, more than ever, she needed to be in control.

She had to get out of here. Her legs were unsteady as she walked across the room. She wanted to double over from the pain but kept walking until she found the bag she had packed in the closet.

Her legs felt heavy and she just wanted to fall into a heap and curl in a protective ball. She blinked as her eyes burned with unshed tears. *Don't cry now*, Ashley thought. *Cry when no one can see you or use your weakness against you. Cry when you're alone.*

Alone. She was all alone with no support system. No home. There was no comfort or peace in her life. Sebastian had taken it all away.

Ashley exhaled slowly, but the pain radiated in her body. She knew she had been different from the other women in his life. She questioned how she'd gained his attention, how she'd attracted him, but hadn't wanted to inspect it too closely. She had been too afraid to poke at her good luck in case it fell apart.

Ashley bent to the waist as the agony ripped through her. It had all been an illusion. All of it.

Even the sex. She leaned against her bedroom door as the nausea swept through her. Especially the sex. He had made her feel special and desirable. Powerful and sexy. Sebastian had introduced her to pleasure. Passion. She thought he had felt the same.

Her body burned with humiliation. She wanted the floor to open up and swallow her whole. Ashley quickly grabbed her bag, knowing she only had a few moments to escape.

She was crossing the floor of the master suite when she heard Sebastian's footsteps down the hall. She barely had time to brace herself when the door swung open.

Her heart gave a brutal leap when Sebastian stood in front of her. She felt so small and insignificant next to him, like a peasant standing before an all-powerful emperor.

"Why didn't you tell me?" she asked in a hiss.

Sebastian noticed her stricken expression and the bag clutched in her hand. He glanced at the doors that led to the balcony and immediately assessed the situation. A shadow crossed his harsh features. He closed the door behind him and leaned against it. He didn't speak as he crossed his arms and watched her.

She felt trapped, weak, and had a fierce need to hide it by striking first. She was never more aware of his intimidating height and powerful build than right at this moment. The button-down shirt and faded jeans didn't hide the fact that he was solid muscle. There was no way she could move him.

"You look upset," he drawled.

Did he still think this was a game? Had he no remorse? "What is Inez Key to you?"

He paused. "It was my childhood home."

"And you felt the need to steal it from me? It was my childhood home as well."

"I didn't steal Inez Key," he pointed out calmly, but she saw the anger flash in his eyes. "Your father did."

"What exactly are you accusing him of?" she asked hoarsely. She knew Donald Jones probably did something underhanded. It was how he approached life.

"He won our home in a poker game," Sebastian said. "But he had cheated."

That sounded like dear old Donald, but maybe this was the one time when her father's reputation automatically made him the culprit. "You don't know that. You have no proof."

Sebastian's eyes narrowed. "He bragged about it years later. His friend Casillas confirmed the story."

Ashley wanted to be ill. "Why did he want the island? It doesn't make sense. My father didn't care about property. He rarely used this island."

The anger whipped around Sebastian. "He wanted something else and tried to use the island as a bargaining chip."

"What?" Ashley couldn't shake off the dread. "What did he really want?"

"My mother." His voice was cold and harsh. "Jones said he wouldn't take the island if he could take my mother to bed instead."

The words drew blood like the lash of a whip. She could easily imagine her father trying to make a deal like that. She'd seen him try many times. And he occasionally succeeded. "Is that why you slept with me?" she asked.

"No," he said in a raspy voice. "I took you to bed because I wanted you and I couldn't stop myself."

She wasn't going to believe that. Not anymore. He had already proven that she had no power over him. He didn't stop himself because he wanted to continue playing the game.

"Don't lie to me," she warned. "It was an eye for an eye. My father tried to blackmail your mother into bed. You did the same to me. Only you were successful." Because apparently she had a price.

"My father wasn't going to let Jones touch my mother. She was his wife. The mother of his children. He should have killed that man for suggesting it."

"And I was a spoiled heiress living the life you should have had," she whispered. She gripped her bag until her knuckles turned white. She wanted to get out. She needed to escape before she said too much or crossed the line.

"Put down the bag," Sebastian ordered. "You're not going anywhere."

"I believed every word you said," she said and scoffed at her ignorance. "You said you would look after me if I got pregnant. I actually thought you meant it."

"I still mean it." Sebastian froze and his gaze quickly traveled down the length of her body.

"Don't worry, Sebastian. I'm not pregnant. Or was that part of the plan too?"

He took a step toward her. "I would never do that to an innocent child."

Ashley backed away. She didn't trust herself around Sebastian. She'd already made a few assumptions and poor choices. He had the ability to make her forget her best intentions with one simple touch. Worse, he knew it.

"But you would do it to me because I couldn't possibly be innocent. I'm Donald Jones's daughter, right? I must be punished."

"Let me explain," Sebastian said as he reached for her.

"No! Don't you touch me. You no longer have that right."

He held up his hands. "Listen to me. When we thought my mother was dying, she made a request. If she survived the surgery, she wanted to live out her remaining years on Inez Key."

Ashley remembered Patricia's faraway look when she'd talked about her home. She was remembering Inez Key. It had been lovingly re-created in the watercolors her husband had painted. It was the paradise she had lost.

"Oh, well, that makes all the difference," Ashley said with heavy sarcasm. "Your mother wanted the island. That excuses the fact that you seduced me and stole my home."

"I'm not making any excuses," he said as he watched her reach the door.

"No, you don't think you need to. You were only getting justice, right?"

"What he did—"

"My father stole the island from you. You stole it from me," she said as she swung open the doors and fled down the stairs. She heard Sebastian's footsteps behind her. "My father wanted to humiliate your parents by blackmailing Patricia into bed. You blackmailed me and tried to humiliate me by making me a mistress. My father's action drove you into poverty. Your actions leave me homeless and broke. Have I missed anything?"

"I had no plans for revenge," Sebastian said as he followed her. "My goal was to buy Inez Key and make it my mother's home."

"Oh, you didn't *plan* to repeat history," she said as she marched to the front door. "You *accidentally* fell into the same pattern that my father followed. What a relief! You don't know how *happy* it makes me feel that you are exactly like Donald Jones."

Sebastian glared at her. "I didn't start this twisted game. I finished it."

"Congratulations, Sebastian. You won." She almost choked on the words as she opened the door and crossed the threshold before she slammed the door shut. "I hope it was worth it."

Ashley didn't notice the aggressive lines of steel and glass as she strode into the Cruz Conglomerate headquarters. The impressive lobby and stunning artwork no longer intimidated her. The anger coursing through her body silenced the noise and the crowds of people surrounding her. She didn't care about anything other than saying a few choice words to Sebastian.

She crushed the buff envelope in her hand as she waited impatiently at the reception desk. She wasn't looking forward to seeing Sebastian. It had been a month since she'd left Inez Key and she didn't feel ready.

She still loved the rat bastard. She shook her head in self-disgust. It was a sign that she was definitely her mother's daughter.

Her first instinct had been to ignore the letter he sent. But how could she? She had felt numb for the last few weeks until she had seen his name on the envelope. She had been pathetically pleased that he knew where she lived. That he was still aware of her.

That ended when she read the letter. Her body shook with anger and hurt, confusion and despair. Every dark emotion whipped through her body until she leaned on the wall and slid to the floor.

This was why she'd cut him out of her life. She couldn't go through this pain. She wasn't going to let her unrequited love tear her apart.

The elegant receptionist hung up the phone and gave her a curious look. "Mr. Cruz will see you right away, Miss Jones."

Ashley nodded as the surprise jolted her system. The last time she was here she had been ignored and forgotten. Now she was given immediate access to Sebastian? She hadn't been prepared for that. Ashley glanced at the exit and took a deep breath. She wasn't going to hide from him. Not anymore.

She was here. Ashley was here to see him. Sebastian stood in the center of his office and buttoned his jacket.

His fingers shook and he bunched his hands into fists. This was an opportunity he couldn't squander. His future, his happiness, was riding on the next few minutes.

The door opened and Ashley rushed inside. "What the hell is this?" she asked as she held up the envelope.

He barely noticed his assistant closing the door and leaving them alone. Sebastian greedily stared at Ashley. This time she didn't feel the need to dress up. He was glad. She looked stunning in her black T-shirt, cutoff shorts and sandals. Her hair was a wild mane and her skin carried the scent of sunshine.

He frowned as he saw that Ashley was vibrating with anger. "That is payment for Inez Key," he said. He thought he had explained everything in the letter.

"Why would you give this to me?" Ashley asked, shaking the envelope close to his face. "You got the island because I couldn't pay back the loan."

"I want to pay you my highest offer because I made a mistake. I went after this island even though it wasn't for sale. My actions were legal but unforgiveable," he admitted through gritted teeth.

"And you think throwing money around is going to make it all go away?" she asked, tossing the envelope onto the floor. "Typical. You rich and powerful men are all the same."

Ashley may look sweet and innocent, but she knew just how to hurt him. "Stop comparing me to your father."

She raised her eyebrows. "Oh, is that what this is all about? You're uncomfortable with the idea that you are just like Donald Jones? Refuse to believe it even though you think like him. You act like him. You destroy lives like him. The only difference is that you out–Donald Jones the original."

"The difference is that I regret what I did. It's tearing me up inside, knowing that you hate me. That your opinion of me is so low." He cursed in Spanish and thrust his hand in his hair. *That you loved me once but I destroyed those feelings.*

"And so you send me a check because you feel responsible? Because you think if you throw enough money at me you think I'll forgive you?" Her voice rose. "Don't get me wrong, Sebastian. I could use the money. I'm flat broke and I don't know if I can make rent next month. But I won't take a penny from you. You think this will absolve what you did? It won't."

"I know that. I can't erase what I did." Sebastian would never forget the hurt in Ashley's eyes when she realized his original plan. He wanted to be a hero in her eyes. He wanted her to look at him in wonder and admiration the way she used to. "The only thing I can do is repair the damage and make amends."

"It's too late."

"I refuse to believe that," he said as the hope died a little inside him. "I want what we had and I am willing to do whatever is necessary to make it happen. Tell me what you need from me. What can I do to regain your trust?"

She glanced up and met his gaze. "There is nothing you can do."

Sebastian felt as if his last chance was disintegrating in his hands. He didn't know what to do and the panic clawed at him. If she gave him a mission, he could earn her trust. But she didn't want anything from him.

"Stay with me," he urged. His request was pathetically simple. He couldn't dazzle her with his wealth and connections. "Give me a chance."

She shook her head. "You don't have to make this offer. I'm not pregnant."

"That's not what I'm asking." Sebastian tasted fear. This reunion wasn't going the way he had envisioned. He was losing her. If she didn't want to be with him, he had nothing to use as leverage. She wasn't interested in his money or power. Those were disadvantages in her eyes. All he could give her was himself. It wasn't enough, but it was a start.

"I need you," he said quietly. "You left this giant hole in my life. I can't sleep. I can't concentrate. All I do is think of you."

Ashley looked away. "You'll get over it."

"I don't want to," he said harshly. "I knew you would be my downfall the moment we met. I didn't care. Nothing mattered but you."

"Getting the island back mattered," she said as the tears shimmered in her eyes. "You used me and betrayed my trust. You planned to cut me out with nothing because that is what my father did to your family. I was just part of your revenge. You would have tossed me to the wolves if you hadn't been attracted to me."

"That's not true! I love you, Ashley."

"Stop playing games with me," Ashley said in a broken whisper. She took a step back and he grabbed her hand. He wasn't going to let her go again.

"You don't have to forgive me at this moment." It hurt that she didn't believe him, but he was willing to work hard at regaining her love and her trust. "Just be with me and I'll prove my love to you every day."

She looked down at their joined hands. Sebastian took it as a good sign that she didn't let go. "I want to but I can't go through this again," she whispered.

He knew how much it cost her to say those words. She risked so much. Maybe even more than when she had declared her love. She still may have feelings for him, that she was willing for another chance. "I want to be the man you need. I want you to believe in me. In us."

The tears started to fall down her cheeks. "I want that, too."

"Stay with me, Ashley," he urged her as his heart pounded fiercely. "I will give you everything you need. Everything you want."

"Stay as what?" she asked as she stepped closer and pressed her hand against his chest. "Your lover? Your mistress?"

"I'm going to make you my wife very soon."

Ashley tugged his tie. "You have to ask first."

"I will," he promised as he covered her mouth with his. "And I'll keep asking until you say yes."

Five years later

Ashley heard the incessant chirping of the nighthawks as she stepped out onto the patio. It had been weeks since she and Sebastian had visited Inez Key. Every time she stepped on the wooden dock, she was struck by how much the island had changed and how much it remained the same.

Sebastian had painstakingly restored the main house, adding a few touches to accommodate his mother's age and mobility. The antebellum house was no longer stark and silent. It was always filled with the shrieking laughter of children and the waft of spices in the big kitchen as everyone had a hand in cooking for the large family dinners.

But this dinner was different, Ashley decided as she caught Sebastian's eye and slowly walked to him. The sky was streaked with orange and red and the birthday candles flickered on the cake she held.

The guests at the long table clapped and cheered when they saw her. She smiled when they began to sing "Happy Birthday." She walked barefoot as the ocean breeze pulled at her casual sundress.

Everyone on Inez Key was there to celebrate. The main house was festooned with streamers, bunting and balloons. The bright colors and loud music reflected the festive spirit of the day. The islanders and the Cruz family mingled at the party that had started early in the day and showed no signs of fading.

Ashley glanced at her mother-in-law. She knew it had been a long and emotional day for Patricia. The older woman, dressed in a vibrant red, was dabbing her eyes with one hand while holding Ashley's infant daughter with the other. Patricia continued to fulfill the wish she'd made almost thirty years ago. She was home surrounded by her family.

Ashley carefully set the cake down in front of Sebastian as he held their boisterous three-year-old twin boys in each arm. She felt his heated gaze on her as the guests sang the last verse.

"Happy birthday, Sebastian," she murmured as she scooped up one of the boys who tried to lunge for the cake. "Make a wish."

"I have everything I want, *mi vida*."

"Ask for anything," she encouraged her husband, "and I'll make it happen."

Ashley saw the devilish tilt of his mouth as the desire flared in his eyes. Anticipation licked through her veins as she watched Sebastian blow out the candles.

As the guests clapped, Ashley saw Sebastian's satisfied smile at the blown-out candles. The curiosity got the better of her. "What did you ask for?"

"If I tell you, it won't come true," he teased. "But this is going to be one birthday wish I'll never forget."

* * * * *

AFTER HOURS
WITH HER EX

MAUREEN CHILD

To La Ferrovia in Ogden, Utah
Thanks for the best calzones ever.

Maureen Child writes for the Mills & Boon Desire line and can't imagine a better job. A seven-time finalist for a prestigious Romance Writers of America RITA® Award, Maureen is an author of more than one hundred romance novels. Her books regularly appear on bestseller lists and have won several awards, including a Prism Award, a National Readers' Choice Award, a Colorado Romance Writers Award of Excellence and a Golden Quill Award. She is a native Californian but has recently moved to the mountains of Utah.

One

"You actually *can* go home again," Sam Wyatt murmured as he stared at the main lodge of his family's resort. "The question is, will anyone be happy to see you."

But then, why should they be? He'd left Snow Vista, Utah, two years before, when his twin brother had died. And in walking away, he'd left his family to pick up the pieces strewn in the wake of Jack's death.

Guilt had forced Sam to leave. Had kept him away. And now, a different kind of guilt had brought him home again. Maybe it was time, he told himself. Time to face the ghosts that haunted this mountain.

The lodge looked the same. Rough-hewn logs, gray, weathered shingles and a wide front porch studded with Adirondack chairs fitted with jewel-toned cushions. The building itself was three stories; the Wyatt family had added that third level as family quarters just a few years ago. Guest rooms crowded the bottom two floors and there were a few cabins on the property as well, offering privacy along with a view that simply couldn't be beat.

Mostly, though, the tourists who came to ski at Snow Vista stayed in hotels a mile or so down the mountain. The Wyatt resort couldn't hold them all. A few years ago, Sam and his twin, Jack, had laid out plans for expanding the lodge, adding cabins and building the Wyatt holdings into the go-to place in the Utah mountains. Sam's parents, Bob and Connie, had been eager to expand, but from the looks of it, any idea of expansion had stopped when Sam left the mountain. But then, a lot of things had stopped, hadn't they?

His grip tightened on his duffel bag, and briefly Sam wished to hell he could as easily get ahold of the thoughts racing maniacally through his mind. Coming home wouldn't be easy. But the decision was made. Time to face the past.

"Sam!"

The voice calling his name was familiar. His sister, Kristi, headed right for him, walking in long brisk strides. She wore an electric blue parka and ski pants tucked into black boots trimmed with black fur at the tops. Her big blue eyes were flashing—and not in welcome. But hell, he told himself, he hadn't been expecting a parade, had he?

"Hi, Kristi."

"Hi?" She walked right up to him, tilted her head back and met his gaze with narrowed eyes. "That's the best you've got? 'Hi, Kristi'? After two years?"

He met her anger with cool acceptance. Sam had known what he would face when he came home and there was no time like the present to jump in and get some of it over with. "What would you like me to say?"

She snorted. "It's a little late to be asking me what

I want, isn't it? If you cared, you would have asked before you left in the first place."

Hard to argue that point. And his sister's expression told him it would be pointless to try even if he could. Remembering the way Kristi had once looked up to him and Jack, Sam realized it wasn't easy to accept that her hero worship phase was over. Of course, he'd pushed that phase over a cliff himself.

But this wasn't why he'd come home. He wasn't going to rehash old decisions. He'd done what he had to do back then, just as he was doing today.

"Back then, I would have told you not to go," Kristi was saying and as she stared up at him, Sam saw a film of tears cover her eyes. She blinked quickly, though, as if determined to keep those tears at bay—for which he was grateful. "You left us. Just walked away. Like none of us mattered to you anymore…"

He blew out a breath, dropped his duffel bag and shoved both hands through his hair. "Of course you mattered. All of you did. *Do.*"

"Easy to say, isn't it, Sam?"

Would it do any good to explain that he had thought about calling home all the time?

No, he told himself. Because he hadn't called. Hadn't been in touch at all—except for a couple of postcards letting them know where he happened to be at the time—until his mother had found a way to track him down in Switzerland last week.

He still wasn't sure how she'd found him. But Connie Wyatt was a force to be reckoned with when she had a goal in mind. Probably, she had called every hotel in the city until she'd tracked him down.

"Look, I'm not getting into this with you. Not right

now anyway. Not until I've seen Dad." He paused, then asked, "How is he?"

A flicker of fear darted across her eyes, then was swept away in a fresh surge of anger. "Alive. And the doctor says he's going to be fine. It's just sad that all it took to get you to come home was Dad having a heart attack."

This was going great.

Then it seemed her fury drained away as her voice dropped and her gaze shifted from him to the mountain. "It was scary. Mom was a rock, like always, but it was scary. Hearing that it was a warning made it a little better but now it feels like…"

Her words trailed off, but Sam could have finished that sentence for her. A warning simply meant that the family was now watching Bob as if he were a live grenade, waiting to see if he'd explode. Probably driving his father nuts.

"Anyway," she said, her voice snapping back to knifelike sharpness. "If you're expecting a big welcome, you're in for a disappointment. We're too busy to care."

"That's fine by me," he said, though damned if it didn't bother him to have his little sister be so dismissive. "I'm not here looking for forgiveness."

"Why are you here, then?"

He looked into his sister's eyes. "Because this is where I'm needed."

"You were needed two years ago, too," she said, and he heard the hurt in her voice this time.

"Kristi…"

She shook her head, plastered a hard smile on her face and said, "I've got a lesson in a few minutes. I'll talk to you later. If you're still here."

With that, she turned and left, headed for one of the

bunny runs where inexperienced skiers got their first introduction to the sport. Kristi had been one of the instructors here since she was fourteen. All of the Wyatt kids had grown up on skis, and teaching newbies had been part of the family business.

When she disappeared into the crowd, Sam turned for the main lodge. Well, he'd known when he decided to come home that it wasn't going to be easy. But then, nothing in the past two years had been easy, had it?

Head down, strides long, he walked toward home a lot slower than he had left it.

The lodge was as he remembered it.

When he left, the renovations had been almost finished, and now the place looked as though the changes had settled in and claimed their place. The front windows were wider; there were dozens of leather club chairs gathered in conversational groups and huddled in front of the stone hearth where a fire burned brightly.

It might be cold outside, with the wind and snow, but here in the lodge, there was warmth and welcome. He wondered if any of that would extend to him.

He waved to Patrick Hennessey, manning the reception desk, then skirted past the stairs and around the corner to the private elevator to the third floor. Sam took a breath, flipped open the numerical code box and punched in the four numbers he knew so well, half expecting the family to have changed the code after he left. They hadn't, though, and the door shushed open for him to step inside.

They'd installed the elevator a few years ago when they added the third story. This way, none of their guests accidentally gained access to the family's space and the Wyatt's kept their privacy. The short ride ended, the door swished open and Sam was suddenly standing in the family room.

He had time for one brief glance around the familiar surroundings. Framed family photos hung on the cream-colored walls alongside professional shots of the mountain in winter and springtime. Gleaming tables held handcrafted lamps and the low wood table set between twin burgundy leather sofas displayed a selection of magazines and books. Windows framed a wide view of the resort and a river-stone hearth on one wall boasted a fire that crackled and leaped with heat and light.

But it was the two people in the room who caught and held his attention. His mother was curled up in her favorite, floral upholstered chair, an open book on her lap. And his father, Sam saw with a sigh of relief, was sitting in his oversize leather club chair, his booted feet resting on a matching hassock. The flat-screen TV hanging over the fireplace was turned to an old Western movie.

On the long flight from Switzerland and during the time spent traveling from the airport to the lodge, all Sam had been able to think about was his father having a heart attack. Sure, he'd been told that Bob Wyatt was all right and had been released from the hospital. But he hadn't really allowed himself to believe it until now.

Seeing the big man where he belonged, looking as rugged and larger than life as usual, eased that last, cold knot in the pit of Sam's stomach.

"Sam!" Connie Wyatt tossed her book onto a side table, jumped to her feet and raced across the room to him. She threaded her arms around him and held on tightly, as if preventing him from vanishing again. "Sam, you're here." She tipped her head back to smile up at him. "It's so good to see you."

He smiled back at her and realized how much he'd missed her and the rest of the family. For two years, Sam had been a gypsy, traveling from one country to another, chasing the next experience. He'd lived out of the duffel bag he still held tightly and hadn't looked any further ahead than the next airport or train connection.

He'd done some skiing of course. Sam didn't compete professionally anymore, but he couldn't go too long without hitting the slopes. Skiing was in his blood, even when he spent most of his time building his business. Designing ski runs at some of the top resort destinations in the world. The skiwear company he and Jack had begun was thriving as well, and between those two businesses, he'd managed to keep busy enough to not do much thinking.

Now he was here, meeting his father's studying gaze over the top of his mother's head. It was both surreal and right.

With a deliberate move, he dropped the duffel bag, then wrapped both arms around his much-shorter mother and gave her a hard hug. "Hi, Mom."

She pushed back, gave his chest a playful slap and shook her head. "I can't believe you're really here. You must be hungry. I'll go fix you something—"

"You don't have to do that," he said, knowing nothing could stop her. Connie Wyatt treated all difficult situations as a reason to feed people.

"Won't be a minute," she said, then shot her husband a quick glance. "I'll bring us all some coffee, too. You stay in that chair, mister."

Bob Wyatt waved one hand at his wife, but kept his gaze fixed on his son. As Connie rushed out of the room and headed for the family kitchen, Sam walked over to his father and took a seat on the footstool in front of him. "Dad. You look good."

Scowling, the older man brushed his gray-streaked hair back from his forehead and narrowed the green eyes he'd bequeathed to his sons. "I'm fine. Doctor says it wasn't anything. Just too much stress."

Stress. Because he'd lost one son, had another disappear on him and was forced to do most of the running of the family resort himself. Guilt Sam didn't want to acknowledge pinged him again as he realized that leaving the way he did had left everyone scrambling.

Frowning more deeply, his father looked over to the doorway where his wife had disappeared. "Your mother's bound and determined to make me an invalid, though."

"You scared her," Sam said. "Hell, you scared me."

His father watched him for several long minutes before saying, "Well now, you did some scaring of your own a couple years ago. Taking off, not letting us know where you were or how you were…"

Sam took a breath and blew it out. And there was the guilt again, settling back onto his shoulders like an unwelcome guest. It had been with him so long now, Sam thought he would probably never get rid of it entirely.

"Couple of postcards just weren't enough, son."

"I couldn't call," Sam said, and knew it sounded cowardly. "Couldn't hear your voices. Couldn't—hell, Dad. I was a damn mess."

"You weren't the only one hurting, Sam."

"I know that," he said, and felt a flicker of shame. "I do. But losing Jack…" Sam scowled at the memory as if that action alone could push it so far out of sight he'd never have to look at it again.

"He was your twin," Bob mused. "But he was our child. Just as you and Kristi are."

There it was. Sam had to accept that he'd caused his parents more pain at a time when they had already had more than enough loss to deal with. But back then, there had seemed to Sam to be only one answer.

"I had to go."

One short sentence that encapsulated the myriad emotions that had driven him from his home, his family.

"I know that." His father's gaze was steady and there was understanding there as well as sorrow. "Doesn't mean I have to like it, but I understand. Still, you're back now. For how long?"

He'd been expecting that question. The problem was, he didn't have an answer for it yet. Sam ducked his head briefly, then looked at his father again. "I don't know."

"Well," the older man said sadly, "that's honest at least."

"I can tell you," Sam assured him, "that this time I'll let you know before I leave. I can promise not to disappear again."

Nodding, his father said, "Then I guess that'll have to do. For now." He paused and asked, "Have you seen... anyone else yet?"

"No. Just Kristi." Sam stiffened. There were still minefields to step through. Hard feelings and pain to be faced. There was no way out but through.

As hard as it was to face his family, he'd chosen to see them first, because what was still to come would be far more difficult.

"Well then," his father spoke up, "you should know that—"

The elevator swished open. Sam turned to face who-ever was arriving and instantly went still as stone. He hardly heard his father complete the sentence that had been interrupted.

"—Lacy's on her way over here."

Lacy Sills.

She stood just inside the room, clutching at a basket of muffins that filled the room with a tantalizing scent. Sam's heart gave one hard lurch in his chest. She looked good. Too damn good.

She stood five foot eight and her long blond hair hung in a single thick braid over her left shoulder. Her navy blue coat was unbuttoned to reveal a heavy, fisherman's knit, forest-green sweater over her black jeans. Her boots were black, too, and came to her knees. Her features were the same: a generous mouth; a straight, small nose; and blue eyes the color of deep summer. She didn't smile. Didn't speak. And didn't have to.

In a split second, blood rushed from his head to his lap and just like that, he was hard as a rock. Lacy had always had that effect on him.

That's why he'd married her.

Lacy couldn't move. Couldn't seem to draw a breath past the tight knot of emotion lodged in her throat. Her heartbeat was too fast and she felt a head rush, as if she'd had one too many glasses of wine.

She should have called first. Should have made sure the Wyatts were alone here at the lodge. But then, her mind argued, why should she? It wasn't as if she'd expected to see Sam sitting there opposite his father. And now that she had, she was determined to hide her reaction to him. After all, she wasn't the one who'd walked out on her family. Her *life*. She'd done nothing to be ashamed of.

Except of course, for missing him. Her insides were

jumping, her pulse raced and an all too familiar swirl of desire spun in the pit of her stomach. How was it possible that she could still feel so much for a man who had tossed her aside without a second thought?

When Sam left, she had gone through so many different stages of grief, she had thought she'd never come out the other side of it all. But she had. Finally.

How was it fair that he was here again when she was just getting her life back?

"Hello, Lacy."

His voice was the deep rumble of an avalanche forming and she knew that, to her, it held the same threat of destruction. He was watching her out of grass-green eyes she had once gotten lost in. And he looked so darn good. Why did he have to look so good? By all rights, he should be covered in boils and blisters as punishment for what he'd done.

Silence stretched out until it became a presence in the room. She had to speak. She couldn't just stand there. Couldn't let him know what it cost her to meet his gaze.

"Hello, Sam," she finally managed to say. "It's been a while."

Two years. Two years of no word except for a few lousy postcards sent to his parents. He'd never contacted Lacy. Never let her know he was sorry. That he missed her. That he wished he hadn't gone. Nothing. She'd spent countless nights worrying about whether he was alive or dead. Wondering why she should care either way. Wondering when the pain of betrayal and abandonment would stop.

"Lacy." Bob Wyatt spoke up and held out one hand toward her. In welcome? Or in the hope that she wouldn't bolt?

Lacy's spine went poker straight. She wouldn't run.

This mountain was her home. She wouldn't be chased away by the very man who had run from everything he'd loved.

"Did you bake me something?" Bob asked. "Smells good enough to eat."

Grateful for the older man's attempt to help her through this oh-so-weird situation, Lacy gave him a smile as she took a deep, steadying breath. In the past two years, she had spent a lot of nights figuring out how she would handle herself when she first saw Sam again. Now it was time to put all of those mental exercises into practice.

She would be cool, calm. She would never let on that simply looking at him made everything inside her weep for what they'd lost. And blast it, she would never let him know just how badly he'd broken her heart.

Forcing a smile she didn't quite feel, she headed across the room, looking only at Bob, her father-in-law. That's how she thought of him still, despite the divorce that Sam had demanded. Bob and Connie Wyatt had been family to Lacy since she was a girl, and she wasn't about to let that end just because their son was a low-down miserable excuse for a man.

"I did bake, just for you," she said, setting the basket in Bob's lap and bending down to plant a quick kiss on the older man's forehead. "Your favorite, cranberry-orange."

Bob took a whiff, sighed and gave her a grin. "Girl, you are a wonder in the kitchen."

"And *you* are a sucker for sugar," she teased.

"Guilty as charged." He glanced from her to Sam. "Why don't you sit down, visit for a while? Connie went off to get some snacks. Join us."

They used to all gather together in this room and

there was laughter and talking and a bond she had thought was stronger than anything. Those times were gone, though. Besides, with Sam sitting there watching her, Lacy's stomach twisted, making even the thought of food a hideous one to contemplate. Now, a gigantic glass of wine, on the other hand, was a distinct possibility.

"No, but thanks. I've got to get out to the bunny run. I've got lessons stacked up for the next couple of hours."

"If you're sure..." Bob's tone told her he knew exactly why she was leaving and the compassion in his eyes let her know he understood.

Oh, if he started being sympathetic, this could get ugly fast and she wasn't about to let a single tear drop anywhere in the vicinity of Sam Wyatt. She'd already done enough crying over him to last a lifetime. Blast if she'd put on a personal show for him!

"I'm sure," she said quickly. "But I'll come back tomorrow to check on you."

"That'd be good," Bob told her and gave her hand a pat.

Lacy didn't even look at Sam as she turned for the elevator. Frankly, she wasn't sure what she might do or say if she met those green eyes again. Better to just go about her life—teaching little kids and their scared mamas to ski. Then she'd go home, have that massive glass of wine, watch some silly chick flick and cry to release all of the tears now clogging her throat. Right now, though, all she wanted was to get out of there as quickly as she could.

But she should have known her tactic wouldn't work.

"Lacy, wait."

Sam was right behind her—she heard his footsteps on the wood floor—but she didn't stop. Didn't dare. She made it to the elevator and stabbed at the button.

But even as the door slid open, Sam's hand fell onto her shoulder.

That one touch sent heat slicing through her and she hissed in a breath in an attempt to keep that heat from spreading. Deliberately, she dipped down, escaping his touch, then stepped into the elevator.

Sam slapped one hand onto the elevator door to keep it open as he leaned toward her. "Damn it, Lacy, we have to talk."

"Why?" she countered. "Because you say so? No, Sam. We have nothing to talk about."

"I'm—"

Her head snapped up and she glared at him. "And so help me, if you say 'I'm sorry,' I will find a way to make sure you are."

"You're not making this easy," he remarked.

"Oh, you mean like you did, two years ago?" Despite her fury, she kept her voice a low hiss. She didn't want to upset Bob.

God, she hadn't wanted to get into this at all. She never wanted to talk about the day Sam had handed her divorce papers and then left the mountain—and *her*—behind.

Deliberately keeping her gaze fixed to his, she punched the button for the lobby. "I have to work. Let go of the door."

"You're going to have to talk to me at some point."

She reached up, pulled his fingers off the cold steel and as the door closed quietly, she assured him, "No, Sam. I really don't."

Two

Thank God, Lacy thought, for the class of toddlers she was teaching. It kept her so busy she didn't have time to think about Sam. Or about what it might mean having him back home.

But because her mind was occupied didn't mean that her body hadn't gone into a sort of sense memory celebration. Even her skin seemed to recall what it felt like when Sam touched her. And every square inch of her buzzed with anticipation.

"Are you sure it's safe to teach her how to ski so soon?" A woman with worried brown eyes looked from Lacy to her three-year-old daughter, struggling to stay upright on a pair of tiny skis.

"Absolutely," Lacy answered, pushing thoughts of Sam to the back of her mind, where she hoped they would stay. If her body was looking forward to being with Sam again, it would just have to deal with disappointment. "My father started me off at two. When you begin this young, there's no fear. Only a sense of adventure."

The woman laughed a little. "That I understand." Her gaze lifted to the top of the lift at the mountain's summit. "I've got plenty of fear, but my husband loves skiing so…"

Lacy smiled as she watched her assistant help a little boy up from where he'd toppled over into the soft, powdery snow. "You'll love it. I promise."

"Hope so," she said wistfully. "Right now, Mike's up there somewhere—" she pointed at the top of the mountain "—with his brother. He's going to watch Kaylee while I have my lesson this afternoon."

"Kristi Wyatt's teaching your class," Lacy told her. "And she's wonderful. You'll enjoy it. Really."

The woman's gaze swung back to her. "The Wyatt family. My husband used to come here on ski trips just to watch the Wyatt brothers ski."

Lacy's smile felt a little stiff, but she gave herself points for keeping it in place. "A lot of people did."

"It was just tragic what happened to Jack Wyatt."

The woman wasn't the first person to bring up the past, and no doubt she wouldn't be the last, either. Even two years after Jack's death, his fans still came to Snow Vista in a sort of pilgrimage. He hadn't been forgotten. Neither had Sam. In the skiing world, the Wyatt twins had been, and always would be, rock stars.

The woman's eyes were kind, sympathetic and yet, curious. Of course she was. Everyone remembered Jack Wyatt, champion skier, and everyone knew how Jack's story had ended.

What they didn't know was what that pain had done to the family left behind. Two years ago, it had been all

Lacy could think about. She'd driven herself half-crazy asking herself the kind of what-if questions that had no answers, only possibilities. And those possibilities had haunted her. Had kept her awake at night, alone in her bed. She'd wondered and cried and wondered again until her emotions were wrung out and she was left with only a sad reality staring her in the face.

Jack had died, but it was the people he'd left behind who had suffered.

"Yes," Lacy agreed, feeling her oh-so-tight smile slipping away. "It was." And tragic that the ripple effect of what happened to Jack had slammed its way through the Wyatt family like an avalanche, wiping out everything in its path.

While the kids practiced and Lacy's assistant supervised, the woman continued in a hushed voice. "My husband keeps up with everything even mildly related to the skiing world. He said that Jack's twin, Sam, left Snow Vista after his brother's death."

God, how could Lacy get out of this conversation?

"Yes, he did."

"Apparently, he left competitive skiing and he's some kind of amazing ski resort designer now and he's got a line of ski equipment and he's apparently spent the last couple of years dating royalty in Europe."

Lacy's heart gave one vicious tug and she took a deep breath, hoping to keep all the emotions churning inside her locked away. It wasn't easy. After all, though Sam hadn't contacted the family except for the occasional postcard, he was a high-profile athlete with a tragic past who got more than his share of media attention.

So it hadn't been difficult to keep up with what he'd been doing the past couple of years. Lacy knew all about his businesses and how he'd put his name on everything from goggles to ski poles. He was rich, famous and gorgeous. Of course the media was all over him. So naturally, Lacy had been treated to paparazzi photos of Sam escorting beautiful women to glamorous events—and yes, he had been photographed with a dark-haired, skinny countess who looked as though she hadn't had a regular meal in ten years.

But it didn't matter what he did, because Sam was Lacy's *ex*-husband. So they could both date whomever they wanted to. Not that she had dated much—or any for that matter. But she could if she wanted to and that's what mattered.

"Do you actually know the Wyatts?" the woman asked, then stopped and caught herself. "Silly question. Of course you do. You work for them."

True. And up until two years ago, Lacy had been one of them. But that was another life and this was the one she had to focus on.

"Yes, I do," Lacy said, forcing another smile she didn't feel. "And speaking of work, I should really get to today's lessons."

Then she walked to join her assistant Andi and the group of kids who demanded nothing but her time.

Sam waited for hours.

He kept an eye on Lacy's classes and marveled that she could be so patient—not just with the kids but with the hovering parents who seemed to have an opinion on everything that happened. She hadn't changed, he thought with some small satisfaction. She was still patient, reasonable. But then, Lacy had always been the calm one. The cool head that invariably had smoothed over any trouble that rose up between Sam and Jack.

He and his twin had argued over everything, and

damned if Sam didn't still miss it. A twinge pulled at his heart and he ignored it as he had for the past two years. Memories clamored in the back of his mind and he ignored them, as well. He'd spent too much time burying all reminders of the pain that had chased him away from his home.

Muttering under his breath, he shoved one hand through his hair and focused on the woman he hadn't been able to forget. She hadn't changed, he thought again and found that intriguing as well as comforting. The stir of need and desire inside him thickened into a hot flow like lava through his veins.

That hadn't changed, either.

"Okay, that's it for today," Lacy was saying and the sound of her voice rippled along his spine like a touch.

Sam shook his head to clear it of any thoughts that would get in the way of the conversation he was about to have and then he waited.

"Parents," Lacy called out with a smile, "thanks for trusting us with your children. And if you want to sign up for another lesson, just see my assistant Andi and she'll take care of it."

Andi was new, Sam thought, barely glancing at the young woman with the bright red hair and a face full of freckles. His concentration was fixed on Lacy. As if she felt his focused stare, she lifted her head and met his gaze over the heads of the kids gathered around her.

She tore her gaze from his, smiled and laughed with the kids, and then slowly made her way to him. He watched every step. Her long legs looked great in black jeans and the heavy sweater she wore clung to a figure he remembered all too well.

Despite the snow covering the ground and the surrounding pines, the sun shone brilliantly out of a bright blue sky, making the air warm in spite of the snow. Lacy flipped her long blond braid over her shoulder to lie down the center of her back and never slowed her steps until she was right in front of him.

"Sam."

"Lacy, we need to talk."

"I already told you we have nothing to say to each other."

She tried to brush past him, but he caught her arm in a firm grip and kept her at his side. Her gaze snapped to his hand and made her meaning clear. He didn't care. If anything, he tightened his hold on her.

"Time to clear the air," he said softly, mindful of the fact that there was a huge crowd ebbing and flowing around them.

"That's funny coming from you," she countered. "I don't remember you wanting to talk two years ago. All I remember is seeing you walk away. Oh, yeah. And I remember divorce papers arriving two weeks later. You didn't want to talk then. Why all of a sudden are you feeling chatty?"

He stared at her, a little stunned at her response. Not that it wasn't justified; it was only that the Lacy he remembered never would have said any of it. She was always so controlled. So…soft.

"You've changed some," he mused.

"If you mean I speak for myself now, then yes. I have changed. Enough that I don't want to go back to who I was then—easily breakable."

He clenched his jaw at the accusation that *he* had been the one to break her. Sam could admit that he'd handled everything badly two years ago, but if she was so damaged, how was she standing there glaring at him?

"Looks to me like you recovered nicely," he pointed out.

"No thanks to you." She glanced around, as if to make sure no one could overhear them.

"You're right about that," he acknowledged. "But we still have to talk."

Staring into his eyes now, she said, "Because you say so? Sorry, Sam. Not how it works. You can't disappear for two years, then drop back in and expect me to roll over and do whatever it is you want."

Her voice was cool, and her eyes were anything but. He could see sparks of indignation in those blue depths that surprised him. The new attitude also came with a temper. But then, she had every right to be furious. She was still going to listen to him.

"Lacy," he ground out, "I'm here now. We'll have to see each other every day."

"Not if I can help it," she countered, and the flash in her eyes went bright.

Around them, the day went on. Couples walked hand in hand. Parents herded children and squeals of excitement sliced through the air. Up on the mountain, skiers in a rainbow of brightly colored parkas raced down the slopes.

Here, though, Sam was facing a challenge of a different kind. She'd been in his thoughts and dreams for two years. Soft, sweet, trusting. Yet this new side of Lacy appealed to him, too. He liked the fire sparking in her eyes, even if it was threatening to engulf him.

When she tugged to get free of his grip, he let her go, but his fingertips burned as if he'd been holding on to a live electrical wire. "Lacy, you work for me—"

"I work for your father," she corrected.

"You work for the Wyatts," he reminded her. "I'm a Wyatt."

Her head snapped up and those furious blue eyes narrowed to slits. "And you're the one Wyatt I want nothing to do with."

"Lacy?"

Kristi's voice came from right behind him and Sam bit back an oath. His sister had lousy timing was his first thought, then he realized that she was interrupting on purpose. As if riding to Lacy's rescue.

"Hi, Kristi." Lacy gave her a smile and blatantly ignored Sam's presence. "You need something?"

"Actually, yeah." Kristi gave her brother one long, hard look, then turned back to Lacy. "If you're not busy, I'd like to go over some of the plans for next weekend's End of Season ski party."

"I'm not busy at all." Lacy gave Sam a meaningful look. "We were done here, right?"

If he said no, he'd have two angry women to face. If he said yes, Lacy would believe that he was willing to step away from the confrontation they needed to have—which he wasn't. Yeah, two years ago he'd walked away. But he was back now and they were both going to have to find a way to deal with it.

For however long he was here.

"For now," he finally said, and saw the shimmer of relief in Lacy's eyes. It would be short-lived, though, because the two of them weren't finished.

After Lacy and Kristi left, Sam wandered the resort, familiarizing himself with it all. He could have drawn the place from memory—from the bunny runs to the slalom courses to the small snack shops. And yet, after being gone for two years, Sam was looking at the place through new eyes.

He'd been making some changes to the resort, beginning the expansion he'd once dreamed of, when Jack died. Then, like a light switch flipping off, his dreams for the place had winked out of existence. Sam frowned and stared up at the top of the mountain. There were other resorts in Utah. Big ones, small ones, each of them drawing away a slice of tourism skiing that Snow Vista should be able to claim.

While he looked around, his mind worked. They needed more cabins for guests. Maybe another inn, separate from the hotel. A restaurant at the summit. Something that offered more substantial fare than hot dogs and popcorn. And for serious skiers, they needed to open a run on the backside of the mountain where the slope was sheer and there were enough trees and jumps to make for a dangerous—and exciting—run.

God knew he had more than enough money to invest in Snow Vista. All it would take was his father's approval, and why the hell wouldn't he go for it? With work and some inventive publicity, Sam could turn Snow Vista into the premier ski resort in the country.

But to make all of these changes would mean that he'd have to stay. To dig his heels in and reclaim the life that he'd once walked away from. And he wasn't sure he wanted to do that. Or that he could. He wasn't the same man who had left here two years ago. He'd changed as much as Lacy had. Maybe more.

Staying here would mean accepting everything he'd once run from. It would mean living with Jack's ghost. Seeing him on every ski run. Hearing his laugh on the wind.

Sam's gaze fixed on a lone skier making his way

down the mountain. Snow flared up from the sides of his skis and as he bent low to pick up speed, Sam could almost feel the guy's exhilaration. Sam had grown up on that mountain and just seeing it again was easing all of the rough edges on his soul that he'd been carrying around for two years. It wouldn't be easy, but he belonged here. A part of him always would.

And just like that, he knew that he would stay. At least as long as it took to make all of the changes he'd once dreamed of making to his family's resort.

The first step on that journey was laying it out for his father.

"And you want to oversee all of this yourself?"

"Yeah," Sam said, leaning back in one of the leather chairs in the family great room. "I do. We can make Snow Vista the place everyone wants to come."

"You've only been back a couple hours." Bob's eyes narrowed on his son. "You're not taking much more time over this decision than you did with the one to leave."

Sam shifted in his chair. He'd made his choice. He just needed to convince his father that it was the right one.

"You sure you want to do this?"

The decision had come easily. Quickly, even though he'd barely arrived. Maybe he should take some time. Settle in. Determine if this was what he really wanted to do. But even as he considered it, he dismissed it.

Looking at his father, Sam realized that his first concern—the worry that had brought him home—had been eased. His dad was in no danger. His health wasn't deteriorating. But still, the old man would have to rest up, take it easy, which meant that Sam was needed here. At least for the time being.

And if he didn't involve himself in the family resort, what the hell would he do with himself while he was here? He scrubbed one hand across the back of his neck. If he got right to work he could have most of the changes made and completed within a few months. By then, his dad should be up and feeling himself again and Sam could... "Yeah, Dad. I'm sure I want to do it. If I get started right away, most of it can be finished within a few months."

"I remember you and Jack sitting up half the night with drawings and notebooks, planning out what you were going to do to the place." His father sighed heavily and Sam could feel his pain. But then his father nodded, tapped the fingers of his right hand against his knee. "You'll supervise it all? Take charge?"

"I will." Heat swarmed through the room, rushing from the hearth where a fire burned with licks and hisses of flames.

"So this means you're staying?" His father's gaze was wise and steady and somehow way too perceptive.

"I'll stay. Until I've got everything done anyway." That was all he could promise. All he could swear to.

"Could take months."

"To finish everything? I figure at least six," Sam agreed.

His father shifted his gaze to stare out the window at the sprawling view of the Salt Lake Valley. "I shouldn't let you put your money on the line," he finally said quietly. "You've got your own life now."

"I'm still a Wyatt," Sam said easily.

Bob slowly turned his head to look at his son. "Glad to hear you remember that."

Guilt poked at Sam again and he didn't care for it. Hell, until two years ago, guilt had never been a part of his life, but since then, it had been his constant companion. "I remember."

"Took you long enough," his father said softly. "We missed you here."

"I know, Dad." He leaned forward, braced his elbows on his knees and let his hands hang in front of him. "But I had to go. Had to get away from—"

"Us."

Sam's head snapped up and his gaze fixed on his father's face, wreathed in sorrow. "No, Dad. I wasn't trying to get away from the family. I was trying to lose myself."

"Not real smart," the older man mused, "since you took you with you when you left."

"Yeah," Sam muttered, jumping to his feet and pacing. His father's point made perfect sense when said out loud like that. But two years ago, Sam hadn't been willing or able to listen to anyone. He hadn't wanted advice. Or sympathy. He'd only wanted space. Between himself and everything that reminded him he was alive and his twin was dead.

He stalked back and forth across the wide floor until he finally came to a stop in front of the man sitting quietly, watching him. "At the time, it seemed like the only thing to do. After Jack…" He shook his head and bit back words that were useless.

Didn't matter now why he'd done what he had. Hearing him say that he regretted his choices wouldn't change the fact that he had walked out on the people who loved him. Needed him. But they, none of them, could understand what it had meant when his twin— the other half of himself—had died.

His dad nodded glumly. "Losing Jack took a huge chunk out of this family. Tore us all to pieces, you more than the rest of us, I'm guessing. But putting all that aside, I need to know, Sam. If you start something here, I need to know you'll stay to see it through."

"I give you my word, Dad. I'll stay till it's done."

"That's good enough for me," his father said, and pushed out of his chair. Standing, he offered his hand to Sam and when they shook on it, Bob Wyatt smiled and said, "You'll have to work with our resort manager to get this up and running."

Sam nodded. Their resort manager had been with the Wyatts for twenty years. "Dave Mendez. I'll see him tomorrow."

"Guess you haven't heard yet. Dave retired last year."

"What?" Surprised, Sam asked, "Well who replaced him?"

His father gave him a wide grin. "Lacy Sills."

First thing the next morning, Lacy was sipping a latte as she opened the door to her office. She nearly choked on the swallow of hot milk and espresso. Gasping for air, she slapped one hand on her chest and glared at the man sitting behind *her* desk.

"What're you doing here?"

Sam took his time looking up from the sheaf of papers in front of him. "I'm going over the reports for the hotel, the cabins and the snack bar. Haven't gotten to the ski runs yet, but I will."

"Why?" She managed one word, her fingers tightening on the paper cup in her hand.

God, it was a wonder she could think, let alone talk. Her head was fuzzed out and her brain hadn't quite clicked into top gear. It was all Kristi's fault, Lacy told herself. Sam's sister had come over to Lacy's cabin the night before, carrying two bottles of wine and a huge platter of brownies.

At the time it had seemed like a great idea. Getting a little drunk with her oldest friend. Talking trash about the man who was such a central part in both of their lives.

Sam.

It always came down to Sam, she thought and wished to heaven she had a clear enough head to be on top of this situation. But, she thought sadly, even without a hangover, she wouldn't be at her best facing the man who had shattered her heart.

It was still hard for her to believe that he'd come back. Even harder to know what to do about it. The safest thing, she knew, would be to keep her distance. To avoid him as much as possible and to remind herself often that no doubt he'd be leaving again. He had left, he said at the time, because he hadn't been able to face living with the memories of Jack.

Nothing had changed.

Which meant that Sam wouldn't stay.

And Lacy would do whatever she had to, to keep from being broken again.

"When I left," Sam said quietly, "we had just started making changes around here."

"Yes, I remember." She edged farther into the office, but the room on the first floor of the Wyatt lodge was a small one and every step she took brought her closer to *him*. "We finished the reno to the lodge, but once that was done, we put off most of the rest. Your folks just weren't..." Her voice trailed off.

The Wyatts hadn't been in the mood to change anything after Jack's death changed *everything*.

"Well, while I'm here, we're going to tackle the rest of the plans."

While he was here.

That was plain enough, Lacy thought. He was making himself perfectly clear. "You talked to your dad about this?"

"Yeah." Sam folded his hands atop his flat abdomen and watched her. "He's good with it so we're going to get moving as quickly as possible."

"On what exactly?"

"For starters," he said, sitting forward again and picking up a single piece of paper, "we're going to expand the snack bar at the top of the lift. I want a real restaurant up there. Something that will draw people in, make them linger for a while."

"A restaurant." She thought of the spot he meant and had to admit it was a good idea. Hot dogs and popcorn only appealed to so many people. "That's a big start."

"No point in staying small, is there?"

"I suppose not," she said, leaning back against the wall, clutching her latte cup hard enough she was surprised she hadn't crushed it in her fist. "What else?"

"We'll be building more cabins," he told her. "People like the privacy of their own space."

"They do."

"Glad you agree," he said with a sharp nod.

"Is there more?" she asked.

"Plenty," he said and waved one hand at the chair in front of the desk. "Sit down and we'll talk about it."

A spurt of anger shot through her. He had commandeered her office and her desk and now she was being relegated to the visitor's chair. A subtle move for power?

Shaking her head, she dropped into the seat and

looked at the man sitting opposite her. He was watching her as if he knew exactly what she was thinking.

"We're going to be working together on this, Lacy," he said quietly. "I hope that's not going to be a problem."

"I can do my job, Sam," she assured him.

"So can I, Lacy," he said. "The question is, can we do the job together?"

Three

It went wrong right from the jump. For the next hour, they butted heads continuously until Lacy had a headache the size of Idaho.

"You closed the intermediate run on the east side of the mountain," he said, glancing up from the reports. "I want that opened up again."

"We can't open it until next season," Lacy said, pausing for a sip of the latte that had gone cold over the past hour.

He dropped a pen onto the desk top. "And why's that?"

She met his almost-accusatory stare with cool indifference. "We had a storm come through late December. Tore down a few pines and dropped a foot and a half of snow." She crossed her legs and held her latte between her palms. "The pines are blocking the run and we can't get a crew in there to clear it out because the snow in the pass is too deep."

He frowned. "You waited too long to send in a crew."

At the insinuation of incompetence in his voice, she stood up and stared down at him. "I waited until the storm passed," she argued. "Once we got a look at the damage and I factored in the risks to the guys of clearing it, I closed that run."

Leaning back in his chair, he met her gaze. "So you ran the rest of the season on half power."

"We did fine," she said tightly. "Check the numbers."

"I have." Almost lazily, he stood so that he loomed over her, forcing her to lift her gaze. "You didn't do badly..."

"Thanks so much." Sarcasm dripped from every word.

"It would have been a better season with that run open."

"Well yeah," she said, setting her latte cup onto *her* desk. "But we don't always get what we want, do we?"

His eyes narrowed and she gave herself a mental pat on the back for that well-aimed barb. Before Sam had walked out on her and everyone else, she couldn't remember a time when she'd lost her temper. Now that he was back, though, the anger she used to keep tamped down kept bubbling up.

"Leaving that alone for the moment," he said, "the revenue from the snack bar isn't as high as it used to be."

She shrugged. This was not news to her. "Not that many people are interested in hot dogs, really. Most people go for a real lunch in town."

"Which is why building a restaurant at the summit is important," he said.

She hated that he was right. "I agree."

A half smile curved his mouth briefly and her stomach gave a quick twist in response. It was involuntary, she consoled herself. Sam smiled; she quivered. Didn't mean she had to let him know.

"If we can agree on one thing, there may be more."

"Don't count on it," she warned.

He tipped his head to one side and stared at her. "I don't remember you being so stubborn. Or having a temper."

"I learned how to stand up for myself while you were gone, Sam," she told him, lifting her chin to emphasize her feelings on this. "I won't smile and nod just because Sam Wyatt says something. When I disagree, you'll know it."

Nodding, he said, "I think I like the new Lacy as much as I did the old one. You're a strong woman. Always have been, whether you ever chose to show it or not."

"No," Lacy said softly. "You don't get to do that, Sam. You don't get to stand there and pretend to know me."

"I do know you, Lacy," he argued, coming around the desk. "We were married."

"*Were* being the operative word in that sentence," she reminded him, and took two steps back. "You don't know me anymore. I've changed."

"I can see that. But the basics are the same," he said, closing the distance between them again. "You still smell like lilacs. You still wear your hair in that thick braid I used to love to undo and spill across your shoulders…"

Lacy's stomach did a fast, jittery spin and her heartbeat leaped into a gallop. How was it fair that he could still make her body come alive with a few soft words and a heated look? Why hadn't the need for him drowned in the sea of hurt and anger that had enveloped her when he left?

"Stop it."

"Why?" He shook his head and kept coming, one long, slow step after another. "You're still beautiful. And I like the way temper makes your eyes flash."

The office just wasn't big enough for this, Lacy told herself, and crowded around behind the desk, trying to keep the solid piece of furniture between them. She didn't trust herself around him. Never had been able to. From the time she was a girl, she had wanted Sam and that feeling had never left her. Not even when he'd broken her heart by abandoning her.

"You don't have the right to talk to me like that now. You left, Sam. And I moved on."

Liar, her mind screamed. She hadn't moved on. How could she? Sam Wyatt was the love of her life. He was the only man she had ever wanted. The only one she still wanted, damn it. But he wasn't going to know that.

Because she had trusted him. More than anyone in her life, she had trusted him and he'd left her without a backward glance. The pain of that hadn't faded.

He narrowed his gaze on her. "There's someone else?"

She laughed, but the sharp edge of it scraped her throat. "Why do you sound so surprised? You've been gone two years, Sam. Did you think I'd enter a convent or something? That I'd throw myself on our torn-up marriage certificate and vow to never love another man?"

His jaw tightened, the muscle there twitching as he ground his teeth together. "Who is he?"

She sucked in a gulp of air. "None of your business."

"I hate that. But yeah, it's not," he agreed, moving

closer. So close that Lacy couldn't draw a breath without taking the scent of him—his shampoo, the barest hint of a foresty cologne—deep into her lungs. He looked the same. He felt the same. But *nothing* was the same.

Lacy felt the swirl of need she always associated with Sam. No other man affected her as he did. No other man had ever tempted her into believing in forever. And look how that had turned out.

"Sam." The window was at her back, the glass cold through her sweater and still doing nothing to chill the heat that pulsed inside her.

"Who is he, Lacy?" He reached up and fingered the end of her braid. "Do I know him?"

"No," she muttered, looking for a way out and not finding one. She could slip to the side, but he'd only move with her. Too close. She took another breath. "Why does it matter, Sam? Why would you care?"

"Like I said, we were married once," he said as if he had to remind her.

"We're not now," she told him flatly.

"No," he said, then lifted his fingers to tip up her chin, drawing her gaze to meet his. "Your eyes are still so damn blue."

His whisper shivered inside her. His touch sent bolts of heat jolting through her and Lacy took another breath to steady herself and instead was swamped by his scent, filling her, fogging her mind, awakening memories she'd worked so hard to bury.

"Do you taste the same?" he wondered softly, and lowered his head to hers.

She should stop him, she knew, and yet, she didn't. Couldn't. His mouth came down on hers and everything fell away but for what he could make her feel. Lacy's heart pounded like a drum. Her body ached; her mind

swirled with the pleasure, the passion that she'd only
ever found with Sam.

It was reaction, she told herself. That was all. It was
the ache of her bones, the pain in her heart, finally
being assuaged by the man who had caused it all in
the first place.

He pulled her in tightly to him and for a brief, amazing moment, she allowed herself to feel the joy in being
pressed against his hard, muscled chest again. To experience his arms wrap around her, enfolding her. To
part her lips for his tongue and know the wild rush of
sensation sweeping through her.

It was all there. Two years and all it took was a single kiss to remind her of everything they'd once shared,
they'd once known. Her body leaned into him even as
her mind was screaming at her to stop. She burned and
in the flames, felt the heat sear every nerve ending. That
was finally enough, after what felt like a small eternity,
to make her listen to that small, rational internal voice.

Pulling away from him, Lacy shook her head and
said, "No. No more. I won't do it."

"We just did."

Her head snapped up, furious with him, but more so
with herself. How could she be so stupid? He'd *abandoned* her and he's back on the mountain for a single
day and she's kissing him? God, it was humiliating.
"That was a mistake."

"Not from where I'm standing," Sam said, but she
was pleased to see he looked as shaken as she felt.

Small consolation, but she'd take it. The office suddenly seemed claustrophobic. She had to get out. Get
into the open where she could think again, where she
could force herself to remember all of the pain she'd
been through because of him.

"You can't touch me again, Sam," Lacy said, and it cost her, because her body was still buzzing as if she'd brushed up against a live wire. "I won't let you."

Frowning, he asked, "Loyal to the new guy, huh?"

"No," she told him flatly, "this is about me. And about protecting myself."

"From *me*?" He actually looked astonished. "You really think you need protection from me?"

Could he really not understand this? "You once asked me to trust you. To believe that you loved me and you'd never leave."

His features went taut, his eyes shuttered. She *felt* him closing himself down, but she couldn't stop now.

"But you lied. You *did* leave."

His eyes flashed once—with hurt or shame, she didn't know, couldn't tell. "You think I planned to leave, Lacy? You think it was something I wanted?"

"How would I know?" she countered, anger and hurt clawing at her insides. "You didn't talk to me, Sam. You shut me out. And then you walked away. You hurt me once, Sam. I won't let you do it again. So you really need to back off."

"I'm here now, Lacy. And there's no way I'm backing off. This is still my home."

"But *I'm* not yours," she told him, accepting the pain of those words. "Not anymore."

He took a breath, blew it out and scrubbed one hand across the back of his neck. The familiarity of that gesture tugged at her.

"I thought of you," he admitted, fixing his gaze to hers as his voice dropped to a low throb that seemed to rumble along her spine. "I missed you."

Equal parts pleasure and pain tore at her heart. The taste of him was still on her mouth, flavoring every breath. Her senses were so full she felt as if she might explode. So she held tight to the pain and let the pleasure slide away. "It's your own fault you missed me, Sam. You're the one who left."

"I did what I had to do at the time."

"And screw anyone else," she added for him.

Pushing one hand through his hair, he finally took a step back, giving Lacy the breathing room she so badly needed. "That's what it looked like, I guess."

"That's what it was, Sam," she told him, and took the opportunity to slip out and move around until the desk once again stood between them like a solid barrier. "You left us all. Me. Your parents. Your sister. You walked away from your home and left the rest of us to pick up the pieces."

"I couldn't do it." He whirled around to face her, green eyes flashing like a forest burning. "You need to hear me say it? That I couldn't take it? That Jack died and I lost it? Fine. There." He slapped both hands onto the desk and glared at her. "That make it better for you? Easier?"

Overwhelmed with fury, Lacy thought she actually *saw* red. So many emotions surged inside her, she could hardly separate them. Lacy felt the crash and slam of the feelings she'd tried to bury two years ago as they rushed to the surface, demanding to be acknowledged.

"Better? Really?" Her voice was hard, but low. She wouldn't shout. Wouldn't give him the satisfaction of knowing just how deeply his words had cut her. "You think it can get better? My *husband* left me with all the casualness of tossing out an old shirt."

"I didn't—"

"Don't even try to argue," she interrupted him before he could.

"I won't." He fisted his hands on the desktop, then carefully, deliberately, released them again. "I can't explain it to myself, so how could I explain it to you or anyone else? Yeah, I left and maybe that was wrong."

"Maybe?"

"But I'm back now."

Lacy shook her head and swallowed the rest of her temper. Clashing with him was no way to prove to Sam that she was over him. She would *not* get pulled into a Wyatt family drama. She wasn't one of them anymore. Sam returning had nothing to do with her. In spite of the heat inside her, the yearning gnawing at her, she knew she had to protect herself.

"You didn't come back for me, Sam. So let's not pretend different, okay?"

"What if I had?" he whispered, gaze locked with hers.

"It wouldn't matter," she told him, and hoped to heaven he believed her. "What we had is done and gone."

He studied her for a long minute. Seconds ticked past, counting off with every heartbeat. Tension coiled and bristled in the air between them.

"I think," he said at last, "we just proved that what we had isn't completely gone."

"That doesn't count."

Surprised, he snorted, and laughter glinted in his eyes for a split second. "Oh, it counts. But we'll let it go for now."

She released a breath she hadn't realized she was holding. Ridiculous to feel both relieved and irritated all at once. How easily he turned what he was feeling on and off. How easily he had walked away from his life. From her.

"Back to business, then," he said, voice cool, dispassionate, as if that soul-shaking kiss hadn't happened. "Yesterday, you and Kristi were talking about the End of Season party."

"Yes. The plans are finalized."

Fine. Business she could do. She had been running the Wyatt resort for the past year and she'd done a damn good job. Let him go over the records and he would see for himself that she hadn't curled up and died just because he left. Lacy had a life she loved, a job she was good at. She was *happy*, damn it.

Coming around the desk, she ignored him and hit a few keys on the computer to pull up the file. "You can see for yourself, everything's in motion and right on schedule."

She moved out of the way as he stepped in to glance at the monitor. Scrolling down, he gave the figures there a quick look, then shifted his gaze to hers. "Looks fine. But end of season's usually not until March. Why are we closing the slopes early?"

Lacy was on familiar ground here and she relaxed a little as she explained, "There hasn't been any significant snowfall since early January. Weather's been cold enough to keep the snowpack in good shape, but we're getting icy now. Our guests expect the best powder in the world—"

"Yeah," he said wryly, "I know."

Of course he knew. He had, just like Lacy, grown up skiing the very slopes they were discussing now. He'd built a life, a profession, a reputation on skiing.

"Right. Then you should appreciate why we're doing the official closing early." Lacy walked around the desk until it stood between them again. She sighed and said, "Numbers have been falling off lately. People know there's no fresh snow, so they're not in a rush to come up the mountain.

"Throwing the End of Season party early will bring them up here. The hotel's already booked and we just have two of the cabins left empty…"

"One," he said, interrupting the flow of words while he continued to scan the plans for the party.

"One what?"

"One cabin's empty." He shrugged. "I moved my stuff into Cabin 6."

A sinking sensation opened up in the pit of her stomach. Cabin 6 was close to her house. Way too close. And he knew that. So had he chosen that cabin purposely? "I thought you'd be staying in the family quarters at the lodge."

He shook his head. "No. The cabin will suit me. I need the space."

"Fine," she said shortly, determined not to let it matter where he stayed. "Anyway, locals will still come ski whether we're 'officially' closed or not. We'll keep the lifts running and if we get more snow, then others will come, too. But holding the party early gives us publicity that could keep tourists coming in until the snow melts."

"It's a good idea."

He said it grudgingly and Lacy scowled at him. "You sound surprised."

"I'm not," he said, then dropped into the desk chair. "You know this place as well as I do. You were a good choice to run the resort. Why would I be surprised that you're good at your job?"

Was there a compliment in there?

"I want to go over the rest of the records, then, since you're the manager now, I'll want to talk tomorrow about the plans for the resort."

"Fine," she said, headed for the door. "I'll see you here tomorrow, then."

"That'll work."

She opened the door and stopped when he spoke again.

"And Lacy…"

She looked over her shoulder at him. His eyes met hers. "We're not done. We'll *never* be done."

There was nothing she could say to that, so she left, closing the door softly behind her.

That kiss stayed with him for hours.

For two years, he'd lived without her. It hadn't been easy, especially at first. But the grief and rage and guilt had colored everything then and he'd buried her memory in the swamp of other emotions. He'd convinced himself she was fine because the reality was too brutal. She'd come to haunt him at night of course. His sleep was crowded with her image, with her scent, with her taste.

And now he'd had a taste of her again and his system was on fire.

Need crouched inside him, clawing at his guts, tearing at what was left of his heart. He'd loved her back then. But love hadn't been enough to survive his own pain. Now there was desire, rich and thick and tormenting him in ways he hadn't felt since the last time he'd seen Lacy Sills.

She'd said she had a new man. Who the hell was touching her? Who heard her whisper of breath when she climaxed? Who felt her small, strong hands sliding up and down his skin? It was making Sam crazy just thinking about it. And yet, he couldn't seem to stop, either.

Yeah, none of it was rational. He didn't care.

When he'd headed home, his only thought had been for his father. Worry had driven every action. He hadn't stopped to think what it would be like to be near Lacy again. To face her and what he'd done by leaving. His heart told him he was a bastard, but his brain kept reminding him that he'd had to leave. That he might have made even more of a mess of things if he'd stayed.

Now he was here, for at least a few months. How was he going to make it without touching her? Answer—he wouldn't. The truth was, he was *going* to touch her. As soon and as often as possible. Her response to his kiss told him that whether she wanted to admit it or not, she wanted him, too. So to hell with the new guy, whoever he was.

Sam turned in the chair and looked out at the night. The lights glittering in the Salt Lake Valley below smudged the horizon with a glow that dimmed the stars. His gaze shifted, sweeping across the resort, where lights were golden, tossing puddled yellow illumination on the snow. It was pristine, beautiful, and he'd missed the place.

Acknowledging it was hard, but Sam knew that coming back here eased something inside him that had been drawn tight as a bowstring for two years. Coming home hadn't been easy. He'd spent the past two years trying to convince himself that he'd never come back. Now that he was here, though, there were ghosts to face, the past to confront and, mostly, there was the need to make a kind of peace with Lacy.

But then, he thought as he stood and walked out of the office, maybe it wasn't peace he was after with her.

For the next few days, Lacy avoided him at every turn and Sam let her get away with it. There was time to settle what was between them. He didn't have to rush, and besides, if he made her that nervous, drawing out the tension would only make her more on edge.

And that could only work to his benefit. Lacy cool and calm wasn't what he wanted. The temper she'd developed intrigued him and made him think of how passionate she had always been in bed. Together, they had been combustible. He wanted that back.

He glanced at her and almost smiled at the deliberate distance she kept. As if it would help. As if it could cool the fires burning between them. The day was cold and clear and the snow-covered ground at the summit crunched underfoot as they walked toward the site for the restaurant he was planning.

Tearing his gaze from Lacy momentarily, Sam studied the snack shop that had been there since before he was born. Small and filled with tradition, it had outlived its purpose. These days, most people wanted healthy food, not hot dogs smothered in mustard and chili.

"What're you thinking?" Lacy looked up at him, clearly still irritated that he'd dragged her away from the inn to come up here and look around.

He glanced at her. "That I want a chili dog."

For a split second, the ice in her eyes drained away. "You always did love Mike's chili."

"I've been all over the world and never found anything like it."

"Not surprising," Lacy answered. "I think he puts rocket fuel in that stuff."

Sam grinned and she gave him a smile in return that surprised and pleased him. A cold wind rushed across the mountaintop and lifted her blond braid off her shoulder. Her cheeks were pink, her blue eyes glittering and she looked so good it was all he could do not to grab her. But even as he thought it, her smile faded.

"I think we'll keep the snack shack for old time's sake," he said, forcing himself to look away from her and back out over the grounds where he would build the new restaurant. "But the new place, I'd like it to go over there," he pointed, "so the pines can ring the back of it. We'll have a deck out there, too, a garden area, and the trees will provide some shade, as well."

She looked where he pointed and nodded. "It's a good spot. But a wood deck requires a lot of upkeep. What about flagstone?"

Sam thought about it. "Good idea. Easier to clean, too. I called Dennis Barclay's construction company last night and he's going to come up tomorrow, make some measurements, draw up some plans so we can go to the city and line up the permits."

"Dennis does good work." She made a note on her iPad. "Franklin stone could lay the gravel paths and the flagstone. They've got a yard in Ogden with samples."

"Good idea. We can check that out once we get the permits and an architect's drawing on the restaurant."

"Right." Her voice was cool, clipped. "We used Nancy Frampton's firm for the addition to the inn."

"I remember." He nodded. "She's good. Okay, I'll call and talk to her tomorrow. Tell her what we want up here."

She made another note and he almost chuckled. She was so damn determined to keep him at arm's length. To pretend that what they'd shared in the office last night hadn't really happened. And he was willing to let that pretense go on. For a while.

"As long as you're making notes, write down that we want to get some ideas for where to build an addition to the inn. I want it close enough to the main lodge that it's still a part of us. But separate, too. Maybe joined by a covered walkway so even during storms, people can go back and forth."

"That'd work." She stopped, paused and said, "You know, a year ago, we put in a restaurant-grade stove, oven and fridge in the main lodge kitchen. We're equipped to provide more than breakfast and lunch now."

He turned his head and looked at her. "Then why aren't you?"

"We need a new chef." Lacy sighed and pulled her sunglasses off the top of her head to rest on the bridge of her nose. "Maria's ready to retire but she won't go until she's sure we'll survive without her."

Sam smiled, thinking of the woman who'd been at the lodge since he was a boy. Maria was a part of Sam's childhood, as much a fixture on the mountain as the Wyatt lodge itself. "Then she'll never leave."

Lacy smiled, too, and he wondered if she realized it. "Probably not. But if we want to serve a wider menu to more people, we need another chef to take some of the work off her shoulders. Maria doesn't really want to retire anyway, but she can't handle a larger load, no matter what she says. Another chef would make all the difference."

"Make a note," he said.

"Already done."

"Okay then." Sam took her elbow and turned her toward the snack bar. "Come on. We've got to go down and finalize the party setup. But first—chili dogs. On me."

"No thanks. I'm not hungry."

"As I remember it, you're always hungry, Lacy," he said, practically dragging her to the snack bar.

"Oh, for—" She broke off, gave in and started walking with him. "Things change, you know."

She was right. A lot had changed. But that buzz of something hot and electric that hummed between them was still there. Stronger than ever. Two years away hadn't eased what he felt for her. And since that kiss, he knew she felt the same.

"Mike's chili hasn't changed. And that's all I'm thinking about right now."

Of course, he was also planning ahead. So no onions.

Four

"Dad's really glad Sam's home." Kristi drained the last of her wine, then reached out and snagged the bottle off the coffee table for a refill.

"I know," Lacy said, sipping hers more slowly. She remembered the too-much-wine-and-brownies fest she and Kristi had had just a few days ago, and Lacy could live without another morning-after headache. "Your mom's happy, too."

Kristi sighed and snuggled deeper into the faded, overstuffed chair opposite Lacy. "I know. She hasn't stopped baking. Pies, cakes, the cookies I brought over to share. It's nuts, really. I don't think the oven's cooled off once since Sam arrived. Between Mom's sugar overload and Maria making all of Sam's favorites for dinner…I think I've gained five pounds."

While her best friend talked, Lacy stared at the fire in the brick hearth. Outside, the night was cold and still, moonlight glittering on snow. Inside, there was warmth from the fire and from the deep threads of friendship.

It felt good to sit here relaxing—or as much as she could relax when the conversation was about Sam. But at least he wasn't *here*. He wasn't walking through the resort with her, hunched over her desk going over plans, smelling so good she wanted to crawl onto his lap, tuck her head against his chest and just breathe him in.

Oh, God.

It had been days now and her very righteous anger kept sliding away to dissolve in a puddle of want and need. She didn't *want* to want Sam, but it seemed there was no choice. And damn it, Lacy told herself, she should know better.

What they had together hadn't been enough to keep him with her two years ago. It wouldn't be enough now. Wanting him was something she couldn't help. That didn't mean that she would surrender to what she felt for him again, though.

"They're all so happy he's back," Kristi was saying. "It's like they've forgotten all about how he left."

"I can understand that," Lacy told her, pausing for another sip of wine to ease the dryness in her suddenly tight throat. It was different for his family, of course. Having Sam back meant filling holes in their lives that had stood empty for too long. There was no second-guessing what they felt at his return. They weren't focused on their pain now, but on the alleviation of it.

Taking a breath, Lacy gave her friend a smile she really didn't feel. "Your parents missed him horribly. They're just grateful to have him home."

"Yeah, I get it." Kristi frowned into her straw-colored wine. "But how do they just ignore how he left? What he did to all of us by leaving *when* he did?"

"I don't know." Lacy reached out to snag a chocolate chip cookie off the plate on the table. Taking a bite, she chewed thoughtfully while Kristi continued to rant about her older brother, then she said, "I think for your mom and dad, it's more about getting their son back than it is punishing him for leaving."

"He hurt us all."

"Yeah. He did." Lacy knew how the other woman felt. *She* couldn't get past how Sam had left, either. Having him here now was so hard. Every time she saw him. Every time he stepped close to her, her heartbeat staggered and the bottom dropped out of her stomach.

Plus, there was the whole kiss thing, too. She hadn't been able to forget it. Hadn't been able to stop thinking about it. Had spent the past several days on red alert, waiting for him to try it again so she could shut him down flat.

And he hadn't tried.

Damn it.

"I used to think," Kristi said softly, "that everything would be better if Sam just came home." She paused for a sip of wine. "Now he has and it's not better. It's just... I don't know."

"He's your brother, Kristi," Lacy said, propping her feet on the coffee table and crossing them at the ankles. "You're still mad at him, but you love him and you know you're glad he's back."

"Do you?"

"Do I what?"

"Still love him."

Lacy's heart gave a hard thump. "That's not the point."

"It's completely pointy."

"Funny." Lacy took a long drink of her wine and

when she'd swallowed, said, "But this isn't about me. Or what I feel."

"So," Kristi mused, a half smile on her face, "that's a yes."

"No, it's not." Because her heart hammered every time he was near didn't necessarily mean *love*. Desire would always be there and that she could accept. Love was something else again and, "Even if it was, it wouldn't matter."

"You're still mad, too."

Lacy sighed. "Yeah. I am."

"He's worked really hard on the End of Season party," Kristi grudgingly admitted. "Sam even called one of his old friends. Tom Summer? He has a band that's really popular now and Sam talked Tom into bringing the band in for the party. Live music's going to be way better than the stereo we had arranged."

"Yes, it will." Irritating to admit that Sam had so easily arranged for a good band when everyone Lacy had spoken to about playing at the party had already been booked. He had friends everywhere and they were all as pleased to have him back as his family was. Here at Snow Vista, it was a regular *Celebration of Sam*. And Lacy was the only one not playing along. Well, okay, there was Kristi, as well. But she would eventually join the parade—Sam was her brother and that connection would win in the end.

When that happened, Lacy would be off by herself. Standing on the sidelines. Alone.

"It's like he's stepped right back into his life without a miss." Kristi shook her head again. "He steers away from most of the skiers—I think that's because everyone wants to ask him about Jack and he doesn't want to talk about him. I can't blame Sam for that." Her index finger ringed the rim of her wineglass. "None of us do."

"True." Lacy herself had seen Sam keep away from strangers, from the tourists who flocked to ski at Snow Vista. Just as she had watched him visit all of the runs on the mountain but the one that Jack had favored. She knew that memories were choking him just as her own had for two years.

Even this cabin—where she had grown up—wasn't a sanctuary anymore. Instead of memories of days spent with her father, the images in her mind were all of her and Sam, starting their life together. Lacy glanced around the familiar room, seeing the faded but comfortable furniture, the brightly colored throw rugs, the photos and framed prints hanging on the wall.

When she and Sam had married, they'd moved into her place—the plan had been to stay there and add on to the simple cabin until they had their dream house. The cabin was in a perfect spot—great views, close to the lodge and the ski runs—plus it was hers, free and clear, left to her after her father's death. Of course, those building plans were gathering dust in a closet and the rooms for the children they'd planned to have had never been built.

But staying here in this cabin had been a sort of exquisite torture. She'd heard Sam's voice, felt his presence, long after he left. Even her bed felt too big without him sharing it with her. Sam had torn up the foundation of her life and left her sitting in the rubble.

"Sam's even talking to Dad about building a summer luge ride. One like Park City has, to give tourists something to do up here in summer." Frowning, she took a sip of wine and grumbled, "I hate that it's a good idea."

"I know what you mean," Lacy admitted, chewing

on another cookie. "I want him to be out of step, you know? To stumble a little when he takes charge after two years gone. And yet, he's doing it all and he's getting a lot done. He's already had a contractor up at the summit to see about building the new restaurant and he's hired Nancy Frampton to draw up plans." She took a huge bite of the cookie and ground her teeth together. "He's gotten more done in the last few days than we have in two years."

"Irritating as hell, isn't it?" Kristi muttered.

"Really is."

"I don't know if I want him here or not. I mean, I'm glad for Mom and Dad—they missed him so much. But seeing him every day…" She stopped, her eyes widened and she groaned out loud. "God, I'm spewing all over the place and this has got to be so much worse on you." Instantly, Kristi looked contrite, embarrassed. "How are you handling it?"

"I'm fine." Lacy figured if she said those two words often enough, they might actually click in and she'd *be* fine.

At the moment, though, not so much. Her gaze shifted to the closest window. Through it, she had a view of the snow-covered forest, a wide sweep of sky, and there, she thought, through the trees, a glimpse of Cabin 6.

Most of the time she could pretend he wasn't there, but at night, when he had the lights on, he was impossible to ignore. As she watched, she saw his shadow pass a window and her heartbeat fluttered. Having him that close was a new kind of torture, she told herself.

For two years, she hadn't known where he was or what he was doing, except for the occasional updates from his parents or snippets in the media. Being apart from him tore at her—at least in the first few months. Now he was here, and still out of reach—not that she wanted to reach out and touch him. But having him close by and yet separate was harder than she'd imagined it could be.

When he first told her he'd be staying in the cabin closest to her home, Lacy had worried that he'd be coming over. But not once had Sam walked to her door. And she didn't know if that made her feel better or worse. The only thing she was sure of was that her nerves were stretched taut and sooner or later, they were going to snap.

"You're not fine." Kristi's voice was soft and filled with understanding.

Lacy might have argued that point, but Kristi was her best friend. They'd seen each other through high school, college courses, mean girls and heartbreak. What would be the point of trying to hold out now?

"Okay, no, I'm not." Nodding, Lacy held her wineglass a little tighter and drew a long, deep breath. "But I can be. It's just going to take some time."

"I hate that you're getting all twisted up by him again."

"Thanks," Lacy said, forcing a smile. "Me, too."

"The problem is, we're letting him get to us," Kristi said, grabbing another cookie and taking a bite. "That gives him all the power. What we have to do is take it back."

"You've been reading self-help books again." Lacy shook her head.

A quick grin flashed over Kristi's face. "Guilty. But you know, some of what they say makes sense. He can only bug us if we allow it. So we just have to stop allowing it."

"What a great idea," Lacy said, laughing, and God it felt good to laugh. "Got any ideas on how?"

Kristi shrugged. "Haven't gotten to that chapter yet."

"How does Tony maintain sanity around you?"

Tony DeLeon was smart, gorgeous and hopelessly in love with Kristi. For the past year or so, they'd been inseparable and Lacy really tried to be happy for her friend and not envious.

"He loves me." Kristi sighed dreamily. "Who would have guessed that I'd fall for an accountant?"

"Good thing you did—he's done a great job handling the inn's books."

"Yeah, he's pretty amazing," Kristi mused. "And so not the issue here. The problem is Sam."

Lacy's problem had always been Sam. She'd known from the time she was fifteen that he was the one she wanted. Oh, Jack was what the newspapers had always called "the fun twin" and she supposed that was true. Sam was quieter. More intense. Jack had been larger than life. His laugh was loud and booming; his love for life had been huge.

And when he died, he'd taken pieces of everyone who loved him with him. The largest piece had come from Sam. Those had been dark, terrible days. Lacy had helplessly watched Sam sink into a pit of misery and grief. Even lying beside him in their bed here at the cabin, she'd felt him slipping away from her.

He'd gotten lost, somehow, in the pain and he hadn't been able to find his way out.

But knowing that didn't make what had happened between them any easier to bear.

"Kristi," she said, "he's your brother. You can't stay mad at him forever."

Unexpectedly Kristi's eyes filled with tears, but she

blinked them back. "We *all* lost Jack and Sam didn't seem to understand that. He hurt me. Hurt all of us. Are we just supposed to forgive and forget?"

"I don't know," Lacy said, though she knew that she would never forget that she'd been left behind. Shut out. Made to feel that she didn't matter. She'd lived through that as a child and she'd trusted Sam when he promised he would never leave her—then he did, and that pain would never completely disappear.

"I don't think I can," Kristi admitted. She set her wineglass on the table and stood up. Then she walked to a window and stared out at the lamplight streaming from Sam's cabin. "I want to," she said, sending a short glance over her shoulder at Lacy. "I really do. And Tony keeps telling me that I'm only hurting myself by hanging on to all of this anger..."

Smiling, Lacy asked, "Gave him one of your books to read, did you?"

A soft, sad chuckle shot from Kristi's throat. "Yeah, guess I'm going to have to stop that." She turned her back on the window and shrugged. "It shouldn't be this hard."

No, it shouldn't.

"You'll just have to keep trying," Lacy told her.

"What about you?" her friend asked quietly. "Are you going to try?"

"My situation's different, Kristi. He's your family." Lacy stood up and cleared the coffee table of the cookies and wine. It had been a long day and clearly this girlfest was winding down into a pit of melancholy. She'd rather take a hot bath and go to bed. Straightening, she looked at the woman watching her. "He was my family, now he's not. So it doesn't really matter what I think of him."

Kristi gave her a sad smile. "Of course it matters. *You* matter, Lacy. I don't want him to hurt you again."

Winking, Lacy deliberately brought up Kristi's self-help advice. "He can only hurt me if I *allow* it. And trust me, I won't."

The party was a huge success. It was still early in the evening and Snow Vista was packed with locals and tourists who were enjoying the clear, cold weather and the hum of energy. The crowds were thick; music pumped into the air with a pounding beat that seemed to reverberate up from the ground. All around Sam, people were talking, laughing, dancing. The party was a success. So why the hell was he so on edge?

Then he realized why.

It had been two years since he'd been in a crowd this size. He'd avoided mobs of people like the plague. It was always Jack who'd enjoyed the adoring masses. Sam's twin had fed off the admiration and applause. He'd loved being the center of attention, always making his ski runs faster, his jumps higher, his freestyle twists riskier.

All to push the edges of an envelope that never had a chance to hold him. Jack was the adventurer, Sam thought, a half smile curving his mouth as he remembered. Even as kids, Jack would go off the beaten path, skiing between trees, jumping over rocks, and once he'd even gone over a cliff edge and landed himself in a thigh-high cast for eight weeks.

Basically, Jack had loved the rush of speed. If he hadn't, maybe he wouldn't have died in a fiery car wreck. So useless. Such a waste. And so like Jack to drive himself to his own limits and beyond. He hadn't considered risks. Hadn't worried about consequences.

It was almost as if he'd come into his life hungry for every experience he could find. There was a time Sam had admired—envied—Jack's ability to cruise through the world getting exactly what he wanted out of it.

Jack had loved the publicity, the reporters, seeing himself on the glossy pages of magazines. Adulation had been his drug of choice.

"Hell," Sam muttered, "this party would have been a showcase for Jack. He'd have been right in the center of it all, holding court, laughing." Shoving his hands into his jeans pockets, Sam glanced at the black sky overhead. "Damned if I don't miss you."

"Mr. Wyatt!"

Sam's head swiveled and he spotted a slim blonde woman with short hair clutching a microphone, headed right at him. Worse, there was a cameraman hot on her heels.

A reporter.

Everything in him tightened, like fists ready for battle. There was a time when Sam had handled the media like a pro. When he was skiing, competing, he was used to being in front of a camera and answering what always seemed like moronic questions. But then Jack died and the questions had changed and ever since, Sam had dodged as many reporters as he could.

That wasn't an option tonight, though, and he knew it. The End of Season party was big news around here, and as Lacy had pointed out, the more publicity they got, the better it was for Snow Vista's bottom line.

So he gritted his teeth, planted his feet wide apart in a fighting stance and waited.

"Mr. Wyatt," the woman said again as she got closer. She gave him a fabulous smile, then turned and looked at her cameraman. "Scott, just set up right here. We'll get the party in the background for atmosphere."

She hadn't even asked if he'd speak to her. Just assumed he would. The reporter was probably used to most people wanting to do anything to get on camera for a few minutes.

When the light flashed on, Sam squinted briefly, then looked to the woman. Around him, the curious began to gather, with the occasional teenager making faces and waving to the camera.

"I'm Megan Short reporting for Channel Five," the woman said, her smile fake, her voice sharp and clipped. "I'd like to talk to you about this event, if you've got a few minutes."

"Sure," he said with what he hoped was more enthusiasm than he felt.

"Great." She turned, faced the camera and, when the guy behind the lens gave her a signal, she started right in "This is Megan Short and I'm reporting from Snow Vista resort where the annual End of Season party is under way."

Sam forced himself to relax, taking a deep breath. While he half listened to the reporter, he let his gaze slide over the raucous crowd. More gathered behind him, jostling to get on camera, but most were too busy partying to pay attention. The music still pounded, people were laughing, kids were ice-skating on the pond. The air was cold and the sky was clear. A perfect night really—but for the reporter.

"In recent years, the party at Snow Vista just hasn't been the same, some residents have claimed," Megan was saying as she turned from the camera to look up at Sam. "But tonight, it looks like everything is as it should be. And I think that's due to the return of local champion Sam Wyatt." She turned, gave him another fatuous smile and continued, "What's it like for you, Sam, to be back here where you and your twin, Jack, once ruled the slopes?"

He sucked in a gulp of frosty air and pushed it forcefully into his lungs. *Of course she would bring up Jack. Tragedy made for great TV, after all.*

"It's good to be home." He hoped she let it go at that, but he knew she wouldn't.

"Your brother's tragic death two years ago left the entire state reeling," she was saying, with a thread of insincere sympathy coloring the words. "We were all invested in the success of the Wyatt twins. How does it feel, Sam, to be here without Jack?"

Under the building rage ran a slender thread of helpless frustration. Why did reporters always ask *how does it feel*? Could they really not guess? Or did they not care that they were digging into open wounds and dumping handfuls of salt into them? He had a feeling it was a little of both along with the hope of getting an emotional reaction out of their victims—and if there were tears, that was a bonus.

Well she wouldn't get what she wanted from him. He had plenty of experience dealing with those who sought to pry into feelings best left alone. His features shuttered as he locked away emotions and buried them deep.

"Jack loved the End of Season party," he said, keeping his voice even and steady, though the effort cost him. "So it's good to be here, watching locals and visitors alike enjoy the festivities."

"I'm sure, but—"

He cut her off and pretended not to see the flash of anger in her eyes. "Tom Summer's band is great. If you'll swing your camera around, you'll see we've got the kiddie pond open for ice-skating and there are more than two dozen food booths set up offering everything from pizza to Korean barbecue to funnel cakes." He smiled into the camera and ignored the sputtering reporter beside him.

"Yes," she said, determined to steer him back on the course she'd chosen. "And yet, how much more special would it be for you to be here tonight if your twin hadn't died so tragically? Is that loss still resonating within the Wyatt family?"

He'd tried, Sam assured himself. He'd put on a good face, pushed the resort and made an effort to ignore the woman's painful digging. But there was only so much a man could take. Damned if he'd let this woman feed off his family's pain. He sent her a steely-eyed glare that had her backing up one small step. But the determination in her eyes didn't dim.

"No comment," he said tightly even though he realized that a statement as simple as that one to a reporter was like waving a red flag at a bull.

"The loss of a twin has to be difficult to deal with—"

"Difficult?" Such a small, weak word to describe what Jack's loss had done to him. To the family. "I think this interview is finished."

She was relentless. Obviously, she'd set a goal for herself and had no intention of walking away until she'd succeeded in her mission.

"I can't imagine what it must have been like for you," she was saying, moving in closer so that she and Sam shared the same camera frame. "Competing with your twin, then becoming a bone-marrow donor during his battle with leukemia…"

Sam kept breathing—that was all he could do. If he spoke now, it wouldn't be pretty. It all rushed back at him. The stunning news that Jack had cancer. The treatments. Watching his strong, fit brother weaken under the stress of the chemo. And finally, Sam, donating his bone marrow in a last-ditch attempt to save the other half of himself.

The transplant worked. And over the span of several weeks, Jack's strength returned. His powerful will and resolve to reclaim his life drove him to recover, become the man he used to be.

Just in time to die.

"...helping him win that battle," the reporter was saying, "defeat cancer only to die in an horrific car accident on his way to the airport to compete in the international ski trials." She pushed the microphone up higher. "Tell us," she urged, "in your own words, what it cost you and your family to survive such a personal tragedy."

His brain was buzzing. His heartbeat thundered in his own ears. His mouth was dry and once again, he clenched his hands into useless fists. Sam gritted his teeth because he knew, if he opened his mouth to speak, he was going to blast the woman for her feigned sympathy in the name of ratings.

"Megan Short!" Lacy stepped up beside Sam, smiled at the reporter and said, "This is great! I'm Lacy Sills, manager of the resort. We're so happy to have Channel Five at Snow Vista. I hope everyone in your audience will come on up to join the party! We've got free food, a skating rink for the kids, dancing to a live band and the best desserts in Utah. The evening's young so come up and join us!"

Undeterred, Megan shifted her attention to Lacy. "Thank you, Lacy, for that invitation. Maybe you could answer my question, though. Our viewers watched Sam and Jack Wyatt over the years, as the twins scooped up pretty much every available prize and award available for skiing. Now, since you were once married to Sam, maybe you could share with our viewers just how hard it is for you to deal not only with the ghost of Jack Wyatt, but with your own ex-husband."

For a split second, Sam had been torn when Lacy hurried up. Glad to see her, but irritated that she'd obviously believed he needed rescuing. What was most surprising, though, was that she would come to his aid in the first place. He'd been home nearly a week and she'd done everything she could to avoid him. Now she rushed in? Why?

He looked at her, wearing a navy blue sweater, jeans and boots, her thick blond braid hanging over one shoulder. No one else would have noticed, but Sam could see what it cost Lacy to stand there and smile at the woman taunting her.

Lacy's chin lifted, her eyes flashed and Sam felt a swell of pride. When she met the reporter's gaze, he remembered all of the times over the years when Lacy had stood her ground in spite of everything. Damn, she was something to see. Admiration and desire twisted together inside him.

"I really can't talk about Jack Wyatt other than to say we all miss him. Always will." Face frozen into a tight smile, Lacy added, "Thanks so much for coming to the resort tonight and I hope all of your viewers will come up the mountain to enjoy the End of Season party! Now, if you'll excuse us, Sam and I have a few things to take care of…"

Not waiting for an assent, Lacy threaded her arm through Sam's and tugged. He took the escape she offered. Leading her away from the crowds, Sam stalked around the peripheries of the noisy mob until they were far enough away from everyone that he felt he could draw an easy breath again. They stood in the shadows behind the main lodge. Here, the music was distanced and so were the shouts and conversations and laughter.

If Lacy hadn't shown up when she did, Sam thought he might have told that reporter exactly what he thought of her. And that wouldn't have been good for him or the resort. "Thanks," he said when he could unclench his teeth enough for words to sneak past.

"No problem," she assured him, and leaned against the building. "I've been dealing with Megan Short for the last two years. She's relentless."

"Like a damn shark," he muttered, shoving one hand through his hair, furious that he'd allowed the woman to get to him.

"Please," Lacy said on a snort of laughter. "She makes sharks look like fluffy kittens. Everyone she interviews on camera either ends up crying or screaming at her or threatening her."

"You handled her."

She shrugged.

"What I'm wondering is why," he said. "You could have left me swinging in the wind and didn't. So... why?"

Lacy pushed away from the wall. "I saw the look on your face. Another minute or two alone with her and you'd have ruined all the good publicity we're getting."

"That's it? For the good of the resort?"

She tipped her head back to look up at him. "Why else, Sam?"

"That's what I want to know." His gaze moved over her, sweeping up and down before settling finally on her eyes. "See, I think there's more to it than that. I think you still feel something."

She snorted. "I feel plenty. Just not for you."

A grin curved his mouth as Sam watched her fiddle with the end of her braid. She'd always done that when she was skirting the truth. "You're playing with your hair and we both know what that means."

Instantly, she stopped, tossed her braid behind her back and glared at him. "You know, here in the real world, when someone helps you out, you just say 'thanks.'"

"Already said thanks."

"Right. You did. You're welcome."

She turned to go and he stopped her with one hand on her arm. "We're not done."

Then he kissed her.

Five

Lacy should have pushed him away.

Should have kicked him, stomped on his foot, *something*.

Instead, she kissed him back.

How could she not? Two years of hungering for him made her just crazy enough to want his arms around her again. To feel his mouth on hers. His breath on her cheek.

For a heart-stopping moment, there was just the heat of him, holding her, tasting her. The erotic slide of his tongue against hers sent sparks of awareness dazzling through her body like tiny flames, awakening and dying and starting up again.

She leaned into him, the sound of the party nothing more than a buzz in her ears. How could she hear more, when her own heartbeat was crashing so loudly it drowned out everything else?

The black leather jacket he wore felt cold and slick

beneath her hands as she clung to his shoulders. Reaching up, she threaded her fingers through his hair, holding his mouth to hers, reveling in the sensations rushing inside.

He moved her backward until she was pressed against the back wall of the inn. The thick, cold logs sent chills down her spine even as the heat Sam engendered swamped them both. Years fell back, pain slipped away and all she was left with was the amazing sensations she'd only experienced with Sam. Anger fell beneath layers of passion and she *knew* it would be back, stronger than ever. Anger at him. At herself.

But right at the moment, she didn't care.

It was crazy. A party attended by crowds of people was going on not a hundred yards from them. They were out in the open, where anyone could stumble across them. And yet, all she could think was, *yes. More.*

His hands slid beneath the hem of her sweater to stroke across her abdomen and the chill of his touch warred with the heat—and lost. Lacy pushed herself into him, moving as close as she could and still it wasn't enough to feed the raw need pulsing within.

He tore his mouth from hers and they stared at each other, breaths coming fast and harsh, clouds of vapor pushing into the air between them. His gaze moved over her face. His eyes were shadowed in the dim light and still they seemed to shine a brilliant green.

A moment later, raucous laughter and a girl's flirty squeal shattered the spell holding them in a silent grip. Sam stepped back from her with a muttered curse just as a young couple ran around the side of the inn.

They came to a sliding stop on the snowy path. "Oh hey, man. Sorry. We were just looking…um…"

Clearly the young couple had been looking for the same privacy she and Sam were just enjoying.

Sam stuffed both hands into his jeans pockets. "It's fine. Enjoy the party."

"Yeah," the boy said and shot his girlfriend a quick grin. "We are."

They left as quickly as they'd appeared.

"Well, that was embarrassing." Lacy blew out a long breath, straightened her sweater and stepped back from Sam so she wouldn't be tempted to leap at him again.

"Lousy timing," he mumbled, his gaze locked on her.

"I think it was pretty good timing," she said, though her body disagreed. Another minute or two of Sam's kisses and she might have forgotten everything. Might have just given in to the need still clamoring inside her. Oh, there was no *might* about it, she admitted silently.

She'd wanted to be touched, kissed, loved. She'd wanted Sam as she had always wanted him. Knowing better didn't seem to help. Lacy had nearly drowned in the sea of her own anger and misery when Sam first left. To survive, she'd clawed her way out then closed and locked the door on those feelings, good and bad. She had had to forget—or at least try to forget, just how much she loved Sam.

Life would be a lot easier right now, she thought, if she'd only been able to hold on to that anger. Instead, it was the heat of lost love she felt, not the ice of pain.

"Lacy…"

"Don't," she said, holding up one hand and shaking her head. Talking to him was almost as dangerous to her as kissing him. His voice alone was a kind of music to her, that seemed to seep into her heart and soul whether she wanted it to or not. "Just…don't say anything."

"I want you."

"Damn it," she snapped, walking now, with long strides, moving toward the light and sound of the party, "I asked you not to say anything." Especially *that*.

"Not saying it doesn't change anything." He followed her, his much longer legs outpacing hers easily.

She whipped her head up to look at him. "This was a kiss, Sam. Just a kiss." It had been more and she knew it but damned if she'd admit it to him. Heck, she wasn't entirely comfortable admitting it to herself. "We were both strung a little tight and the tension snapped. That's *all*."

If that were true, she told herself, she'd be feeling a heck of a lot better right now. Instead, she was wound tighter than ever. It was a wonder her body wasn't throwing off sparks with every slam of her heartbeat.

He moved closer and Lacy held her ground. Probably dumb, but she wasn't going to give him the satisfaction of thinking that she couldn't handle being near him. Especially since she couldn't.

"If those kids hadn't come crashing around the corner, we'd still be having at each other."

"Call it fate," she said with a shrug that belied the tension still coursing through her. "Someone somewhere knows that this shouldn't have happened and they were cutting us a break."

"Or trying to kill me," he said, and one corner of his mouth lifted, though there wasn't a sign of humor in his eyes.

"The easy answer is," she pointed out, "keep your lips to yourself."

"I never did 'easy.' You should know that."

"Not fair," she said, shaking her head and giving him a hard look. "You don't get to do the 'remember when' thing with me, Sam." She backed up a step for good measure, but when he followed that move, she didn't bother backing up farther.

"It's our past, Lacy," he reminded her, his voice dropping to a low, sexy rumble.

"*Past* being the operative word." Lacy sighed and told herself to gather up the wispy threads of what had once been her self-control. "There's nothing between us anymore, so you shouldn't have kissed me again."

"Wasn't just me," he reminded her, and a cold wind whipped around the edge of the building and lifted his dark hair. "Won't be just me when it happens next time, either."

The band finished one song and the pause between it and the next hung in the sudden stillness. When the pounding beat of the drums kicked in once more, Lacy forced herself to say, "It won't happen."

"You said that the last time and yet, here we are."

She had said it. At the time, she had meant it, too. Lacy didn't want to get drawn back into the still-smoldering feelings she had for Sam. Didn't want to put herself through another agonizing heartbreak. It was just a damn shame that her body didn't have the same resolve as her mind.

"Why are you kissing me at all, Sam?" She asked the question again because she still didn't have an answer. "Why do you even want to? *You* left *me*, remember? You walked away from us and never gave me another thought. Why pretend now that this is anything more than raging hormones with nowhere else to go?"

He looked at her, but didn't speak. But then, what could he say?

With her words hanging in the cold, clear air, Lacy turned and walked hurriedly back to the safety of the crowd, losing herself in the mob of people.

* * *

By midnight, the party was over. Everyone had gone home or to their hotel rooms and the mountain was quiet again. The Snow Vista crew had taken care of cleanup, so all that was left to clear out in the morning were the booths that would have to be disassembled and stored until the next time they were needed.

The mountain was dark, but for the sprinkling of lamplight shining through windows at the main lodge and surrounding cabins. The sky was black and starlit, leaving a peaceful, serene night.

In contrast, Sam felt like a damned caged tiger. He couldn't settle. Couldn't relax. Just like he couldn't get Lacy out of his mind. She remained there, a shadow on his thoughts, even when he knew he shouldn't be thinking of her at all. Even when he knew it might be easier for all of them if he just did as she asked and left her alone.

But hell. Easier wasn't always what it was cracked up to be. He'd grown up skiing the fastest, most dangerous runs he could find. Memories crowded his mind. But they weren't of skiing. They weren't of him and his twin, Jack, chasing danger all over the mountain. These memories were all Lacy. Her kiss. Her touch. The way she laughed one night when they'd walked through a snowstorm, tipping her head back and letting the fat flakes caress her cheeks. The shine in her hair, the warmth of her skin. All the things that had haunted him for the past two years.

Every moment with her stood out in his mind with glaring clarity and he knew he wouldn't be able to stay away from her.

Leaning against the doorjamb of his cabin, he looked through the woods toward Lacy's place. What had once been *their* place. There were lights in the windows and smoke curling lazily from the chimney.

His guts fisted. This was the hardest part of being home. Facing his family had been tough but being close to Lacy and not *with* her was torture. Leaving her had torn him up, coming home was harder still. A couple of kisses had only fed the banked fires inside him, and yet, all he wanted was another one.

"No," he muttered, one hand tightening on the wood door frame. "You want more than that. Much more."

He thought back over the past several days and realized that beneath the lust was a layer of annoyance. The Lacy he had left behind two years ago had been cool, calm. And crazy about him.

Sam could privately admit that he'd half expected her to jump into his arms with a cry of joy when he came back. And the fact that she hadn't, stung. Not only that, he had thought he'd be dealing with cool dispassion from her. Instead, there had been temper. Fury. Which, he had to say, was arousing. He liked that flash of anger in her eyes. Liked the heat that spilled off her whenever they were together. And he knew Lacy liked it, too.

She could argue all she wanted, fight what lay simmering between them, but the truth was, she still felt it, whether she wanted to or not.

Those kisses proved him right on that score.

Now his skin felt too tight. There was an itch inside him—damned if he'd ignore it any longer. This all began and ended with Lacy, he told himself. When he left Snow Vista two years before, he'd been wrapped up in his own grief and fury. Losing his twin had sliced at Sam's soul to the point where even breathing had seemed an insurmountable task. He'd deliberately exiled himself from this place. From her.

He'd picked up Jack's dreams and carried them for his dead twin—believing that he owed it to his brother. But dreams were damned empty when they weren't your own. Now Sam was back. To stay? He didn't know. But while he was here, he and Lacy were going to straighten out a few things.

Behind him, the heat of the room swelled, while in front of him, the cold and the dark beckoned. And he knew that whatever was between him and Lacy, it was time they settled it. He reached back to snatch his jacket off a hook. He was shrugging it on as he stepped into the night and closed the door behind him.

It didn't take him long to cross the distance separating his cabin from hers. And in those few moments, Sam asked himself why the hell he was doing this. But the simple fact was, he had to see her again. Had to get beyond the wall she had erected between them.

Stars were out and a pale half-moon lit the path, though he didn't need it. He could have found his way to Lacy's place blindfolded. On her wide front porch, he looked through the windows and saw a fire in the hearth, a couple of lamps tossing golden puddles across a hardwood floor. And he saw Lacy, curled up in a chair, staring at the flames as flickering shadow and light dazzled over her.

Even now, his heart gave a hard lurch and his body went like stone—but then, passion had never been a problem between them. He knocked on the door and watched as she frowned, pushed to her feet and walked to it.

She opened the door and her features went stiff. "Go away."

"No."

Lacy huffed out a breath. "What do you want?"

"To talk."

"No, thank you." She tried to close the door, but he slapped one hand to it and held it open.

He stepped past her and walked into the main room, ignoring her sputter of outrage. "You should close that door before you freeze."

Glaring at him, she looked as though she might argue the point, even though all she wore was a flannel sleep shirt, scooped at the neck, high on her thighs. Her long, toned legs were bare and the color of fresh cream. Her feet were bare, too, and he noted the sinful red polish on the nails. Her blond hair was free of its braid, hanging in heavy waves around her shoulders, making him want nothing more than to fist his hands in that thick, soft mass again. But her blue eyes were narrowed and there was no welcome there.

Finally, though, the winter cold was enough to convince her to shut the door, sealing the two of them in together. Still, she didn't cross the room, but stayed at the door, her back braced against it, her arms folded across her chest. "You don't have the right to come here. I didn't invite you."

"Didn't used to need an invitation."

Her mouth worked as if she were biting back words struggling to escape. The flannel nightshirt she wore shouldn't have been sexy, but it really was. Everything about this woman got to him as no one else ever had. He had thought he could walk away from her, but the truth was, he'd taken her with him everywhere he went.

"What do you want?"

"You know the answer to that." He shrugged out of his jacket and tossed it on the back of the nearest chair.

"Don't get comfortable. You won't be here that long."

One dark eyebrow lifted. "You don't want me to go, Lacy, and we both know it."

Frowning, she stared at him. "Sometimes we want things that aren't good for us."

"Been reading Kristi's self-help books?"

A brief smile curved her mouth and was gone again in an instant.

The wind whistled under the eaves and sounded like a breathless moan. The fire in the hearth jumped and hissed as that wind passed over the chimney and the golden light in the room swayed as if it was dancing.

"You left once. Why can't you just stay away?" she whispered.

"Because I can't get you out of my head."

She looked at him. "Try harder."

Sam laughed shortly, shook his head and moved toward her. "Won't do any good. Been trying for two years."

Those memories, images of her, were so ingrained inside him, Sam had about convinced himself that the reality of her couldn't possibly be as good as he remembered. And maybe that's why he was here now. To prove to himself, one way or another, what exactly it was that burned between him and Lacy.

"Sam…" She sighed and shook her head, as if denying what he was saying, what the two of them were feeling.

"Damn it Lacy, I want you. Never stopped wanting you." He moved in close enough to touch her and then stopped. He took a breath, drawing her scent deep inside.

Silence crowded down around them, the only sound the hiss and crackle of the flames in the hearth. His heart pounding, Sam waited for what felt like an eternity, until she finally lifted her eyes to his and said simply, "Me, too."

In a blink, Sam reached for her and she came into his arms as if they'd never been apart. He fisted his hands in the back of her soft, flannel gown and held her tight, pressing her length against him until he felt her heart thundering in time with his own. Bending his head, he took her mouth in a kiss that was both liberation and surrender.

Fires leaped within, burning him from the inside out and it was still only a flicker of the heat he felt just holding her. His tongue tangled with hers in a desperate dance of need. She gave herself up to the moment, leaning into him, running her hands up and down his arms until the friction of his own shirt against his skin added a new layer of torture.

Lost in the blinding passion spinning out of control, Sam reached down for the hem of her gown and in one quick yank, pulled it over her head and off. Lacy's blond hair spilled across her bare shoulders and lay like silk over his hands. His first look at her in two long years hit him hard. She was even more beautiful than he'd remembered and he couldn't wait another second to get his hands on her. He tossed the nightgown to the chair beside him and then covered her breasts with his palms.

She sighed, letting her head fall back as a murmured groan of pleasure slid from her throat. His thumbs and fingers stroked and rubbed her hardened nipples and he watched those summer-blue eyes of hers roll back as sensations took her over.

Burying his own groan, Sam's gaze swept up and down her body briefly before he shifted his hold on her, catching her at the waist and lifting her up so he could taste her. First one breast, then the other, his mouth moved over her sensitized skin, licking, nibbling, suck-ling. The warm, tantalizing scent of her wrapped around him, driving him mad with a hunger he had only known with Lacy.

She clutched at his shoulders and lifted those long legs of hers to wrap around his waist. Having her there, in his arms, was so…*right*.

He cupped her bare bottom and held her steady as she looked into his eyes, showing him the passion, the desire that he knew was glittering in his own.

"Sam, Sam…" she asked, her voice breathless, "what're we doing?"

"What we were *meant* to do," he murmured, dip-ping his head to nibble at the slender length of her neck.

She shivered and that tiny reaction reverberated in-side him, setting off what felt like earthquake after-shocks that rippled through his system. Who would have guessed that as great as his memories of her had been, they weren't even *close* to how good she felt in reality.

Her fingers threaded through his hair and she pulled his head back to meet his gaze. "What're we waiting for, then?"

"No more waiting at all," he ground out.

Sam squeezed and caressed her behind until she was writhing against him and every twist of her hips hard-ened his body further until he felt as though he'd ex-plode with one wrong move. *Not yet*, his brain screamed, but his body was in charge now and rational or logical or *slow* didn't come into it.

Two long years it had been since he'd touched her last and now that he had her—naked, willing, wanting—he couldn't wait any longer.

Lacy, it seemed, felt the same. She shook her long hair back from her face, kissed him hard and deep, then reached down to undo his fly. Buttons sprang free under her fingers and in a second, she was holding him, stroking him from base to tip and back again. Sam gritted his teeth, struggling for control and losing, since he felt as wild as a hormonal teenager.

Need was a living, breathing animal in the room, snapping its jaws, demanding release. Sam's brain blanked out, every thought whipping away in the surge of his reaction to her touch. With her fingertips smoothing over him, he couldn't think beyond breathing. That was all he needed anyway. Air—and Lacy.

Shifting his grip on her, he stroked the hot, damp core of her. She sucked in a breath and trembled, but she didn't release her hold on him. If anything, her grip tightened, her caresses became more determined, more demanding. As did his. He rubbed the small bud of sensation at her center and each time she quivered and moaned, it fed his need to touch her more deeply. More completely.

She twisted in his grasp; her heels dug into the small of his back. "Sam, if you don't take me right this minute, I might die."

"No dying allowed," he muttered, and fused his mouth to hers. Their tongues tangled together again, even more desperately this time.

He'd come here with the idea to either talk through the barriers standing between them or seduce her into a sexual haze. Now neither one was happening. This wasn't seduction. It was raw urgency. Sam took two long steps to the closest wall, braced her back against it and then broke the kiss so he could look into her eyes as he filled her in one long, hard stroke.

She gasped and he was forced to pause, willing himself to be still. She was so tight. So hot, it stole his breath and left him gasping. A moment passed, and then as if of one mind they moved together, Lacy taking him deep inside her and each of them groaning when he retreated only to slide back inside, even deeper.

Again and again, they moved frantically, the rhythm they set a punishing pace that left no margin for smooth, for slow, lazy loving. It was all passion and lust and a desperate craving for the release that rose within them, higher and higher as they chased it. Emotion, sensation poured through them both, and then were drowned in the immediate demands of bodies too long denied.

He felt the cold of the wall on the palms of his hands as he braced her there, pinned like a butterfly to a board. He felt her fingers, digging into his shoulders as she urged him higher, faster, deeper. He heard their breaths coming fast and sharp.

Sam reached between their laboring bodies and flicked his thumb across that tight, sensitive bud at the junction of her thighs. Instantly, she screamed out his name as she shuddered, splintering in his arms.

Her body tightened around his; those internal shivers driving him over the edge. When the first explosion took him, Sam groaned aloud and emptied himself into her.

Seconds, minutes...maybe *days* passed with neither of them willing to move. Frankly, Sam didn't think he could move even if he had to. His knees were weak and the only thing holding them both up at the moment was sheer willpower.

"Oh. Wow." Her voice was a whisper that sounded like a shout to him. "Sam. I think I might be blind."

He looked at her. "Open your eyes."

She did. "Right. Good. Wow."

"You said that already," he told her, hissing in a

breath as she moved on him and sent his still-willing body into overdrive.

Nodding, Lacy murmured, "It was two *Wows* worthy."

"Yeah," he agreed, slapping one hand to her butt to try to hold her still. "Gotta say it really was."

Breathing still strained, Lacy looked at him and said, "I should probably tell you to leave now."

"Probably," he agreed, even as he felt his body hardening inside her again.

She felt it, too, because she inhaled sharply and let that breath slide from her on a soft moan of pleasure. "But I'm not."

"Glad to hear it." Sam tightened his grip on her, swung her away from the wall and walked, their bodies still linked, to the hall. "Bedroom?"

"Yeah," she said, dipping her head for another taste of his mouth. "Bedroom."

It was a small cabin and Sam took a moment to be grateful for that. He laid her down on the bed they used to share and reluctantly drew out of her heat just long enough to strip out of his clothes. Then he was back on the bed, looming over her, sheathing himself inside her on a sigh of appreciation. His hips moved as he reclaimed her body in the most elemental way. She met his pace and rocked with him in a dance they'd always been good at. Their rhythms meshed, their breaths mingled and the sighs crashing in the quiet seemed to roll on forever.

Lifting her legs, she locked them at the small of his back and pulled him tighter, deeper. She groaned as he kissed first one hardened nipple then the other, sending a cascade of sensations pouring into her body. Again and again, he licked, tasted, nibbled, all the while his body rocked into her heat, taking her as she took him.

There was no hesitation. No question. There was only the moment and the moment was *now*. They'd been heading toward this night since Sam had arrived back on the mountain.

Her hands swept up and down his back, her short, neat nails scraping at his skin as she touched him, everywhere. Her scent rose up and enveloped him. Surrounded by her, in her, Sam pushed them both to the brink of oblivion, and when she cried out his name, she held him tight and took him over the edge with her.

Six

Lacy stared up at the ceiling and, just for a second or two, enjoyed the lovely, floaty feeling that filled her. It had been so long since she'd felt anything like this. For the past two years, she'd forced herself to forget just how good it had always been between her and Sam. She'd had to, to survive his absence. Had to put it out of her mind so that she could try to rebuild her life without him.

Now he was back.

And in her bed.

God, how could she be such an idiot? Those lovely sensations of completion and satisfaction emptied away like water going down a tub drain.

"We should talk."

A short, sharp laugh shot from her throat. "Oh, I so don't want to talk about this." She wanted to forget again. Fast.

He went up on one elbow, looked down at her, and Lacy steeled herself against the gleam in his grass-green eyes. If she wasn't careful, her oh-so-foolish heart would slide gleefully right into danger. Why did he have to come back?

Why did he ever leave?

His jaw tight, he stared into her eyes and asked, "You're still taking the Pill, right?"

She blinked at him. Not what she'd been expecting. Yet, now that he'd said it, a single, slender thread of panic began to unwind inside her. His words echoed over and over again in her mind, because now her stupidity had reached epic proportions. Sam Wyatt walked in her door and every brain cell she possessed just whipped away. Which explained why she hadn't thought of protection. Hadn't paid any attention. She really was an idiot.

"Since you just went white," he said wryly, "I'm guessing the answer is no."

"Well, now's a great time to ask," she muttered, wishing she could blame this situation on him, as well. But she was a grown-up, modern woman who took responsibility for her own body, thanks very much. So it was as much her fault as his that she was suddenly thinking she might be in really big trouble here.

"We didn't do much talking before."

"True." She sighed and stared at the ceiling again. Easier than meeting his eyes. Easier than looking at him while she was wondering if she might have just gotten pregnant by her ex-husband. At that thought, she slapped one hand over her eyes.

Unprotected sex. She had never once—even at seventeen when she'd given Sam her virginity at the top of the mountain under a full, summer moon—been that reckless. Lacy was the careful one. The cautious one. The one who looked at every step along a path before she ever started down it. Now she couldn't even see the path. Oh, this was a mistake on so many levels she couldn't even count them all.

He pulled her hand aside and she looked at him.

"Now we have even more to talk about."

"No thanks." She didn't want to have a conversation with him at all. And certainly not about the possibility of an unplanned baby. *Oh, God.*

No way would fate do that to her, right? Hadn't it screwed with her life enough?

"No thanks?" He repeated her words with a snort of derision. "That's not gonna cover it. We just had sex. Twice. With zero protection."

"Yeah, I was there."

"Damn it, Lacy—"

"Look," she cut him off neatly and tried to get him off the subject, away from the thoughts that were already making her a little crazy. "It's the wrong time for me. The odds are astronomical." Please let her be right about this. "So don't worry about it, all right?"

He didn't like that. She could see the light in his eyes and recognized it. Sam Wyatt never had been a man to be told what to do and take it well.

"Yeah," he said flatly. "That's not gonna happen. I want to know when you know."

"And I want a brand-new camera with a fifteen-zoom lens. Looks like we're both going to be disappointed."

"Damn it, Lacy," he repeated. "You can't cut me out of this. I'm here. I'm involved in this."

"For now." A part of her couldn't believe that she was lying in bed with Sam, both of them naked and having an argument about a possible pregnancy. That was the sane part, she thought reasonably. The panicked portion of her was trying not to think about any of this.

Once he left the cabin she wouldn't be bringing up tonight with him at all. And she was going to use every part of her legendary focus to forget everything that had just happened—mainly out of self-protection. She couldn't think about being with him and *not* be with him. That was a recipe for even more craziness and more late-night crying sessions, so thanks, she'd pass.

When she didn't speak, he seemed to accept her silence as acquiescence, which worked for her—until he started talking again.

"I came over here tonight to talk to you," he said.

"Yeah," she said on a sigh, "that went well."

"Okay," he admitted, "maybe talking wasn't the only thing on my mind." He dropped one hand to her hip and slowly slid his palm up until he was cupping her breast, sending tingles of expectation and licks of heat sinking down into her bones.

Just not fair, she told herself sternly even as she felt that heat he engendered begin to spread. Not fair that the man who broke her heart could still have such an effect on her. Even when she *knew* it was a mistake to allow his hands on her, she couldn't bring herself to make him stop. And if she kept lying there, letting him touch her, it would start over again and where would that get her? Deeper into the hole she could already feel herself falling into.

Quickly, before she could talk herself out of doing the smart thing, she rolled out from under his hand and off the bed in one fluid motion. Just getting a little distance between them cleared her mind and soothed all those buzzing nerve endings.

He stared at her as she snatched up the robe she had

tossed over a chair only that morning. Slipping into the soft terry fabric she tied it at the waist and only briefly considered making a knot, just to make it harder to slip off again. Once she was covered up, Lacy felt a bit more in control. Tossing her hair back from her face, she said, "I think you should go."

"I came to talk, remember? We haven't done that yet."

"And we're not going to," she told him. "I don't feel like talking and you don't live here anymore, so I want you to go."

"As soon as we have this out." He settled on the bed, carelessly naked, clearly in no hurry to get up and get moving. "I've got a few things to say to you."

"Now you have things to say? *Now* you want to share?" She laughed shortly and the sound of it was as harsh as the scrape of it against her throat. Through the miasma of emotions coursing through her, rage rose up and buried everything else. "Two years ago, you left without a word of explanation. Just came home from the funeral, threw some clothes in your bag and went."

In a blink, she was back there. In this very cabin two years ago when her world had come crashing down around her.

The funeral had been hideous. Losing Jack to a senseless accident after he'd survived cancer had cut deeper than she would have thought possible. The Wyatt family had closed ranks, of course, pulling into a tight circle where pain shared had become pain more easily borne.

All of them but Sam. Even within that circle, he had stood apart, forcing himself to be stoic. To be solitary. He hadn't turned to Lacy once for comfort, for solace.

Instead, he'd handled all of the funeral arrangements himself, taken care of details to keep his parents from having to multiply their grief by dealing with the minutia of death. He'd given the eulogy and brought everyone to tears and laughter with memories of his twin.

But after everyone had gone home, after the ceremony had faded into stillness, she'd hoped he would finally turn to her.

He hadn't.

Instead he walked straight into their bedroom and pulled his travel bag out of the closet.

Stunned, shaken, Lacy could only watch as he grabbed shirts, rolled them up and stuffed them into the bag. Jeans were next, then underwear, socks and still she didn't speak. But as he zipped it closed and stood staring down at the bag, she asked, "Sam, what are you doing? Are we going somewhere?"

He looked at her then and his green eyes were drenched with a sorrow so deep it tore at her to see it. "Not *we*, Lacy. *Me*. I'm going. I have to—"

She swallowed hard against the knot in her throat. "You're leaving?"

"Yeah." He stripped out of his black suit, and quickly dressed in boots, jeans and a thermal shirt, then shrugged into his leather jacket

The whole time, she could only watch him. Her mind had gone entirely blank. It couldn't be happening. He had promised her long ago that he would never leave. That she would always be able to count on him. To trust him. So none of this made sense. She couldn't understand. Didn't believe he would do this.

"You're leaving me?"

He snapped her a look that said everything and nothing. "I have to go."

She couldn't breathe. Iron bands tightened around her chest, cutting off her air. It had to be a dream. A nightmare, because Sam wouldn't leave. He walked across the room then, his duffel swung over one shoulder, and she stepped back, allowing him to pass because she was too stunned to try to stop him.

He stopped at the front door for one last look at her. "Take care of yourself, Lacy." He left without another word and closed the door behind him quietly.

Alone in her cabin, Lacy sank to the floor, since her knees were suddenly water. She watched the door for a long time, waiting for it to open again, for him to come back, tell her he'd made a mistake. But he never did.

Now, thinking about that night, Lacy wanted to kick her former self for letting him stroll out of her life. For crying for him. For missing him. For hoping to God he'd just come home.

"I had to."

"Yeah," she said tightly, amazed that as angry as she was, there was still more anger bubbling inside her. "You said that then, too. You *had* to leave your wife, your family." Sarcasm came thick. "Wow, must have been rough on you. All on your own, free of your pesky wife and those irritating parents and sister. Wandering across Europe, dating royalty. Poor little you, how you must have suffered."

"Wasn't why I left," he ground out, and Lacy was pleased to see a matching anger begin to glint in his eyes. A good old-fashioned argument was at least honest.

"Just a great side benefit, then?"

"Lacy I couldn't explain then why I had to leave—"

"Couldn't?" she asked. "Or wouldn't?"

"I could hardly breathe, Lacy," he muttered, sitting up to shove both hands through his hair in irritation. "I needed space. It had nothing to do with you or the family."

Lacy jerked back as if he'd slapped her. "Really? That's how you see it? It had everything to do with us. You couldn't breathe because your family needed you? Poor baby. That's called *life*, Sam. Bad stuff happens. It's how we deal with it that decides who we are."

"And I didn't deal."

"No," she said flatly. "You didn't. You ran. *We* were the ones left behind to sweep up the pieces of our lives. Not you, Sam. You were gone."

His mouth worked as if he were trying to hold back words just itching to pour out. "I didn't run."

"That's what it looked like from the cheap seats."

Nodding, he could have been agreeing or trying to rein in his own temper. "You didn't say any of this at the time."

"How could I? You wouldn't *talk* to me," she countered. "You were in such a rush to get out of the cabin, you hardly saw me, Sam. So you can understand that the fact you want me to be all cooperative because *now* you want to talk, is just a little too much for me."

Scowling at her, he wondered aloud, "What happened to quiet, shy Lacy who never lost her temper?"

She flushed and hoped the room was dark enough to disguise it. "Her husband walked out on her and she grew a spine."

"However it happened, I like it."

"Hah!" Startled by the out-of-the-blue compliment when she was in no way interested in flattery from him, Lacy muttered, "I don't care."

He blew out a breath and said, "You think I wanted to go."

"I know you did." She could still feel his sense of eagerness to be gone. Out of the cabin. Away from her.

"Damn it, Lacy, Jack *died*."

"And we all lost him, Sam," she pointed out hotly. "You weren't the only one in pain."

He jumped off the bed and stood across from it, facing her. "He was my twin. My identical twin. Losing him was like losing a part of me."

Torn between empathy for the pain he so clearly still felt and fury that he would think she didn't understand, she blurted out, "Did you think I didn't know that? That your parents, your sister, were clueless as to what Jack's death cost you?" Her voice climbed on every word until she heard herself shouting and deliberately dialed it back. "We were here for you, Sam. You didn't see us."

"I couldn't." He shook his head, glanced around for his clothes, then reached down and snatched up his jeans. Tugging them on, he left them unbuttoned as he faced her again. "Hell, I was half out of my mind with grief and rage. I couldn't be around you."

"Ah," she said, nodding sagely as she silently congratulated herself for not throwing something at him. "So you left for *my* sake. How heroic."

"Damn it, you're not listening to me."

"No, I'm not. Not much fun being ignored, is it?" She gathered up her hair with trembling fingers and in a series of familiar moves, tamed the mass into a thick braid that frayed at the edges. "Why should I listen to you anyway?"

"Because I'm back now."

"For how long?"

He frowned again and shook his head. "I don't know the answer to that yet."

"So, just passing through." Wow, it was amazing how much that one statement hurt. And Lacy knew that if she allowed herself to get even more involved with him, when he left this time, the pain would be more than she could take. So she drew a cloak of disinterest around her and belted it as tightly as her robe. "Well, have a nice trip to...wherever."

The pain was as thick and rich as it had been two years ago. She'd gotten through it then, curling up in solitude, focusing on her job at the lodge and on her photography. The pictures she'd taken during that time were black-and-white and filled with shadows that seemed to envelop the landscape. She could look at them now and actually *feel* the misery she'd been living through. And damned if she would go back to that dark place in her life.

He took a breath and huffed it out again in a burst of frustration. "I'm not proud of what I did two years ago, Lacy. But I had to go, whether you believe that or not."

"I'm sure you believe it," she countered.

"And I'm—"

"Don't you dare say you're sorry." Her voice cracked into the room like a whip's snap.

"I won't. I did what I had to do at the time." His features were tight, his eyes shining with an emotion she couldn't read in the dim light. "Can't be sorry for it now."

Flabbergasted, Lacy stared at him and actually felt her jaw drop. "That's amazing. Really. You're *not* sorry, are you?"

Again, he pushed his hands through his hair and

looked suddenly as if he'd rather be anywhere but there. "What good would it do?"

"Not an answer," she pointed out.

"All I can give you."

Cold. She was cold. And her thick terry-cloth robe might as well have been satin for all the warmth it was providing at the moment. For two years, she'd thought about what it might be like if he ever came home. If he ever deigned to return to the family he'd torn apart with his absence. But somehow, she'd always imagined that he'd come back contrite. Full of regret.

She should have known better. Sam Wyatt did what he wanted when he wanted and explained himself to no one. Heck, she'd known him most of her life, had married him, and he'd still kept a part of himself locked away where she couldn't touch it. He'd gone his own way always and for a while, he'd taken her with him. And she, Lacy thought with a flash of disgust, had been so glad to be included, she'd never pushed for more—that was her fault. His leaving? His fault.

"God," he said on a short laugh, "I can practically *see* you thinking. Why don't you just say what you have to and get it out?"

"Wow. You really have not changed one bit, have you?"

"What's that supposed to mean?"

"You even want to be in charge of when I unload on you."

"We both know you've got something to say, so say it and get it done."

"You want it?" she asked, hands fisting helplessly at her sides. "Fine. You walked out on all of us, Sam. You walked away from a family who loved you. Needed you. You walked away from *me*. You never said goodbye.

You just disappeared and then the next thing I know, divorce papers are arriving in the mail."

He blew out a breath.

"You didn't even warn me with a stinking phone call." Outrage fired in her chest and sizzled in her veins. "You vanished and Jack was dead and your family was shattered and you didn't care."

"Of course I cared," he snapped.

"If you cared, you wouldn't have left. Now you're back and you're what? A hero? The prodigal returned at last? Sorry you didn't get a parade."

"I didn't expect—"

She rolled right over him. "Two years. A few post-cards to let your parents know you were alive and that was it. What the hell were you thinking? How could you be so heartless to people who needed you?"

He scrubbed both hands over his face as if he could wipe away the impact of her words, but Lacy wasn't finished.

Her voice dropping to a heated whisper that was nearly lost beneath the moan of the icy wind outside, she said, "You broke my heart, Sam. You broke *me*." She slapped one hand to her chest and glared at him from across the room. "I trusted you. I believed you when you said it was forever. And then you left me."

Just like her mother had left, Lacy thought, her brain firing off scattershot images, memories that stole her breath and weakened her knees. When she was ten years old, Lacy's mother had walked away from the mountain, from her husband and daughter, and she had never once looked back. Never once gotten in touch. Not a phone call. Or a letter. Nothing. As if she'd slipped off the edge of the earth.

Lacy had spent the rest of her childhood hoping and

waiting for her mom to come home. But she never had, and though he'd stayed, Lacy's father had slowly, inexorably pulled away, too. Lacy could see now that he hadn't meant to. But his wife leaving had diminished him to the point where he couldn't remain the man he had once been. Her family had been shattered.

And when Sam convinced her to trust him, to build a life with him and then left, she'd been shattered again. She wouldn't allow that to happen a third time. Lacy was stronger now. She'd had to change to survive and there was no going back.

"You know what? That's it. I'm done. We have to work together, Sam," she said. "For however long you're here. But that's all. Work."

"Damn it, Lacy…" His features were shadowed, but somehow the green of his eyes seemed to shine in the darkness. After a second or two, he nodded. "Fine. We'll leave it there. For now."

She was grateful they had that much settled, at least. Because if he tried to apologize for ripping her heart out of her chest, she might have to hit him with something. Something heavy. Better that they just skate over it all. She'd had her say and it was time to leave her scars alone.

"And what about what just happened?" he asked, and she wondered why his voice had to sound like dark chocolate. "What if you're pregnant?"

That word sent a shiver that might have been panic—or longing—skating along her spine. "I won't be."

"If you are," he warned, "we're not done."

Another flush swept through her, heating up the embers that had just been stoked into an inferno. "We're already done, Sam. Whatever we had, died two years ago."

Her whisper resounded in the room and she could only hope he didn't read the lie behind the words.

Because she knew, that no matter what happened, what was between them would never really die.

Two days later, Sam was still thinking about that night with Lacy.

Now, standing in the cold wind, staring up at the clear blue sky dotted with massive white clouds, his brain was free to wander. And as always, it went straight to Lacy.

Everything she'd said to him kept replaying through his mind and her image was seared into his memory. He'd never forget how she'd looked, standing there in her robe, eyes glinting with fury, her mouth still full from his kisses. The old Lacy wouldn't have told him off—she'd have hugged her anger close and just looked…hurt.

What did it say about him that this new Lacy—full of fire and fury—intrigued him even more than the one he used to know?

Being with her again had hit him far harder than he had expected. The feel of her skin, the sound of her sighs, the brush of her lips on his. It was more than sexual, it was…*deeper* than that. She'd reclaimed that piece of his heart that he had excised so carefully two years before. And now he wasn't sure what to do about that.

Of course, he'd steered clear of the office for the past two days, giving himself the time and space to do some serious thinking. But so far, all he'd come up with was…he still wanted her.

Two years he'd denied himself what he most wanted—Lacy. Now she was within reach again and he wasn't about to deny himself any longer. She might think that what was between them had died...but if he had killed it, then he could resurrect it. He had to believe that, because the alternative was unacceptable.

He tossed a glance at the office window and considered going in to—what? Talk? No, he wasn't interested in more conversation that simply ended up being a circular argument. And what he *was* interested in couldn't be done in the office when anyone could walk in on them. So he determinedly pushed aside those thoughts and focused instead on work. On his plans.

Sam walked into the lodge and headed straight through the lobby for the elevator. He paid no attention to the people gathered in front of a blazing fire or the hum of conversations rising and falling. There were a few things he needed to go over with his father. One idea in particular had caught his imagination and he wanted to run it past his dad.

He found the older man in his favorite chair in the family great room. But for the murmuring of the TV, the house was quiet and Sam was grateful for the reprieve. He wasn't in the mood to face Kristi's antagonism or his mother's quiet reproach.

"Hey, Sam," his father said, giving a quick look around as if checking to make sure his wife wasn't around. "How about a beer?"

Sam grinned. His father had the look of a desperate man. "Mom okay with that?"

"No, she's not," he admitted with a grimace. "But since you got home, she's stocked the fridge. So while she's in town, we could take advantage."

He looked so damn hopeful, Sam didn't have the heart to shoot him down. "Sure, Dad. I'll risk it with you."

His father slapped his hands together, then gave them

a quick rub in anticipation. Pushing out of his chair, he led the way to the kitchen, his steps long and sure. It was good to see his father more himself. Bob Wyatt wasn't the kind of man to take to sitting in a recliner for long. The inactivity alone would kill him.

In the kitchen, Sam took a seat at the round oak table and waited while his dad pulled two bottles of beer out of the fridge. He handed one to Sam, kept the other for himself and sat down. Twisting off the top, Bob took a long drink, sighed in pleasure and gave his son a wide smile. "Your mother's so determined to have me eating tree bark and drinking healthy sludge, this beer's like a vacation."

"Yeah," Sam said, taking a sip of his own, "but if she comes in suddenly, you're on your own."

"Coward."

Sam grinned. "Absolutely."

With a good-natured shrug, Bob said, "Can't blame you. So, want to tell me why you're stopping by in the middle of the day?"

He couldn't very well admit to avoiding Lacy, so Sam went right to the point. "You know we've got a lot of plans in motion for the resort."

"Yeah." Bob took another sip and nodded. "I've got to say you've got some good ideas, Sam. I like your plan so far, though I'm a little concerned about just how much of your own money you're pumping into this place."

"Don't worry about that." Sam had enough money to last several lifetimes, and if he couldn't enjoy spending it, what was the point of accruing it?

"Well," his father said, "I'll keep worrying over it and you'll keep spending, so we all do what we can."

Sam grinned again. God, he hadn't even realized

how much he'd missed being able to sit down and talk to his dad. Just the simplicity of being in this kitchen again, sharing a beer with the man who had raised him, eased a lot of the still-jagged edges inside him.

"If you like the plans so far, you'll like this one, too." Sam cupped the beer bottle between his palms and took a second to get his thoughts in order. While he did, he glanced around the familiar kitchen.

Pale green walls, white cabinets and black granite countertops, this room had been the heart of the Wyatt family for years. Hell, he, Jack and Kristi had all sat around this table doing homework before the requisite family dinner. This room had witnessed arguments, laughter and tears. It was the gathering place where everyone came when they needed to be heard. To be loved.

"Sam?"

"Yeah. Sorry." He shook his head and gave a rueful smile. "Lots of memories here."

"Thick as honey," his father agreed. "More good than bad, though."

"True." Even when Jack was going through cancer treatment, the family would end up here, giving each other the strength to keep going. He could almost hear his brother's laughter and the pain of that memory etched itself onto his soul.

"You're not the only one who misses him, you know." His father's voice was soft, low.

"Sometimes," Sam admitted on a sigh, "I still expect him to walk into the room laughing, telling me it was all a big mistake."

"Being here makes it easier and harder all at the same time," his father said softly. "Because even if I can fool myself at times, when I see his chair at the table sitting empty, I have to acknowledge that's he's really gone."

Sam's gaze shot to that chair now.

"But the good memories are stronger than the pain and that's a comfort when you let it be."

"You think I don't want to be comforted?" Sam looked at his father.

"I think when Jack died you decided you weren't allowed to be happy."

Stunned, Sam didn't say anything.

"You take too much on yourself, Sam," Bob said. "You always did."

As he sipped his beer, Sam considered that and admitted silently that his father was right. About all of it. Maybe what had driven him from home wasn't only losing Jack and needing to see his twin's dreams realized—but the fact that he had believed, deep down, that with Jack gone, Sam didn't deserve to be happy. It was something to consider. Later.

Shaking his head, he said, "About this latest idea…"

Apparently accepting that Sam needed a change of subject, his father nodded. "What're you thinking?"

"I want to initiate a new beginner's ski run on the backside of the mountain," Sam said, jumping right in. "The slope's gentle, there're fewer trees and it's wide enough we could set it up to have two runs operating all the time."

"Yeah, there's a problem with that," Bob said, and took another drink of his beer.

The hesitation in his father's voice had Sam's internal radar lighting up. "What?"

"The thing is, that property doesn't belong to us anymore."

The radar was now blinking and shrieking inside him. "What're you talking about?"

"You know Lacy's family has lived on that slope for years..."

"Yeah..." Sam had the distinct feeling he wasn't going to like where this was going.

"Well, after you left, Lacy was in a bad way." Bob frowned as he said it and Sam knew his father was the master of understatement. Guilt pinged around inside him like a wildly ricocheting bullet. "So, your mother and I, we deeded the property to her. Felt like it was the least we could do to try to ease her hurt."

Sam muffled the groan building in his chest. His decision to leave was now coming back to bite him in so many different ways. Most especially with the woman he still wanted more than his next breath.

"So, if you're determined to build that beginner run, you're going to have to deal with Lacy."

Letting his head hit his chest, Sam realized that *dealing with Lacy* pretty much summed up his entire life at the moment. He thought about the look in her eyes when he left her cabin the other night. The misery stamped there despite what they'd just shared—hell, maybe *because* of that.

Leaving here was something he'd *had* to do. Coming back meant facing the consequences of that decision. It wasn't getting any easier.

"She never mentioned that you and mom gave her the land," Sam said.

"Any reason why she should?"

"No." Shaking his head, Sam took another pull on his beer. He wanted that land. How he was going to get it from Lacy, he didn't know yet. As things stood between them at the moment, he was sure that she would never sell him that slope. And maybe it'd be best to just forget about getting his hands on it. The land was Lacy's, and he ought to back off. But for now, there were other things he wanted to talk to his father about. "You know that photo of the lodge in spring? The one hanging over the fireplace here?"

"Yeah, what about it?"

"I'd like to use it on the new website I'm having designed so I'll need to talk to the photographer. I want to show the lodge in all the seasons with photos that rotate out, always changing. The one I'm talking about now, with Mom's tulips a riot of color and that splash of deep blue sky—the picture really shows the lodge in a great way."

"It's one of Lacy's."

Sam looked at his dad for a long moment, then actually laughed, unsurprised. "Of course it is. Just like I suppose the shot of the lodge in winter, with the Christmas tree in the front window is hers, too?"

His father nodded, a smile tugging at the corner of his mouth as he took a sip of his beer. "You got it. She's made a name for herself in the last year or so. We've had hotel guests buy the photos right off the walls." He shook his head, smiling to himself. "Lacy does us up some extra prints just so we can accommodate the tourists. She's been making some good money selling her photos through a gallery in Ogden, too."

"She never mentioned it."

And it was weird to realize that he was so out of touch with Lacy. There had been a time when they were so close, nothing between them was secret. Now there was an entire chunk of her life that he knew nothing about. His own damn fault and he knew it, but that didn't make it any easier to choke down.

His father nodded sagely. "Uh-huh. Again, any reason why she should have?"

"No." Blowing out a breath in frustration, Sam leaned back in his kitchen chair and studied his father. There was a sly expression on the older man's face that told Sam his father was enjoying this. "She doesn't owe me a thing. I get that. But damn it, we shared a lot of great times, too. Don't they mean something? Okay fine. I left. But I'm back now. That counts, too, doesn't it?"

"It does with me. Lacy may be harder to convince."

"I know."

"And Kristi."

"I know." Sam snorted. "And Mom."

Bob winced. "Your mother's damn happy to have you back, Sam."

"Yeah," he said, turning his head to look out the window at the pockets of deep blue sky visible between the pines. He'd felt it from his mom since he'd returned. The reluctance to be too excited to see him. The wary pleasure at having him home. "But she's also holding back, waiting for me to go again."

"And are you?"

Guilt reared up and gnawed at the edges of his heart. "I don't know yet. Wish I did. But I promised you I'd stay at least until these plans are complete and the way I'm adding things I might never be finished."

"All true," his father said. "You might ask yourself sometime why it is you keep thinking of more things to do. More things that will give you an excuse to stay here longer."

He hadn't thought of it like that but now that he was, Sam could see that maybe subconsciously he had been working toward coming home for good. Funny that he hadn't noticed that the more involved his plans became the further out he pushed the idea of leaving again.

"Anyway," his father said, "while you're doing all this thinking, you'll have to talk to Lacy about using her photos in the advertising you're planning."

"I will," he said.

"She's really good, isn't she?"

"She always was," Sam acknowledged and knew he was talking about much more than her talent for photography.

Seven

Seven

"You want to use my photos?"

Sam grinned at Lacy an hour later and told himself it was good to actually surprise her. He enjoyed how her eyes went wide and her mouth dropped open.

"I do. And not just on the website, I'd like to use them in print advertising, as well."

"Why—"

He tipped his head. "Don't pretend you don't know how good a photographer you are."

"I don't know how to respond to that without sounding conceited."

"Well, while you're quiet, here's something else to think about." He planted both palms on the edge of the desk and leaned in until he was eye to eye with her. "I'll want some of your photos made into postcards that we can sell in the lobby of the lodge."

"Postcards."

"Hey, some people actually enjoy *real* mail," he told

her and straightened up. "We can have a lawyer draw up terms—all nice and legal, but I'm thinking a seventy-thirty split, your favor, on the cards and any prints we sell. As for the advertising, we'll call that a royalty deal and you'll get a cut every time we use one of your photos."

She blinked at him and damned if he didn't enjoy having her off balance. "Royalty."

Sam leaned over, tipped her chin up with his fingers and bent to plant a hard, quick kiss on her mouth. While she was flustered from that, he straightened up and announced, "Why don't you think it over? I'm heading out to meet with the architect. Be back later."

He left her staring after him. His own heart was thundering in his chest and every square inch of his body was coiled tight as an overwound spring. Just being around her made him want everything he'd once walked away from.

Sam shrugged into his jacket as he left the hotel and headed out into a yard that boasted green splotches of grass where the snow was melting under a steady sun. He took a deep breath, glanced around at the people and realized that it had taken him two years of being away to discover that his place was *here*.

His life was here.

And he wanted Lacy in his life again. Smiling to himself, Sam decided he was going to romance the hell out of her until he got just what he wanted. That slope he needed for the lodge expansion was going to have to wait, he told himself as he headed for his car. Because if Lacy found out he wanted the property she owned, she would never believe he wanted her for herself.

Lacy's nose wrinkled at the rich, dark scent of the latte Kristi carried as the two of them walked along

Historic Twenty-Fifth Street in downtown Ogden. The street was narrow with cars parked in front of brick and stone buildings that had been standing for more than a hundred years. Twenty-Fifth Street had begun life as the welcome mat for train travelers, then it morphed into a wild blend of bars and brothels.

But in the 1950s, it had been reborn as a destination for shopping and dining, and today, it retained all of the old-world charm while it boasted eclectic shops and restaurants that drew tourists from all over. And depending on the time of year, Historic Twenty-Fifth hosted farmer's markets, art festivals, Pioneer Days, Witchstock and even a Christmas village.

Lacy loved it, and usually, strolling along the street and peeking into storefronts cheered her up. But today, she was forcing herself into this trip with Kristi.

"Since when do you say no to coffee?" her friend asked after another sip of her latte.

"Since my stomach's not so sure it approves of food anymore." She swallowed hard, took a deep breath and hoped the fresh air would settle her stomach.

"Well, that sucks," her friend said, shrugging deeper into her jacket as a cold wind shot down the street as if determined to remind everyone that winter wasn't over yet. "Something you ate?"

"Hopefully," Lacy murmured. She didn't want to think about other causes of her less than happy stomach. It had been two weeks since her night with Sam and she couldn't help but think that her sudden bouts of queasiness had more to do with a nine-month flu than anything else. Still, she didn't want to share any of this with Kristi yet, so more loudly, she said, "It's probably the cold pizza I had for dinner last night."

"That'd do it for me," Kristi acknowledged with a

grimace. "You do know how to use a microwave, right? Now that we've struggled out of the caves there is no need to settle for cold pepperoni."

"I'll make a note." They passed a gift store, its front window crowded with pretty pots of flowers, gardening gloves and a barbecue apron that proudly demanded Kiss The Cook, all lovely promises of spring. But the sky was overcast and the wind whistling down from Powder Mountain, looming over the end of the street, made the thought of spring seem like a fairy tale.

Unwell or not, it was good to be away from Snow Vista, wandering down Ogden's main street where she had absolutely zero chance of running into Sam. The man hadn't left the mountain since he got back. And for the past two weeks, she'd hardly spoken to him at all. After that wild bout of earth-shattering sex, Lacy had figured he'd be back wanting more—heaven knew she did. But he'd kept his distance and she knew she should be grateful. Instead, she was irritated.

"So you want to tell me what's going on between you and Sam these days?"

Kristi's question jolted Lacy and her steps faltered for a second. This woman had been her best friend for years. There was nothing they hadn't shared with each other, from first kisses to loss of virginity and beyond. Yet, Lacy just didn't feel comfortable talking about Sam right now. Especially with his little sister.

She gave a deliberate shrug. "Nothing. Why?"

"Please," Kristi said with a snort. "I'm not speaking to him, either, but *you're* not speaking to him really loudly."

"That doesn't even make sense." Lacy paused outside the cupcake shop to stare wistfully at a rainbow confetti cupcake. Normally, she would have gone in and bought herself one. Or a dozen. Today, though, it didn't seem like a good idea to feed her already-iffy stomach that much sugar. Just the pizza she'd eaten, she told herself. She'd be fine in a day or two.

"Sure it does. Mom says you were at the house a couple days ago, visiting Dad. And when Sam showed up you left so fast there were sparks coming up from your boot heels."

Lacy sighed. "Your mom's great but she exaggerates."

"I've seen those sparks, too, when you're in full retreat." Kristi gave her a friendly arm bump as they walked. "I know it's probably hardest on you, Sam being back and everything. But I thought you were over him. You *said* you were over him."

"I exaggerate, too," Lacy mumbled and stopped at the corner, waiting for a green light to cross the street. Her gaze swept along the street.

One of the things she liked best about Ogden was that it protected its history. Relished it. The buildings were updated to be safe, but the heart and soul of them remained to give the downtown area a sense of the past even as it embraced the future.

At the end of the street stood the Ogden train station. Restored to its beautiful Spanish Colonial Revival style, it boasted a gorgeous clock tower in the center of the building. Inside, she knew, were polished wood, high-beamed ceilings and wall murals done by the same artist who did the Ellis Island murals in the 1930s.

Today there was an arts-and-crafts fair going on inside, and she and Kristi were headed there to check out the booths and see how Lacy's photographs were selling.

"I knew you weren't over him," Kristi said with just a touch of a smug smile. "I told you. You still love him."

"No. I won't." Lacy stopped, took a breath. "I mean I don't." She wanted to mean it, even as she felt herself weakening. What kind of an idiot, after all, would she be to deliberately set herself up to get run over again? The light turned green and both women crossed the street.

"Any decent self-help book would tell you that what you just said has flags flying all over it." Still smug, Kristi gave Lacy a smile and took another drink of her latte. "You're trying so hard, but it's hopeless. You do love him—you just don't want to love him. Or forgive him. And I so get that." Shaking her head, Kristi added, "Tony keeps telling me that I've got to let it go. Accept that Sam did what he had to do just like we did. We all stayed and he had to go. Simple."

"Doesn't it just figure that a guy would defend another guy?"

"That's what I thought, too," Kristi admitted. "But in a way, he has a point."

Lacy snorted. "Hard to believe that Sam *had* to leave."

"Yeah," Kristi said on a sigh, and crossed the street, matching her strides to Lacy's. "That urge to bolt out of a hard situation was really more Jack than Sam. Jack never could stand any really deep emotional thing. If a woman cried around him, he'd vanish in a blink."

"I remember," Lacy said wistfully. Hadn't they all teased Jack about his inability to handle any relationship that looked deeper than a puddle?

"I love both of my brothers," Kristi told her, "but I always knew that Sam was the dependable one. Jack was fun—God, he was fun!" Her smile was wide for a split second, then faded. "But you never knew if he'd be home for dinner or if he'd be on his way to Austria for the skiing instead."

Kristi was right. Sam had always been the responsible one. The one you could count on, Lacy thought. Which had made his leaving all that much harder to understand. To accept. As for forgiving, how did you forgive someone you had trusted above everyone else for breaking their word and your heart along with it?

"I kind of hate to admit it, but Tony may be right," Kristi was saying. "I mean, I'm still mad at Sam, but when I see him with Dad, it makes it harder to stay mad, you know?"

"Yeah, I do." That was part of her problem, Lacy thought. She so wanted to keep her sense of righteous anger burning bright, but every time she saw Sam with his father, she softened a little. When she watched him out on the slopes just yesterday, helping a little boy figure out how to make a parallel turn. When she saw him standing in the wind, talking future plans with the contractor. All of these images were fresh and new and starting to whittle away at the fury she had once been sure would be with her forever.

"Dad's so pleased he's back. He's recovering from that heart attack scare faster I think, because Sam's over every day and the two of them are continuously going over all of the plans for Snow Vista." She took another gulp of coffee and Lacy envied it. "Mom's a little cooler, almost as if, like you, she's half expecting him to disappear again, but even she's happy about Sam being home. I can see it in her eyes and on the bathroom scale since she's still cooking the fatted calf for her prodigal nearly every night. Maybe," Kristi said thoughtfully, "it would be easier to forgive and be glad he was here if I knew he was staying."

Lacy's ears perked up. Here was something important. Had he decided to stay after all? And if he did, what would that mean for her? For *them*?

"He hasn't said anything to any of you?"

"No. Just sort of does his work, visits with the parents and avoids all mention of the future—outside of the plans he's got cooking for the resort." Kristi tossed her now-empty cup into a trash can. "So every day I wait to hear that he's gone. He left so fast the last time—" She broke off and winced. "Sorry."

"Nothing to be sorry about," Lacy said as they walked up to the entrance of the train station. "He did leave, and yeah, I'm not convinced he's staying, either."

And she didn't know if that made her life easier or harder. If he was going to leave again, she had to keep her distance for her own heart's sake. She couldn't let herself care again. And if he was staying...what? Could she love him? Could she ever really trust him not to leave her behind again?

What if she didn't have the flu? What if she had gotten pregnant that one night with him? What then? Did she tell him or keep it to herself?

Feeling as if her head might explode, Lacy pushed it all to one side and walked into the train station, deliberately closing her mind to thoughts of Sam for the rest of the day. Instantly, she was slapped with the noise of hundreds of people, talking, laughing, shouting. There were young moms with babies in strollers and toddlers firmly in hand. There were a few men looking as if they'd rather be anywhere else, and then there were the grandmas, traveling in packs as they wandered the crowded station.

Lacy and Kristi paid their entrance fee and joined the herd of people streaming down the narrow aisles. There were so many booths it was hard to see everything at once, which meant that she and Kristi would be making several trips around the cavernous room.

"Oh, I love this." Kristi had already stopped to pick up a hand-worked wooden salad bowl, sanded and polished to a warm honeyed gleam. While she dickered with the artisan, Lacy wandered on. She studied dry floral wreaths, hand-painted front-door hangers shouting WELCOME SPRING and then deliberately hurried past a booth packed with baby bibs, tiny T-shirts and beautifully handmade cradles.

She wouldn't think about it. Not until she had to. And if there was a small part of her that loved the chance that she might be pregnant, she wasn't going to indulge that tiny, wistful voice in the back of her mind.

Lacy dawdled over the jewelry exhibit and then the hand-tooled leather journals. She stopped at the Sweet and Salty booth and looked over the bags of snacks. Her stomach was still unhappy, so she bought a small bag of plain popcorn, hoping it would help. Nibbling as she went, her gaze swept over the area. There were paintings, blown-glass vases and wineglasses, kids' toys and outdoor furniture made by real craftsmen. But she moved through the crowd with her destination in mind. The local art gallery had a booth at the fair every year and that's where Lacy was headed. She sold her photographs through the gallery and she liked to keep track of what kind of photos sold best.

She loved her job at the lodge, enjoyed teaching kids how to ski, but taking photographs, capturing moments, was her real love. Lacy nibbled at the popcorn as she climbed the steps to the gallery's display. The owner was busy dealing with a customer, so Lacy busied herself, studying the shots that were displayed alongside beautiful oil paintings, watercolors and pastels.

Seeing her shots of the mountain, of sunrises and sunsets, of an iced-over lake, gave her the same thrill it always did. Here was her heart. Taking photographs, finding just the right way to tell a story in a picture—that was what fed her soul. And now, she reminded herself, Sam wanted to use her work to advertise the resort. She was flattered and touched and sliding down that slippery slope toward caring for him again.

The owner of the gallery, Heather Burke, handed Lacy's black-and-white study of a snow-laden pine tree to a well-dressed woman carrying a gorgeous blueberry-colored leather bag.

Pride rippled through Lacy. People valued her work. Not just Sam and those at the lodge, but strangers, people who looked at her prints and saw art or beauty or memories. And that was a gift, she thought. Knowing that others appreciated the glimpses of nature that she froze in time.

Lacy smiled at Heather as the woman approached, a look of satisfaction on her face. "I loved that picture."

"So did she," Heather said with a wink. "Enough to pay three hundred for it."

"Three hundred?" The amount was surprising, though Heather had always insisted that Lacy priced her shots too low. "Seriously?"

"Yes, seriously." Heather laughed delightedly. "And, I sold your shot of the little boy skating on the ice rink for two."

"Wow." Exciting, and even better, if she did turn out to be pregnant, at least she knew she wouldn't have to worry about making enough money to take care of her child.

"I told you people are willing to pay for beautiful things, Lacy. And," Heather added meaningfully, "now that spring and summer tourists are almost here, I'm going to need more of your photographs for the gallery. My stock's getting low and we don't want to miss any sales, right?"

"Right. I'll get you more by next week."

"Great." Heather gave her an absent pat on the arm and whispered, "I've got another live one I think. Talk to you later." Then she swept in on an older man studying the photo of a lone skier, whipping down Snow Vista's peak.

Lacy's heart gave a little lurch as it always did when she saw that shot. It was Sam, of course, taken a few years ago just before the season opened and the two of them had had the slopes to themselves. In the photo, the snow was pristine but for the twin slashes in Sam's wake. Trees were bent in the wind, snow drifting from heavy branches. She could almost hear his laughter, echoing in her memory. But, she thought as a stranger lifted the photo off its display board, that was then— this was now.

"I remember that day."

Sam's voice came from right behind her and Lacy was jolted out of her thoughts. She turned to look at him, but he was watching the photograph the older man carried.

"Jack was in Germany and it was just you and me on the slopes."

"I remember." She stared up at him and saw the dreaminess in his green eyes. Caught up in the past, she followed him down Memory Lane.

"Do you also remember how that day ended?" He ran one hand down the length of her arm, giving her a chill that was filled with the promise of heat.

"Of course I do."

As if she could ever forget. They'd made love in the ski-lift cabin as snow fell and wiped away the tracks they'd left on the mountain. She remembered feeling as though they were the only two people in the world, caught up in the still silence of the falling snow and the wonder of Sam loving her.

It had all been so easy back then. She loved Sam. Sam loved her. And the future had spread out in front of them with a shining glory. Then two years later, Jack was dead, Sam was gone and Lacy was alone.

Now he was watching her with warmth in his eyes and a half smile on his lips, and Lacy felt her heart take a tumble she wasn't prepared to accept. Love was so close she could almost touch it. Fear was there, too, though. So she pushed memories into the back of her mind.

"What are you doing at a craft fair?" she blurted out.

He shrugged. "Kristi told Tony where the two of you would be, so we decided to come down and meet up. Thought maybe we could join you for lunch."

Just the thought of lunch made her stomach churn enough that even her popped corn wasn't going to help. She swallowed hard and breathed deeply through her nose. Honestly, she was praying this was something simple. Like the plague.

"Hey." He took her arm in a firm grip. "Are you okay? You just went as pale as the snow in your pictures."

"I'm fine," she said, willing herself to believe it. "Just an upset stomach, I think."

He stared at her, his gaze delving into hers as if he could pry all her secrets loose. Lacy met his gaze, refusing to look away and give him even more reason to speculate. "You're sure that's the problem?"

He was thinking *baby*, just as she was. But since she didn't have the answer to his question, she sidestepped it. "I'm sure. Just not very hungry is all."

"Okay…" He didn't look convinced, but at least he was willing to stop staring at her as if she were a bomb about to explode. Glancing back at the prints being displayed in the booth, he said, "Your photography's changed as much as you have."

"What does that mean?"

He shifted his gaze back to her, then reached out and helped himself to some of her popcorn. "You've grown. So have your photos. There's more depth. More—" he looked directly into her eyes "—layers."

Lacy flushed a little under the praise and was more touched than she was comfortable admitting. Over the past two years, she *had* changed. She'd been forced to grow up, to realize that though she had loved Sam, she could survive without him. She could have a life she loved, was proud of, without him. And though the empty space in her heart had remained, she'd become someone she was proud of. Knowing that he saw, recognized and even liked those changes was disconcerting. To cover up the rush of mixed feelings, she asked, "Is that a backhanded compliment?"

"No," he said with a shake of his head. "Nothing backhanded about it. Just an observation that you're a hell of a woman."

He was looking at her as if he was really *seeing* her—all of her—and she read admiration in his eyes. That was a surprise, and damned if she didn't like it.

A little too much. He was getting to her in a big way. What she was beginning to feel for Sam Wyatt now was so much more than she'd once felt and that worried her. When he left before, she'd survived it, but she didn't know if she could do that again.

"Well, I should look for Kristi—"

"Oh, she left with Tony," Sam told her with a half smile that made him look so approachable, so like the Sam she used to know that it threw her for a second. The then and now blended together and became a wild mix of *throwing Lacy for a loop*. When his words finally clicked in, though, she said, "Wait. She left?"

"He offered to buy her a calzone at La Ferrovia."

"Ah." Lacy nodded, understanding why her best friend had ditched her for her boyfriend. "He does know her weak spots. But who can blame her? Those calzones are legendary."

"Yeah," he said, and started walking alongside her as she turned to move down the crowded aisle. "When I was in Italy, I tried to find one as good as their spinach-cheese calzone and couldn't do it."

"Italy, huh?" Her heart tugged a little, thinking about the time he was away from her. What he'd done, seen. And yes, fine, who he'd been with. She shouldn't care. He'd left her, after all. But it was hard to simply shut down your own feelings just because someone else had tossed them in your face.

"It was beautiful," he said, but he didn't look pleased with whatever memories were rising. "Jack always loved Italy."

"Did you?"

He took more of the popcorn and munched on it. "It was nice. Parts of it were amazing. But seeing something great when you're on your own isn't all that satisfying, as it turns out." He shrugged. "There's no one to turn to and say, *isn't that something*? Still, it was good to be there. See it the way Jack did. But I never did find a calzone as good as La Ferrovia's."

An answer that wasn't an answer, Lacy thought, and wondered why he was bothering to be so ambiguous. She would have thought that he'd love seeing the top skiing spots in Europe. The fact that he clearly hadn't, made her wonder. And she hated that she cared.

"But you're happy to make do now with my popcorn," she said.

"And the company," he added, dipping one hand into the bag again. "This stuff is great, by the way."

"Chelsea Haven makes it, sells it at all the craft fairs and at one of the shops on Twenty-Fifth." She took another handful and added, "I got plain today because, you know. Stomach trouble."

His eyebrows lifted, but she ignored it.

"She's got lots of great flavors, too. Nacho, spicy and—my personal favorite—churro."

He laughed a little. "You're a connoisseur of corn?"

"I try," she said with a shrug, and stopped at the next booth. Wooden shelves and a display table held colorful, carefully wrapped bars of handmade soaps. From bright blue to a cool green, the soaps were labeled with their scents and the list of organic ingredients. Lacy picked up two pale blue bars and held on to them until she could pay for all of her purchases at once at the exit.

Sam studied the display for a long moment before he picked up a square of green soap, sniffed and asked, "Who makes all of this stuff?"

"A small company in Logan. I love it."

She sniffed at the bar of soap, smiled, then held it up for him to take a whiff.

"It's you," he said, giving her a soft smile. "The scent that's always clinging to your skin." He thought about it a moment, then said, "Lilac."

"Good nose," she told him, and started walking again.

"Some things a man's not likely to forget." He bent his head to hers, lowered his voice and whispered, "Like the scent of the woman he's inside of. That kind of thing is imprinted onto your memory."

She quivered from head to toe and, judging by his smile, he approved of her reaction. Her body was tingling, her brain was just a little fuzzed out and breathing seemed like such a chore. When she looked into his eyes and saw the heat there, Lacy felt her heart take another tumble, and this time she didn't try to deny it. To stop it.

When it came to Sam, there was no stopping how her body, her soul, reacted. Her brain was something else, though. She could still give herself a poke and remind herself of the danger of taking another plunge with Sam Wyatt. And yet, despite the danger, she knew there was nothing else she'd rather do. Which meant she was in very big trouble.

Then he straightened, scanned the crowd surrounding them and muttered, "I feel sort of outnumbered around here. Can't be more than a handful of men in the whole building."

"Gonna leave?" she asked, shooting him a quick look.

He met her gaze squarely. "I'm not going anywhere."

And suddenly, she knew he was talking about more than just the craft fair.

Sam stayed with her for another hour as they cruised through a craft fair that normally he wouldn't have been caught dead in. But being with Lacy on neutral ground made up for the fact that he felt a little out of place in what was generally considered female territory.

But while they walked and Lacy shopped, his mind turned over ideas. He carried her purchases in a cloth bag she'd brought with her for that purpose, and together they stepped out of the train station. Sam paused to look up, to the end of Historic Twenty-Fifth and beyond to the snow-covered mountain range in the distance. Trees were budding, the air was warmer and the sun shone down, as if designed to highlight the place in a golden glow.

"I missed this," he said, more to himself than Lacy. "I don't think I even knew how *much* I missed it until I was home again." The wind kicked up as if reminding everyone that spring was around the corner but winter hadn't really left just yet.

"Are you?" she asked, and Sam turned his head to look down at her. That long, silky braid of blond hair fell across one shoulder and loosened tendrils flew around her face, catching on her eyelashes as she watched him. "Are you home?"

Reaching out, Sam gently stroked the hair from her face and tucked it behind her ear. He'd wondered this himself for days. He hadn't been able to give his father a direct answer because he was still too torn. Leave? Walk away from the memories this mountain held and spend the rest of his life running from his own past? Or stand and face it all, reclaim the life—and the woman—he'd left behind?

And wasn't it just perfect now to realize that the woman he wanted owned the property he wanted? If he tried romancing her now, she'd never believe he wanted her for herself. Seemed as though fate was really enjoying itself at his expense.

He'd have to find a way around it, Sam told himself. Because he was done trying to hide from the past. It was time to set it all right. Starting now.

"Yeah, Lacy. I'm home. For good this time."

Eight

"I want to open a gift shop," Sam said, and watched as surprise had Lacy goggling at him. He'd been doing a lot of thinking since the two of them had walked through the arts-and-crafts fair the day before. Though he hadn't been tempted into buying anything himself, Sam was astute enough to realize that other people were. He figured that tourists would be just as anxious to shop for items made by local artisans.

He smiled at Lacy's confusion, then said, "Yeah, I know. Not exactly what you'd expect me to say. But I can see possibilities in everything."

"Is that right?"

"You bet." He eased down to sit on the corner of the desk in her office. "I already talked to you about using the photos you have of the lodge…"

"Yes?"

He grinned at her, enjoying having knocked her a

little off balance, and said, "It struck me when we were at that craft and art fair. There's a hell of a lot of talented people in the area."

"Sure," she said, warily.

"That's why I'm thinking gift shop. Something separate from the lodge, but clearly connected, too. Maybe between the lodge and the new addition that's going up." He nodded as the image filled his mind and he could actually envision what it would look like. "I'd want to have some refrigerated snacks in there, too. For people who are hungry but don't really want a full meal. Like prepackaged sandwiches, drinks, fruit, that kind of stuff…"

"Okay, that's a good idea, but—"

"But more than a snack shop—I want to display local artists. Not just your stuff, which is great, but like the wood-carver at the fair, the glass artist I saw there. I'll still want your postcards and we can sell framed prints, too."

"I don't know what to say."

Shaking his head, he said, "Knowing you, that won't last long. But my point is, if we're expanding Snow Vista, we could bring a lot of the local artists along with us for the ride. I think the tourists would love it and it would give the artists another outlet beyond the fairs to sell their stuff."

"I'm sure they'd love that," she said slowly, cautiously.

That was fine. He could deal with her suspicion. She'd see soon enough that he meant what he was saying. "We'll have a lawyer draw up agreements, of course. Specific to each artisan and what they sell."

"Agreements."

He nodded. "I'm thinking a seventy-thirty split with everyone, same as you and I will have."

"That's amazing," she said, tipping her head to one side and looking up at him as if she'd never seen him before.

"Okay, I know what you're thinking," he said. "I've never really involved myself in anything beyond the lodge or skiing itself."

"Yeah…"

"Like I told you before. People change." He shrugged and mentally brushed off whatever else might be running through Lacy's mind. "Back to the financial aspect, I think what we'll offer is fair. And we'll do well by each other, the lodge and the artists." His gaze met hers. "I want a range of different products in this shop. I want to showcase local talent, Lacy. Everyone from the artists to the chefs, to the woman who makes the blackberry preserves we use at the restaurant."

"Beth Howell."

"Right." He grabbed a piece of paper off the desk and scribbled down the name. "You know her, right? Hell, you probably know all of the artists around here."

"Most, sure…"

"That's great—then as resort manager you can be point on this. Talk to them. See what they think. When it gets closer to opening time, we'll set down the deals in legalese."

She blinked at him. "You want me to take charge of this?"

"Is that a problem?" He smiled, knowing that he'd caught her off guard again.

"No," she said quickly with a shake of her head. "I'm just surprised is all."

"Why?" He came off the desk and stood in front

of her before leaning down, bracing his hands on the arms of her chair. "You know your photos are great. Why would you be surprised that I'd want to showcase them, help you sell them?"

She blew out a breath and fiddled nervously with the end of her blond braid. "I suppose, because of our past, I wonder why you're being so...nice."

"I want you, Lacy. That one night with you wasn't enough. Not by a long shot."

She sucked in air and a faint flush swept up her cheeks, letting him know she felt the fire still burning between them.

"I'm home to stay. That means we're going to be part of each other's lives again."

Shaking her head, she started to speak, but he cut her off. "It's more than that, though. I want to dig in, make the kind of changes that are going to put Snow Vista on the map. And mostly, I want to convince *you* that I'm here and I'm not leaving."

"Why is that so important to you? Why do you care what I think?" Her voice was whisper soft and still it tore at him.

"You don't trust me," he said, and saw the flash in her eyes that proved it. He hated that she was wary of him, but again, he could understand it. "I get that. But things are different now, Lacy. I told you I've seen how much you've changed. Well, I've changed, too." He reached out and captured her nervous fingers in his. "I'm not the same man I was when I left here two years ago."

"And is that a good thing?" she asked quietly. "Or a bad thing?"

Leave it to this new Lacy to lay it out there so bluntly.

His mouth quirked. "I guess you'll have to discover that for yourself."

"It shouldn't matter to you what I think," she said.

"Yes, it should," he argued, and briefly looked down at her fingers, caught in his. "You more than anyone. I had a lot of time to think while I was gone."

"Yeah," she said shortly. "Me, too."

He nodded, acknowledging what she said even as he mentally kicked himself for putting her through so much pain. He hadn't been able to see anything beyond his own misery two years ago. Yet now everything looked clear enough to see that he'd set this whole situation in motion. He had to dig his way out of the very mess he'd created.

"My point is, I took some long, hard looks at my life. Choices made. Decisions. I didn't like a lot of them. Didn't much care for where those decisions had taken me. So now I'm home and I'm going to live with whatever it was that brought me back here."

She took a breath when he rubbed his thumb across her knuckles and he felt the soft whoosh of heat simmering into life between them. Her summer-blue eyes narrowed in caution. He understood why she was looking at him as if expecting him to turn and bolt for the door. But he was done looking for escape. He was here to stay now and she had to get used to it.

"I understand your suspicion," he said, capturing her gaze with his and willing her to not look away. "But I'm home now, Lacy. I'm not leaving again and you're gonna have to find a way to deal." He leaned in closer. "I left two years ago—"

She took a breath. "You keep reminding me of that, and trust me, it's not necessary."

"The point is, those two years changed us both—but

nothing can change what's still between us and I'm not going to let you deny that fire."

She licked her lips, clearly uneasy, and that slight action shot a jolt of heat right to his groin.

"Sam—"

Oh, yeah. She felt it. She was just determined to fight it. Well hell, he'd always liked a challenge. "I'm going to *romance* you, Lacy."

"What? Why?" She pulled her fingers from his grasp, but he saw her rubbing her fingertips as if they were still buzzing with sensation.

"Because I want you," he said simply. He wasn't going to use the *L* word—not only because she wouldn't want to hear it, but because he didn't know if he could say it again. He'd had that love once before but it hadn't held him. He wasn't ready to try and fail again. Failure simply wasn't an option, to quote some old movie. So he was going to keep this simple.

Looking deeply into her eyes, he added, "It's not just what I want, Lacy. You want me, too."

She looked as if she wanted to argue, but she didn't, and Sam called that a win. At least she was admitting, if only to herself, that the burn between them was hotter than ever.

"You're really trying to keep me off balance, aren't you?" she asked.

He gave her a slow, wicked smile. "How'm I doing?"

"Too well."

"Glad to hear it." He stood up abruptly and announced, "I'm headed over to the architect's office. I want to talk to her about designing this gift shop."

"You've already got so much going on…"

"No point in wasting time, is there?" And he meant

both the building and what lay between them. He was sure she understood that, too.

"I suppose not."

"So, talk to a few of your friends," he said, heading for the door. "See if they'd be interested in being involved."

"I'm sure they will…"

"Good," Sam said, interrupting her as he opened the office door. "We can have dinner later and talk about everything."

He took one last look at her and was pleased to see she looked completely shaken. That's how he wanted her. A little unsteady, a little unsure. If he kept her dancing on that fine edge, she'd be less likely to pull back, to cling to her anger. Sam was determined that he would find a way back into her life. To have her in his. And he knew just the way to do it.

Back in the day, he hadn't given Lacy romance. They'd simply fallen into love and then into marriage, and it had all been so easy. Maybe, he thought as he stalked through the lobby and out the front door, that was why it had fallen apart. It was all so easy he hadn't truly appreciated what he'd had until he'd thrown it away.

He wasn't going to make that mistake again.

Two hours later, Lacy was at home, closed up in the bathroom, staring down at the counter and the three—count them, *three*—pregnancy tests.

She'd driven into Logan to buy them just so she wouldn't run into anyone she knew in the local drugstore. She'd bought three different kinds of early-response tests because she was feeling a little obsessive and didn't really trust results to just one single test. And for the first time in her life, she got straight A's on three separate tests.

Positive.

All three of them.

Lacy lifted her gaze to her own reflection in the bathroom mirror. She waited for a sense of panic to erupt inside her. Waited to see worry shining in her own eyes. But those emotions didn't come. Her mind raced and her heart galloped just to keep pace.

"Oh, my God. Really?" Her voice echoed in the quiet cabin. All alone, she took a moment to smile and watched herself as the smile became a grin. She was going to have a baby.

Instinctively, she dropped one hand to lay it gently against her abdomen as if comforting the child within. When she and Sam were together, she had daydreamed about building a family with him. About how she might tell him the happy news when she got pregnant.

"Times change," she muttered. "Now it's not *how* to tell him, but *if* to tell him."

She had to, though, didn't she? Sure she did. That was just one of the rules people lived by. They'd made a baby together and he had a right to know. "Oh, boy, not looking forward to that."

Funny, a couple of years ago, there would have been celebration, happiness. Now she was happy. But what about Sam? He said he wanted her, but that wasn't love. Lust burned bright but went to ash just as quickly. And love was no guarantee anyway. He had loved her two years ago, but he'd left anyway. She loved him now, but it wasn't enough.

"Oh, God." She stared into her own eyes and watched them widen with realization. Kristi was right. Lacy *did* still love Sam. But that love had changed, just as she had. It was bigger. More grown-up. Less naive. She knew there were problems. Knew she wasn't on steady ground, and it wasn't enough to wipe away what she felt. Especially when she didn't know if she *wanted* it wiped away. God, she really was a glutton for punishment. Just pitiful.

The baby added another layer to this whole situation. Yes, Sam had to know.

"But," she told the girl in the mirror, "none of the rules say *when* you have to tell him."

The problem was, she wanted him to be here right now. Wanted to turn into his arms and feel them come around her. She wanted to share this…magic with him and see him happy about it. She wanted him to love her.

Stepping away from the counter, she plopped down onto the closed toilet seat and just sat there in stunned silence. She was still in love with the man who had once shattered her heart. She might have buried her emotions and her pain for two long years, but she hadn't been able to completely cut him out of her heart. He had stayed there because he belonged there, Lacy thought. He always had.

But loving him was a one-way ticket to misery if he didn't love her back. And if she told him about the baby, he'd say and do all the right things—she knew him well enough to know that for certain. He'd want to get married again maybe. Raise their child together, and she would never really know if he would have chosen *her* without the baby. Would he have come not just back home, but back to *her*?

She couldn't live an entire life never knowing, never sure.

Slowly, she pushed to her feet, stared at the test kits, then swept all three of them into the trash can. Patting her abdomen, she said, "No offense, sweetie, but I need to know if your daddy would want me even if you weren't here. So let's keep this between us for a while, okay?"

"You all right?" Sam asked the next morning when he caught her staring off into space. "Still have an upset stomach?"

"What?" Lacy jolted a little. "Um, no. Feel much better." Not a lie at all, she told herself. Once she got past the first fifteen or twenty minutes of feeling like death, everything really lightened up. Of course, she really missed coffee. Herbal tea was just…disappointing.

"Okay." He gave her a wary look as if trying to decide if she was telling the truth or not. "You were acting a little off last night when I stopped by your place with dinner, too."

Because she had still been reeling with the shock of finding herself pregnant. She hadn't really expected him to show up, especially bringing calzones from La Ferrovia. And once he was in the cabin, she had assumed that he would make a move to get her back into bed. But he hadn't. Instead, they'd talked about old times, his new plans for the resort, everything in fact, except what was simmering between them.

For a couple of hours, they'd shared dinner, laughter and a history that was made up of a lifetime of knowing each other. And darn it, Lacy thought, she had been completely charmed and thrown off balance again. He'd said he was going to give her romance, and if last night was the beginning of that, he was off to a great start.

"Have you had a chance to talk to any of your friends about the gift shop?"

"Oh, I did get a couple of them on the phone and

they're very interested." Excited, actually. Thrilled to be asked and to have another venue to sell their wares.

"Good." He shoved both hands in his pockets and stared out the office window at the view. "I'm meeting with the architect in an hour. I want the plans drawn up as soon as possible."

"I don't think that'll be a problem," she said wryly.

He glanced at her. "Why's that?"

"Nobody says no to you for long, do they?"

Sam's mouth quirked. "That include you?"

She felt her balance dissolving beneath her feet. One smile from him, one whispered comment sent jagged shards of heat slicing through her. It just wasn't fair that he had so much ammunition to use against her.

Rather than let him see that he was getting to her, Lacy replied, "As I recall, I also said 'yes' a couple of weeks ago."

"Yeah," he said, gaze moving over her like a touch. "You did."

She squirmed in her chair, then forced herself to settle when she noticed him noticing.

"Don't get jumpy," he said, coming around the desk to lean over her.

"If you don't want me jumpy, you should back up a little."

That smile came again. "Seduction in the office isn't romance, so you're safe from me at the moment."

It could be, she thought wistfully. Lock the door, draw the blinds and—oh, yeah, the office could work. Oh, boy.

He kissed her light and quick, then straightened up. "I'm heading into Ogden to the meeting with the architect. If you need me, you've got my cell number."

"Yeah. I do." *If you need me.* She smothered a sigh. She did need him, but probably not in the way he meant.

"Okay then."

He was almost at the door when she remembered something she had to run by him. "I hired an extra chef to give Maria some help in the kitchen. He starts tomorrow."

"That works," he said, and gave her a long look. "You don't have to run this stuff by me, Lacy. You've done a hell of a job managing the resort for a long time now. I trust you."

Then he left and Lacy was alone with those three words repeating in her mind. *He trusted her.*

And she was keeping his child a secret from him. Was she wrong to wait? To see if maybe his idea to romance her had more to do with reigniting love rather than the flash and burn of desire?

How could she know? All she had to go on were her instincts and they were screaming at her to protect herself—because if he shattered her again, she might not be able to pick up all the pieces this time.

For the next few weeks, Sam concentrated on setting his plans into motion. As February became March and spring crept closer day by day, he was busier than ever. It felt good, digging back into Snow Vista, making a new place for himself here. And Lacy was a big part of that. They had dinner together nearly every night—he'd taken to showing up at the cabin bringing burgers or Italian or Chinese. They talked and planned, and though it was killing him not to, he hadn't tried to smooth her into bed again yet.

He was determined to give her the romance neither of them had had the first time around. And that included sending her flowers, both at work and at her house. The wariness in her eyes was fading and he was glad to see it go.

A roaring engine from one of the earth movers working on the restaurant site tore through his thoughts and brought him back to the moment. The construction team was digging out and leveling the ground for the foundation. As long as the sun kept shining and temperatures stayed above freezing, they'd be getting the lodge addition started by next week. The hard-core, hate-to-see-winter-end skiers were still flocking to the mountain, but for most of the tourists, the beginning of spring meant the end of looking for snow.

Which brought him back to the latest plan he'd already set in motion. Right now there was an engineer and a surveying crew laying out the best possible route for his just-like-Park-City forest ride. There would be rails for individual cars and the riders would be able to slow down if they didn't like the speed attached to careening down a mountain slope. The architects were busily drawing up plans and making the changes that the Wyatt family insisted on.

Sam smiled to himself, stuffed his hands into the pockets of his battered black leather jacket and turned his face into the wind. Here at the top of Snow Vista, the view was, in his opinion, the best in the world. Damned if he hadn't missed it.

He'd been all over the planet, stood on top of the Alps, skied amazing slopes in Germany, Italy and Austria, yet this was the view that for him couldn't be beaten. The pines were tall and straight in the wind, and the bare branches of the oaks and aspens chattered like old women gossiping. Soon, the trees would green up, the wildflowers would be back and the river through the canyon would run fresh and clear again.

His gaze swept across the heavily wooded slope that was unusable for skiing. The alpine ride he wanted installed would make great use of that piece of land. Like a roller coaster but without the crazy dips and climbs. It would be a slower, open-air ride through the trees, displaying the fantastic views available from the top of the mountain. Like Park City, Snow Vista could become known for summer as well as winter fun.

He could see it all. The lifts, the alpine coaster, the restaurant offering great food at reasonable prices. Hell, Sam told himself, as he turned to shift his view to the meadow, still blanketed in snow, with a gazebo and a few other additions, they could open the resort to weddings, corporate getaways…the possibilities were endless.

And he'd be here, to see it all. He waited for the urge to leave and when it didn't come, he smiled. It really was good to be back.

"I know the sun's out, but it's still too cold to be standing around outside."

Chuckling, Sam turned to face his sister.

"It's spring, Kristi," Sam said. "Enjoy the cool before the summer heat arrives."

She walked toward him, her hair pulled back from her face, a black jacket pulled over a red sweater and jeans. As she approached, her features were as cool as the wind sliding across the mountain. His little sister hadn't really said anything about his decision to stay and Sam knew that she and Lacy were the ones he'd have to work hardest to convince. He was pretty sure he had Lacy halfway there, but maybe now was his chance to get through to his sister.

"You haven't even been back a full month and you've

got the whole mountain running to catch up with your ideas."

Sam shrugged. "Now that I've decided to stay, there's no point in holding back." He looked away from Kristi and sent a sharp-eyed look at the men working the half-frozen ground. "I want the resort to be up and offering new things as quickly as possible."

"Hence the bonus money offered the crew if they get both foundations poured before April 1?"

Sam grinned. "Money's a great motivator."

"It is," she acknowledged. "And Dad's really happy with everything you're doing."

"I know." It felt good, knowing that his father was excited about the future. That meant he was thinking ahead, not about the past or about his own health issues. Sam was still stopping in at the lodge every day to go over the plans with his father. To keep the older man engaged in what was going on. To get his input and, hell—just to be with him. Sam had missed that connection with his parents over the past two years. Being here with them again was good for the soul— even with the ghost of Jack hanging over all of them, whether he was spoken of or not. But even with that, with the memories of sorrow clinging close, even with the complications nearly choking him, it was good to be on familiar ground again.

"What about you, Kristi?" His gaze shifted to her again. "How are you feeling about all of this? About me?"

She took a breath and let it out. "I like all of the plans," she said, lifting her eyes to meet his. "But the jury's still out on what I'm thinking of you."

Sam felt his good mood drift away and decided that now was the time to get a few things straightened out with his little sister. "How long are you going to make me pay?"

"How long have you got?" Kristi shrugged, but her eyes were clouded with emotion rather than anger.

"I can't keep saying I'm sorry." Apologizing had never come easy for Sam. Not even when he was a kid. Having to swallow the fact that he'd screwed up royally two years ago wasn't exactly a walk in the park. But he was doing it.

"I came back," he told her. "That has to count, too."

"Maybe it does, because I am glad you're back, Sam. Really." She shoved both hands into her jacket pockets and tossed a strand of hair out of her eyes with a single jerk of her head. "You being here is a good thing. But what you did two years ago affected all of us and that's not so easy to get past."

"Yeah, I know." He nodded grimly, accepting the burden of past decisions. "Lacy. Mom. Dad."

"Me," she snapped out, and stepped up close enough to him that the toes of their boots collided. Tipping her head back, she glared up at him, her eyes suddenly alive with anger, and said, "You leaving taught me that trusting *anyone* was too risky. Did you know Tony's asked me to marry him twice now and twice I told him no?"

He inhaled sharply. "No, I didn't know that."

"Well, he did. And I said no because—" her voice broke off, she swallowed hard and pinned him with a hot look designed to singe his hair. "Because if *you* could leave Lacy, how could I possibly trust that Tony would stay with me? What's the point, right? I couldn't make myself believe, because you ripped the rug out from under me."

"Damn it, Kristi." Talk about feeling lower than he would have thought possible. Somehow in screwing over his own life, he'd managed to do the same for his baby sister. One more piece of guilt to add to the burden he already carried. Sam gritted his teeth and accepted it. Then he dropped both hands onto her shoulders and held on.

"You can't use me as an excuse for not trying. I messed things up pretty well, but they were *my* decisions." Bitter pill to choke down, but there it was. "You can't judge everyone else by what I did. Tony's a great guy and you know it. You're in charge of your own life, Kristi. Make it or break it on your own. Just like the rest of us."

"Easy to say when you're not the one left behind."

She had a point, though it cut at him to admit it. Damn, the repercussions of what he'd done two years ago just kept coming. It was like dropping a damn rock into a pond and watching the ripples spread and reach toward shore. But even as he acknowledged that, he tried to cut himself a break, too.

When Jack died, Sam hadn't been able to think. Hadn't been able to take a breath through his own pain, and he'd reacted to that. Escaping the memories, the people, who were all turning to him for answers he didn't have. The emptiness he'd felt at his brother's death had driven him beyond logic, beyond reason. Now, his decision to come home again meant he was forced to face the consequences of his actions. Acknowledging the pain he'd dealt others was hard to swallow.

He looked at Kristi and saw her in flashing images through his mind at every stage of her life. The baby his parents had brought home from the hospital. The tiny blonde girl chasing after him and Jack. The prom date Jack and he had tortured with promises of pain if he got out of line with their sister. The three siblings laughing together at the top of the mountain before hurtling down the slope in one of the many races they'd indulged in. Slowly, though, the memories faded and he was looking into her eyes, seeing the here and now, and love for her filled him.

Going with instinct, he pulled her, resisting, in for a hug, and rested his chin on top of her head. It only took a second or two for her to wrap her arms around his waist and hold on. "Damn it Sam, we needed you—I needed you—and you weren't here."

"I am now," he said, waiting until she looked up at him again. She was beautiful and sad, but no longer furious and he was silently grateful that the two of them had managed to cross a bridge to each other. "But, Kristi, don't let my mistakes make you miss something amazing. You love Tony, right?"

"Yes, but—"

"No." He cut her off with a shake of his head. "No buts. You've always been nuts about him and it's clear he loves you, too, or he wouldn't put up with all of those self-help books you're always quoting."

She snorted and dipped her head briefly. The smile was still curving her mouth when she looked up at him again.

Shaking his head, Sam said softly, "Don't use me as an excuse for playing it safe, Kristi. Nobody's perfect, kid. Sometimes, you have to take a chance to get something you want."

She scowled at him, then chewed at her bottom lip.

He smiled and planted a kiss on her forehead. "Trust Tony. Hell, Kristi, trust *yourself*."

"I'll try," she said, then added, "I'm so glad you're home."

"Me, too, kid. Me, too."

Nine

The talk with his sister was still resonating with him when Sam stopped at Lacy's cabin later that night. For hours, he'd heard Kristi's voice repeating in his mind as he came to grips with what he'd put everyone through two years ago. Realizing what he'd cost himself had brought him to the realization that he not only wanted but *needed* Lacy in his life again. Now he had to find a way to make that happen.

The occasional night with her wasn't enough. He wanted more. And Sam wasn't going to stop until he had it.

He brought pizza and that need to be with her. To just be in the same damn room with her. To be able to look into those eyes that had haunted him for too long and realize he had a second chance to make things right.

"Bringing a pizza is cheating," Lacy told him, settling back into the couch with a slice of that pizza on a stoneware plate.

He laughed. "How? Gotta eat. You always loved pizza."

"Please." She rolled her eyes and shook her head. "Everyone loves pizza."

"Not many people love it with pepperoni and pineapple."

She took a bite and gave a soft groan of pleasure that had his body tightening in response. "Peasants who don't know what's good," she said with a shrug.

Ordinarily he might enjoy bantering with her, but tonight, he couldn't seem to settle. Sam set his pizza aside and looked into the fire that burned cheerily in the hearth. The hiss and crackle of flames was a soothing sound, but it did nothing for the edginess he felt. He couldn't shake that conversation with Kristi.

"What's wrong?"

He looked at her, firelight dancing across her face, highlighting the gold of her hair lying loose across her shoulders. That same flickering light glittered in her eyes as she watched him. She wore jeans, a deep red sweater and a pair of striped socks, and still, she was the most beautiful woman he'd ever seen.

"Sam? What is it?"

He got to his feet, stalked to the fireplace and planted both hands on the mantel as he stared into the flames. "I talked to Kristi today."

"I know. She told me."

Of course she had. Women told each other everything—a fact that gave most men cold chills just to think about it. He turned to look at her. "Did she tell you that she's been putting her whole damn life on pause because of what I did two years ago?"

"Yeah, she did."

He pushed one hand through his hair, turned his back

on the fire and faced her dead on. His brain was racing; guilt raked his guts with sharpened claws. "I never realized, you know, how much my decisions two years ago affected everyone else."

Lacy set her pizza aside and folded her hands in her lap as she looked at him. "How could they not, Sam?"

Scrubbing the back of his neck, he blurted, "Yeah, I see that now. But back then, I couldn't see past my own pain. My own misery."

"You wouldn't let any of us help. You shut us all out, Sam."

"I know that," he said tightly. "I do. But I couldn't reach out to you, Lacy. Not when the guilt was eating me alive."

"Why should you feel guilty about what happened to Jack? I don't understand that at all."

He blew out a breath, swallowed hard and admitted, "When Jack first got sick—diagnosed with leukemia—that's when the guilt started."

"Sam, why? You didn't make him sick."

He choked out a sharp laugh. "No, I didn't. But I was healthy and that was enough. We were *identical twins*, Lacy. The same damn egg made us both. So why was he sick and I wasn't? Jack never said it, but I know he was thinking it because I was. Why him? Why not me?"

A soft sigh escaped her and he didn't know if it was sympathy or frustration.

Didn't matter now anyway. He was finally telling her exactly what had been going through his head back then, and he had to get it finished. But damn, it was harder than he would have thought. Shaking his head, he reached up to scrub one hand across the back of his neck and started talking again.

"I was with Jack through the whole thing, but I

couldn't share it. Couldn't take my half of it and make it easier on him." His hand fisted and he thumped it uselessly against his side as his mind took him back to the darkest days of his life. "I felt so damn helpless, Lacy. I couldn't *do* anything."

"You did do something, though, Sam," she reminded him. "You gave him bone marrow. You gave him a chance and it worked."

He snorted at the reminder of how high their hopes had been. Of the relief Sam had felt for finally being able to help his twin. To save his life. "For all the good it did in the end."

"I never knew you were feeling all of this." She stood up, walked to him and looked into his eyes. "Why didn't you talk to me about this then, Sam?"

He blew out a breath. Meeting her eyes was the hardest thing he'd ever done. Trying to explain the unexplainable was just as difficult. "How could I tell my wife that I felt guilty for being married? Happy? Alive?" He pushed both hands through his hair, then sucked in air like a drowning man hoping for a few more seconds of life before the sea dragged him down. "God, Lacy, you were loving me and Jack had no one."

"He had *all* of us," she countered.

"You know what I mean." He shook his head again. "He was *dying* right in front of me."

"Us."

She was right, he knew. Jack's loss was bigger than how it had affected Sam. He could remember his parents' agony and worry. The whispered prayers in the mint-green, soulless, hospital waiting room. He saw his father age and watched his mother hold back tears torn from her heart and still... "I couldn't feel that then," he admitted. "*Wouldn't* feel it. I was watching my twin die and I was so messed up I couldn't see a way out."

"But you finally found one…"

"Yeah," he said softly, looking into those eyes of hers, seeing the sorrow, the regret, and hating himself for causing it then and reawakening it now. "I don't know if you can understand what I did, Lacy. Hell, I don't even know if I do, now."

"Try me." She folded her arms across her chest and waited.

God, two years he'd been holding everything inside him. Letting it all out was like—he couldn't even think of the right metaphor. It was damned painful but it was long past time he told Lacy exactly what had happened then. Why he'd done what he'd done.

"After the bone-marrow transplant, after it worked and Jack was in remission, it was like…" He paused, looking for the right words, and was sure he wouldn't be able to find them. Not to explain what he had felt. Finally, he just started talking again and hoped for the best. "It was like fate had suddenly said, 'Okay, Sam. You can go ahead and be happy again. Your brother's alive. You saved him. So everything's good.'"

He could remember it so well, the nearly crippling relief, the laughter. Watching his brother recover, get strong again, believing that their world was righting itself.

Lacy reached out and gently laid one hand on his forearm. It felt like a damn lifeline to Sam, holding him to this place, this time, not letting him go too deeply into a past filled with misery. He covered her hand with his, needing that warmth she offered him as he finished.

Sam looked down at their joined hands and said softly, "Jack was full of plans, Lacy. He was well again, and after so long feeling like crap, he couldn't wait to get back out into the world."

"I remember," she said quietly.

The snap and hiss of the flames was the only sound in the room for a few seconds. "He showed me his 'list.' Not a bucket list, since he wasn't dying anymore. It was a *life* list. A *life* list. His first stop was going to be Germany. Staying with some friends while he skied the slopes and reclaimed everything the cancer stole from him."

She didn't speak, just kept looking at him through eyes gleaming with the shine of tears she wouldn't allow to fall.

"He was well, damn it." Sam pulled away from her and scrubbed both hands over his face like a man trying to wake up from a nightmare. "Jack was happy again and on the road and then he *dies* in a damn car wreck on the freeway? It was crazy. Surreal."

"I know, Sam. I was with you. We all were."

"That's the thing, Lacy." His gaze caught hers again as he willed her to understand how it had been for him. "You were there but I couldn't have you. Couldn't *let* myself have you because Jack was dead and his dreams with him. I *saved* him and he died anyway. It was like fate was screwing with us just for the hell of it. None of it made sense. I couldn't bring him back. So I told myself I had to do the next best thing. I had to at least keep his dreams alive."

Seconds ticked past before Lacy stared up at him and said, "That's why you left? To pick up the list Jack left behind and make it happen?"

"He had all these plans. Big ones. And with him gone, those plans were all I had left of him. How could I let them die, too?"

"Sam—" She broke off, took a breath and said, "Did you really think fulfilling Jack's list was going to keep him with you?"

God, why did it sound stupid when she said it? It hadn't been at the time. But that's exactly what he'd thought. By living his twin's dreams, in essence, his twin's *life*, it would be as if Jack never died.

"It was important to me," he muttered thickly. "I had to keep him alive somehow."

"God, Sam…" She lifted one hand to cover her mouth and her beautiful eyes shone with tears.

"Keeping Jack with me meant distancing myself from the reality of his death. That's why I had to leave. I couldn't be here, facing the fact, every day, that he was gone."

God, he felt so stupid. So damn weak somehow for having to give up his own life because he'd been unable to accept his twin's death. He rubbed one hand across his mouth, then said, "I took Jack's dreams and lived them for him. For a while, I lost myself in ski slopes, strangers and enough alcohol to sink a ship." He snorted ruefully as memories of empty hotel rooms and staggering hangovers rose up to taunt him. "But drinking only made the pain more miserable and even skiing and being anonymous got old fast."

"You should have talked to me, Sam."

"And said what?" he asked, suddenly weary to his bones. His gaze locked on hers and everything in him wished that they were still what they had once been to each other. It rocked him a little to realize just how much he wanted her back. How much he still loved her. "What could I possibly have told you, Lacy? That I wasn't allowed to be happy because Jack was dead? You couldn't have understood."

"You're right," she said, nodding. "I wouldn't have. I'd have told you that *living* was the best way to honor Jack. Living your own dreams. Not his."

He sighed. She was right and he could see that now. He wouldn't have then. "My dreams didn't seem to matter to me once his were over."

"Did it help?" she asked quietly. "Leaving. Did it help?"

"For a while." His mouth quirked briefly. "But not for long. I couldn't find satisfaction in Jack's dreams because they weren't mine. But I owed it to him to try."

She reached up to cup his face in her palms and the soft warmth of her touch slid deep inside to ease away the last of the chill crouched in his heart. God, how had he lived for two years without her touch? Without the sound of her voice or the soft curve of her mouth? How had he been able to stay away from the one woman in the world who made his life worth living?

"Sam," she said quietly, "you don't owe Jack your life."

"I know," he said, covering her hands with his. It was too early to tell her he loved her. Why the hell should she believe him after what he'd done to their lives? Their marriage? No, he'd sneak up on her. Be a part of her world every day, slowly letting her see that he was here to stay and that he would never leave her again. "That's why I'm back, Lacy. To rebuild my life. And I want that life to include you."

"Sam..."

"Don't say anything yet, Lacy," he told her. "Just let me prove to you that I can be the man for you."

Her breath hitched and her eyes went shiny with emotion.

"Let's just take our time and discover each other again, okay?"

She nodded slowly, and in her eyes he read hope mingled with caution. Couldn't blame her for it, but he silently vowed that he'd wipe away her trepidation.

"You can trust me, Lacy. I swear it."

"I want to, Sam," she whispered, "for more reasons than you know…"

"Just give me a chance." When he pulled her close, bent his head and kissed her, she leaned into him, curving her body to his, silently letting him know that she was willing to try. And that was all he could hope for. For now.

Tenderness welled up between them and in the soft, flickering firelight, they came together as if it were the first time and the shining promise that was the future was almost in reach.

Lacy was still smiling the next morning.

She felt as though she and Sam had finally created a shaky bridge between the past and present. At long last, he'd told her what had driven him to leave, and though it still hurt, she could almost understand. As sad as they'd all been when Jack died, for Sam it had to have been even more devastating. Like losing a part of himself. And she could admit, too, that she hadn't been capable of being what he needed back then. She'd been too concerned with her own insecurities.

When Jack died, all she'd been able to think was *thank God it wasn't Sam*. She'd been too young and too untried—untested—to be able to see what Sam was going through, so how could she have helped him?

Now it was as if they were both getting a second chance to do things right. She laid one hand on her belly and whispered to the child sleeping within, "I think it's going to be all right, baby. Your daddy and I are going to make it happen. Build a future in spite of the past."

And just to prove to herself—and him—that she was willing to trust him, willing to believe, she had decided to tell him about the baby that night at dinner.

Whoa. Her stomach did a quick twist and spin at the thought. Nervous, yes, but it was the right thing to do. If they were going to work this out between them and have it stick this time, she had to be as honest as he had been the night before.

She gave the baby a gentle pat, then, smiling, she headed through the lobby. There were guests sprinkled around the great room, enjoying the fire, having a snack, chatting. She ignored them all, stepped outside and took a deep breath of the chill spring air. Tulips and daffodils were spearing up, trees were beginning to green.

It was as if the snow was melting along with the ice in her heart. Lacy felt lighter than she had in two years. And she was ready to let go of the past and rush to a future that was suddenly looking very bright.

"Lacy! Hey, Lacy!"

She turned and grinned at Kevin Hambleton as he jogged toward her. Kevin was young, working his first season at the lodge. He was helping out at the ski-rental shop, but had been angling for an instructor's position.

"Hi, Kevin," she said as he started walking with her toward the ski lift that would take her to the new construction site. Not only did she want to see how the building was coming along, she could admit to herself that she wanted to see Sam, too. And she knew that if he wasn't at the lodge, working in the office, he would be at the site, watching his plans come to life. "I'm just going up to check on the guys, see what progress they're making."

"It's great, isn't it?" His face practically shone with excitement. "A lot of things happening around here now that Sam's back."

"There are, with more to come," she said, thinking about the gift shop, the portico and the expansion to the lodge. Within a couple of years, Snow Vista would be a premier tourist destination.

"I know, I read that in the paper this morning."

"What?" She looked up at him. As far as she knew, the gift shop hadn't been announced.

"Yeah, there was this article, talking about all the changes and how Sam's going to put in a new beginner's run on the back side of the mountain and all…"

Lacy shook her head, frowned and tried to focus on what he was saying. But her heart was pounding and her brain was starting to short-circuit. "He's building a run on the backside?"

"Yeah, and I wanted to put my name in with you early, you know?" He grinned. "Get in on the ground floor. I really want to be an instructor and I figured starting out with the newbies would be a good idea, you know?"

"Right." Mind racing, Lacy heard Kevin's excited voice now as nothing more than a buzz of sound. The cold wind slapped at her, people around her shouted or laughed and went about their business. It was all she could do to put one foot in front of the other.

"With a new run going in, you'll need more instructors, so I just, you know, wanted to see if maybe you'd think about me first."

He was standing there, staring at her with a hopeful

grin on his face, the freckles across his cheeks bright splashes of gold.

The edges of her vision went dark until she was looking at Kevin as if through a telescope. She felt faint, her head was light and there was a ball of ice in the pit of her stomach. Through the clanging in her brain and the wild thumping of her heart, Lacy knew she had to say *something*.

"How did you hear about the new run?"

"Like I said," he told her, his eyes a little less excited now, "I saw it in the paper. Well, my mom did and she told me."

He was looking worried now, as if he'd done something wrong, so Lacy gave him a smile and a friendly pat on the shoulder to ease him. No reason to punish him just because *her* world was suddenly rocking wildly out of control. "Okay then, Kevin. I'll put your name down."

"Thanks!" Breath whooshed out of him in relief. "A lot, really. Thanks, Lacy."

When he ran off again, she watched him go, but her mind wasn't on Kevin any longer. It was fixed solely on Sam Wyatt. The lying bastard. God. She thought about the night before—as she had been doing all morning—only now she was looking at it through clearer eyes.

And heck, it wasn't just last night, it was the past few weeks. Romancing her. She nearly choked. He'd said he was going to romance her, but that wasn't what he'd been doing. This whole time, he'd been conducting a sort of chess match, with her as the pawn, to be moved wherever he wanted her. He'd spent weeks softening her up, until he could apply the coup de grâce last night. Then he rolled her up in sympathy, let her shed a few tears for him, for them, then he'd swept her into bed, where rational thinking was simply not an option.

"Oh, he was good," she murmured, gaze fixed on the top of the mountain where she knew he was, but not really seeing it. "He actually convinced me. He had me."

And wasn't that a lowering thing to admit? Lacy cringed internally as she remembered just how easily she'd fallen for charm and lies. Sam had slipped beneath her radar and gotten past every one of her defenses. He'd made her feel *sorry* for him. Made her forgive him for what he'd done to her two years ago. Made her *believe* again. Last night, he'd convinced her at last that maybe they had a chance of rebuilding their lives.

But he wasn't really interested in that at all. Or in *her*. She was a means to an end. All he wanted from her was the land his family had given her. For his plans. For his changes. He was sweeping her aside just as he had two years ago. And just like then, she hadn't noticed until she had tire tracks on her back.

Temper leaped into life and started pawing at her soul like a bull preparing to charge. Well, she wasn't the same Lacy now. She was tougher. Stronger. She'd had to be.

And this time, he wasn't going to get away with it.

She found him at the construction site, just where she'd expected him to be. Sam spent half his time up here, talking to the men, watching the progress of the new restaurant going up. And all the while, he was probably planning his takeover of her property, too.

The ride on the ski lift hadn't calmed or soothed Lacy as it usually did. Normally, the sprawling view spreading out beneath her, the sensation of skimming through the sky was enough to ease away every jagged edge inside her. But not today. The edges were too sharp. Cutting too deeply.

The rage she'd felt when Kevin first stopped her and spilled his news had grown until it was a bubbling froth rising up from the pit of her stomach to the base of her throat. Her hands shook with the fury and her eyes narrowed dangerously against the sun glinting off what was left of the snowpack. Shaking her head, she jumped off the lift when it reached the top and before she could even *try* to cool down, she followed the steady roar of men and machines to the site.

Sam stood there, hands in the pockets of his black leather jacket, wind tossing his dark hair into a tumble and his gaze fixed on the men hustling around what looked to her like the aftermath of a bombing. He couldn't have heard her approach over the crashing noise, but as she got closer, he somehow sensed her and turned to smile. That smile lasted a fraction of a second before draining away into a puzzled frown.

"Lacy?" His voice was pitched high enough to carry over the construction noise. "Everything okay?"

"*Nothing* is okay and you know it," she countered, sprinting toward him until she was close enough to stab her index finger against his chest. "How could you do that? You lied to me. You used my own pain against me. You played me, Sam. Again."

"What the hell are you talking about?"

Oh, he was a better actor than she'd given him credit for. The expression of stunned surprise might actually have been convincing if she didn't already know the truth. "You know damn well what I'm talking about so don't bother playing innocent."

God, she was so furious she could hardly draw a breath.

But the words clogging her throat didn't have any trouble leaping out at him. "Kevin told me what's really going on around here. I should have known. Should have guessed. Romancing me," she added snidely. "Flowers. Dinner."

If anything, the confusion on his face etched deeper until Lacy wanted to just smack him. She'd never been a violent person, but at the moment she sorely wished she was.

"Why don't you calm down," he was saying. "We'll go talk and you can tell me what's bothering you?"

"Don't you tell me to calm down!" She reached up and tugged at her own hair, flying loose in the wind. "I can't believe I fell for it. I was this close—" she held up her thumb and index finger just a whisker apart "—to trusting you again. I thought last night meant something—"

Now anger replaced confusion and his features went taut as his eyes narrowed. "Last night *did* mean something."

"Sure," she countered, through the pain, the humiliation of knowing it had all been an act. "It was the cherry on top of the sundae of lies you've been building for weeks. The grand finale of the Romance Lacy Plan. My God, I went for it all, didn't I? Your sadness, your grief." She huffed in a breath, disgusted with him, with herself, with everything. "I've got to give you credit— it really did the job on me. Then slip me into bed fast and make me remember how it used to be for us. Make me *want* it."

A couple of the machines went silent and the drop in the noise level was substantial, but she kept going. She was aware of nothing beyond the man staring at her as if she were speaking in tongues.

"You set this whole thing up, didn't you? Right from the beginning."

"Set *what* up?" He threw both hands in the air and let them fall to his sides again. "If you'll tell me what you're talking about maybe I could answer that."

"The backside of the mountain," she snapped. "*My* land. The land your folks deeded to me." Her breath was hitching, her voice catching. "You want it for a new beginner run. Kevin told me he saw it in the paper this morning. Your secret's out, Sam. I know the truth now, and I'm here to tell you it's not going to work."

"The *paper*?" he repeated, clearly astonished. "How the hell did—"

"Hah!" she shouted. "Didn't mean for the word to get out so soon, huh? Wanted a little more time to sucker me in even deeper?"

"That's not what I meant—never mind. Doesn't matter."

She gasped. "You son of a bitch, of *course* it matters. It's *all* that matters. You lied to me, Sam. You used me. And damn it, I let you." She was so stupid. How could she have been foolish enough to let him get into her heart again? How could she have, even for a moment, allowed herself to hope? To dream?

"Now just wait a damn minute," Sam blurted out. "I can explain all of this."

She took a step back and didn't even notice when the last of the construction machinery cut off and silence dropped on the mountain like a stone. "Oh, I bet you can. I bet you've got stories and explanations for any contingency."

"Just a minute here, Lacy…"

"How far were you willing to go, Sam, to get what you wanted from me? Marriage?"

"If you'll just shut up and listen for a second…"

"Don't you tell me to shut up! And for your information, I'm done listening to you." She backed up a step, lifted her chin and gave him the iciest glare she could manage. "You want the land? Well you're not going to get it. The one thing you want from me, you can't have."

He moved toward her. "That's not what I want from you."

"I don't believe you." She shook her head and her gaze fixed with his. "I know the truth now. I know the real reason you've been spending so much time with me, *reconnecting*."

"You don't know anything," he said, moving in closer. "I admit, I wanted a new beginner run on the backside, but—"

"There. Finally. *Truth*." She jerked her head back as if he'd slapped her. "Did it actually hurt to say it?"

"I'm not finished."

"Oh, yes," she told him, "you are. *We* are. Whatever there was between us is done."

"It'll never be done, Lacy." His voice was dark, deep and filled with determination. "You know that as well as I do."

"What I know, is that once I believed you when you said you would never leave me. You *knew* what that meant to me. Because my own mother left me. You promised you wouldn't. You swore to love me forever." Oh, God, this was so hard. She couldn't breathe now. There were iron bands around her chest, squeezing her lungs, fisting around her heart. "And then you left. You walked away. Broke your word *and* my heart. You don't get a second chance at that. Damned if I'll bleed for you again, Sam."

"You're upset," he said, his voice carrying the faintly

patient tone that people reserved for dealing with hysterics. "When you settle down a little, we can talk this out."

She laughed and it scored her throat even as it scraped the air. "I've said what I came to say to you—and I don't want to hear another word from you. Ever."

Lacy spun around and hurried to the ski lift for a ride back down the mountain.

Sam watched her go, his own heart pounding thunderously in his chest. Silence stretched out around him, and it was only then he noticed all the men had stopped working and were watching him. They'd probably heard every word. He turned his head and caught sight of Dennis Barclay.

"Seems you're in some deep trouble there, Sam," the man said.

Truer words, he thought, but didn't let Dennis know just how worried he was. He'd never seen Lacy in a tear like that before. Even when she was furious when he first got home, even when she had yelled at him about past sins, there'd been some control. Some sort of restraint. But today there had been nothing but sheer fury and bright pain. Pain he'd caused her. Again. That thought shamed him as well as infuriated him.

How the hell had that tidbit about the beginner run made it into the paper? He hadn't told anyone. Hadn't said a word.

"She'll cool off," Dennis said, offering hope.

"Yeah," Sam agreed, though a part of him wasn't so sure. The pain and fury he'd just witnessed wasn't something that would go away quickly. If ever. Had he screwed things up so badly this time that it really was over?

Misery blossomed in his chest and wrung his heart

until the pain of it nearly brought him to his knees. A life without Lacy?

Didn't bear thinking about.

Ten

Sam's instincts told him to go to Lacy right away. Follow her. Force her to listen to him so he could straighten all this out. But his instincts two years ago had been damned wrong, so he was hesitant to listen to them now—when it mattered so much.

He denied himself the urge to go to Lacy and instead went to the lodge and upstairs to the family quarters. He wasn't even sure why, but he felt as if he needed more than being alone with the black thoughts rampaging through his mind.

The great room was empty, so he followed his nose to the kitchen. The scent of spaghetti sauce drifted to him, and in spite of everything, his stomach growled in appreciation. Another thing he'd missed while he was gone was his mother's homemade sauce. Sam stopped in the doorway and watched her at the stove while his father sat at the round oak pedestal table, laying out a hand of solitaire.

"Sam!" His father spotted him first and his mother whirled around from the stove to smile in welcome. "Good to see you," his father said. "How's the work on the mountain going? Tell me all about it since your mother won't let me go up yet."

"Everything's fine," Sam said, and walked to the table to take a seat. The kitchen was bright, cheerful, with the sunlight pouring in through windows sparkling in the light.

"You don't look too happy about it," his mother said.

He glanced at her and forced a smile. "It's not that. It's…"

"Lacy," his mother finished for him.

"Well," Sam chuckled darkly, "good to know that your mother radar is still in good shape."

Connie Wyatt grinned at her son. "It wasn't that hard to guess, but I'll take the compliment, thanks."

"So, what's going on?" his father asked as Sam sat down opposite him.

He hardly knew where to start. But hell, he'd come here to talk, to get this all off his chest. He just had to lay it all out for them, so he took a breath and blurted out, "Apparently someone talked to a reporter. It was in the paper today about me wanting to build a beginner run on Lacy's property."

"Ouch." His father winced.

"And she found out," Connie said.

"Yeah." Sam drummed his fingers on the table. "She let me have it, too. I just can't figure out how the reporter heard about it. I mean, I changed my plans when I heard the land was Lacy's."

"That's probably my fault."

"Bob," his wife demanded, "what did you do?"

Grumbling, the older Wyatt glanced first at his son,

then his wife. "A reporter called here the other day," he said, with a rueful shake of his head. "Asking questions about all the changes happening around here. Got me talking about the different runs we have to offer, then she said something about how she was a novice skier and I told her we could teach her and that you had wanted to build a brand-new beginner run on the back of the mountain, but that the plans weren't set in stone so not to say anything...and I guess she did anyway."

Sam groaned. At least that explained how it had made the paper. And, it would be a lot simpler if he could just blame this latest mess on his father. But the reality was, if Sam had just been honest with Lacy from the jump, none of this would be happening.

"Don't worry about it, Dad. She was bound to hear about it sooner or later anyway."

"Yeah, but it would've been better to hear it from you," his father pointed out.

"That ship sailed when I didn't tell her." Sam slumped back in the chair and reached for the cup of coffee his mother set in front of him. Taking a long sip, he let the heat slide through him in a welcome wave.

"So what're you going to do about all of this?" his mother asked quietly.

He looked at her. Connie was standing with her back braced against the counter, her arms folded over her chest.

"That's the thing," Sam said honestly. His chest ached like a bad tooth and he suspected his heart wasn't going to be feeling better anytime soon. Not with the way things stood between him and Lacy. "I just don't know."

And that was the truth. With Lacy's words still echoing in his mind, the wounded glint in her eyes still fresh in his memory, Sam couldn't see clearly what he should do. He knew what he *wanted* to do. Go to her. Tell her he loved her. But damned if she'd believe that *now*. It had been easier—if more selfish—two years ago, when he hadn't considered how his decision to take off would affect anyone but himself. Now, though, there was too much to think about. Just one more rock on the treacherous road his life had become.

"I almost went after her—"

"Bad idea," his father said. "Never beard a lioness in her den when she's still itching to take a bite out of you. I speak from experience," he added with a sly glance at his wife.

"Very funny," Sam's mother quipped, then turned back to Sam. "And just how long do you think it's going to take for her to cool off?"

"A decade or two ought to do it," Sam mused, only half joking. He raked one hand through his hair and sighed. "Hell, me coming home has thrown everyone off their game. Maybe it'd be best for everyone if I just left again and—"

"Don't you even say that," his mother warned, her voice cold steel. "Samuel Bennett Wyatt, don't you even *think* about leaving here again."

Shocked at the vehemence in her tone, Sam could only look at her. "I really wasn't going to leave again. I was just thinking that maybe it would be easier on everyone if I—"

"If you what?" his mother finished for him. "Disappear again? Leave us wondering if you're alive or dead again? Walk away from your home? Your family? *Again?*"

Now it was his turn to wince. Damned if Sam didn't feel the way he had at thirteen when he'd faced down his mother after driving a snowmobile into the back of the lodge.

"Mom," he said, standing up.

"No," she interrupted, pushing off the counter as if she were leaping into battle. And maybe she was. Connie took three short steps until she was right in front of her son, tipping her head back to glare at him. "Ever since you got back, I've kept my peace. I didn't say all the things I was bursting to say to you because I didn't want to rock the boat. Well, brace yourself because here it comes."

"Uh-oh," his father whispered.

His mother's eyes were swimming with tears and fury, her shoulders were tense and her voice was sharp. "When you left right after Jack died, it was like I'd lost both of my sons. You might as well have been dead, too," she continued. "You walked away, left us grieving, worrying." Planting both hands at her hips, she continued, "Four postcards in two years, Sam. That's it. It was as if you'd disappeared as completely as Jack. As if you were as out of reach as he was."

No one could make a grown man feel quite as shameful and guilt-ridden as his mother. Sam looked down at her and knew he'd never be able to make it up to her for what he'd done. "I had to go, Mom."

"Maybe," she allowed tightly with a jerking nod. "Maybe you did, but you're back now, and if you leave again, you'll be no better than Jack was, always running away from life."

"What?" Staggered, Sam argued, "No, that's wrong. Jack was all about living life to the fullest. He grabbed every ounce of pleasure he could out of every single day."

She sighed heavily and Sam watched the anger drain

from her as she shook her head and reached up to cup his cheek in her palm. "Oh, honey. Jack was all about *experiences*, not living. The fastest cars. Best skis. Highest mountain. That's not *life*. That's indulgence."

He'd never really thought about his brother in those terms. It would have been disloyal, he guessed, but with his own mother pointing it out, it was impossible to argue.

"I loved Jack," she said, fisting her hand against her chest. "When he died, I lost a piece of my heart I'll never get back. But I'm not blind to my children's faults just because I love them to distraction." Connie gave him a wistful smile. "When it came to adventure, there was no one better than Jack. But he never had the courage to love one woman and build a life with her. To face the everyday crises that crop up, to pay bills, get a mortgage, take the kids to the dentist. *That's* life, Sam. A real life with all the ups, downs, tears and laughter that come with it. That kind of thing terrified him and he did everything he could to avoid it."

Sam thought about that and realized his mother was right. Jack had always gone for the one-night stand kind of woman. The kind who hated commitment as much as he did himself.

"You had that courage once, Sam. When you married Lacy and began to build a life together." She sighed a little and stared into his eyes. "You walked away from that, and I'm not going to say now whether that was right or wrong because it's done and can't be undone. My question is, do you still have that courage, Sam? Do you still want that life with Lacy?"

The question hung in the air between them and seemed to reverberate inside him, as well. He looked at his mother, then at his father. At the room around them and the memories etched into the very walls. His life was here. It was time he picked it up and claimed it once and for all. He did want that life that he'd once been foolish enough to throw away. He wanted another chance to build what his parents had built.

He wasn't Jack. Sam wanted permanent. He wanted the everyday with the one woman who would make each single day special. All he had to do was find the way to make Lacy listen. To make her understand that he damn well loved her, and she loved him, too.

"Yeah, Mom," he said softly, reaching out to pull his mother close. "I do."

She hugged him hard—no more wary caution from her—and for the first time since he'd come back to Snow Vista, he really felt as if he was home again.

"You're *pregnant*?"

"Yes, and don't tell your brother."

"Not a word," Kristi swore, fingers crossing her heart, then flying up into a salute of solidarity. "How far along are you? Never mind. Can't be far. He's only been home a month. It *is* Sam's, right?"

Lacy gave her an exasperated look.

"Right, right," Kristi said, using both hands to wipe away her words, "it's Sam's. The idiot."

"That about covers how I'm feeling about him right now."

Lacy had been ranting about Sam for the past hour, and when news of the baby had slipped out, she'd had to swear her friend to silence. But she couldn't regret sharing her big secret with her best friend. It had felt too good to tell *someone*.

Lacy was still so furious she could hardly see straight, but mostly at herself, for falling for Sam's stories again. Seriously. *If you're going to make mistakes*, she thought, *at least have the good sense to make some new ones along the way.* But how could she have avoided letting herself be sucked back in? She still loved him. Though she was going to find a way to get over it. Maybe *she* should start reading those self-help books that Kristi was so addicted to. What she needed was a book called *How to Wipe That Man Out of Your Life*.

"What're you going to do?"

Lacy dropped into the closest chair and stared at the fire in her hearth. "I'm going to have a baby and never speak to your brother again."

"Hmm…" Kristi leaned into her own chair. "I applaud the sentiment, but it's gonna be tough. What with you both living here and all."

"He won't stay," Lacy muttered. "Soon enough, he'll be gone again, chasing his dead brother's dreams."

"I used to think Jack was the dummy, but I'm sorry to say," Kristi mused, "turns out Sam's the lucky winner there."

Lacy cringed a little. "I'm sorry. I shouldn't be dumping all of this on you. He's your brother. You shouldn't be in the middle."

"Are you kidding? In matters like these, it's all about girls versus boys as far as I'm concerned."

She smiled. "You're a good friend, Kristi."

"I could be better if you'd let me go kick Sam."

"No." Anger was now riding hand in hand with misery, and the two were so tangled up inside her, Lacy could hardly breathe. But she did know enough to realize that giving Sam any more attention at all would be just what he wanted. So she was going to ignore him. Forever.

Oh, for heaven's sake, how would she ever be able to

pull that off? It wouldn't be long before she'd be showing and Sam would know about the baby and...

"Maybe I'm the one who should move."

"Don't you dare," Kristi countered in a flash. "What
would I do here without you to talk to? Besides, you've
got my niece or nephew in there—" she waved one hand
at Lacy's tummy "—and I want to meet them."

"Yes, but—"

"Mostly, though," Kristi said smugly, "if you leave,
you let Sam think you were too afraid to stay in your
own home."

Oh, she didn't like the sound of that at all. Plus, the
truth was, Lacy didn't want to move. She loved her
cabin. She loved her job. She loved the mountain. She
loved *Sam*, damn it.

"Can your head actually explode?" she wondered
aloud.

"I hope not," Kristi said solemnly. "Now, why don't
we go out for dinner or something? Get your mind off
my idiot—er, brother."

Lacy smiled as she'd been meant to, but shook her
head. "No thanks. I just want to stay home and bury
my head under a pillow."

"Sounds like a plan." Kristi pushed up from the chair.
"I'll leave you to it."

Lacy got up, too, and wrapped her friend in a tight
hug. "Thanks. For everything."

"You bet. This'll work out, Lacy. You'll see." There
was a knock at the door and Kristi asked, "Want me to
get that and send whoever it is away?"

"God, yes. Thanks."

Kristi opened the door and Lacy heard Sam's voice
say "I want to talk to her."

"Surprise," Kristi shot back, "she doesn't want to talk to you."

Lacy groaned and went to face Sam because she couldn't put siblings at war over her. It was too soon, was all she could think. It had only been a few hours since that horrible scene at the top of the mountain. She needed a day or two or a hundred before she was willing to speak to Sam again. Yet it seemed fate didn't care about what she needed.

"It's okay, Kristi, I'll handle it."

"You sure?" Her friend's eyes narrowed in concern.

"Yeah, I'm fine." Of course she wasn't, but she wouldn't give Sam the satisfaction of knowing just how off balance she was with him here. She would be calm. Cool. Controlled, damn it!

"Okay, I'll leave," Kristi announced with a glare at Sam. "But I won't be far. Idiot."

"Thanks," he said wryly, "that's nice."

"Be grateful Lacy made me promise not to kick you," she called back over her shoulder.

Lacy watched him give his sister a dirty look, then grit his teeth as he turned around to face the door. Sadly, she didn't have enough time to slam it shut before he slapped one palm to it and held it open.

He was still wearing the black jacket and jeans. His dark hair still looked windblown and completely touchable. His eyes were shadowed, his mouth grim, and in spite of everything, her heart leaped and her body hummed with a desire that would probably never end. Mind and heart were at war inside her, but for her own good, for the sake of her baby, she had to be strong.

Behind him, she saw the soft, dying streaks of sunlight spearing through the pines. The dark green stalks of soon-to-bloom daffodils popped up all over her yard and the last of the snow lay in dwindling, dirty mounds.

"Lacy, you had your say on the mountain," Sam told her, dragging her gaze to his. "At least hear me out now."

"Why should I?"

He looked at her for a few long seconds, then admitted, "I can't think of a single damn reason. Do it anyway."

Sam walked into the main room and took a moment to gather himself. He looked around at the familiar space, the comfortable furnishings, the hominess of it all and felt his heart ease. Funny, he'd spent most of his life thinking of the mountain as home. But it was this place. It was *Lacy*.

Wherever she was, that was his home. He only hoped she would take him back.

An invisible fist tightened around his heart and gave a vicious squeeze. Was she still so furious she wouldn't listen to him? Wouldn't let him fix this? What could have been panic scratched at his guts, but he shoved it down, ignored it. He wouldn't fail at this, the most important thing he'd ever done. He'd make her listen. Make her understand and then make her admit she loved him, damn it.

Lacy walked into the room behind him, but stopped three feet away. She crossed her arms over her chest, lifted her chin in what could only be a fighting stance and said, "Say what you came to say, then leave."

She'd been crying. Her lashes were still wet, her face was flushed and her mouth trembled even as she made an attempt to firm it. *Bastard*, he thought, bringing her to this, and if he could have punched himself in the face, he would have. But it wouldn't have solved anything.

"First," he said tightly, "let's get this off the table. Keep your land. I don't want it."

Her eyebrows lifted into twin blond arches. "That's not what the newspaper reported."

"They were wrong." He pushed one hand through his hair. "Okay, I admit that I did have the idea for building a new beginner run on the backside of the mountain."

Her mouth tightened further into a grim slash that didn't bode well for Sam. But he kept going, determined to say everything that needed to be said.

"But Dad told me they'd deeded the property to you, so I let that idea go."

"How magnanimous of you."

Scowling, he snapped, "Damn it, Lacy, I didn't know you owned the land. When I found out, I changed my plans."

"And I'm supposed to take your word for that?"

"Believe me or not, doesn't matter," he countered, and took a step toward her. She didn't move away and he didn't know if that was sheer stubbornness or a willingness to listen. He took it as the latter. "The only thing you need to believe is that I love you."

Her eyes flickered with emotion but he couldn't tell if that was good or bad, so he kept talking. "Took me two damn years to realize what I had. What I lost. But I know now, we belong together, Lacy."

She huffed out a breath and shook her head. Her hands tightened on her own arms until her knuckles whitened, but she didn't speak. Didn't order him to get out. That had to mean something.

"I know I hurt you when I left."

She snorted. "You crushed me."

He winced and kept talking. "I did and I'm sorry for it. But even when we were first married, things were shaky between us. You kept waiting for me to disappoint you. To walk away, like your mother did."

"I was right, wasn't I?" She whispered it, but he heard and ached for her.

"Yeah, I guess you were. But you know, you always looked at what your mother did—leaving—as what love was really all about. So you thought I'd do what she did. You never really believed that I'd stay. Admit that much at least."

She took a breath and said, "To ease your guilt? Why would I? I can tell you that I wanted to believe you, but if I had believed, completely, your leaving would have killed me."

Pain slammed into the center of his chest and he deserved it for putting both of them through this.

"But I trusted you, Sam," she said, adding to the misery he felt now. "And you broke my heart."

Sunset was streaking across the sky outside, but inside, where the light was dim, shadowy and still, he could see the hurting in her summer-blue eyes.

"I know and I'll always regret that, wish I could go back and change it." His voice dropped into a husky whisper that tore at his throat even as her words clawed at his heart. "But, Lacy, your mother wasn't an example of love. Your father was. He *stayed*. He stayed with you. Right here. He lived through the unhappiness and never let it affect how he treated his daughter. That's the kind of love I'm offering you now."

A couple of long seconds ticked past as she considered what he said.

"You're right about my father," she agreed. "I never

thought about it like that, but you're right. She left. He stayed. He was lonely. Sad. But he stayed. *You* didn't."

"No." He hated admitting to that. "But I'm back now. And I'm not going anywhere."

She shook her head again, unwilling to take him at his word, and he only had himself to blame for it.

"I'm here forever, Lacy," he told her, willing her to believe. To trust. "I want a life with you. Children with you. I want to grow old and crotchety on this mountain and watch our kids and grandkids running Snow Vista."

She swayed a little and Sam took that as hope and moved another step closer. "If I have to spend the next ten years romancing you to get you to believe me, then that's what I'll do," he vowed. "I'll bring you flowers every day, dinner every night. I'll kiss you, touch you, make promises to you and eventually, you'll believe in me again."

"Will I?"

"Yeah," he said softly, a smile curving his mouth. "Because you love me, Lacy. As much as I love you."

She took a fast, shallow breath and held it for a long moment.

Sam looked at her standing there, her long hair loose and soft, her features tight, unsure, her eyes damp with tears, and his heart swelled until he thought it might burst from his chest.

"Lacy, I hurt you. I know that and if I could change the past I would. But all I can do is promise you tomorrow and all the tomorrows afterward." Breathing ragged, he took another step toward her. "You know, last night, after we talked, after I told you everything, I realized something I never had before."

"What?"

One word only, but he took that as a good sign, too.

"It wasn't just losing Jack that drove me from here—though that was devastating. I was scared. See, I loved you so much more than my own twin, the thought of losing you was unimaginable."

"Sam..."

"No," he said quickly, "just hear me out. I couldn't stand the thought of maybe losing you, as well. Seems stupid now, to leave you because I was afraid of losing you."

"Yeah," she agreed wryly. "It does."

"But leaving didn't stop the fear," he told her. "I still thought about you. Worried about you. *Loved* you. Staying with you is the only thing that can stop that fear. I know that now. I want to be with you. Dream with you, for however long we live." He took a long breath, let it out and said, "I want to risk the pain to have the love."

Lacy's heart was galloping in her chest. Her mind was reeling. She looked up into his eyes and knew that he was right. About everything. At the start of their marriage, she had been waiting for Sam to let her down. She'd kept her guard up, prepared to be hurt. As much as she'd loved Sam, she'd never really gone all in. She'd held a part of herself back. Always cautious.

She *had* forgotten that her father had always been there for her. In her pain over the loss of her mother, she'd refused to see that love doesn't always leave. Sometimes it stayed. And it was something to count on. To trust in. *That* was the love she wanted to believe in. The kind that never left. The kind that lasted forever.

Yes, she thought, looking up at him, Sam had made mistakes, but so had she. If she had been stronger in her own right, more self-confident, she might have forced him to talk to her in those days after Jack's death. They might have worked this out together. But she'd been half expecting him to leave, so when he did, she'd let it happen instead of fighting for what she wanted.

Now she was willing to fight.

He was watching her through those beautiful green eyes of his and she knew that the next step was hers to take. It always had been. She had to forgive. Had to believe. And looking into his eyes, she knew she did.

Love wasn't perfect. No doubt in the future they'd both make mistakes. But they would both stay. Together.

"You're right," she said, and watched as some of the tension drained out of him. "About a lot of things. But mostly," she said, "you're right that risking the pain is the only way to have the joy I feel when I'm with you."

"Will you risk it?" he asked, gaze never leaving hers. "Will you marry me again, Lacy? Will you trust me to be there for you and to always love you? Will you have my children and build a family with me?"

There it was, she thought. Everything she wanted, shiny and bright and laid at her feet. All she had to do was reach out and take it.

She held her hand out for his, and when his fingers closed around hers, she felt the warmth of him slide down inside and ease away the cold. "Yes, Sam. I'll marry you. I'll believe in you. And I'll love you all my life."

He gave a tug and she flew into his arms. As he held her, he whispered, "Thank God. I love you, Lacy. Now, always, forever, I love you."

"I love you, too, Sam. I always have. Always will." She nestled her head on his chest and listened to the thundering beat of his heart.

His arms encircling her, he asked softly, "What do you say we start making babies right away?"

A slow, satisfied smile crossed her face as she leaned

back to look up at him. "You can cross that one off your to-do list, Sam."

"What do you—" Understanding dawned and his eyes widened even as his jaw dropped. "You mean... are you...already?"

She nodded, waiting for the pleasure to ease past the shock. It didn't take long. His grin spread across his face and lit his eyes with the kind of joy she had once dreamed of seeing. Reality was so much better.

"We're going to have a great life," he promised her as one hand dropped to tenderly cup her flat belly.

She laid her hand over his and said, "We've already started."

Then he kissed her and Lacy's world opened up into a bright, beautiful place.

Epilogue

Lacy had a private room in the maternity ward at McKay-Dee Hospital in Ogden. Outside, it was snowing, but inside, there was a celebration going on.

Sam looked down at his wife, cuddling their newborn son, and felt everything in him surge with happiness. Contentment. The past few months had been full and busy and *great*. The restaurant opened in the fall and was already packed daily. The gift shop was a huge hit not only with the tourists, but also with the local artisans, and the lodge addition was nearly ready to take in guests.

But best of all was the time spent with Lacy. Rediscovering just how good they were together. They were living at her cabin, though they'd added so many rooms to the place, it was barely recognizable now. There were four more bedrooms, a couple of baths and a country kitchen that Lacy rarely wanted to leave. They had plans to fill that cabin with kids and laughter, and they'd gotten their start today.

"You were amazing," he told her, bending down to kiss her forehead, the tip of her nose and then her lips.

Lacy smiled up at him. "Our son is amazing. Just look at him, Sam. Isn't he beautiful?"

"Just like his mom," Sam said, trailing the tip of one finger along his son's cheek. He never would have believed how deeply, how completely, you could love a person not even an hour old. He was a *father*. And a very lucky man.

"He's got your hair and my eyes. Isn't that incredible? His own little person but a part of both of us." She sighed happily and kissed her son's forehead.

"How are you feeling?" Worry colored his words, but he could be forgiven for that. Hadn't he just watched her work and struggle for eight hours to give birth? A harrowing experience he was in no hurry to repeat. "Tired? Hungry?"

She laughed a little at that, caught Sam's hand in hers and gave it a squeeze. "Okay, yeah, I could eat one of Maria's steak sandwiches and swallow it whole. But I feel *great*. I have so much energy, I could get up and ski Bear Run."

The fastest, most dangerous slope at Snow Vista. Shaking his head, he said, "Yeah. You can forget about that for a while."

Lacy grinned and shrugged. "I suppose, but I'm really not tired." Narrowing her gaze on him, she said, "But you're exhausted. You should go home and rest."

"I'm not going anywhere without you." Thankfully, the hospital provided cots for new fathers to sleep on in their wives' rooms. Though he'd have stayed, even if he'd had to sleep in the chair by her bed. He kissed her again, kissed the top of his son's head, and then straightened and threw a glance at the door. "The family's waiting to come in. You ready to face them?"

"Absolutely."

He walked over, waved in the crowd of Wyatts and moved to the head of Lacy's bed as everyone crowded around. His parents were beaming, his father clutching an impossibly bright purple teddy bear, his mother carrying a vase of sunshine-yellow roses. His sister, Kristi, was there, holding her husband Tony's hand. The two of them had finally married last May, and Kristi was already pregnant with their first child.

"He's gorgeous," Connie Wyatt exclaimed.

"Handsome boy," Bob agreed.

"What's his name?" Kristi asked, looking from Lacy to Sam.

He looked down at his beautiful wife and smiled when she said, "You tell them, Sam."

He dropped one hand to Lacy's shoulder, linking them, making them the unit they'd become. Sam looked at his family and said, "His name is Jackson William Wyatt. Named for Jack and for Lacy's dad."

Sam watched his mother's eyes well with tears and she didn't try to stop them as they spilled along her cheeks even as she gave them both a proud smile. "Jack would be pleased. We are, aren't we, honey?"

Bob Wyatt dropped one arm around his wife and pulled her in tight. "We are. It's a good thing you've done, you two."

Sam watched the family talk in excited whispers and half shouts. He saw Lacy hand baby Jack over to his mother and watched as she turned to Sam's father and the two of them cuddled and cooed at their first grandchild.

Life was good. Couldn't be better. All that was missing, he thought with a lingering touch of sorrow, was his brother. He wished that Jack could know somehow that they had survived his loss. Found happiness, in spite of missing him.

A flicker of movement caught Sam's eye and he turned his head, shooting a look at the corner of the room, where the watery winter sun painted a pillar of golden light.

Sam's breath caught.

Jack was there, in the light, a part of it. Heart thudding in his chest, Sam could only stare at his twin in disbelief. The buzz of conversation around him softened and drifted away as he and his twin stared at each other from across the room, across the chasm between life and death.

Jack nodded, as if he understood just what Sam was feeling. Then he gave his twin a slow, wide smile, just as he used to. And in moments, as Sam watched, Jack drifted away with the last of the light until the corner of the room was empty and dark again.

"Sam?" Lacy called his name, and still bemused by what he'd seen, he turned to her, a half smile curving his mouth. "Are you okay?"

He glanced back at the corner of the room. Had it happened? Or was it wishful thinking? Did it matter? Jack was a part of them, always would be. Maybe he'd just found a way to let Sam know that he was okay, too.

Turning back to Lacy, Sam let go of the last of his pain and welcomed the joy he was being offered.

"I'm more than okay," he assured her. "Everything's perfect."

Then he turned his back on the past and stepped into the future with his wife and son.

* * * * *

Join Britain's BIGGEST Romance Book Club

- **EXCLUSIVE offers every month**
- **FREE delivery direct to your door**
- **NEVER MISS a title**
- **EARN Bonus Book points**

50% OFF your first parcel

Call Customer Services
0844 844 1358*

or visit
millsandboon.co.uk/subscriptions

* This call will cost you 7 pence per minute plus your phone company's price per minute access charge.

BKCB3

MILLS & BOON®

Why shop at millsandboon.co.uk?

Each year, thousands of romance readers find their perfect read at millsandboon.co.uk. That's because we're passionate about bringing you the very best romantic fiction. Here are some of the advantages of shopping at www.millsandboon.co.uk:

* **Get new books first**—you'll be able to buy your favourite books one month before they hit the shops

* **Get exclusive discounts**—you'll also be able to buy our specially created monthly collections, with up to 50% off the RRP

* **Find your favourite authors**—latest news, interviews and new releases for all your favourite authors and series on our website, plus ideas for what to try next

* **Join in**—once you've bought your favourite books, don't forget to register with us to rate, review and join in the discussions

Visit **www.millsandboon.co.uk** for all this and more today!